Mexico Redux

The Most Obscure, Hardest Fought, Least Understood,
and Most Significant War in American History

Philip F. Rose

iUniverse, Inc.
Bloomington

Mexico Redux

iUniverse books may be ordered through booksellers or by contacting:

iUniverse
1663 Liberty Drive
Bloomington, IN 47403
www.iuniverse.com
1-800-Authors (1-800-288-4677)

ISBN: 978-1-4759-4330-6 (sc)
ISBN: 978-1-4759-4332-0 (hc)
ISBN: 978-1-4759-4331-3 (ebk)

Printed in the United States of America

iUniverse rev. date: 09/17/2012

Table of Contents

Introduction

Mexico Redux was written as a result of watching a four hour PBS television special entitled "U. S. Mexican War 1846-1848." The PBS special was a visually stunning production covering all the aspects of the Mexican war. The author hopes this book will in some way supplement the television program in somewhat greater depth.

Various well known historians and authors were highlighted in the film and included such well known names as General John Eisenhower, Robert Johannsen, David Pletcher, David Edmunds, Sam Haynes, Jesus Velasco-Marquez, and Josefina Zoraido Vasquez. They have provided many of the references for this volume.

The author was particularly interested in the conflicting personal drives and bad judgment of the various commanders in this war. In general it was during the Mexican War that many of the famous generals in American history emerged. Specifically the Mexican war was a training ground for the Civil War, but it was also a clash between neighbors who were strangers.

The chapters have been kept brief and especially void of excessive military details. Many of the chapters are autobiographical in nature. I have tried to cover all the aspects of the war covered in the television special except for the U. S. Far West.

Chapter 1

A Mexican War Primer

Territorial disputes with Mexico plagued the United States from an early date. In the Spring of 1825 President John Quincy Adams sent Mr. Joel R. Poinsett as the first United States Minister to the Republic of Mexico. Poinsett carried instructions requiring him to attempt to persuade the government of Mexico to sell all the provinces of Texas to the United States.

In December 1829 Joel Poinsett was replaced by President Andrew Jackson's good friend Anthony Butler. Butler schemed and maneuvered for six years but no good came of anything he tried. In the winter of 1835 the Mexican government asked for his recall.

Powhatan Ellis, the next American Minister, had no better success in his effort to secure some Mexican territory. Early in 1842 President John Tyler named Waddy Thompson to replace him as American Minister to Mexico. Waddy Thompson was a vigorous advocate of the Americanization of Texas.

In January 1843 Thompson was replaced by Benjamin E. Green who was soon thereafter replaced by Wilson Shannon. At this later time Mexican President Santa Anna sent his long time aide Juan N. Almonte to Washington to represent his government. In Mexico those opposed to Santa Anna rallied behind José de Herrera, a moderate. Wilson Shannon informed the State Department that he would have nothing to do with any attempts to negotiate with Mexico, and in mid-summer 1844 he recommended that Congress act on his request. In November Shannon broke off all his diplomatic relations with Mexico. In December 1844 Santa Anna was forced into exile to Cuba, and José de Herrera was inaugurated as the president of Mexico. Herrera hoped to put his country's international relations back on a realistic footing.

President John Tyler signed a Texas annexation bill on March 3, 1845 at the end of his term. Mexican Minister to the United States, Juan Almonte, screamed that the annexation was an act of aggression against Mexico. He demanded his passport and left the country. Almonte, being a Santa Anna man, could have been expected to be replaced momentarily. He had nothing to lose.

In the summer of 1845 the annexation of Texas was the critical issue on the political scene. In July the Texas convention accepted the offer of annexation by the United States and the Texas Congress rejected any Mexican peace offer. President James Knox Polk ordered General Zachary Taylor, then in Louisiana, to occupy Texas and prepare to defend it. Taylor took the "Army of Occupation" as it was then called to the mouth of the Nueces River and set up camp on the south bank. The territory south of the Nueces River up to the Rio Grande was totally unsettled and could not provide any logistical support for a military encampment.

Mexican president José de Herrera let it be known that he would receive a minister from the United States. President James K. Polk's special agent William S. Parrat was confirmed by the American Consul and the British minister. The Texas electorate ratified a state Constitution in October 1845. Also in October 1845 Herrera's Congress met in secret session and declared that the Mexican government would receive a representative from the United States with full power to settle the present dispute. A few weeks later President Polk promptly appointed John Slidell of Louisiana to negotiate with the Herrera government and gave him wide powers of discretion. In Polk's instructions to Slidell settlement problems in California were addressed. Polk told John Slidell to actually attempt to purchase California from Mexico.

Herrera's overthrow in Mexico was imminent and war seemed inevitable. It mattered little whether Polk was interested in California or not. In California Santa Anna's appointee as governor, Manuel de Micheltorena, had been driven out. Pío Pico was established as provisional governor with José Castro in command of Northern California. Soon conflict erupted between Pico and Castro and for all practical purposes the Mexican government in California disintegrated. Observers declared that California was ready for separation from Mexico.

John Slidell was empowered to:

(1) Accept the Nueces River as the southern boundary of Texas if Mexico would settle all claims.
(2) Accept the Rio Grande as far as El Paso del Norte if the United States assumed all claims.
(3) Add an additional $5 million dollars if Mexico would cede New Mexico to the United States.
(4) Add an additional $5 million dollars for Northern California, and
(5) Offer as much as $25 million dollars for all of California not including Baja California.

In the first part of December John Slidell arrived at Vera Cruz and was informed that Herrera would not receive any minister from the United States until Texas was returned to Mexico. With Santa Anna in exile another opportunist Marciano Paredes chased fortune. Shouting denunciations of the Herrera government and its conciliatory attitude toward Texas and the United States, he mustered enough support to take over the City of Mexico without firing a shot. In his manifesto of December 14, 1845 Paredes charged that Herrera had thwarted the army from attacking the Americans in Texas. On December 29th when President Polk admitted Texas into the Union, Paredes entered the City of Mexico and assumed the powers of government.

On receiving word of Slidell's rejection by Herrera, President Polk sent out orders to General Zachary Taylor to take up a position on the Northern bank of the Rio Grande, and he sent instructions to Slidell to try to negotiate with the new strong man Marciano Paredes. A Mexican revolutionary junta named Paredes as acting president and rewarded Juan Almonte with an appointment as Secretary of War. The junta reiterated their intentions of going to war with the United States for the recovery of Texas. Paredes at once began to mobilize his forces.

President Paredes ordered General Francisco Mejía, then in command of Mexican troops amassed at Matamoros, to attack General Zachary Taylor on April 4, 1846. Taylor was encamped north of the Rio Grande since March 23, 1846. For some reason Mejía did not comply with the April 4th order to attack. He was replaced by General Pedro de Ampudia, who ordered Taylor to withdraw to the Nueces River and ordered American civilians to leave Matamoros because a state of war existed. Taylor responded by blockading the mouth of the Rio Grande with chains. He requested American gunboats to deny the use of the river to Mexico.

General Ampudia was replaced in command on April 24th by Mariano Aresta who ordered General Torrejón to cross the Rio Grande with about 1600 cavalry troops. Torrejón sent a message to Taylor that he was commencing hostilities. Torrejón isolated Captain William Thornton and about sixty American dragoons that afternoon, and after an intensive skirmish forced Thornton to surrender the next day. Taylor sent a dispatch to President Polk which arrived in Washington at about 6:00 PM on Saturday evening, May 9th. On Sunday Polk drafted a war message, and on Monday, May 11, he presented it to Congress. In the late afternoon of May 12th, following a spirited debate, a declaration of war was voted. On Wednesday May 13, 1846 Polk signed the declaration into law. He did not know that Mexican forces had crossed the Rio Grande again and attacked General Taylor at the battles of Palo Alto and Resaca de la Palma. At this point we were officially at war.

Chapter 2

Intrigue at the Rio Grande

Robert Field Stockton

My grandfather Richard Stockton was a member of the Continental Congress and a signer of the Declaration of Independence. Doctor Richard Rush, of Philadelphia, married my grandfather's daughter Julia. The noted Reverend Witherspoon was the minister who performed the marriage in January 1776. Witherspoon was then the president of the College of New Jersey[1] and the institution was located on a portion of the Stockton estate. For the next 75 years the Stockton family was one of the most influential and one of the wealthiest families in New Jersey. George Washington was a friend of the family and visited on many occasions. Richard Stockton died in 1781.

Richard Stockton's son, also named Richard, was better known as "Old Duke." He was a judge and a United States Senator. His close friend was Daniel Webster. He was unsuccessful, however, in his aspirations for the governorship of New Jersey.

---

[1]   Now Princeton University.

I was the second son of Old Duke, and was born in 1795. I attended the College of New Jersey, but I quit at an early age to enlist in the navy. I was quickly appointed a midshipman. Between 1823 and 1838 I was on furlough and managed the Stockton estate. In 1829 the State of New Jersey issued a charter for a new canal which would serve as a transit across New Jersey from the Delaware River to the Atlantic Ocean just below New York City. I invested $400,000 in the venture. The Raritan canal, as it was called, was completed in 1834. The canal enterprise and railroads were my major business interests, but much of my wealth was also in New Jersey land. I also invested in mining properties in Virginia and agricultural land in Arkansas and California.

My career as a naval officer covered two periods of time. I began with my service in the War of 1812 and later in the late 1830's when I was engaged in developing new methods of propulsion and armaments for warships.

I was also involved in the major domestic issue of slavery. During the years 1819 to 1821 I was one of the few American naval officers who made a determined effort to suppress the illicit trade in slaves off the African coast. In 1821 I captured four ships which were engaged in the slave trade. I was a vigorous supporter of the "Society for Colonizing the Free People of Color in the United States." The first effort of the society to establish a colony on Sherbro Island near Sierra Leone was a failure. In 1821 the society tried again, founding Cape Mesurado, also near Sierra Leone. They negotiated with "King" Peter who at first agreed to cede the region to the society, but then reneged and disappeared into the interior.

King Peter was run down and at gun point he signed a contract for $500 in goods. The lands were forever ceded to me and Eli Ayres, "To Have and to forever Hold the said Premises for the use of the said Citizens of America."

My political activity lead me to be President Polk's agent in Texas on the eve of the war with Mexico. Politically I tended toward the Whig Party and supported John Quincy Adams in 1824. I backed Jackson in 1828 and again in 1832. I supported Martin Van Buren in 1836, and had considerable influence in the Tyler administration. My support of the Democratic party was not continuous and I often identified myself with the Know-Nothings, a nativist group whose principles were anti-Catholic and anti-foreign.

In October 1838 I was given the command of the U.S. Battleship *Ohio* with orders to sail to the Mediterranean. In January 1839 I was granted a two months leave of absence to deliver dispatches to the American minister in London. At Liverpool I met the Swedish inventor John Ericsson, who was working on an internal combustion engine for marine applications. Ericsson devised a ship using a screw propeller. In England during the summer of 1839 I arranged with Ericsson for the construction of a small iron boat driven by steam power applied to a screw propeller as an experimental craft. I named it the *Robert F. Stockton*, and I ran it up and down the Thames River. From London I eventually returned to the United States and was placed on furlough again.

The small boat designed by Ericsson demonstrated the feasibility of this form of propulsion for a powerful warship. Ericsson produced detailed plans for a full sized warship and brought his plans to the United States in November 1839. I applied for an authorization to build the ship and received the approval of the Navy department soon after John Tyler acceded to the presidency, following Harrison's death.

On May 27, 1841 I submitted a ship model to the Secretary of the Navy and on June 1st I was requested to report to the Navy Yard at Philadelphia for the purpose of preparing drafts of such a vessel. Construction began in 1842. The ship was launched in the fall of 1843 and I named it the *Princeton*. The *Princeton* was both a sailing vessel and a steamship. The funnel was retractable and she burned anthracite rather than soft coal, thus putting out very little smoke. I claimed she was the "cheapest, fastest and most powerful ship-of-war in the world." She was armed with two cannons and twelve 42-pound cannonades. One of the big guns was named the "Oregon" and the other the "Peacemaker." The triumph was overshadowed by the catastrophic explosion of the Peacemaker gun on February 28, 1844. Those killed included Abel P. Upshur, Secretary of State; Thomas W. Gilmer, Secretary of the Navy; Captain Beverly Kennon of the Navy; Virgil Maxey of Maryland and David Gardiner of New York. Seventeen sailors were wounded. A Naval Board of Inquiry found that I had not been negligent in the construction or testing of the gun, but the accident left a heavy mark upon my soul.

In the middle of February 1845 John Y. Mason, who had been appointed Secretary of the Navy following the death of Thomas Gilmer on the *Princeton* asked me to come to Washington on naval business. On

February 28th I was given orders to prepare to take the *Princeton* and other vessels back to some of the principal ports in the Mediterranean, where I could exhibit the unique construction of the *Princeton*.

Andrew Jackson Donelson, charge d'affaires, or official representative of the United States in Texas, was looking forward to a Texan acceptance of the terms of annexation in early 1845. The president of the Republic of Texas, Anson Jones, worked to maintain Texas's status as an independent nation, but in the beginning of April 1845 he acquiesced to the popular will of the people. There had been attempts to exert pressure on President Anson Jones to accept annexation for quite some time. Memucan Hunt, former Minister from the Republic of Texas to the United States, regarded Jones as a traitor. Hunt wrote that he was going to the capital to tell Jones that if the people were not allowed to vote on annexation "a convention would be called to do so by the people."

I was probably Polk's most important and influential supporter in New Jersey, and when Polk won the presidential election I anticipated some special attention. On April 2nd I was given orders countermanding those of February 28th sending me to the Mediterranean. I was to report to Commodore David Conner, in command of the Home Squadron, in the Gulf of Mexico. Conner was stationed near the Mexican port of Vera Cruz. I was told that further orders would be given to me by Commodore Conner.

On April 15th I took the *Princeton* to Philadelphia to pick up a new gun. I returned to Norfolk on April 22nd and received further orders from President Polk's Secretary of the Navy, George Bancroft. I was handed two letters:

1. Instructions placing me at the disposition of Commodore Conner.
2. A copy of my instructions to be handed to Commodore Conner.

I was ordered to go ashore at Galveston, Texas and make myself acquainted with the disposition of the people of Texas, and there negotiate with Mexico and remain there as long as in my judgment it may seem necessary.

Charles A. Wickliffe, a Kentucky politician, had been a member of the House of Representatives for ten years, then lieutenant governor of Kentucky for three years and governor for the years 1839-1840 following the death of the elected governor. He was adamant in his desire for the annexation of Texas. He was appointed Postmaster General by President Tyler in October 1841. Wickliffe was specifically sent to Texas by President Polk in a scheme to make Polk's aggressive designs on Mexico's territory look legitimate. Polk sought to make it appear that Wickliffe went to Texas for personal reasons and with a view to emigrate there. Archibald Yell, a former governor of Arkansas, and now an agent for President Polk in Texas, wrote the president on May 5, 1845 that Wickliffe had arrived on May 2nd. He told Polk, "you may now rest assured that nothing but presidential interference can prevent annexation—so far as Texas is concerned." Andrew J. Donelson felt comfortably certain that Texas would accept annexation and he set sail for New Orleans.

The squadron under my command arrived off Galveston on May 12, 1845. It was the first extensive cruise of the *Princeton* and I was intent on demonstrating her worth. I was received at Galveston with ceremony on May 14th. I immediately sought out Charles Wickliffe whom I knew President Polk had sent to attempt to manipulate the foreign policy of the Republic of Texas. I was prepared to use my personal fortune to finance any fighting if necessary. I next sought out Major General William T. Sherman, the chief officer of the Militia of Texas, the result of which were plans for organizing a volunteer force for an invasion of Mexico. I proposed that President Anson Jones should authorize Major General Sherman to raise a force of two thousand or more men.

On the evening of May 21st a Great Ball was given in my honor in Galveston. On the same evening and the next day I was in consultation with Wickliffe and General Sherman about descending upon the Mexican town of Matamoros, to capture and hold it, and that I would provide assistance with my fleet under the pretext of giving protection promised by the United States to Texas. The purpose of this action was not to protect Texas. It was not to defend the territory, it was simply to initiate an attack on Mexico. General Sherman, in an interview with Anson Jones, urged him to agree with my proposal asserting that it was popular among the people, and that he would have no difficulty in obtaining the requisite number of men upon my assurance that they would be provisioned and paid.

After the Great Ball I wrote Secretary of the Navy Bancroft saying, "the question of annexation is settled in my opinion. In truth seven-eights of the people are in favor of it, and every man in the Republic seems to despise the threats of Mexico and to spurn all European interference in the matter." I further said that the Mexicans were "crossing the Rio Grande and taking possession of an immense and valuable portion of the territory on the east side of the river." In truth the Republic had never had any jurisdiction there. I then wrote that the Mexicans "certainly in my judgment, ought to be driven back to the other side of the Rio Grande *at least* before annexation takes place." I closed my letter with the comment, "I will send one of my ships to Vera Cruz with the letters for Commodore Conner, as it will be impossible for me to go there and at the same time give the necessary attentions to the important interests in Texas." With that revelation I should have taken my squadron to join Commodore Conner at once. But I never did.

President Anson Jones was expecting the return of British Minister Elliot from Mexico with a proposition of peace and an acknowledgment of Texan independence. He calculated that such an offer from the Mexican government, even if conditional, would squash any movement for an attack on Mexico. Anson Jones contacted me and said he would take a few days longer to reflect upon the matter. Elliot returned from Mexico in the meantime and then President Jones publicly issued a proclamation announcing the Mexican offer and declaring a state of peace with Mexico until such time as the government of Texas should act on the matter.

Charge d'affaires Andrew J. Donelson was worried that the U.S. government might take some precipitous military action in Texas in a movement toward the Mexican border. On May 24th he wrote to Secretary of State John Buchanan urging that no United States military forces be introduced into Texas. He said that after the Texas government had accepted annexation American troops could be properly sent to the Rio Grande—and then he struck out "Rio Grande" and wrote "frontier." Donelson wrote a second letter to Mr. Buchanan expressing his anxiety about me and my activities, He said he hoped the State Department would ask Navy Secretary Bancroft to restore my *Princeton* cruise.

On May 27, 1845 I sent a letter to Secretary Bancroft to let him know how I proposed to settle the matter without committing the United States. I said, "The major general will call out three thousand men and

R. F. Stockton Esquire will supply them in a private way with provisions and ammunition." The facts were incontestible; an officer of the United States Navy in command of a squadron sent to Texas by the United States government, an officer who was at the same time a wealthy and influential businessman and politician, was attempting to initiate an attack upon Mexico by an army which I would finance secretly from my own personal funds. I sailed from Galveston with Wickliffe and several other Texan friends on the same day, but by June 2nd we were back in Galveston. Andrew J. Donelson met with us that day and he wrote the State Department:

> I adverted in my last dispatch from New Orleans to the presence of Captain Stockton's squadron here, and to a rumor that he had sailed to Santiago, to cooperate with General Sherman of the Texan militia in defending the occupation of the Rio Grande. This was not correct. Captain Stockton weighed anchor at this port a few days ago for the purpose of examining the coast; but he has since returned, and has taken no step susceptible of construction as one of aggression upon Mexico, nor will he take any unless ordered to do so. His presence here has had a fine effect, and operates, without explanation, as an assurance to Texas that she will receive the protection due to her when she comes into the Union.

Of course Donelson had talked to me and warned me against involvement in any military action against Mexico. The possibility that I might yet engage in some overt military action against Mexico gave Donelson continuous concern until I left Galveston on June 23rd and proceeded towards Washington. President Polk held to his plan of instigating a military movement, ostensibly Texan, to the Mexican border. Polk had the Department of State and the Department of the Navy send dispatches to Texas with instructions to urge the Texans to attack the Mexicans in the contested border area. Bancroft instructed me to defend Texas "against aggressions as promptly as you would defend any of the states," as soon as the Texas Congress and the Texas convention had accepted annexation.

I reached the port of Annapolis on July 3rd, and I proudly said I made it in nine days by using only 93 tons of coal. I immediately sent a certified copy of the joint resolutions of the Congress of Texas accepting annexation by a unanimous vote. The news was immediately relayed to President Polk by Bancroft and Dr. Wright, my medical officer and also my secretary. Bancroft wrote a letter back to me in which he said the president wanted to express his "extreme satisfaction" at the "agreeable tidings" and his "gratification at the astonishing dispatch with which you have brought" the news. The following March I was given the command of the *United States Ship Congress*. On Wednesday, May 13, 1846 President Polk signed the measure declaring war on Mexico, and in October I sailed away to the Pacific Ocean.

Chapter 3

Viva Mexico!

William Selby Harney

I n the early days Texas, then a province of Mexico, received a great number of American settlers. This was caused by the lure of liberal grants of land, a refuge for fugitives from justice, and by debtors who were forced by hard times. The settlers were mostly Caucasian and were a tough and determined lot. They recognized themselves as part of the "United States of Mexico," and were loyal to that government.

In 1835 General Santa Anna became president of Mexico and changed the Federal character of the Mexican government and destroyed states sovereign rights. The states of Texas and Tamaulipas protested against this as a violation of the Mexican Constitution. The result was rebellion and ultimate independence after the battle of San Jacinto on April 21, 1836.

During the revolution volunteers from the United States went to the assistance of the Texans. In 1837 the people of the Republic of Texas expressed the desire to be annexed to the United States. Their request was rejected. Another attempt was made during John Tyler's administration but nothing happened. Powers at Washington were afraid that the Texans might put themselves under the protection of Great Britain. The acquisition of Texas by Great Britain would probably involve us in a war with that power, while annexation threatened war with Mexico. General Houston was in favor of English control. He was an early Texas patriot who had won many civic and military laurels, and he was the one who had defeated Santa Anna at San Jacinto. The annexation of Texas was finally ratified by the United States Senate with certain conditions on March 1st, 1845. The Mexican Minister at Washington exerted his influence to prevent the annexation, making his formal protest on March 6th. Meeting no success he quit his post and went home.

Upon the Mexican Minister's return to Mexico all official intercourse between the two countries was closed, but President Herrera had a conciliatory attitude toward Texas. On November 9th an official message from the Mexican government consented to renew diplomatic relations which had been suspended in March. President Polk sent Mr. Slidell to the City of Mexico for negotiations but President Herrera would not receive a minister from the United States until Texas was returned to Mexico. It was a foolish gesture designed to save face for Herrera, who was being desperately pressed by radical centralists. On receiving word of Slidell's rejection by Herrera, President Polk decided to send troops, and the American Squadron took up a position in the Gulf of Mexico. He announced in his message of December 2, 1845, that the moment the terms of annexation offered by the United States were accepted by Texas, the latter became so far a part of our own country as to make it our duty to afford such protection and defense. In the summer of 1845 General Taylor was stationed at Corpus Christi, Texas where he remained for the balance of the year.

After my leave of absence in October 1845 I returned to my command of six companies of dragoons back in San Antonio, Texas. I had heard stories that the Mexicans were assembling on the Rio Grande, west of San Antonio. I was determined to push forward, for the purpose of reconnaissance and the protection of the frontier, and before the arrival of General Wool I had collected a force of seven hundred men. My officers called my attention to the fact that we lacked artillery, and suggested that I request two cannons from Victoria. I knew this would involve loss of valuable time so I inquired if the Mexicans had any artillery. I was told that they had field pieces and ordnance of good quality, and so I decided to go into Mexico and take them forcefully, as they would suit me satisfactorily.

I crossed the Rio Grande and advanced to the Mexican town of Presidio. From there I determined to move upon Monterey and called a council of my officers. They all opposed the project, and so I was forced to abandon it. In the meantime General Wool reached San Antonio and assumed command of the military district. He sent an order for me to return immediately, but before the order was dispatched I was on my way from Presidio back to San Antonio.

The news of my crossing the Rio Grande reached San Antonio and quite a number of Texans who had seen service in the war of 1836 organized a volunteer force to reinforce me. They could not reach me until I had returned to Texas. I had collected a quantity of supplies at Presidio which I left behind under a guard of sixty men. After my departure these men, being alone, became panic-stricken. They burned all the stores to the ground, and retreated back after me.

General Wool's order was followed by another one ordering me arrested, and he placed Major Bell in command of my troops. On reaching San Antonio I reported directly to General Wool. I would not shake hands with the general and demanded to know what charges he had lodged against me. General Wool replied that he ordered me arrested because he feared I would disobey the order to return and the people of San Antonio assured him that *I would not return* under his orders. I reproached the general for paying attention to such idle gossip.

General Zachary Taylor remained at Corpus Christi until March 11th, 1846 when he started his offensive and pushed forward to the Rio Grande. At the Arroyo Colorado General Taylor was met by Mexican stragglers who opposed his crossing but they soon fled and dispersed. On March 24th 1846 General Taylor took possession of Point Isabel. He continued to move forward and on March 28th occupied a point on the Rio Grande opposite Matamoros. Here General Taylor sent Brigadier General Worth with dispatches to the Mexican authorities. A Mexican delegation refused to receive Worth and denied him an interview with the American consul at that city.

There were poor prospects for peace there so General Taylor commenced the construction of a fortification which the men fondly called "Fort Texas." General Taylor mounted a battery of two eighteen-pounders covering the city of Matamoros and extended his field works and armaments. In the meantime the Mexicans, under the command of General Ampudia, were not idle and they entrenched themselves for a two mile stretch in front of the Americans on the opposite side of the river. The Mexican government claimed that the Nueces River, and not the Rio Grande, was the border of Texas, and that any territory west of the Nueces was Mexican territory. On the 17th of April the mouth of the Rio Grande was declared in a state of blockade. General Ampudia sent an angry communication to General Taylor in which he made threats of serious consequences if the blockade was not lifted. General Taylor replied that the blockade had been rendered necessary by the belligerent action of the Mexican authorities.

At Fort Texas Captain Thornton was placed in command of a reconnoitering party of dragoons. He had proceeded about twenty-four miles when he was ambushed by a party of Mexicans concealed behind a chaparral fence. After a severe conflict the Americans were forced to surrender and they were made prisoners-of-war. The Mexicans were jubilant over their first victory. They crossed the Rio Grande and invaded the country between Fort Texas and Point Isabel, threatening Taylor's communications. Captain Walker, a noted Texas Ranger, attempted to open a path to Taylor and started out from Point Isabel with seventy-five troops. He was defeated by a large body of Mexicans and driven back on April 28th. When General Taylor heard that Point Isabel was threatened he determined to march his army to its relief. He left Major Jacob Brown in command of Fort Texas, and with six hundred men started out for the Point on May 1st. On May 3rd a battery at Matamoros opened fire on the fort. It was answered by the American battery of eighteen-pounders. On the next day, Major Brown, the gallant commander was killed and Captain Hawkins took command. Fort Texas was now renamed to Fort Brown.

On May 8th General Taylor attacked the Mexican army under General Arista and on the next day defeated him. The Mexicans threw away their arms and fled in all directions. In these engagements Colonel Twiggs commanded the left wing and I commanded the 2nd dragoons. It was only a few more days until our army was in possession of Matamoros and on June 30th 1846 I was promoted to the rank of full colonel, in place of Colonel Twiggs, who was promoted to the rank of brigadier-general.

After the occupation of Matamoros I was ordered to rejoin my regiment. In company with Brigadier General Shields and an escort of only fifteen men I set out to report to General Taylor. We passed through dangerous enemy country. On reaching Monterey I was ordered to report to General W. O. Butler. This placed me, very much against my will, under the command of General Wool from whom I had suffered the indignity of an arrest at San Antonio.

Hell I had to obey those orders! I reported to General Wool at a place beyond Saltillo, and I refused to shake the general's hand again. He ordered me to Agua Caliente with my dragoons. We failed to see any enemy at that place and I took up quarters in a nearby church. I was just relaxing at Agua Caliente when a courier arrived late in the afternoon with a dispatch from General Wool, ordering my immediate return, as the "enemy," so the dispatch said, was advancing on him. I read the dispatch to my officers and knowing that there was no "enemy," I bivouacked for the night. The next morning we marched back where all was quiet and I reported to General Wool, who reproached me for my tardiness. I told the general that if he had inquired of me, I could have told him from my own personal knowledge, there was **no enemy**.

General Wool had a disgusted and pained look and said little. He then ordered me to continue on my way and to report back to General Zachary Taylor, where I was assigned to my new duty with General Worth.

Chapter 4

El Presidente

Antonio López de Santa Anna

I was born on February 21, 1794 at Jalapa, Mexico in the province of Vera Cruz and christened Antonio López de Santa Anna. I was of Spanish parentage but tainted by the fact that my birthplace was geographically located in the New World. I had little education in a formal sense, but I developed an early interest in military life.

On June 9th, 1810 I joined the Spanish army as a cadet in the Vera Cruz Fixed Regiment. I falsified my age to get in and soon transferred to the calvary which I admired. My first military action came on March 13, 1811 when I sailed to Tampico under the command of General Arredondo. We captured and executed a bandit leader in the area north of the Pánuco River. On May 10th I pursued the insurgent Villerías and took a small number of prisoners. I was lauded by General Arredondo for my brave conduct.

For the next few years I fought guerilla leaders and insurgent bands of the Mexican independence movements. I was promoted to second lieutenant on February 6, 1812 and on October 7th of the same year I advanced to first lieutenant.

Arredondo received orders to take his regiment to Texas to combat the rebellion there. We reached the Rio Bravo at Laredo and began the Texas campaign on July 26, 1813. On August 18th our forces soundly trounced the rebel forces led by Bernardo Gutiérrez de Lara. Before returning to Vera Cruz in March 1814 Arredondo ordered many cruelties upon the defeated Texans including numerous executions. I carried out most of these punishments as his subordinate and devoted student.

After my return to Vera Cruz I spent most of my time chasing guerilla bands. In 1817 I was appointed an aide-de-camp and made my first important visit to the Capital, where I especially enjoyed a presence "among the ladies." During this period I found time to further my neglected education. My later reading concentrated on the great Napoleon whom I took on as a model.

Starting in 1819, when relative peace existed in Mexico, I participated in a venture to construct new towns in my native province. I helped build many churches and forts. In resisting insurgent revolts and Indian uprisings in the North, I received the Shield of Honor and the Certificate of the Royal and Distinguished Order of Isabella the Catholic. Colonel Agustín de Iturbide was appointed to command the rebellious district of the South on November 9, 1820 and departed on November 19th to combat guerilla bands south of the City of Mexico.

In early 1821 the Mexican wars for independence took a new turn. In Spain King Ferdinand VII was forced to restore the Spanish Constitution of 1812, insuring that the empire would be governed by liberal principles, but conservatives in Mexico, including church officials, opposed the provisions. I was promoted to captain and a bit later I was breveted as a lieutenant colonel. I watched Colonel Iturbide develop political-military ideas when he came out with his famous Plan of Iguala on February 24, 1821. This document served as the basis for an "Army of Three Guarantees":

1. Preservation of the Catholic religion and the toleration of no other faiths.
2. Absolute Independence of Mexico.
3. Union of all European and native Mexicans into a new nation.

In the City of Mexico Viceroy Apodaca refused to support the Plan of Iguala. He ordered the royalist forces to combat the Army of the Three

Guarantees. I was sent with 200 men to quell the disturbances of the rebels at Jalapa and Orizaba. Up to this point I was a loyal Spanish officer who fought for Spain's interests. While combating the rebels at Orizaba in March 1821 I transferred my allegiance from Spain to Iturbide's cause. On March 29th I broke with Spain completely and joined the rebel leader José Joaquín de Herrera whom I had been sent to defeat. The rebel Herrera offered me a colonelship and the command of the Province of Vera Cruz. I proclaimed my allegiance to the Plan of Iguala and joined Herrera for a joint campaign against my former superiors and the royalists of Vera Cruz. My first successful campaign was an assault upon the port of Alvarado, south of Vera Cruz. I told my troops:

> Comrades! You are going to put an end to the great work
> of the reconquest of our liberty and independence. You are
> going to plant the eagle of the Mexican empire, lost three
> centuries ago on the plains of Otumba . . .

Hearing of royalist successes in the interior I marched inland to Córdoba and issued a challenge to meet my opponents in battle. The challenge was refused and the royalists retreated from the city. I intercepted the retreat and inflicted heavy losses on the enemy. For this I received an award known as the Córdoba Cross, and became a commandant general of the Province of Vera Cruz. There were still pockets of royalist opposition to be overcome. Two of these were in my province;—the fortress of Perote, near Jalapa, and the port city of Vera Cruz with its fortress of San Juan de Ulúa in the harbor. On October 7, 1821 Perote surrendered to me and I then concentrated my efforts on the siege of Vera Cruz. After eight days José Dávilla agreed to withdraw from the city to the fortress in the harbor, which he did so on October 26th.

At about this time I was having second thoughts about my allegiance to Iturbide. He had appointed Manuel Rincón to succeed me as governor of the province of Vera Cruz, which I felt was unfair. Also his failure to promote me as a general sewed the seeds of future trouble.

I made my second visit to the capital in early January 1822 and returned home to Vera Cruz still without my promotion. Finally in May Iturbide called me to the capital again and issued my promotion and named me commanding general of the Province of Vera Cruz. I reluctantly pledged my regiment to the defense of the "immortal

Iturbide as Emperor." Scarcely six months later I was instrumental in initiating an open political and military revolt against him. My inability to overcome the resistance of the Spaniards at San Juan de Ulúa started it all. Iturbide suspected me of treachery, even to the extent of negotiating with the enemy. I resented his feelings.

Iturbide came to Jalapa on November 16th where he held a conference with me. It was obvious that the emperor did not intend to grant me the powers I had requested and had come to remove me. I professed dissatisfaction of Iturbide's dissolution of the Constitutional Congress. He ordered me to return to the capital but I refused on the pretext that I lacked money and had some debts to pay. The Emperor offered to loan me 500 pesos but I begged for time to settle some business affairs. This Iturbide granted and left Jalapa on December 1, 1822.

At this point I left in secret for Vera Cruz. I knew I would have to hasten there to defend it against Iturbide's forces when I would announce my opposition to the emperor. I was determined to protect my personal interests in Vera Cruz, justifying my actions by allegations that Iturbide had become a tyrant when he dissolved the Congress and disregarded the freedoms guaranteed by the Plan of Iguala. At 4:00 PM on December 2, 1822, at the head of my soldiers, I proclaimed the Republic. I had little idea of what a republican form of government resembled. When I proclaimed the Republic I unfolded a tricolored flag of black, green and red, with a rifle volley of three shots. I then paraded through the streets of Vera Cruz with my new flag unfurled. I declared that I would observe the guarantees from the Plan of Iguala—**Independence**, **Catholicism** and **Union** and grant an armistice to my opponents.

I denounced Iturbe for bringing ills to the nation, obstructing commerce, paralyzing agriculture and failing to improve work in the mines. I obtained some assistance for formulating my plans from my former rival, Manuel Rincón. On December 6, 1822 I formally proclaimed the Plan of Vera Cruz. The basic plan consisted of sixteen articles in which I stated that Mexican Sovereignty rested with the Congress and that Iturbe might not be recognized as Emperor. During the month of December I speedily acquired both allies and opponents.

When I was subsequently moved to Jalapa in mid December Iturbe declared that I was a traitor and stripped me of my military rank. On December 21st the Emperor's troops overran my army near Jalapa. The disaster was so drastic I informed the insurgent leader Guadulupe

Victoria that I was thinking of fleeing to the United States. I went to Vera Cruz to prepare its defenses for the expected assault. Other leaders waiting for an opportunity to launch a campaign against the emperor now formulated a new plan to establish a Federal Republic. The Plan of Casa Mata was proclaimed on February 1, 1823 and its articles called for a new Congress and solicited the endorsement of the various provisional military leaders. I accepted the Plan on February 2nd and before the end of the month Iturbe's empire had been reduced to the City of Mexico and its immediate environs. I played no direct part in the defeat of Iturbe or his departure into exile.

In those past two years I had emerged as a major military figure with considerable influence. I had gone from royalist to a supporter of Iturbide's empire, and finally to promotion of a true Republic. At age 29 I was on top of the world. I became president of the Provisional Junta of Vera Cruz for a short time in March, 1823, but that type of work did not appeal to me. In January 1824 a revolt occurred in the Capital and I was again appointed to a military command. I suppressed the revolt in three days, and was then appointed Commandante General of Yucatán, as well as governor of that distant province. My orders stated that the "Military Commander shall not leave the province without its written permission." My first effort in the province was to suppress all opposition to my policies, especially from the press, and this enabled me to consolidate control over the region. I soon learned of the death of Iturbide, who had been shot by paid assassins. I told my friends, "he was never my personal enemy. In Yucatán he would not have been shot."

I resolved the trade conflict which I had been sent to settle in January 1825. I finally lost prestige when I proposed a scheme to free Cuba from the Spanish yoke with an assault on the fortress of El Moro at the entrance of Havana Harbor. I lacked sufficient funds to finance such an expedition, and the government denounced my schemes. I lashed back and submitted my resignation to Guadalupe Victoria on April 25, 1825 and left on April 30th for Vera Cruz.

I now spent a good amount of time in retirement, managing my newly acquired properties, receiving distinguished visitors and attending to family matters. I acquired a wife before returning to Vera Cruz. A lovely Creole, Doña Inés García was fourteen years of age. She became the unofficial manager of my estates and concentrated upon the raising of a family. I had purchased the hacienda of Manga de Clavo [2] near Vera Cruz on the Jalapa Road. I found time to enjoy cock fighting which demonstrated my interest in gambling and my appreciation for skill and aggression. My estate also became a launching point for revolutions and a refuge in times of trial and adversity. At this time author Lorenzo de Zavala wrote a little observation about me which I cherished:

> The soul of General Santa Anna does not fit in his body. It lives in perpetual motion. It permits him to be dragged along by his insatiable desire to acquire glory. It estimates the value of his outstanding qualities. He gets angry with the boldness that denies him immortal fame . . .

Towards the end of 1827 I came out of retirement to become involved in conflicts among two Masonic lodges, the Yorkinos and the Escoceses. The Escoceses had been brought from Spain largely by the army to establish a monarchy. To counteract this the Yorkinos were organized to promote Federalism and Republicanism. I offered my services to the Yorkinos and to Vincente Guerrero against Nicholás Bravo, who was Grand Master of the Escoceses in the town of Tulancingo. We assaulted Tulancingo on January 7, 1828, routed the enemy forces, and took Bravo prisoner. For this act of loyalty I was again appointed governor of Vera Cruz.

On September 1, 1828 the presidential elections took place. Guadulupe Victoria, the incumbent, could not run for a second consecutive term. The two announced candidates were Guerrero and Manuel Gómez Pedraza who had been Victoria's Minister of War, and who was supported by the Escoceses. I actually hated Pedraza because he opposed my plan to invade Cuba when I was Governor of Yucatán in 1825.

In the election Gómez Pedraza received more votes than Guerrera but I refused to abide by the constitutional decision, and charged the supporters of Pedraza with "intimidation" during the election. I collected 800 men near Jalapa and marched to the fortress of San Carlo de Perote which I took on September 11, 1828 only ten days after the election. Here I issued my "Grito de Perote," declaring that I would not recognize

---

[2]   Literally Clove Spike.

the election of Pedraza, urged the formation of a liberating army, and announced that I would only lay down my arms when Guerrero was announced president. The Congress announced that I was "outside the law" and sent troops to defeat my forces and seize me!

Confronted by the government's army I abandoned San Carlos de Perote and fled south to Oaxaca and occupied the Convent of Santo Domingo. I seized the city, but in turn was besieged within its confines by the pursuing army, led by General José Maria Calderón. On the night of October 29th I made a sortie to the Convent of San Francisco. Finding the church occupied with worshipers I called for a forced contribution to my cause.

My situation was desperate and I soon realized the futility of my revolt without outside help, so I negotiated an armistice with General Calderón. I took advantage of this lull to supply my small army and induce some of Calderón's officers to join my forces. I had learned at an early age that it paid to establish brief armistices with the enemy in order to reinforce one's own forces. The rebellion of others in support of my movement eventually forced Gómez Pedraza to relinquish the presidency. Vincente Guerrero and Lorenzo de Zavala undermined the military support for the president and it was the revolt in the City of Mexico on November 30th that insured the success of the rebellion. The siege against me in Oaxaca was lifted and on December 4th Guerrero became president and Anastasio Bustamante vice-president.

For my patriotism I was returned as governor of the Vera Cruz province. On August 29th, 1829 I was promoted to General of Division. In September I resisted a Spanish invasion of Tampico, and I was now a hero in the eyes of most Mexicans. I left Tampico on September 20th and returned to Vera Cruz where I received a hero's welcome. Congress authorized that my name should be inscribed on a pillar to be erected on the site of the Spanish surrender. As a final act of tribute the people of Mexico officially renamed Tampico after me as Santa Anna de Tamaulipas.

I had hoped to be named Minister of War in the Guerrero government. I was not appointed so I returned to Manga de Clavo where I remained for two years in retirement. When Bustamante successfully forced Guerrero into relinquishing his presidency on January 1, 1830, I remained at my hacienda and recognized the new government while remaining in retirement. Secretly I agreed with Joel Poinsett, United

States Minister, who denounced the move. Guerrero was treacherously shot after being captured by a ruse carried out by government forces.

Two years went by and on January 2, 1832 General Pedro Landero revolted against Bustamante from San Juan de Ulúa, in the harbor of Vera Cruz. I offered to mediate the dispute between Landero and Bustamante, but I insisted that the president make certain changes in his Cabinet first. While awaiting a reply from Bustamante I made preparations for military action if necessary. I organized a ragged army whose weapons included rusty swords and worn out muskets. Bustamante sent General Calderón to suppress my actions and he soundly trounced my forces and I retreated to Vera Cruz. However, Calderón failed to follow up his initial victory giving me time to prepare my defenses. Calderón's forces now decimated with Yellow fever, lifted their siege on May 13th. I immediately went to Jalapa, which I seized on June 12th. The next day I reached a temporary armistice at Corral Alto, near Jalapa.

Remember Gómez Pedraza who had been elected president in 1828 and who I opposed? While I was resisting Calderón's forces at Vera Cruz other revolts were occurring in northern and western Mexico in favor of him. One of the generals, Velentín Gómez Farías, now issued the famous Plan of Zacatecas favoring the return of Pedraza and the overthrow of Bustamante. I quickly embraced the plan as a means of extricating myself from the stalemate of midsummer.

I reorganized my army and resumed fighting against the legal government in the early fall of 1832. I defeated the government forces near Orazaba in September and seized Puebla on October 4th. I then advanced toward the City of Mexico, arriving at Tacubaya on October 22nd and at Guadalupe on the 28th. Bustamante was forced to capitulate. On December 21st he met with Gómez Padraza and myself at the hacienda of Zavaleta and a peace accord was signed. By its terms Bustamante retired from the presidency and Pedraza assumed that post until April 1833, when a new president and vice president would be elected.

I was not a strong supporter of the new interim president because he was my opponent for nearly a decade, but I was instrumental in sending a commission to return Gómez Pedraza from his exile at Bedford Springs in Pennsylvania, the United States. I then returned to Manga de Clavo to await the call to the presidency which I felt certain would result from the victory arranged for at the end of March.

Santa Anna

I ascended to the presidency on April 1, 1833 having been elected by a "free and unanimous election of the Legislatures." General Farías was elected vice president. I did not appear in the City of Mexico for the inauguration, having invited Farías to take the oath for me. I planned to let my vice president run things while I enjoyed the glory from Manga de Clavo.

Mexican Federalism was subjected to severe stresses and strains, as well as the threat of continued revolts from dissidents. I was not a dedicated Federalist and my friends called me an opportunist. Gómez Farías, on the other hand, was a sincere Federalist interested in preserving the rights of the individual states in relation to the central government. Thus Farías and I were completely incompatible.

Two disasters occurred during my presidential office. The first was an epidemic of Asiatic Cholera which killed thousands of people during the period from June through September 1833. The second was legislation sponsored by Farías to deprive the Catholic Clergy of its privileged position. I was bombarded by letters from Catholic Priests who wanted me to come to their aid and reoccupy the presidential chair. I had never really embraced the cause of Federalism, so I adopted a program to achieve these objectives and denounced the reform of Gómez Farías, my own vice president. By December 1834 I suppressed the anti-clerical laws and drove Farías into exile.

The turmoil of the period from 1832 to 1834 caused foreigners to make derogatory observations about the Mexican nation in general and me in particular. But I had reached the pinnacle of political and military power. When the new Mexican Congress assembled on January 4, 1835 it was dominated by my followers and those devoted to the principle of Centralism. But I was getting tired of government. Pleading ill health I named General Miguel Barragán as an interim president in my absence. I was able to gracefully retire to Manga de Clavo where I could still manipulate the government in relative comfort.

Once again the religious orders reestablished their rights over the California missions, and over the nation's educational system. It wasn't long before trouble arose in the Department of Zacatecas where Governor Francisco García refused to comply with governmental decrees in early 1835. I was appointed to command the army that would force the submission of that rebellious Department. On May 11, 1835 I encountered Governor García's forces at Guadalupe near the city of Zacatecas. I had a great victory and sacked the city. Congress named me "*El Benemérito*,"[3] of the country. On October 3, 1835 Barragán, with my concurrence decreed that Centralism was the governing principle of the Mexican Government and that Federalism was officially suppressed. A new Constitution was drawn up in 1836, which stated that states would be replaced with "departments" and that the national government, the "Supreme Government" would dominate the country.

Trouble with Texas, however, was now going to be my undoing. Texas was the last frontier region occupied by Spain. It remained a sparsely populated area with only a few Franciscan missions and some scattered Presidios. Adventurers and filibustering expeditions from the United States often illegally entered the region at the beginning of the nineteenth century. To establish a greater control over Texas and to populate the region Spain accepted the offer of Moses Austin to bring colonists in from the United States in the early 1820's. Moses' son, Stephen F. Austin, inherited his father's grant and received confirmation from the Mexican government. The difference between Anglo-Americans in Texas and their Spanish-American countrymen in the South caused great antagonism, both with Texas and the rest of Mexico. The Constitution of 1824 endorsed the Catholic religion as the exclusive faith of the Mexican nation, whereas the Texas colonists were largely Protestants. There also was a desire for self-government at first and later the demand for total independence. Other conflicts included the introduction of slavery into Texas whereas Mexico had abolished slavery upon the achievement of her independence. The Centralist coup d'état in 1834 convinced the Texans that they were fighting a losing battle in their desire for self-government.

It was the agitation of the Federalist Lorenzo de Zavala in 1835 that started the movement. In the spring of 1835 he quarreled with me and the Centralists, lost his arguments, and look refuge in Texas. There he urged the department to revolt, obtaining assistance from many friends of the Texans residing in New Orleans. He and Sam Houston led an uprising at Velasco and promoted the declaration of Texan independence on

---

[3]   Savior.

November 3, 1835. The newly established government named David G. Burnet as president of Texas and Lorenzo de Zavala as vice president.

I could not sit idly by while my administration was thus openly challenged. I secured the authorization of the government to come out of retirement and lead a campaign against the rebellious Texans. I reached San Luis Potosí on December 5, 1835 determined to suppress the rebellion. My big problem was the recruitment of an army and supplies for the long march to Texas. I received no local aid and there was silence from the City of Mexico. But I was resourceful and mortgaged some of my property to provide seed money. I negotiated a few bank loans and went ahead to organize some six thousand poorly equipped soldiers. As an incentive I created a special award called the Legion of Honor to be awarded to those who fought bravely against the Texans. Officers would receive this medal in solid gold.

Accompanied by my aide Juan Nepomuceno Almonte and my secretary Ramón Martínez Caro I began the march northward on January 2, 1836. Difficulties in crossing the Rio Bravo del Norte[4] and Nueces River hindered the march. The assault on the Alamo, on the outskirts of San Antonio de Bexar took place about eight days after my exhausted army reached that town. The Texans, under the command of William B. Travis, took refuge in an old Franciscan mission. The attack, conducted over a period of one and a half hours on Sunday morning, March 6, 1836 resulted in the death of 183 men. I spared three women, two children and a Negro servant boy during the final assault. I had to reduce the Alamo so that my army would not be exposed to an attack from the rear. Seventy of my men died and 300 were wounded.

After my success at the Alamo I divided my forces into four divisions. One remained at Bexar under General José Andrade, another was dispatched under General José Urrea to the south to maintain a point for the loading of supplies, a third force under General Gaona was sent north, and I led the main element eastward towards the Colorado River. Urrea's division encountered a Texan force near the town of Goliad. The Texans believed they had surrendered on terms but General Urrea informed them in no uncertain terms that it was an unconditional surrender. Colonel Portilla, left behind by General Urrea to take charge of the prisoners was notified on March 26th to execute all the prisoners.

---

[4]   The Rio Grande.

On the next day Portilla marched them out of town and carried out the sentence. I explained that the prisoners at Galiad were condemned by law since they surrendered unconditionally. I agreed that the law was unjust, but that it was not my job to be a judge.

The massacre at Galiad and the annihilation of the Alamo garrison caused the Texans to rally and concentrate on saving their cause. The Texans abandoned towns, scorched the earth and burned buildings to deny our advancing forces. My Army reached the San Jacinto River on April 20th. After reinforcements arrived the size of my force numbered around 1150, thus exceeding the strength of Houston's army by about 300. A major clash occurred on the next day. After a day of marching to reach Buffalo Bayou and an all night vigil followed by an entire morning marching on horseback I was forced to stop and rest.

I picked a location under some shade trees on a small rise overlooking an area where the Texans were known to be hiding. I ordered Captain Miguel Aguírre to keep a vigilant observation and instructed General Castrillón to take care of the scouts and maintain an alert watch. Both officers failed miserably in their tasks. Houston's army completely surprised our forces and engaged in an 18 minute battle starting at 3:27 PM in the afternoon. I was awakened from a deep sleep by the noise of the assault, but by then it was too late. I yelled out, **"The enemy is upon us! The enemy is upon us!"**

I then mounted my horse and succeeded in riding through the Texan lines, although my horse was hit by a stray bullet. Our army was completely annihilated, approximately half killed, and the other half wounded and captured. I learned at a later date that only six Texans were killed in that action.

My horse subsequently died and I had to continue on foot. I continued my journey until a party of Texans, who were pursuing fugitives, captured me on April 22nd without recognizing me. On the morning of April 23, 1836 I asked to see Houston and I showed the American Colonel a letter with my signature on it. I was asked if I might be Santa Anna. I replied, "Sí Señor, General Houston."

Meanwhile other captured Mexican officers recognized me and exclaimed, "El Presidente! El Presidente!" I was then taken to meet Houston where I formally surrendered. Houston still wished to make absolutely sure of my identity and summoned my secretary Ramón Caro and my aide Juan Almonte, both of whom identified me. I was taken to the port of Velasco to complete the negotiations on the terms of the armistice. Colonels Almonte and Gabriel Núñez accompanied me to Velasco as did my secretary Martínez Caro. Most of the negotiations were carried out by Almonte and the son of Lorenzo de Zavala, who had resisted Texan pressure to execute me. On May 14th I signed two treaties with the victorious Texans. In the public Treaty of Velasco I agreed not to take up arms against the people of Texas, private property was to be restored, and prisoners were to be exchanged and all hostilities were to cease. Mexican troops were to evacuate Texas beyond the Rio Grande. In the secret treaty I promised to *try* to have the Mexican Cabinet receive a Commission from Texas to obtain recognition for Texan independence, and to set a boundary at the Rio Grande. In return I was to be guaranteed immediate release to embark for Vera Cruz.

I boarded the ship *Invincible* near Velasco, but some 130 volunteers led by one Thomas J. Green arrived and demanded my death. I was removed forcefully from the *Invincible* and imprisoned in the town. When captured I pleaded to be put to death, but the mob just kicked and pummeled me. I was guarded by some of the Goliad survivors. On June 30th I was moved to Goliad where I was told I would be eventually executed. The execution was to be carried out at the very spot where the Texans had been killed in late March. Stephen F. Austin who had been earlier freed by me from imprisonment in the City of Mexico visited and suggested I write President Andrew Jackson. I advised the U. S. president that a Mexican army under General Urrea would soon invade Texas and that my imprisonment was a violation of the Treaty of Velasco. Jackson wrote back on September 4th that the United States could not support the wishes of a disavowed Mexican president, but that he would show my letter to the Mexican Minister, Manuel Eduardo de Gorostiza.

Back in Mexico my government was undergoing great changes. President *ad interim* Barragán died on March 1st 1836 and was replaced by José Justo Corro who would served until the elections of January 1837. The government issued a decree on May 20, 1836 stating that any agreement I might have entered into while a prisoner in Texas was null and void. This was communicated to Gorostiza in Washington. At the beginning of July the Mexican government formally repudiated the Treaty of Velasco, and exhorted all Mexicans to continue the war.

I was in desperate straits. Even my secretary Martinez Caro turned on me and gained his freedom by revealing an alleged escape plan on my part. As a result of the alleged plot I was moved to Orazimba for better security, and on August 17th they attached a heavy ball and chain on my leg. After I was moved to Orazimba all my friends gave me up for dead.

But all hope was not lost. My chains were removed in the second week of October, soon after the arrival of President Jackson's letter. Since I had been denounced as an authorized government official representing Mexico, deserted by my soldiers, and spurned by President Jackson, Texan President David G. Burnet granted a pardon and honored my request to be allowed to go to Washington to plead my case. On November 25th I left accompanied by my aide Juan Almonte and a small Texan escort. We traveled on the river steamer *Tennessee,* landing at Louisville, Kentucky on Christmas Day 1836. From there we went on to Lexington, Kentucky where I became very sick, caused by the change of climate and the strenuous horseback ride. I was granted medical aid and the trip resumed on January 5, 1837. We halted temporarily at Frederick, Maryland where I met the American General Winfield Scott who was being tried by a court martial for transgressions during a campaign in Florida. We reached Washington on January 18, 1837 after a tiring two-month trek.

Secretary of State John Forsyth called upon me soon after my arrival and requested that I accompany him to see the president. I proposed the cession of Texas to the United States for a "fair" consideration but the United States president could not accept such a proposal, since no official correspondence regarding Texas had been received from the legally constituted Mexican government. Furthermore the Mexican Minister had been instructed not to recognize me while being a prisoner. Failing in our unofficial negotiations I departed for Vera Cruz and arrived there on February 12, 1837 escorted by U. S. Naval Lieutenant J. Tatnall. At Vera Cruz I told General Antonio Castro, Commandant, that all I wanted to do was to return to private life.

I returned to Manga de Clavo after an absence of fourteen months. My popularity was at a low point. Home at last, I reported that I was determined never again to quit my peaceful retreat. I wrote a long manifesto absolving myself from all responsibility for the Texas campaign.

France intervened in Mexico to collect claims on behalf of the French nationals. By March of 1838 France demanded a payment of 600,000 pesos for all of her citizens who had suffered injuries and losses of property during the previous decade. When no restitution was offered the French Navy instituted a blockade of Vera Cruz in April 1838. The Bustamante government appointed General Manuel Rincón to defend the city of Vera Cruz, but, as usual, provided no funds for the effort. Rincón consequently opened negotiations with the French. This effort failed, and the French, under Admiral Charles Baudin, bombarded the fortress of San Juan de Ulúa and the city of Vera Cruz itself in late November 1838.

I had the idea that King Philippe of France wanted to make the Mexicans his subjects and introduce a French monarchy. I offered my services to General Rincón and proceeded to Vera Cruz on November 27th, but as I observed, "the worst had already happened." I met with the garrison commander at San Juan de Ulúa and we decided that capitulation was the best course of action. I so advised Rincón and arrangements were made for the surrender of the fortress on November 28th. However Bustamante became enraged over this suggestion and repudiated the surrender treaty. Not knowing of my involvement Bustamante replaced Rincón at the beginning of December and named me the new commandant to lead the fight against the French. By the time the news of Bustamante's repudiation of the treaty with the French and my appointment had reached Vera Cruz I had returned to my hacienda. Learning of my appointment I immediately returned to Vera Cruz on December 4th and took command of the troops there. I informed Admiral Baudin that the treaty of November 28th had not been ratified by my government. That night I had a lengthy conversation with General Mariano Arista concerning plans for the defense of the city. Three days later President Bustamante officially declared war on France and hostilities were expected at any moment.

Well before day-break on the morning of December 5th the King's son, who was a member of the French expeditionary force, led a daring landing party into the city of Vera Cruz. Some three thousand Frenchmen participated in the landing and complete surprise was achieved. I was awakened by gun fire down the street and escaped, but General Arista was still asleep when he was captured. The French forces then began to withdraw toward the waterfront for re-embarkation. I rallied the troops and citizens within the city and led my forces in pursuit of the French, who fled in the direction of a dock where they had concealed a cannon to cover a possible retreat. The first volley from that cannon killed my horse and ripped open my left leg. Severely wounded I ordered the evacuation of Vera Cruz and we fell back out of range of the French guns.

Medical personnel performed a botched amputation of my left leg, severing it below the knee. I was presented with the amputated and preserved section of my leg as a token of my courageous defense of the homeland. With my flair for the dramatic and really expecting to die on the spot I issued another of my proclamations and stated that this would be my last victory on behalf of my country.

This so called "Pastry War" ended the following spring when the French agreed to settle for 600,000 pesos in payment for their claims. I, of course, did not die and recuperated slowly at Manga de Clavo and became a popular hero to my fellow Mexicans. I even had praise from the United States. David G. Farragut, a young naval officer, witnessed the action of December 5th from the deck of the U. S. S. *Erie* in Vera Cruz harbor, and commended me for my bravery in the face of the surprise attack of the French invaders.

Gómez Farías had returned to Mexico and Federalist uprisings intensified during the early months of 1839. While recovering from my amputation I supported Bustamante against these Federalist rebellions and proceeded to the capital on February 17th seventy-four days after I lost my leg. Bustamante faced the problem of whom to appoint as interim president while he actively directed a campaign in the north.

When Bustamante left for Tampico on March 19th I assumed the presidential chair for the second time. I stated that "the exercise of supreme power is for me the torment of an honored man," and I was resolved to retire when the present trouble had ended so that I could concentrate on domestic affairs and my well being. I wasted little time in suppressing newspapers, imprisoning authors and removing conspirators to more secure locations.

Bustamante did not do well in defeating his rebel forces so I responded to the challenge by recruiting an army within the capital. The rebel General José Antonio Mejía moved southward threatening to cut off the Vera Cruz-Puebla Road. Traveling by litter I met Mejía's forces on May 3rd and directed the operation in which my forces annihilated the rebels and captured all the leaders. Three hours after the battle ended I ordered the immediate execution of General Mejía.

I returned to the capital on May 8th amidst the pealing of bells, cannon fire and acclamations from the crowd. I had reached the apex of my career. Wishing to avoid meeting with Bustamante I pleaded ill health and left for Manga de Clavo. I appointed Nicholás Bravo interim president and left on my litter for Vera Cruz on July 11th. Nine days later Bustamante arrived back at the capital. The revolts of Federalism continued and even intensified in 1841 when the province of Yucatán declared itself independent. The Bustamante government appointed me to the military command of Vera Cruz so that I might organize an expedition to subdue the rebellious Yucateros.

I refused the appointment and remained at Manga de Clavo awaiting better opportunities. In the late summer of 1841 I participated in overthrowing the Bustamante government, shortly after the president completed half of his eight year term under the provisions of the Seven laws of 1836. I denounced President Bustamante officially on August 24, 1841. I criticized the government for not securing the obedience of the departments for the laws; failing to defend the frontiers; and failing to aid the departments that were menaced by adventurers, as in the recent case of Texas. I denounced Bustamante for overtaxing the people and failing to provide fiscal stability.

I announced a new Plan on September 7th and officially pronounced against Bustamante, since the president had taken personal command of the government's troops in violation of the Constitution. With a small force I took Perote, near Jalapa, and moved on Puebla in September. On the 27th I met with General Gabriel Valencia and Mariano Paredes at Tacubaya. We forced Bustamante to agree to a truce and the three of us agreed on a plan for the establishment of a new temporary government on September 29th. It provided that I would appoint two representatives from each department who would then select a new provisional president. This official would then call a Congress to write a Constitution revising the present system of government.

I met the crushed Bustamante on October 5th outside the capital and he signed off on the agreed upon provisional regime. The next day I entered the City of Mexico, but there was no display except for the bells of the cathedral. I did not remain in the capital but returned to the Archbishop's Palace in Tacubaya, preferring it to the presidential palace. There the appointed representatives cast 39 of their 44 votes for my election as provisional president. On October 10, 1841 I was again in charge of all of Mexico. I established what outsiders called a military dictatorship and wrote a new Constitution called the Bases Orgánicas in 1843. I was dedicated to the military and clerical groups within my country. I went home frequently to Manga de Clavo and ran things from there. I would plead ill health and leave my affairs at the Capital to my vice president Nicholás Bravo.

One of the unique aspects of my government was its financial policy. I called in all outstanding copper specie and replaced it with new national coins. This measure failed not because of me but because most of the people were left without any money when the mint delayed replacing the old coins and finally defaulted altogether. I also adopted a law permitting foreigners who subjected themselves to Mexican laws to own land in our country.

I was particularly successful in beautifying the capital, resolving a border dispute with Guatemala, and ending the rebellion in Yucatán. However Texas and California remained a problem. Although I sent out General Adrian Woll on a raid to San Antonio in September of 1842 I never carried out my threat to reconquer the lost province. With respect to California I considered selling it to Great Britain so that I could use the money to fight the United States over the Texas issue. The plan quietly collapsed.

I was now enjoying elaborate state dinners, huge cavalry escorts and great celebrations on my birthday. I had a new theater erected and called it the Teatro Santa Anna. There was even a new bronze statue erected in the Plaza de Volador (of you know who) dominating the plaza with my right hand extended and my finger pointing north to remind everyone of the Texan problem. My opponents said behind my back that my statue was pointing at the mint with the idea of despoiling it. The most remarkable event, however, was the transfer of my shattered and amputated limb from Manga de Clavo to the capital where it was solemnly placed on an urn atop a stone column. I attended this ceremony on September 27, 1842. I believed it was inspiration for the young military officers of the Republic. Thereafter I wore an unadorned wooden leg upon most occasions.

My personal life underwent great changes during my term as president. I invested much of my new wealth in land. Especially important was the purchase of El Encero, my new hacienda, in the spring of 1842. It was located east of Jalapa in a better climate than the hot lowlands near Vera Cruz. El Encero now became my main residence and Manga de Clavo tended to be ignored and gradually decayed. I owned forty or fifty thousand head of cattle and permitted other farmers to graze their cattle on my land in return for a rent of $40 per head per year. I made a lot of money this way. My interest in cock fighting did not diminish and I even treated the United States Minister to Mexico, Waddy Thompson, to a great sporting event. I promised to send Thompson one of my prized cocks if his choice won the contest. It was the only cock I ever lost, but I kept my word and sent him the bird after he returned home.

Tragedy struck my household on August 23, 1844 when Doña Inés García died after a lengthy illness. After a huge funeral procession Doña Inés was buried at Puebla. She had been always content to only live at Manga de Clavo and manage my estate. Her death caused me to go into semi-retirement again. I was shortly remarried to Doña María Dolores de Tosta, a young lady of fifteen, in a ceremony performed on October 3, 1844. I did not have time to go to the wedding so the marriage was accomplished by proxy. My new bride was taken to El Encero, but soon returned to the gaiety of the capital where she remained. My sudden remarriage upset the Mexican populace, their premier not having even observed the conventional mourning period.

All was not well in the fall of 1844. My former ally, Mariano Paredes, led a rebellion in Guadalajara and ultimately brought about the end of my third term as president. Paredes launched his rebellion on October 30, 1844 asserting that I had not performed my duties as Chief Executive, allowed the army to degenerate, and failed in handling the financial crisis, having appropriated 60 million pesos (as he claimed) for my own use.

Early in November Paredes advanced on the City of Mexico with a huge army. I requested Congress to give me extraordinary powers to repel him, but that body denied me. My struggle with Congress and the threat of Paredes' forces caused me to evacuate the capital and flee to Querétero on November 28th. Congress declared my conduct rebellious and on December 2, 1844 they officially terminated my presidency.

Violence inflamed the issues and affected all the personalities involved. By December 5th most of the military had deserted and joined the Paredes revolt. An angry mob broke into the Santa Anna

Theater and tore down my splendid statue. They fastened a rope around the statue's neck, dragged it through the streets, and finally broke it up into little pieces. They then went to Santa Paula cemetery where they profaned and burned my leg.

After I reached Querétero the United States published my correspondence with the British Minister concerning negotiations over the possible sale of California. This really upset the citizens. Uprisings in Puebla were followed by similar occurrences in Oaxaca, Zacatecas, Guanajuato and even San Luis Potosí. In Vera Cruz citizens burned my portrait and denounced me as a traitor to everybody. My presence in Querétero was also being resisted by a hostile populace. The temporary government of Jose Joaquín de Herrera refused my request to go into exile, denied me protection, and refused to pay my salary. I decided it was time to fly the coop.

I traveled with five of my servants towards El Encero. I was surprised by a patrol of residents from Xico about ten miles south of Jalapa at 8:00 PM on the evening of January 15, 1845. I offered the angry mob 2000 pesos to let me go home. The offer was refused and the residents arrested me and turned me over to their village commander, who, in turn, reported the arrest to higher authorities. I was escorted by the military commander to Jalapa and slapped into jail. I said the situation was "worse than that when I was prisoner among the Texan adventurers."

I requested that I be allowed to go into exile, but I was again refused. They ordered me to stand trial, but time was on my side and tempers cooled. On May 24th I was exiled "for life," to reside in Venezuela with half the pay of a general. I offered my properties for sale during April and May of 1845, but without success. Nobody had that kind of money! As May drew to a close I prepared to go into exile. I issued a manifesto to the Mexican people proclaiming my loyalty, my faithful service, my gratitude and my love for them. On June 3, 1845 I boarded a pocket vessel at Antigua, near Vera Cruz, bound for the Caribbean (and not Venezuela).

I arrived at Havana, Cuba after five days at sea and went into retirement on a large hacienda outside the city limits of Havana. While I remained in exile the Mexican nation continued its decline into internal chaos. The Government of Herrera lacked direction and had no following. On December 14, 1845 almost a year after I had been overthrown, Mariano Paredes rebelled for the third time in less than five years. When the military garrison of the City of Mexico joined the revolt on December 30th, Paredes' success was assured, and he rode into the capital on January 2, 1846 to become temporary dictator.

Domestic unity did not occur when Paredes came into power. Factionalism and distrust continued to mount. Federalist insurrections started up again, the treasury was virtually empty, and foreign credit all but disappeared. The army was ready for a mutiny in the spring of 1846. This unstable condition was heightened by the threat of war with the United States. The annexation of Texas by the United States on March 1, 1845 would eventually lead to the outbreak of hostilities between the two nations. Mexico had threatened to go to war with the United States if Texas were annexed, but all that happened was that the Mexican Minister to the United States, Juan N. Almonte, simply asked for his passport, thereby severing diplomatic relations and returned to Mexico. This provided the background for intrigue and I knew that as a master of this art I was going to get into the fray. There was a Federalist group spearheading a movement to promote a war with the United States over the Texas issue. That group also desired to restore the Constitution of 1824 and annul the powers of the clergy and the military, but I couldn't have everything. Valentín Gómez Farías was the main leader of this faction of the Federalists. I wrote him in New Orleans and told him I would like to see the overthrow of Paredes. I tried to convince Farías that I had now become a Federalist.

In March 1846 I stepped up my campaign to return to Mexico. On April 25, 1846 I wrote Farías that "I will give you the affection of the army, in which I have many good friends, and you will give me the affection of the masses over whom you have so much influence."

For nearly a decade I had denounced the United States for its failure to be neutral during the Mexican war with the Texans. Now in exile, I was not above dealing with that hated enemy if such negotiations might aid me in returning to power in Mexico. I was willing to negotiate with friend and foe alike to get what I wanted. Colonel Alejandro J. Atocha played a leading role in my negotiations with the United States. Atocha was a Spaniard who had lived in New Orleans and had resided in Mexico as a supporter of mine until President Herrera ordered me out of the country in early 1845. On February 13, 1846 Atocha had an interview with President James K. Polk in Washington City.

In this confidential interview Atocha stated that I was in constant communication with my friends still in Mexico and that I was receiving hundreds of letters whenever a vessel from Vera Cruz reached Cuba. He advanced the idea that I would soon be in power again. He reported that I favored a treaty with the United States recognizing the Rio Bravo del Norte as a boundary between that nation and Mexico, and ceding all the land north of a line extending along the Colorado River to San Francisco Bay for a payment of $30 million dollars.

Colonel Atocha called on President Polk again on Monday, February 16th, and an audience of about one hour was granted. Atocha went further in his suggestions on Monday. He pointed out that the Mexican government could not afford to make such a proposal for fear of being overthrown. Atocha said it must appear that the terms of such a treaty must appear to be forced upon the Mexicans. To do this I recommended that the United States should send an army to the Rio Grande and a naval force to Vera Cruz. Through Atocha I alleged that I had the concurrence of President Paredes who was supposedly a violent opponent of the United States in this project and that when I returned to Mexico Paredes and I would negotiate the treaty together. Atocha told President Polk that I had told Atocha, "when you see the president, tell him to take strong measures, and such a treaty can be made and I will sustain it."

President Polk distrusted Colonel Atocha and certainly he distrusted my intentions. He therefore did not communicate anything of an official nature to him. But he was perplexed as what to do about the growing crisis in Mexico. The president's subsequent use of his military forces strongly resembled my basic ideas. Taylor centered his advance into the disputed zone between the Nueces River and the Rio Grande and clashes occurred.

War was declared and the U. S. Navy blockaded our ports in the Gulf of Mexico, especially around Vera Cruz. Polk then contacted me at my retreat near the Cuban capital to sound me out on some sort of negotiated agreement. Polk sent out several secret agents to talk with me and on May 13, 1846 the day war was declared he had the following message sent to Commander Conner who was in command of the blockading vessels near Vera Cruz:

Private & Confidential
Navy Department, May 13, 1846

Commodore: If Santa Anna endeavors to enter any
Mexican port you will allow him to pass freely.

GEORGE BANCROFT

As a special agent President Polk sent Commander Alexander Slidell
MacKenzie, nephew of John Slidell, to Havana where he landed on July
5, 1846. Polk had instructed the agent to cease hostilities, to promote
a revolution against Paredes, and replace him with a new government.
MacKenzie was to determine the prospects whether I could conclude
such a peace treaty if I were restored to power in Mexico.

MacKenzie talked with me on July 7th and I told him how well I
had been treated by President Jackson during my visit to Washington
in July 1837. I said that if I were restored to power I would govern
in the interests of the masses instead of parties and classes. If I were
restored to the presidency I would negotiate a peace which would
establish boundaries to avoid the ravages of war. I suggested that Taylor
should advance to Saltillo to bring about the collapse of the Parades
government, and that the U. S. Army should then move on San Luis
Potosí, causing the distressed Mexicans to recall me from exile.

The president decided to gamble on me and grant me egress through
the blockade. He figured he had little to lose and much to gain if I came
through with my promises. On August 8, 1846 President Polk asked
the U. S. Congress to appropriate two million dollars to negotiate the
expected peace settlement with Mexico. That very same day I boarded
the British steamer *Arab* in Havana harbor. Accompanied by some
supporters I arrived off Vera Cruz on August 16th.

Meanwhile a revolt had occurred in Mexico resulting in the
overthrow of Paredes and demands that I be recalled. Since I had
indicated willingness to restore Federalism against the "monarchal"
Paredes, the Federalists decided that an alliance with me provided the
best possibility of their restoration to power. On July 31st a military
revolt began in the City of Mexico favoring Federalism and my return to
power. General José Mariano Salas pronounced against Paredes, forcing

the latter's resignation on August 6th. Salas occupied the National Palace and issued a manifesto calling for my return.

Ten days after the successful Salas revolt I came ashore at Vera Cruz. Commodore Conner's patrol vessels intercepted the *Arab* and I handed the boarding officer my note of identification and the ship was allowed to proceed. I landed at Vera Cruz one year, two months, and thirteen days after I had been sent into permanent exile by President Herrera. I never went to Venezuela.

Upon landing I issued a great pronouncement emphasizing that the people of Mexico had issued a popular call for my return. I ardently desired to work with Valentin Gómez Farías whom I considered my best friend and the staunchest supporter of public liberties.

I neither remained in Vera Cruz nor went to the City of Mexico. Instead I returned to El Encero, staying there until September 14th, when I took up residence at the Archbishop's Palace in Tacubaya again. I entered the City of Mexico on September 16th. I was accompanied by Gómez Farías who rode in the front seat facing me. After this show of identity I returned to Tacubaya where I intended to begin the enlistment of an army to combat the invading forces of the United States.

My first step was to regularize the government by establishing a Counsel of States headed by Gómez Farías, an act which was accomplished by a decree issued by General Salas on September 20th. I left Tacubaya on September 28th, arriving at San Luis Potosí on October 8th, to begin the organization of the army which would halt the invasion of General Zachary Taylor in the North. I was joined by General Pedro Ampudia who had been defeated by Taylor at Monterey in September. I ordered the evacuation of the garrison at Tampico, its troops being directed to join me at San Luis Potosí.

I had virtually nothing with which to start with. I had to raise revenues, and equip and supply a force to move northward. In addition I had to raise my army in the heart of an area in which the people despised me for my former ruthlessness against them. For money I seized ninety-eight silver bars from the mint at San Luis Potosí and ordered them melted down. I offered mortgages on my own property as security to obtain loans from the merchants.

When I was elected by the Congress to the presidency on December 6th, 1846, while at San Luis Potosi, I was once more a president *in absentia*. I did not take the oath of office, leaving Gómez Farías, the elected vice president, to take charge. I was now president of Mexico for the fourth time. I inspected my troops at San Luis Potosí with oratory and boundless energy. In early January 1847 Gómez Farías supported a drastic anti-clerical measure that provided for the raising of fifteen million pesos for our army by the sale or mortgaging of Church property. Mounting pressure forced me to dispatch part of my army from San Luis Potosí on January 28, 1847. The army contained 13,400 infantry and over 4300 cavalry men and an artillery train of seventeen pieces. The men had little training and the artillery had never fired as much as a blank shot. Once on the march towards Saltillo through desolate country desertions started occurring, but other reinforcements arrived from the west bringing my forces up to strength again with the addition of 518 artillerymen. I now had forty pieces of artillery of various calibers. My plans were to trap Taylor at Saltillo, and use surprise and envelopment as tools, but things did not go as planned. The two day battle of Buena Vista on February 22 and 23rd was nearly won, but shortage of food and danger of complete defeat forced me to withdraw beginning on February 24th. Having lost about 1,800 killed and wounded, plus 294 captured and 4000 deserters during the battle I decided to fall back to San Luis Potosí.

The retreat southward was a nightmare. Starvation, lack of medical supplies, battle injuries, dysentery and typhus and wholesale desertion all plagued me. When we reached San Luis Potosí on March 12, I only had one-half of my original complement. Having suffered a military defeat which I concealed from the Mexican people I now faced a political crisis. A rebellion had occurred in the City of Mexico over Gómez Farías' decree announcing the seizure of clerical properties. I spoke out about the revolt and emphasized how this would encourage our enemies and concluded that my opponent, General Taylor, had spoken truthfully at Saltillo when he said, "I am not afraid of Santa Anna. There will be a revolution in Mexico very soon and he will be deposed."

I decided to go to the capital and straighten out the situation. I resumed the office of Chief Executive and accepted an offer of the clergy to provide me with two million pesos if I would support their cause. On March 31st, 1847 I repudiated the legislation of the Liberal, Gómez Farías, and he went into exile. Having temporarily quieted the home front I now turned my attention to the problem of the newly arrived North American troops under the command of General Winfield Scott.

I selected Pedro Maria Anaya as provisional president, and departed for El Encero arriving there on April 5, 1847. I immediately began preparations to resist the advance of General Scott from Vera Cruz. **"My duty is to sacrifice myself. Vera Cruz calls for vengeance—follow me and wash out the stain of her dishonor!"**

Chapter 5

A Side Saddle War

Zachary Taylor

I was born on November 24, 1784 in Orange County, Virginia, the son of Richard Taylor and Sarah Strother. In the summer of 1785 my family immigrated to Kentucky, arriving there ten years after the first settlers. A short time later my brother Hancock was murdered by Indians. I went to a school run by Mr. Elisha Ayres of Connecticut, and received a decent education. I worked at the estate of my father until the death of my favorite military brother, Lieutenant William Taylor. I decided to enter the military service in honor of his name. Through the influence of friends and relatives, among whom was Mr. James Madison, I received a commission as first lieutenant in the 7th Infantry Regiment on May 3, 1808.

My ambition was to fight Indians. When General Harrison was governor of the North Western Territory I received orders to march into the wilderness, where I erected a series of forts. One of these, built on the Wabash, was called Fort Harrison. It was located in the very heart of Indian country. Apparently insignificant as was this small defense, it laid the foundation for my military reputation.

I fell in love with Margaret "Peggy" Mackall Smith and we were married on June 21, 1810. The following year I was back at Fort Harrison. In 1812 I was awarded a captain's commission from President Madison and became commander of the fort. Very soon after Congress declared war against Great Britain I was thrown into the front of hostile operations.

On September 4th, 1812 Fort Harrison repulsed a vicious Indian attack for seven hours. That a handful of men should hold off four hundred assailants astonished and discomfited the savages, and materially altered their views and aspirations. Very soon after this battle I received a large envelope from Washington containing their official thanks for my services along with a commission as a brevet major in the United States Army.

When peace returned I was put back to my former rank of captain but my friends exerted themselves strenuously in my behalf. Their efforts were successful and in 1816 I was restored by President Madison to my former rank. I was ordered to Green Bay, remaining there at that station for two years; after which I returned to my family, spent a year at home, and then joined Colonel Russell at New Orleans.

I remained in the south for several years during which time I built Fort Jesup. In 1819 I was made a lieutenant colonel and in 1826 was appointed to a board of officers of the army and militia. It was there that I met General Winfield Scott who was president of the board. In 1832 I was promoted to the rank of full colonel. Immediately after my promotion I was employed in the expedition against the Indian Chief Black Hawk. I then returned to Fort Snelling as commanding officer. There a subordinate, Jefferson Davis, sought to wed my second daughter, Sarah Knox Taylor. I detested Jeff Davis and forbade his entry into my home. Davis resigned his commission in 1835 and eloped with Sarah. Three months later my poor daughter died of a fever at Davis's Mississippi plantation.

War in Florida owed its progress principally to the efforts of Osceola, a wild Indian chief, whose influence was sufficient to drive the Indians through every danger and trial. In December 1837 I was ordered to wipe out the Seminoles, so I eagerly set out into the swamps. On Christmas Day we formed a line of battle and waded through a four foot depth of slime and water against the enemy. The savages were right out in front and held their fire until we faced each other directly.

Volley after volley was fired and one man after another sunk down into the slime. All around was a blaze of fire. Mowed down by scores, our front line faltered, then rolled back and broke. The Indians poured after us yelling one war-whoop after another. Havoc raged among the 6th Infantry to such a degree that the dark cool water beneath grew warm and red with human blood.

Of the five companies in the advance every minor officer was either killed or disabled. Amidst the horrors of the hour I rushed from rank to rank exhorting my heroes to charge. Then the savages broke in disorder and fell back. Then they rallied. Again they were broken, again they rallied, till the whole swamp seemed to boil with the rapid movements. At length the Indians were driven to the border of Lake Okeechobee. Here their flank was turned by Colonel Davenport, and immediately afterwards they delivered their final volley and fled. The pursuit was continued until nightfall.

The loss of the Americans in battle was 14 officers and 124 men; that of the Indians completely unknown. In any other place than Florida the battle of Okeechobee would have terminated the war. But the nature of the terrain prevented the transportation of supplies and the enemy Indians were able to recover from the heavy blow and muster their strength further into the interior. I was breveted a brigadier-general and was dubbed "Old Rough and Ready" by my troops. In the following April I was entrusted with the full command of the military in Florida, General Jesup having been permitted to resign.

Hostilities continued and savage cruelty increased. An infant was murdered with its mother as it pressed upon her breast. Fathers were shot in the presence of their families and children were surprised in sleep from which they never awoke. Victims were shrieking and screaming for help, but I could do very little. In 1840 I requested permission to retire from Florida and was succeeded by General Armistead. I assumed command of the Department of the Southwest and was ordered to Fort Gibson to relieve General Arbuckle. I purchased a home in Baton Rouge, Louisiana, which I thereafter considered home. Here I remained until the commencement of trouble with Mexico.

In May of 1845 I received a confidential communique from the Secretary of War instructing me to place my troops at such a position as would enable me to defend the territory of Texas. A subsequent

47

letter from the war department contained the following additional instructions:

Should Mexico assemble a large body of troops on the Rio Grande, and cross it with a considerable force, such a movement must be regarded as an invasion of the United States and the commencement of hostilities. You will of course use all the authority which has been or may be given you to meet such a state of things. Texas must be protected from hostile invasion, and for that purpose you will of course employ, to the utmost extent, all the means you possess or can command.

I was 62 years old at the time. Brigadier General William J. Worth was ten years younger and my second in command. Worth had his fits of temper, liked liquor, and had a penchant for bad decisions, yet he complimented my short-comings. My other high ranking officers included Colonel William G. Belknap, David E. Twiggs, William Whistler and Colonel James S. McIntosh. All these men were over fifty years of age. My command numbered 3880 troops of whom 500 were ill with amoebic dysentery, diarrhea, and yellow fever all arising from the unsanitary conditions of the military encampments.

I took up a position at Corpus Christi where I remained until Sunday, March 8, 1846. On that day my advance guard consisting of Twiggs's 2nd Dragoons with light artillery commenced its march for Matamoros on the Rio Grande. The route was well marked and to the Mexicans it was called the Road of the Arroyo Colorado. The next day the 1st Brigade under the command of Brevet Brigadier General William J. Worth marched out; on March 10th the 2nd Brigade under Colonel James S. McIntosh left, and on March 11th the 3rd Brigade under Colonel William Whistler set out. The siege train and field battery were sent by water to Point Isabel with a corps of engineers and the officers of ordnance under the command of Major Monroe.

I stayed behind to see the third brigade off, and then marched thirty miles out and joined the 2nd brigade which was advancing without any difficulty. I planned to catch up with Twiggs before reaching any location where enemy resistance could be expected. The march was hot and dirty. The soldiers went without water. I, of course, shared the hardships with the rest. I was heavily sunburned and my skin was beginning to peel. At the Arroyo Colorado the troops encountered a body of Mexicans, who seemed disposed to dispute our passage. This, however, was not attempted and we pushed forward until we were met by a civil deputation from Matamoros. They were on our right flank bearing a white flag, and protested about our march. They desired an interview with me, and I informed them that I would halt at the first suitable place on the road, and afford them the desired interview. It was, however, necessary for the want of water to continue on for some distance. The deputation halted, while yet some miles from Point Isabel, declining to go any further, and sent me a formal protest of the "Prefect of the Northern District of Tamaulipas" against our occupation of the country.

At this very moment I noticed that the buildings at Point Isabel were in flames. I told the bearer of the protest that I would answer their protest when I arrived at Matamoros, and dismissed the deputation. I considered the fires in the village as a decided evidence of hostility and I was not willing to be trifled with any longer. I had reason to believe the Prefect was but a tool of the Mexican authorities. The cavalry fortunately arrived in time to put out the fire, which consumed three or four houses. The Mexican responsible for the fires, under the orders of General Mejia, made his escape before our arrival.

We pursued our march and on the 28th of March we planted the Stars & Stripes on the banks of the Rio Grande, opposite Matamoros. Fortifications were immediately commenced, and soon a fort was erected, furnished with six bastions, and capable of containing two thousand men. It was called Fort Texas. On the other side of the river the Mexicans also commenced the construction of batteries and redoubts, both parties rapidly assuming the attitude of belligerents.

On April 10, 1846 the first American blood was shed. The victim was our venerable Colonel Cross, Deputy Quartermaster General. As was his custom, he took a ride out into the country every morning for exercise, and appears to have been attacked by some lawless Mexican rancheros, murdered, and stripped of all his belongings. His body was not recovered until April 20th, when it was honored by a military funeral becoming of a colonel's rank.

Mexican General Pedro de Ampudia arrived in Matamoros on the 11th, and as expected, entered at once upon active measures for the expulsion of the American army from Texas. His letter of April 12th to our command concluded as follows:

By explicit and definite orders of my government which neither can, will, nor should receive new outrages, I require you in all for, and at latest in the peremptory term of twenty-four hours, to break up your camp, and retire to the other bank of the Nueces River, while our governments are regulating the pending question in relation to Texas. If you insist on remaining upon the soil of the Department of Tamaulipas, it will clearly result that arms and arms alone must decide the question; and in that case I advise you that we accept the war to which, with so much injustice on your part, you provoke us; and that, on our part, this war shall be conducted conformably to the principles established by the most civilized nations—trusting that on your part the same will be observed. In reply I reminded Ampudia that I was acting for the president of the United States and could not recede from my position. Our fortifications were continued and every precaution made to guard it against attack. A few days later two ships, with supplies for the Mexican Army, were forbidden from entering the river, and the Rio Grande was declared in a state of blockade.

General Zachary Taylor

I then wrote General Ampudia as follows:

HEADQUARTERS Army of Occupation,
Camp near Matamoros, Texas, April 22, 1846.

SIR: I have had the honour to receive your communication of this date, in which you complain of certain measures adopted by my orders to close the mouth of the Rio Bravo[5] against vessels bound to Matamoros, and in which you also advert to the case of two Mexicans supposed to be detained as prisoners in this camp.

After all that has passed since the American army first approached the Rio Bravo, I am certainly surprised that you should complain of a measure which is no other than a natural result of the state of war so much insisted upon by the Mexican authorities as actually existing at this time. You will excuse me for recalling a few circumstances to show that this state of war has not been sought by the American army, but has been forced upon it, and that the exercise of the rights incident to such a state cannot be made a subject of complaint.

On breaking up my camp at Corpus Christi, and moving forward with the army under my orders to occupy the left bank of the Rio Bravo, it was my earnest desire to execute my instructions in a specific manner; to observe the utmost regard for the personal rights of all citizens residing on the left bank of the river, and to take care that the religion and customs of the people should suffer no violation. With this view, and to quiet the minds of the inhabitants, I issued orders to the army, enjoining a strict observance of the rights and interests of all Mexicans residing on the river, and caused said orders to be translated into Spanish, and circulated in the several towns on the Bravo. These orders announced the spirit in which we proposed to occupy the country, and I am proud to say that up to this moment the same spirit has controlled the operations of the army.

On reaching the Arroyo Colorado I was informed by a Mexican officer that the order in question had been received in Matamoros; but was told at the same time that if I attempted to cross the river it would be regarded as a declaration of war. Again, on my march to Frontono I was met by a deputation of the civil authorities of Matamoros, protesting

---

5   Mexican name for the Rio Grande.

against my occupation of a portion of the department of Tamaulipas, and declaring that if the army was not at once withdrawn, war would result. While this communication was in my hands, it was discovered that the village of Frontono had been set on fire and abandoned. I viewed this as a direct act of war, and informed the deputation that their communication would be answered by me when opposite Matamoros, which was done in respectful terms. On reaching the river I dispatched an officer, high in rank, to convey to the commanding general at Matamoros the expression of my desire for amicable relations, and my willingness to leave open to the use of the citizens of Matamoros the port of Brazos Santiago until the question of boundary should be definitively settled. This officer received in reply, from the officer selected to confer with him, that my advance to the Rio Bravo was considered as a veritable act of war, and he was absolutely refused an interview with the American consul, in itself an act incompatible with a state of peace.

Notwithstanding these repeated assurances on the part of the Mexican authorities, and notwithstanding the most obviously hostile preparations on the right bank of the river, accompanied by a rigid non-intercourse, I carefully abstained from any act of hostility—determined that the onus of producing an actual state of hostilities should not rest with me. Our relations remained in this state until I had the honor to receive your note of the 12th instant, in which you denounce war as the alternative of my remaining in this position. As I could not, under my instructions, recede from my position, I accepted the alternative you offered me, and made all my dispositions to meet it suitably. But, still willing to adopt milder measures before proceeding to others, I contented myself in the first instance with ordering a blockade of the mouth of the Rio Bravo by the naval forces under my orders—a proceeding perfectly consonant with the state of war so often declared to exist, and which you acknowledge in your note of the 16th instant, relative to the late Colonel Cross.

If this measure seems oppressive, I wish it borne in mind that it has been forced upon me by the course you have seen fit to adopt. I have reported this blockade to my government, and shall not remove it until I receive instructions to that effect, unless indeed you desire an armistice pending the final settlement of the question between the governments, or until war shall be formally declared by either, in which case I shall cheerfully open the river. In regard to the consequences you mention as resulting from a refusal to remove the blockade, I beg you to understand that I am prepared for them, be they what they may.

In regard to the particular vessels referred to in your communication, I have the honor to advise you that, in pursuance of my orders, two American schooners, bound for Matamoros, were warned off on the 17th instant, when near the mouth of the river, and put to sea, returning, probably to New Orleans. They were not seized, or their cargoes disturbed in any way, nor have they been in the harbor of Brazos Santiago to my knowledge. A Mexican schooner, understood to be the "Juniata," was in or off that harbor when my instructions to block the river were issued, but was driven to sea in a gale, since which time I have had no report concerning her. Since the receipt of your communication, I have learned that two persons, sent to the mouth of the river to procure information respecting this vessel, proceeded thence to Brazos Santiago, when they were taken up and detained by the officer in command, until my orders could be received. I shall order their immediate release. A letter from one of them to the Spanish vice consul is respectfully transmitted herewith.

In relation to the Mexicans said to have drifted down the river in a boat, and to be prisoners at this time in my camp, I have the pleasure to inform you that no such persons have been taken prisoners or are now detained by my authority. The boat in question was carried down empty by the current of the river and drifted ashore near one of our pickets and was secured by the guard. Some time afterwards an attempt was made to recover the boat under the cover of the darkness; the individuals concerned were hailed by the guard, and, failing to answer, were fired upon as a matter of course. What became of them is not known, as no trace of them could be discovered on the following morning. The officer of the Mexican guard directly opposite was informed next day that the boat would be returned on proper application to me, and I have now only to repeat that assurance.

In conclusion, I take leave to state that I consider the tone of your communication highly exceptionable, where you stigmatize the movement of the army under my orders as "marked with the seal of universal reprobation." You must be aware that such language is not respectful in itself, either to me or my government; and while I observe in my own correspondence the courtesy due to your high position, and to the magnitude of the interests with which we are respectively charged, I shall expect the same in return.

I have the honor to be, very respectfully, your obedient servant,

Z. TAYLOR, *Brevet Brig. Gen. U. S. A.,*
Commanding Sr. Gen. D. Pedro de Ampudia,
Commanding at Matamoros.

Alarming reports were reaching the American camp. We learned that about 3000 Mexicans were crossing the river and positioning themselves between our position and Point Isabel, my principal depot. Our only alternative was to put up with a scarcity of supplies, or cut our way through the overwhelming numbers to Point Isabel.

I wanted to be sure of my intelligence so I detached a few parties above and below Fort Texas to discover the exact positions and designs of the enemy. The fate of one of these parties deserves notice. It consisted of about sixty men under the command of Captain Thornton. They proceeded up-river for about twenty-five miles, when their Mexican guide halted, reporting that a large party of the enemy were ahead, and that he would proceed no further. Captain Thornton didn't believe his guide and moved forward until he reached a farm house surrounded by a chaparral hedge. After entering the enclosure, Thornton left his men near the entrance, and rode forward with a few advisers to speak with the owners. He suddenly discovered that the chaparral was swarming with armed Mexicans, who, in a few moments, were pouring forth volleys of musket fire. Shouting to his men to get the hell out, Thornton rushed forward and jumped over the hedge. In the act of leaping his horse received a musket-ball, but he succeeded in penetrating the enemy's line, and recede out of sight. In passing some rocks his horse fell, carrying him along with it, after which he managed to get up and hobble off. He was soon captured and carried off to Matamoros, with most of his party sharing the same fate.

After this affair the Mexicans completely shut off our communications and gradually surrounded the river fort. For three days our little garrison was in a state of gloom, but then Captain Walker, of the Texas Rangers, arrived with the cheering news that all was still safe at Point Isabel. I therefore resolved on marching there immediately with my whole command, except for a small garrison left under Major Brown, sufficient to defend Fort Texas.

I left the Rio Grande on May 1st, 1846 and marched for Point Isabel. My "retreat" was hailed in Matamoros by the ringing of Church bells, wild shouting and gun fire. General Arista, commandant of the city, immediately commenced operations for the destruction of our garrison on the river. On May 3rd, he opened fire on the fort and kept up a brisk cannonade for some hours. The next day Captain Walker returned from the expedition, to ascertain the effect of the cannon fire which had been heard at Point Isabel. Seeing that Major Brown had affairs under control he departed to rejoin our forces.

At his departure the enemy firing was renewed, and bands of Mexicans were seen on the plains as though preparing for a charge. Major Brown found that his six-pounders had little effect, owing to the distance. Wishing to save his ammunition the enemy's fire was not returned. On the morning of May 5th an enemy battery was discovered at the rear of the fort. It must have been erected by the enemy during the night. It opened fire with deadly accuracy. At the same time a tremendous discharge of shell and shot was maintained from the distant guns at Matamoros. On the next day the gallant major was mortally wounded by a cannon ball, and the command passed to Captain Hawkins. The enemy fire let up and an enemy messenger brought a surrender notice from General Arista. Captain Hawkins refused and the assailants renewed their attack with increased vigor. At noon on May 8th the thunder of the Mexican batteries suddenly stopped. Two hours passed, and a different set of guns were heard in the distance, sending echoes from the northeast. A shout of joy and hope went up from the fort!

I reached Point Isabel without interruption, and until the evening of the 7th of May I listened with deep emotion to the dull booming of cannon that told of the danger to those gallant spirits I had left behind. The safe return of Captain Walker brought the encouraging news that the garrison was still enthusiastic in their defense. I set out on the evening of May 7th with 2300 men to return to the fort. After marching about seven miles I halted and camped for the night. The march was continued on the following morning and continued until noon when scouts reported that the enemy was drawn up in force directly across the road. The coolness of my men was admirably displayed. The troops were upon a wide level field, bounded in front by rows of dwarf trees which the Mexicans called Palo Alto[6].

In front the Mexican Army was drawn up in battle array; while on the flanks of both armies were a series of mill ponds, filled with very cold but clear water. As soon as the enemy was observed I halted my men and ordered them to fill their canteens with the fresh water. I let them have an hour's rest at which point the advance took place. The battle line was formed in two wings; the right wing with Colonel Twiggs and Major Ringgold's artillery and two squadrons of dragoons; and the left wing, under Colonel Belknap, was formed with a battalion of artillery under Colonel Childs and Captain Duncan's light artillery. Both wings had infantry support.

While the battle line was being formed Lieutenant Blake suddenly rode forward to within one hundred and fifty yards of the enemy, dismounted, and studied their position. He then remounted, slowly rode along their whole line, and returned to report his impressions to me. A feat so daring filled both armies with admiration. The march commenced. The deep silence of our onward progress seemed in harmony with the dreadful business to which we were moving. Within seven hundred yards the enemy right wing opened with a tremendous discharge of artillery. I hurried along my van, deployed it into line, and exhorted my soldiers to be firm. I gave the order to return the fire and immediately all other sounds were drowned out in the fearful roar of artillery. The infantry watched on in horror. At every discharge, whole ranks of the enemy were mowed down, and scores of horses and horsemen flung into one undistinguishable mass.

Unable to sustain their heavy losses, the Mexican infantry began to give way. Then General Arista ordered a cavalry charge. The lancers rode out in two columns and bore down on our line, with a grace and rapidity peculiar to the Mexicans. Before they reached our line, however, Ridgely and Ringgold opened with their artillery. At the first blast the lancers staggered—again and again, with stern energy, the cannon broke forth; huge gaps opened among the horsemen, and scores sunk down beneath the tramp of their companions. Fear succeeded to enthusiasm. The lancers fled, leaving behind them at every step victims to the iron

---

[6]   Literally tall poles.

storm that pursued them. The losses to the Americans was small, but it included the brave Major Ringgold.

The battle now became general and raged with fearful destruction. Suddenly the long prairie grass was ignited by a discharge from one of Captain Duncan's pieces. Volumes of smoke rolled up which for a while completely blotted out the light of day. The battle then ceased and both sides regrouped their lines. Two thousand Mexicans moved through the smoke to attack our unprotected train, but fortunately a light breeze dispersed the smoke, and revealed their movement. Captain Duncan and his men galloped out, and when the air became clear, they opened fire upon the astonished enemy and arrested their progress.

The Mexican infantry fell back to some neighboring chaparral, but the lancers stood firm before a fire which cut deep gaps in their masses. The Mexican infantry reformed and again advanced from the chaparral, and moved steadily forward in the face of the storm from which they had just fled. But their effort was in vain and soon they were flying in utter confusion. Night settled around the victor and the vanquished. Six hundred Mexicans lay dead or wounded on the battlefield; our loss was but nine killed and forty-four wounded.

On the morning of the 9th the Mexicans were dimly seen in the distance retreating through the chaparral. I anticipated another battle before reaching the Rio Grande so I formed a new line and advanced in battle array. In order to guard against surprise I threw forward a small advance detachment under Captain McCall to ascertain the enemy's size and position. At 3:00 PM reports of musketry were heard, and I was informed that the Mexicans were grouped in a large force near the road.

The position which the Mexicans selected was most admirably adopted to defensive action. A strip of open land interrupted the thick chaparral, and through this open space was a deep ravine crossed by the Matamoros road. The ravine was about four feet deep and from one to two hundred feet wide. In rainy seasons its bed formed a series of pools which subsided in dry weather, and hence the name Resaca de la Palma. In this ditch, and amid the dense thicket on its banks, the Mexicans were entrenched with their artillery in position to sweep the road.

The battle of Resaca de la Palma, like that of the former day, commenced with artillery. Ridgely pushed his guns to within one hundred yards of the enemy and opened fire. At the same time the infantry pushed forward and soon the rattling of musketry joined the roar of the cannon. The Mexican forces were determined to recover their lost honor and heedless of the large numbers that fell their brave sons pushed forward. At length they began to weaken and fall back. Their fire slackened, and finally they crossed the ravine and took shelter in the chaparral. With bloody shouts our forces rushed on to complete the victory with a bayonet charge. But the ravine was still guarded by Mexican artillery. The effect upon the American line was dreadful, and our pursuit was halted.

Perceiving that nothing could be accomplished until these guns were silenced, I ordered Captain May to charge them with his dragoons. May shouted to his men, and in the next instant they were dashing down the narrow road toward the cannon emplacements. Pausing until Ridgeley drew the enemy's fire, they again drove on, and were finally within yards of the fatal guns. Suddenly a volley from the Mexicans crushed seven men and eighteen horses to the earth. But May and his men were upon the battery and the enemy was driven back. Charge after charge was made until only the Mexican general was left at his guns. Surrounded with piles of dead, grim with powder and smoke, he faced his enemy alone. In the act of discharging a cannon, May ordered him to surrender, and finding further resistance useless, he complied.

The struggle was not over yet. The Tampico battalion charged forward to regain the artillery. The chaparral presented greater obstacles to the progress of the Americans than the enemy's cannon. Friend and foe were clutched in desperate disorder along the thickets, and in the open spaces to which the Mexicans were driven.

The camp and headquarters of General Arista was taken and the rout of his troops was becoming general. The Tampico battalion, however, still defied the victors. It had never yielded to an enemy. They fought on until they were all cut down. The standard-bearer resolving to save his honored charge, tore it from its staff and fled. But ridden down by the dragoons, he was made prisoner, and his flag, the noblest trophy of the field was taken.

In this battle 1700 Americans were opposed by 6000 Mexicans. Everything in the Mexican camp was captured. The correspondence of General Arista, his private property, provisions, arms, ammunition standards, pack-saddles, and all the equipment of the six thousand men and two thousand horses fell into our hands. Our loss was only one-hundred and ten—that of the Mexicans somewhere in the vicinity of a thousand.

Thus another victory was won. My return to our fort opposite Matamoros was hailed by the weary garrison with unbounded enthusiasm. All cannonading ceased and the exhausted soldiers were allowed to rest. In honor of the unfortunately dead commandant we re-named the outpost Fort Brown.

On the 11th of May, 1846 I returned to Point Isabel for the purpose of arranging a plan for a combined attack on Matamoros with Commander Conner of the Gulf Squadron. Returning to Fort Brown I prepared for the river crossing and on the 18th I sent a note across river requesting the city to surrender. After some delay a messenger was sent back saying that I might enter Matamoros without opposition. General Arista, with his army, had left the city on the previous night. Formal possession was taken and Colonel Twiggs was appointed military governor. The small town of Barita, near the mouth of the Rio Grande was entered without resistance on May 15th.

Although I had captured an important city and erected the flag of my country on the left bank of the Rio Grande, my forces and military supplies were so limited that I was obliged to remain inactive during the greater part of the summer. When the volunteers arrived they had no means of transportation and they had no military training. I wrote headquarters that the boats on which I depended for this service, were found to be nearly destroyed by worms, and entirely unfit for the navigation of the river . . . . Later I wrote, "as I have previously reported my operations are completely paralyzed due to the lack of suitable steamboats to navigate the Rio Grande. Since the 18th of May the army has lain in camp near this place, continually receiving heavy reinforcements of men, but no facility for water transport, without which additional numbers are but an embarrassment." Again I wrote:

I am altogether dark as to our future operations. I must think that orders have been given by superior authority, to suspend the forwarding of means of transportation from New Orleans. I cannot otherwise account for the extraordinary delay shown by the quartermaster's department in that city. Even the mails, containing probably important dispatches from the government are not expedited.

Volunteer regiments have arrived from Louisville and St. Louis, making those from Louisiana, eight strong and organized battalions—mustering over five thousand men. In addition we have seven companies of Alabama volunteers, and twelve or fifteen companies from Texas. Others from Texas are continually arriving. A portion of these volunteers have been lying in camp at this place for nearly a month, completely paralyzed by the want of transportation. Exposed as they are in this climate to diseases of the camp, and without any prospect so far as I can see of being usefully employed, I must recommend that they be allowed to return to their homes.

In June I was promoted by Congress to the full rank of major general. We did not resume our march into the interior until September 5, 1846. Meanwhile the town of Mier, Camargo, Seralvo, and Reynosa fell and became way stations for different divisions of the army. The day I started my march I received intelligence from General Worth that large reinforcements of the enemy were arriving at Monterey, the capital city of the Northern Division of Mexico. I determined to join Worth at Seralvo with all speed leaving General Patterson in command on the Rio Grande. At Seralvo the whole army rendezvoused and then continued the advance towards Monterey. On the 18th of September we were at Walnut Springs, just three miles from the city.

Monterey, the capital of New Leone, contained about 15,000 inhabitants. It is situated near the base of the Sierra Madre, parallel to which runs the Arroyo San Juan, a small branch of the San Juan River. On the north from whence the road from Camargo approaches, is an enormous plain interrupted only by a dry ravine crossing it about three-quarters of a mile in front of the town. This plain contained patches of chaparral and cultivated corn and sugar-cane fields. The mountains appeared on the southern and western horizon. In front and to the right of the town was a strong and extensive fortress known as the Citadel. It covered an area of some three acres with solid masonry walls and bastions commanding all approaches. On the east side of the city several fortified redoubts were built near the suburbs, forbidding ingress in that quarter.

Following the Arroyo San Juan to the southwest extremity of the city, two forts appear on the hills of its further side; while on the nearer side of it, as well as the Saltillo road, are heights crowned with two other fortifications. The latter of these was a large unfinished structure designed for the Bishop's Palace and was known as such. The upper one, more remote from the city, was a redoubt erected expressly for the defense of the city. Entrance to the town in that quarter was discouraged by the walls of the cemetery, forming a strong breast work with embrasures. These works were mounted with forty-two pounder heavy cannon.

The city itself was excellently adapted for defensive warfare. The streets, being straight, a few pieces of artillery could command their entire length. The stone walls of the houses formed natural parapets providing protection to the occupants. Each dwelling was a separate fort, and the whole city was one grand fortification, for which General Ampudia had 8000 troops with abundant supplies of weaponry.

From the continual appearance of the Mexican cavalry at our front we were convinced that the enemy would strongly defend that place. Upon reaching the vicinity of the city on the 19th this belief was fully confirmed. It was ascertained that new works had been constructed commanding the northern approaches; and that the Bishop's Palace on Independence Hill and some heights in the vicinity near the Saltillo Road had been fortified and occupied with Mexican troops and artillery. It was known, from information previously received, that the eastern approaches were commanded by several small works on the lower edge of the city.

The configuration of the mountains on the Saltillo Road visible on the 19th led me to suspect that it was practicable to turn all attention in that direction and cut off the enemy's line of communication. After establishing my camp at Walnut Springs I ordered a close reconnaissance of the grounds which was executed that evening. At the same time Captain Williams made a reconnaissance of the eastern approaches. Major Mansfield's observations proved the practicability of throwing forward a column on the Saltillo Road. I therefore ordered General Worth, commanding the second division, to march with his command on the 20th and occupy the Saltillo Road and capture the Bishop's Palace. The Texas Volunteers, under Colonel Hays, would also go with the second division.

At 2:00 PM on the 20th of September Worth moved out. The column was guided by a Mexican prisoner who was encouraged to tell them the truth by the presence of a "hempen cravat about his neck." It was soon learned by the general, however, that his movements had been observed by the Mexicans and that the enemy was throwing reinforcements at the Bishop's Palace. To divert the enemy's attention as much as possible General Twiggs and the first division appeared in the vicinity of the town until dark. Worth's men only went about seven miles over the difficult terrain. They had a brief skirmish with a Mexican patrol and took up their attack position by 6:00 PM. They spent an uncomfortable night in a downpour of rain, encamped for the night in a group of peasant huts. The men were able to catch and kill some chickens owned by the local farmers for food.

Early on the morning of the 21st the battle commenced. Worth and his command assembled on the Saltillo Road which brought on a charge of 200 Mexican lancers. The exchange with the Rangers was hand-to-hand combat with pistol and swords, while the American artillery poured a withering fire into the rear ranks of the Mexicans. The road was secured and the Mexicans left more than a hundred bodies behind. At noon Worth ordered an attack on the redoubt on Federation Ridge with four companies of artillerymen acting as infantry and six companies of dismounted Texas Rangers. The Texans calmly advanced while the Mexicans fired grape and cannister shot at them ineffectively. Without any casualties the Rangers reached the base of the hill and charged up it, whereupon the Mexicans abandoned their cannon and fled. The Texans then turned the cannon on the retreating Mexicans.

Across the way on Federation Ridge the same type of assault was taking place against Fort Soldado. Artillery, infantry, volunteers and Rangers swarmed to the top yelling loudly. Captain Richard Gillepsie was first to cross the enemy breastworks, and the Mexicans there likewise fled. General Worth let his men rest while he made plans to assault the Bishop's Palace at 3:00 AM the next morning. The attack began at the appointed hour and 450 men climbed up Independence Hill and stormed the Mexican defenders. Morale disintegrated on the Mexican side and the men fled in panic. The Stars & Stripes were unfurled at the junction and at noon Worth's men started cannonading the Bishop's Palace which was strongly defended. A feint by volunteers brought the Mexican infantry out in a charge, whereupon the volunteers came storming after them. Suddenly a group of Rangers, who had been concealed, rose up and fired with deadly effect, demoralizing the Mexicans who retreated either back into the Bishop's Palace or into the city. The Americans then advanced to the gate of the Bishop's Palace. Worth had taken his major objectives with thirty-two men lost in two days of fighting.

My diversionary attack on the northeastern corner of the city greatly aided Worth's movements. He began his effort at the Bishop's

Palace with an artillery barrage from his heavy guns, then ordered light batteries in an attempt to batter an opening in the walls. Next the 1st division commanded by Colonel John Garland[7] moved forward along with Butler's volunteers and Colonel Jefferson Davis's Mississippi Rifles. A crossfire from the Citadel or "Black Fort" as it was called caused the volunteers to break and run. A small group of men managed to break into part of the city streets and take El Tenería, an armed tannery at the east end of Monterey. When darkness fell I ordered a count of my casualties. This one day cost me 394 killed or wounded.

The next day, September 22nd, I allowed my troops to rest. On September 23rd Worth and his troops entered the city from the west and I ordered our men to attack. It was a day of street fighting. Our troops advanced from house to house, and from square to square, until they reached a street just one square in the rear of the plaza, and near which the enemy's force was mainly concentrated. I was now satisfied that we could operate successfully in the city, and that the enemy had left the lower portion of it to make a stand behind his barricades.

The following account from the pen of Captain Johnson of the Baltimore battalion will serve to show the suffering and bravery of his men:

I saw Colonel Lewis Watson shouting, but as to hearing a command, that was an impossibility, owing to the deafening roar of the cannon and musketry. I reached the head of my column just as Colonel Watson was dismounting from his horse, which the next moment fell from a shot in his head. The colonel cried out to his men, "shelter yourselves, men, the best way you can." Most of the men were already lying down, with the lead balls whizzing over their heads.

I sought shelter next to Colonel Watson, alongside of a hedge, when he jumped up and cried out, "now is the time boys, follow me!" We were now in a street with a few houses on either side, and within a hundred yards of three batteries which completely raked it. In addition two twelve-pound guns were in the castle on the right and completely enfiladed the whole distance we had to make. Add to this the horde of

---

[7]   General David Twiggs who should have been in command had a nervous stomach and was in the habit of taking a laxative the night before any action. But he apparently took an overdose and that particular morning he was indisposed.

musketeers on the house-tops at the head of the street, up which we advanced, and at every cross street, and you may form some idea of the missiles poured upon us. Onward we went, men and horses falling at every step. Cheers, shrieks, groans and words of command added to the din, while the roar of the guns was absolutely deafening.

We advanced up the street nearly two hundred yards, when we reached a cross road where we halted. I sat down on the ground with my back against the wall of a house. On my left were two men torn nearly to pieces. One of them was flat on his back with his legs extending into the street. A shower of grape tore one of his wounded legs off. He struggled to get on his feet, shrieked, and fell back a corpse. Directly opposite me was Second Lieutenant Don Asquith; on the right hand corner Lieutenant Bowie, also of my camp; and close to me sat Colonel Lewis Watson and Adjutant Schoeler. In a few moments our color sergeant, old Hart came past with his right arm shattered, and in a few more minutes came our battalion flag, borne by one of the guards. This was the first American flag in the city of Monterey, an honor which we knew belonged to our battalion.

No man there ever thought for a moment that he would get out alive, and most of them did not. When we were finally ordered to charge up the street, a hesitation was manifested by both regulars and volunteers, but the officers sprang up to the front in double file. I soon became separated from Colonel Watson and never saw him again.

As darkness fell I decided to withdraw in order to join with Worth in a combined attack the next day. Suddenly, however, everything was quiet. General Ampudia was concerned with his position because of the cannon fire. Worth's men had brought a cannon from Federation Hill to a point where it could shell the plaza in town. Captain Lucien B. Webster had placed a twenty-four pounder at El Tenería which was also capable of bombarding the plaza and the cathedral where the Mexican munitions were stored. One shell landed so close that it jolted Ampudia into action. The general sent Colonel Francisco Moreno with a flag of truce to ask that an armistice be arranged and that the Mexican soldiers be allowed to retire from the city with their military equipment and stores.

I listened to Moreno and then demanded an unconditional surrender. I arranged a cease fire with the colonel until 12:00 noon, at which hour I was to receive an answer. The message was relayed to General Ampudia and he countered with a request for a personal interview with me. The upshot of the negotiations was an agreement to meet and work out the details of an armistice. General Worth, Jefferson Davis, and J. Pinckney Henderson represented the American side. The terms of the armistice was that the Mexicans could retain their sidearms and accouterments, along with six pieces of artillery, and that the Americans would not pursue them for eight weeks. The following are the exact terms:

ARTICLE I. As the legitimate result of the operations before this place, and the present position of the contending armies, it is agreed that the city, the fortifications, cannon, munitions of war, and all other public property, with the undermentioned exceptions, be surrendered to the commanding general of the United States forces now at Monterey.

ARTICLE II. That the Mexican forces be allowed to retain the following arms, to wit: the commissioned officers their side-arms, the infantry their arms and accoutrements, the cavalry their arms and accoutrements, the artillery one field battery, not to exceed six pieces, with twenty-one rounds of ammunition.

ARTICLE III. That the Mexican armed forces retire, within seven days from this date, beyond the line formed by the pass of Rinconada, the city of Linares and San Fernando de Preras.

ARTICLE IV. That the citadel of Monterey be evacuated by the Mexican and occupied by the American forces to-morrow morning at ten o'clock.

ARTICLE V. To avoid collisions, and for mutual convenience, that the troops of the United States will not occupy the city until the Mexican forces have withdrawn, except for hospital and storage purposes.

ARTICLE VI. That the forces of the United States will not advance beyond the line specified in the 3rd article, before the expiration of eight weeks, or until orders or instructions of the respective governments can be received.

ARTICLE VII. That the public property to be delivered, shall be turned over and received by officers appointed by the commanding generals of the two armies.

ARTICLE VIII. That all doubts as to the meaning of any of the preceding articles, shall be solved by an equitable construction, or on principles of liberality to the retiring army.

ARTICLE IX. That the Mexican flag, when struck at the citadel, may be saluted by its own battery.

On September 25 General Ampudia withdrew from Monterey and I marched in. I had taken the "impregnable" city in just three days with a loss of 800 killed or wounded. On September 28th I designated William J. Worth to be the governor of Monterey and his divisions moved in. The Americans were exhausted and grateful for a respite. The process of rebuilding and refitting their army would take time. I estimated at least six weeks. On the evening of Sunday, October 11, 1846 news of my victory reached the war department in Washington. That same evening Secretary Marcy took the message to the White House. The news of the fall of Monterey caused celebrations throughout the United States, yet in Washington there were many critics of the eight week armistice. The most severe critics were Democrats, including the president, who feared my growing popularity. Polk announced that "In agreeing to this armistice General Taylor violated his express orders and I regret that I cannot approve of his course." Secretary Marcy's letter directing me to terminate the armistice of September 25th reached Monterey on November 2, 1846. I was furious at the rebuke, but I sent the same messenger on to Saltillo with the required letter terminating the armistice.

While the Americans quarreled over politics General Ampudia retreated from Monterey down to Saltillo and across the desert southward to San Luis Potosí, and arrived there on October 8, 1846. The day before his arrival Santa Anna, the wily villain of Mexican disasters entered the city and prepared to take command with Ampudia reporting to him. He called the reformed troops his "Army of Liberation." Santa Anna spent a busy four months at San Luis Potosí. Though he neglected his military build-up at times because of money, he conducted a good training program and by the end of January 1847 he had an army numbering about 20,000 officers and men. His next decision was where to fight. Serendipity stepped in when Mexican scouts intercepted a letter from General Scott to me ordering me to send him all but 6000 of my troops to the coast for embarkation. Santa Anna deduced that most of my remaining men would be volunteers and raw troops. Here would be a good place for him to win a quick victory! Earlier in the year Santa Anna had approached the Polk administration through diplomatic channels promising a quick end to hostilities if he could leave his exile in Cuba and return to Mexico. Now he was ignoring his promise to seek peace.

I also had other plans and decided to defy Polk's orders to remain on the defensive. My first target was Saltillo, some 70 miles southwest of Monterey and a town of some 15,000 inhabitants. On November 8, 1846 I ordered General Worth to prepare to march on Saltillo in four days. The route to Saltillo took Worth and his men past Santa Catarina, then southward into the gorge of the Rinconada Pass, then upward again ending in a wide valley that led to Saltillo. When Worth's advanced guard approached to within a dozen miles of Saltillo it met the usual deputation carrying a protest from the governor who had departed for San Luis Potosí. Worth's men marched to the town square with drums beating and colors flying.

So the town was taken without a shot being fired, and by mid-January I had a line of troops from Monterey to the Gulf of Mexico. This daring move had been made possible by the arrival of six companies of regulars of the 6th Infantry, three companies of volunteers from Illinois, a company of artillery, and some units of Texas Rangers, all under the command of Brigadier General John Ellis Wool. John Wool was another Whig general President Polk mistrusted, but he was a capable soldier. At the outbreak of war with Mexico General Wool had mustered 12,000 volunteers into service in six weeks, then went to San Antonio, where he took command of 1400 men whom he then marched to Saltillo, arriving there on December 22, 1846.

By mid January intelligence warned of Santa Anna's advance north with a powerful Mexican force. This was warning enough to bring me back to Monterey from Saltillo. On January 26, 1947 Polk issued orders for me to remain in the vicinity of Monterey, while four-fifths of my troops were to be sent to accompany General Winfield Scott in an invasion of Mexico at Vera Cruz. The president reasoned that I would have only enough men left to remain in a defensive position. In fact he so ordered me. I now recalled Wool who was on an expedition northwest against Parras, in Chihuahua. I marched to take up a position some sixteen miles south of Saltillo on the road toward San Luis Potosí and I consolidated my force at the town of Agua Nueva. Counting Wool's troops I now had 4759 men. Only two squadrons of cavalry and three batteries of artillery were regulars, a mere 476 men.

Ben McCulloch with the Texas Regulars reported on February 21st that Santa Anna and his army of 20,000 were approaching. In fact General Vicente Miñón's cavalry was blocking the road between Agua Nueva and Saltillo. With great rapidity I ordered my troops to the Hacienda of Buena Vista southwest of Saltillo, and left them under the command of General Wool. Wool reinforced his position to cover the road to San Luis Potosí on a narrow pass known as La Angostura[8] with an eight-gun battery of artillery. His other 4000 men waited below for events to unfold. Santa Anna, marching northward, was confident of an early victory. On February 22nd I returned to Saltillo and was greeted with a note from Santa Anna:

You are surrounded by twenty thousand men, and cannot in any human probability avoid suffering a rout and being cut to pieces with your troops; but as you deserve consideration and particular esteem, I wish to save you from a catastrophe, and for that purpose give you this notice, in order that you may surrender at discretion, under the assurance that you will be treated with the consideration belonging to the Mexican character; to which end you will be granted an hour's time to make up your mind, to commence from the moment when my flag of truce arrives in your camp. With this view I assure you of my particular consideration—God and liberty!

My reply was brief:

> SIR: In reply to your note of this date summoning me to surrender my forces at discretion, I beg leave to say that I decline acceding to your request.

> With high respect, I am, sir, your obedient servant.

> Z. TAYLOR

Santa Anna's army was worn out and ill fed due to their rapid push north. When Santa Anna arrived at Agua Nueva he learned that I had

---

[8]   The Narrows.

departed in great haste and deduced that we were fleeing in panic and should be pursued. Santa Anna ordered General Ampudia to rush his troops forward without rest towards the Hacienda of Buena Vista. When Santa Anna caught up he discovered to his dismay that we had not fled but had taken up a position at La Angostura. There Wool had set up his eight gun battery of artillery under Brevet Major Jon Macrae Washington in a position to cover the San Luis Potosí road. He also located six companies of troops nearby and the other 4000 men waited below.

Santa Anna's men outnumbered mine by three to one and he had General Miñón in the rear with his reserves. He decided to commit Ampudia's troops against the American left and pin down the artillery, while the rest skirted around the base of the hills to attack from the rear. Ampudia, with 1000 men struck to the left. I sent two regiments of infantry and three large guns under Captain John Paul Jones O'Brien to strengthen that side. O'Brien's troops were strengthened by Colonel Humphrey Marshall's Kentucky Volunteers and the 2nd Indiana Volunteer regiment. At the left, however, the 2nd Indiana regiment retreated, exposing O'Brien and his artillery to the withering Mexican advance. Finally O'Brien had to withdraw, losing one of his large guns. The Mexicans reached the upper slopes of the highest peak and there entrenched themselves before dark. Thus ended the first day of fighting.

During the night Santa Anna's men cooked some food which exhausted their rations. Santa Anna promised his men a good meal the next day from the American supplies they would acquire from a decisive victory. He brought forward an eight pound artillery piece to fire upon O'Brien and he moved the San Patricios[9] up with their eighteen and twenty-four pound guns for use in attempting to break the American line.

It was cold and it rained that night. Dawn revealed that 1500 additional Mexican Infantrymen had scaled the heights during the night to join Ampudia's men. General Wool had only 3300 men now to oppose the 12,000 Mexicans moving forward because I had taken 500 men to Saltillo and 700 were in the gullies for the night. The fighting began as General Santiago Blanco attacked the American right.

---

[9]   Irish American deserters fighting on the Mexican side.

Washington's artillery devastated Blanco's men as they advanced up the road and they were repulsed.

The main Mexican force under General Pacheco and General Lombardini attacked Wool's position on the plateau. Here Captain O'Brien and his two artillery pieces along with three of Washington's guns that were relocated wrecked havoc. General Joe Lane, who had arrived the night before to be given command of that section by General Wool ordered a charge. The Mexicans started to retreat but something unforseen happened. One of Lane's officers, Colonel William A. Bowles, for some unknown reason, ordered his bugler to blow a retreat and the three Indiana Volunteers obeyed. The retreat was joined by others and became a rout. O'Brien and his gunners found themselves unprotected and therefore they had to retreat as well.

The action left Marshall's Kentucky Volunteers exposed and alone before Ampudia's advance. Dragoons, under Captain Braxton Bragg and others rode forward and were able to halt the Mexican advance, however. At this crucial point in time I returned from Saltillo at about 9:00 AM. I immediately ordered Colonel Jefferson Davis and his Mississippi Volunteers up to fight Ampudia's men. Davis responded with a courageous charge, and the Mexicans fell back. Bragg and O'Brien also charged, and shortly before noon the Mexicans began to retreat, with artillery shells crashing in their ranks.

Santa Anna immediately sent an officer forward under a white flag of truce to ask what I wanted. While I discussed the matter with General Wool, the Mexicans were able to withdraw out of cannon range. After regrouping his forces Santa Anna ordered troops forward under General Francisco Pérez. I decided to attack and called for my Illinois and Kentucky Volunteers to charge into them. They were outnumbered six to one and the Volunteers soon broke under withering Mexican fire. The Volunteer's leaders Colonel John J. Hardin and Lieutenant Colonel Clay[10] were killed in the exchange and only the artillery rushing forward under Captain John M. Washington prevented the entire force from being annihilated. Grape and canister again turned the tide of battle. By 5:00 PM on February 23 the center of the Mexican line had collapsed and the Americans were now advancing as darkness fell.

---

[10] Son of Henry Clay the famous politician.

That night I held officers call and conferred with my generals. Casualty reports showed that 673 Americans had been killed or wounded. Santa Anna still had a larger, fresher army capable of doing battle. Wool and the other generals advised a retreat but I wanted to hold my ground. At 3:00 AM the next day reinforcements arrived from Monterey amounting to some 400 men and two 18-pound cannons. I decided to continue prosecuting the war, as I did not realize that it was now all over.

Santa Anna had been assessing his position during that same night. His casualties numbered in the neighborhood of 1800 with great damage to the morale of his remaining troops. Twice they had charged and twice they had been routed by American artillery. They were out of food and their ammunition was almost gone. He ordered his troops to retreat and leave the dead and wounded behind. It turned from an orderly retreat into a race of terror as men discarded their weapons, fled into the hills, and blocked the road. The retreat to San Luis Potosí accounted for 7000 losses and the Army of Liberation was now only 11,000 men strong.

On the morning of February 24th the Americans rose ready to do battle only to see evidence of a full withdrawal of the enemy. Wool and I hugged each other with enormous relief as we had grasped victory. I remained in Northern Mexico with my army knowing that General Scott had captured Vera Cruz and was marching on to the City of Mexico. The war was over for me and I received an official vote of thanks from Congress and a line of criticism from President Polk.

Chapter 6

IN ENEMY TERRITORY

Lew Wallace

My regiment, the First Indiana, finally arrived at Walnut Springs near Monterey, Mexico, the site of General Taylor's headquarters at the time. I do not remember the exact date but it must have been in the first week of February, 1847.

Over a thousand miles of marching and now we had the incentive to keep us going—the hope of battle. The whole region was rife with news of Santa Anna assembling an army to come down and put an end to the audacious gringos at San Luis Potosi. With the exception of Colonel Drake and Lieutenant Colonel Lane, none of the regiments had seen General Zachary Taylor. Although the general had, as we thought, dealt us great unkindness, and needlessly stored the dunes with our dead at the mouth of the Rio Grande, we had a craving to see him, and despite his nickname "Rough and Ready," it was impossible for us to think of him entirely divested of pomp and circumstance. His tent must be special. Horsemen and horses must be at his door signifying martial authority. In a word the feeling was general that even before approaching his headquarters there would be a sign, without the asking, that we were near the general.

Moving forward with lengthening steps, and drawing nearer and nearer, we strained our eyes to catch every point in the surrounding of the hero. A tall white flag-staff was the first thing observable. A flag floated from it high up, but the flag was dingy and worn. Next, back of the staff, about twenty steps we noticed a porch and it, too, was dingy and discolored. There were a few camp-stools, a small table, also dirty, and a long straight-backed bench. No orderlies, not even a sentinel marching his beat. Are these HIS quarters? Where is HE? Now the head of the column passed the dingy flag and the tall pole. One by one the companies reached the prescribed saluting location. Officers glanced to the right. So also the color-bearer swept by. And all there asked themselves, anxiously, where is HE?

It came my turn to salute. I readjusted the sword-grip in my hand, and looked for the reviewing officer out of the corner of my eye. Leaning lazily against the butt of the white pole, I saw a man of low stature, dressed in an unbuttoned and faded blouse, a limp-bosomed shirt, a hang-down collar without a tie of any kind, trousers once light blue now stripeless, and rough marching shoes. He also wore a slouch wool hat drawn down low over a dull, unshaven and expressionless face. I did not salute him, but like all who preceded me, and all who came after me, passed on wondering, where can HE be?

Looking back I noticed Colonel Drake riding over to the man with the slouch hat. That evening, when the good colonel's tent was pitched I went over to see him, unable to contain my indignation.

"Colonel," I said, "did General Taylor tell you that he would review us as we marched past his quarters?"

"Yes. I sent the adjutant to notify him of our coming. Didn't you see him?"

"No, sir, or I would have saluted."

The colonel's face became serious as he said, "Nobody saluted."

"Well, there was nobody to salute," I said.

"Yes there was."

"Who?"

"The man leaning against the flag-staff."

"That was General Taylor? I took him to be a teamster!"

After settling in we cleared a spacious parade-ground. A stream of spring water ran through a grove of pecan trees. A range of cloud-capped mountains rose in the southeast, and the town of Monterey nestled beneath it. Nearby rose Saddle Mountain, a solitary peak accessible only to climbers with muscles of steel. It was said, "the purer the air, the bluer the sky." One did not have to go to Italy to test the saying.

Camp life went on as usual here. We did little but a few training exercises day after day. It was, however, an assured thing—everybody said it—we were to be in the coming battle and it would be the greatest of the war.

I have often been asked if I were ever scared. That answer might be found in an incident which occurred to me while the regiment lay at Walnut Springs. A new paymaster arrived at Monterey and a number of the lieutenants requested to be allowed to go to the city and interview him. Unfortunately the time set overlapped the time I was posted for guard duty. With solemn promises to be back at camp on time for my duty the next morning I was permitted to be one of the party.

The quartermaster had put a wagon at our disposal, and we piled in accommodating ourselves to the loose board seats as best we could. There were a dozen of us. We were a merry, reckless mob ready to laugh at any inconvenience or danger which might befall us. It is not my purpose to describe the ride. The road was in our favor, having been cut through the chaparral for the passage of gun carriages during the siege, and while narrow it was level and rutless. The six mules rolled us safely and without event into Monterey.

After a nice dinner at the hotel we went to the paymaster's office where our several accounts were squared away and we received shiny Liberty silver dollars just minted. At nearly 1:00 AM in the morning, as the one sober Indianian, I succeeded in getting the last man to bed, and left the party in care of the hostelry. I set out alone on foot to do the six miles back to camp because I could not find the teamster. It was not my intention to violate my promise to the colonel to be in camp in the morning on time.

I remember a stone bridge at the city limits with a statue of some holy personage. It had been set out for the convenience of people piously induced. The district beyond the bridge was noted for being dangerous for strangers. Nevertheless I went on. If the view of the statue left an impression on my nerves, I did not at the time notice it. I passed through the bad precinct safely. Only some stray dogs in front of an adobe house assailed me, and I picked up a couple of stones. From the main road—to Marin, I think—I turned into the narrow passageway cut by the pioneers. I made good time. Moreover, the stars were all out twinkling, the brighter because of the absolute lethargy of the air. The hush was soothing and the coolness delicious.

After going about three miles it struck me that I had nothing to defend myself with—not even a pen knife. The truth was that my nerves were going as well as my will. A clump of chaparral had been left at a certain point in the wall of brush on the side of the road large enough to have furnished a hiding place for a horse behind it. I noticed the clump when about twenty feet away and I also noticed something unusually black. I came to a sudden dead stop. I could neither think nor resolve. In a word I stood overwhelmed with terror.

At this point I heard a sharp metallic *click, click* as of the hammer of a gunlock raised first to half, then to full cock, slowly, and with care lest the game should startle and run. Then a loud sputter rang out—the familiar hiss of gunpowder burning in a pan—and the chaparral behind the clump flashed red. I immediately passed out. Upon coming to, I found myself hugging the ground like a snake. I don't know how long I had passed out, whether five minutes or an hour. Springing to the side of the road I dropped down and dragged myself into the chaparral, striking, by happy chance, one of the many paths tunneled through by the wandering wild life.

My heart beat like a brass drum and a cold sweat covered me. I crawled on further and at last I gained an opening and stood up. There was a light signifying morning and I calmly walked around the place of ambush. Fortune favored me. Standing in the road I listened again. There was nothing. Strangely the panic caught me in full force again, and I started running. I ran with all my might. The tents of the camp eventually appeared in view, and I knew now that I was finally safe.

About the middle of February, 1847 General Taylor astonished the command at Walnut Springs by disappearing, leaving nothing of his headquarters except the white flag-staff. Intelligence said he was going in the direction of Saltillo with an escort of cavalry. They said he was riding fast as if the business were urgent. Had Santa Anna showed up?

A few days later a Captain Stanton of the Third Indiana rode into camp to join his missing company. He needed help in finding it before the fight and wanted somebody to go with him. Colonel Drake consented to my going. Borrowing a horse and riding gear, I was on the road with Captain Stanton within thirty minutes. A double-barreled 12-gauge shotgun lay across my lap. After leaving San Katrina we met nobody even though we were on the road connecting the two capital cities; Monterey and Saltillo about sixty miles apart with La Rinconada, a fairly large hacienda, halfway. Tired, hungry and sore, we were glad when a picket from the hacienda halted us. At the house in use as a barracks we identified ourselves to a lieutenant who proved to be a hospitable gentleman. He was a Kentuckian. His reply to our request to be put up for the night went as follows:

> Certainly, gentlemen. You shall be made, man and beast, as comfortable as possible. Sorry, I can't do much for you. Today we were to have received our rations from Saltillo. For some reason our teamsters never arrived. Lancers probably on the road. Anyhow we are reduced to hardtack; with wild onions. Still I can promise you some good American made salt and fresh water from a ditch nearby. If your stomachs work well, then fine. Come in and make yourselves at home.

We sat down at the table. The biscuits were of the cracker variety and the onions artistically sliced. There was no coffee. While we ate the lieutenant told us about everything that was happening in the area. La Rinconada, he said, had been occupied by Brigadier General Marshall. Only that morning the general had set out for Saltillo under orders received during the night, leaving half of his company in garrison. Our host told us that Taylor and Wool were anticipating action. The army was out at Encantados waiting for Santa Anna to advance. When last heard from he was at a village called Encarnacion. There had been some skirmishing and the armies would clash soon—exactly when or where no one could say. "The old man" (Taylor) had a penchant for secrets. In the midst of our discussions about thirty minutes after our arrival a soldier banged on the door and came in highly excited. "The pickets are firing, sir."

"From what direction?"

"From the direction of Saltillo." The lieutenant buckled on his sword with gravity.

"Excuse me gentlemen, I am going to have to leave you for a while," he said. "I think that there is an attack going on. I have been expecting it—it explains why my teamsters weren't on time. If you would like some more dessert go in the kitchen and help yourself."

He left and we could hear the sound of gunfire. We quit munching our crackers. Pretty soon we heard the tramp of soldiers outside. The door flew open due to an energetic kick outside, and half of the garrison marched in. The light was dim—from a candle or two stuck in the red onions—but there was enough to see the soldiers who passed through. The lieutenant was with them and banged the door shut again and secured it tightly. The lieutenant told us:

"It's business, gentlemen. The house is being surrounded."

"What kind of a house is this?" asked Captain Stanton.

"It's adobe, sir, and pretty solid. There is a fence of the same material enclosing it on all sides, except there in front. If the greasy Mexicans have no artillery, we can keep them off."

We were then on our feet and he went on, "I suppose you would like to take a hand with us, so if you are through eating," he smiled grimly, "and will come with me, I'll see that you have grandstand seats."

Captain Stanton was provided with a musket and cartridges. I, of course, had my shotgun. We followed the lieutenant.

"There's the back door," he said. "It's open. I'm taking you to the roof. Here's the ladder."

It was chilly on the roof. It seemed strange that my chronic longing to get into action should be gratified at such an out-of-the-way place. Sure enough the house was surrounded. Then Stanton and I sat down behind the adobe wall rising above the roof, and helped the garrison by filling the right with intermittent musketry. Nobody on our side was hurt. At dawn the enemy retired to the south. The Mexicans were holding the road merely to prevent communication until the crisis up-country had passed.

I remained with Captain Stanton until the morning of the 25th. We satisfied ourselves that crackers and onions, reinforced with American salt and choice ditch water were susceptible to improvement as a ration. That day the Mexicans disappeared in the direction of Monterey and Stanton and I reached Saltillo on the evening of the 25th without further interruption. From there we rode on to Buena Vista five miles further on.

Tired as I was I spent most of the night listening to accounts of the battle of Buena Vista. The first thing next day were calls from General "Joe" Lane and Colonel "Jim" Lane. I reported to the general and explained my presence. Then followed my reports to General Wool, whom many admired extravagantly. General Wool's reputation with volunteers was that of a prim, formal man, and stern to an offensive degree. They said he was always in uniform, began business at daybreak, and ate with his sword on. Some believed he even slept with his sword. In short, there was no limit to the general's unpopularity.

From General Wool I passed on to the field. There I saw dead men and horses, bayonets, broken muskets, hats, caps and fragments of clothing. The earth and rocks were splotched with blood. Details were still digging grave holes and other parties were hauling the unfortunates in and depositing them in ghastly rows by the pits. The civil authorities of Saltillo had been ordered to bury the Mexican dead. They were having the bodies dragged to the nearest ravines and pitched down into the depths, and half covered with stones. Groups of swarthy peons went about clipping the mules and tails of the dead horses so that they could make lariats and saddle—girths.

Though too late to have made the battle of Buena Vista a part of my life I would like to deal with it in some detail. In his official report General Taylor condemned a portion of the Indiana troops. I believe his judgment was unjust and even false, and I believe I should set the record straight. But, first I shall describe the battle.

Blocking the road from north to south brought Santa Anna to a stand still and compelled him to attack. Going south from Saltillo to San Luis, one comes to a sheep ranch called San Juan de la Buena Vista, from which the name of the battle was taken. The hacienda has a corral on the plateau probably one hundred and fifty feet square. The area is desolate, boarded by mountains on the east and west. Cacti are the only green things which vary the dull gray color of the spacious stretch. Crossing a plateau beyond the hacienda the traveler comes to the Pass of Angostura.

At the pass the road descends between rugged heights on the left and gullies on the right. The gullies are shapeless and of such width and depth as to be passable by nothing living except birds. A simple earthwork for the accommodation of a battery across the road up where the descent into the "squeeze" begins would hold the pass against any direct attack along the road. General Wool, quick to see these advantages and accept them as a kindness of nature, caused a breastwork to be thrown up at the point mentioned, and put Captain J. M. Washington in charge. Two companies of the First Illinois Infantry and six other companies manned the breastwork. General Wool, still not content, knowing the pass to be the key to the whole field of battle posted Colonel Lane's Third Indiana in reserve on a summit to the rear of Captain Washington.

Thus La Angostura and the road through it, together with a safe position on which the right of the little army was happily secured, left Santa Anna with only one point of attack. Nine or ten ravines broke up the plateau east of the pass into ridges. These ridges all bore down towards the pass and become gorges sixty or seventy feet in depth. They were immense natural ditches deterring passage except by going around them up by the foot-hills, where there was a passage-way, rough yet practicable for infantry and horsemen. In order to succeed Santa Anna would have to secure that route, no others being left him. General Wool proceeded to fence it in.

I might mention some of the commands:

Regulars
Third Artillery, Sherman and Bragg.
First Dragoons, Captain Enoch Steene.
Second Dragoons, Lieutenant Colonel Charles A. May.

Volunteers
Arkansas, Colonel Archibald Yell.
Kentucky, Colonel Humphrey Marshall.
Texas Volunteers, Captain Ben McCullough.

Infantry
First Illinois, Colonel John J. Hardin.
Second Illinois, Colonel William H. Bissell.
Second Kentucky, Colonel William R. McKee.
First Mississippi, Colonel Jefferson Davis.
Second Indiana, Colonel William A. Bowles.

To put this inadequate force to the best advantage over a ground so inhospitable was indeed a most difficult problem. Let me tell you how it was done Three ravines in the south all led through the pass up to the key passage way along the base of the mountains. They had to be defended. The extreme southern ravine would attract Santa Anna, and General Wool thought it best to establish his left at the head of that ravine. He placed Colonel William A. Bowles's Second Indiana there. At the left of the Second Indiana but some distance to the rear Colonel Marshall's Kentucky Cavalry and a squadron of the Second United States Dragoons were placed. Then in the right rear of the Second Indiana, back about a quarter of a mile Bissel's Second Illinois and a section of Bragg's battery were established. Facing south they were so placed to lend Colonel Bowles a helping hand if need be, and at the same time keep an eye on the second and third ravines. At the left of Bissel there were two guns and a squadron of dragoons. Next, at another interval, Colonel McKee's Second Kentucky Infantry was posted.

The very last ravine—the mother ravine so to speak, was christened La Bosca de la Bestarros. Colonel Yell's Arkansas Cavalry was placed there in reserve. These dispositions were made and put in place by General Wool at mid-afternoon on February 22, 1847. He had done the best with his scanty force.

Heavy clouds of dust seen on the morning of the 22nd in the direction of La Angostura notified General Taylor of the approach of the enemy. At 11:00 AM a lone rider arrived under a flag of truce. The summons to surrender was politely rejected. The summons had ample backing. Twenty thousand men were closing in behind the last ridge out of the arid land in front of Buena Vista. These men were commanded by the ablest generals of the Mexican Republic. Santa Anna began the battle directly after the rejection of the demand for surrender by feigning an attack along the road through the Pass of Angostura. Then General Ampudia's light brigade commenced climbing a ridge facing the American riflemen at General Lane's left. It was late in the day and soon darkness hid all the combatants. It was obvious that Santa Anna planned to gain the passageway at the base of the mountains.

Under the cover of night Santa Anna shifted Ballarta to the right where the shrewd artilleryman planted his five eight-pounder cannons in range to enfilade Bowles and O'Brien. Juvera, Chief of Cavalry, together with Torrejón and Androde, were next posted to support Ballarta. To gain the advantage of surprise, the infantry divisions of Lombardini and

Pacheco, seven thousand strong, were drawn noiselessly into a nearby ravine where they bivouacked.

On the morning of the 23rd a furious outbreak of Mexican artillery announced dawn over the mountains and signaled the call for action. Ampudia rushed his riflemen to the front at the sound. Juvera gained ground, while Villamil and Blanco down in the pass lost heavily repeating the feint of the day before. The desolate valley was still ringing with the thunder of guns when suddenly Lombardini's division burst out of the broad ravine, gained space on the plateau and directly confronted O'Brien and the Second Indiana. While this was going on Pacheco, repeating Lombardini's simple maneuver, took a position on his colleague's right and joined in the battle.

With all their weight the Mexicans wavered. Partly to avoid the enfilading of Ballarta, General Lane ordered an advance. O'Brien obeyed; but right in the midst of the movement Colonel William Bowles ordered, "**Cease firing and retreat!**" Twice he gave the order; whereupon his regiments began breaking up at the right, company after company, until the greater part of the soldiers dissolved into a mob fleeing aimlessly to the rear. O'Brien, left without support, withdrew two of his guns, the horses and men having been killed or disabled.

Momentous events followed rapidly. Juvera advanced trotting. The American riflemen on the mountain, about to be cut off made haste down, and ran, most of them, to the hacienda, stopping at the corral. Between Lombardini and Washington in the pass there now stood only three regiments all seriously reduced in size. These were Bissell's Second Illinois, McKee's Second Kentucky and Hardin's First Illinois. The Mexicans half-wheeled the battle front to the left, and it seemed that the three ravaged regiments must go the way of the Second Indiana; but General Wool kept a clear head. At his orders Bissell fell back, while Hardin and McKee advanced running to him. When the three met they formed a line into which Bragg and Sherman brought up their batteries. Then Lombardini and Pacheco were upon them with a roar of "vivas." The ravines separating them reduced the opposing fronts to an equality and it became a question with the combatants which side could endure the killing the longest. Juvera allowed Marshall and Yell no pause. Crossing La Bosca, the mother ravine, he fell upon them and pushed them back—almost to the corral of the hacienda. Yell, refusing to yield an inch, died with his sword in hand.

In the nick of time at 8:00 AM General Taylor appeared, returning from Saltillo with the First Mississippi and May's dragoons. By every rule of war he was beaten. Lombardini's troops had control of the Pass of Angostura. If then he had a sinking heart no one of those about him saw it in his stolid countenance. Taylor ordered Colonel Lane of the Third Indiana to join Davis where the two would cross La Bosca and crush Pacheco's flank. Kilburn's one gun would accompany them. Lane started on the run. Davis halted once to repel an attack of lancers. Then about two hundred of the Second Indiana now led by Lieutenant Colonel William R. Haddon met Davis, and, without halting formed on his left. Finally the three regiments together reached La Bosca and crossed it. They deployed with cheers, pouring a plunging fire into Pacheco's column at a time when his attention was absorbed by Hardin, McKee and Bissell. In an incredibly short time the plateau down which Lombardini and Pacheco had descended so triumphantly was clear of the living. Lombardini himself rode off wounded.

General Taylor now had the time to give attention to the fight which was going on between Marshall and Juvera, begun at the time when Colonel William Bowles had ordered his regiment to retreat. Following, Marshall Juvera was drawn close to the hacienda. Suddenly a volley of fire from the corral withered the Mexicans. The cheer that followed was as stunning as the volley. Strangely, then, the Mexicans flew in all directions. One part of them sped past the corral, and, crossing the valley, disappeared in a defile of the mountain in the west. The others turned, and in great disorder rode just as madly back over the trail by which they had come, intending to rejoin the main body of their army. Bragg was sent to intercept them, with Jefferson Davis, Jim Lane and William R. Haddon in support. The broken, panic stricken horsemen tried to find refuge in the foot-hills. They would have been forced to surrender had not Santa Anna dispatched a messenger to General Taylor asking what he wanted. It is not often that a white flag of truce is so infamously abused. While it was coming and returning the enemy escaped.

At 2:00 PM the plateau was in possession of the Americans all save a corner in the southeast. Occasionally the loud report of a heavy gun and the scream of a shell in flight over the ridge broke an hour of inactivity. The weary soldiers availed themselves of the calm to rest. Santa Anna was not beat yet. Assembling the remains of the divisions of Lombardini and Pacheco, he joined them with Ampudia's light brigade and Ortega's third division which was intact, having been in reserve. He also moved a column of Villamil's to the right that had been attacking Washington and mobilized a battery of twenty-four pounders.

Santa Anna was then able to make his final attack with twelve thousand men, General Don Francisco Perez in command. Hardin and McKee had undertaken a reconnaissance to expose the enemy in the corner of the plateau. Supporting O'Brien they reached the ground which the Second Indiana had held in the morning. At this point Santa Anna's preparations were completed and Perez advanced. In the words of General Taylor, both regiments were "entirely routed" and O'Brien lost all his guns. Hardin, McKee and young Henry Clay, his lieutenant-colonel, refused to retreat and died facing the foe.

The two regiments carrying their heroic dead retreated down a ravine opening into the pass under Washington's breastwork. The pursuers shot at them from the sides of the ravine and then entered the ravine after them. In their eagerness to attack they kept on until they were in the rockbound area at the exit. There, looking up, they saw the mouths of Washington's five cannons staring upon them with unwavering blackness. They turned to go back, but the soldiers behind pushed them forward. Washington withheld his fire. When the last fugitive was safe, he opened fire upon the enemy all bunched up in the area, his guns all double-shotted with grape and canister.

General Zachary Taylor ordered Braxton Bragg and his supports—Davis and Lane—to fall upon the enemy's left flank. They had to re-cross La Bosca, doing it on the run, at which point they were attacked. Davis swept the assailants from his front and then joined Bragg. In the meantime Bragg pushed on as fast as possible without waiting for support. When he wheeled his guns into a battery formation the enemy was within a few yards of their muzzles, and at first he gave ground as his pieces recoiled. It was then that General Taylor sent his famous order, "a little more grape, Captain Bragg." General Taylor added in his report, "The first discharge of canister caused the enemy to hesitate; the second and third drove him back in disorder, *and the day was saved.*" At 6:00 PM the repulse was complete. Night fell cold, and in the morning Santa Anna and all his men, save the wounded and dead were back at Agua Nueva.

In General Taylor's official report of the battle of Buena Vista there is this sentence, "The Second Indiana, which had fallen back as stated could not be rallied, and took no further part in the action, except a handful of men, who, under the gallant Colonel Bowles, joined the Mississippi regiment and did good service. There is not another sentence in American history which equals that one for cruelty and injustice. None so wanton in misstatement, none of malice so obstinately adhered to by its author, none so comprehensive in its damage, since it dishonored a state and held the state subject to stigma.

General Taylor said the regiment fell back. The regiment did fall back but not from cowardice. General Taylor said the regiment could not be rallied. That I say is untrue! General Taylor said in the third place, that the regiment after it fell back took no further part in the action. To this he makes an exception in favor of a "hand-full of men who, under its gallant Colonel Bowles, joined the Mississippi regiment and did good service." That is one of those cunning partial truths which, by forcing a contrast between the meritorious conduct of a few and the supposed infamous conduct of the many, but intensifies a wrong.

Colonel Jefferson Davis, learning after the battle that Colonel Bowles, of the Second Indiana, had fallen into the ranks of the Mississippi regiment as a private, and behaved well, conceived the idea of specially recognizing Bowles's conduct, so he ceremoniously presented to him the Mississippi rifle used by him. The publicity of the affair upset the survivors of the Second Indiana, who held that the acceptance of the gift was an admission of their dishonor. Then General Joe Lane, hoping to learn the actual facts of the retreat, the regiment having been part of his command in the battle, sought a court of inquiry.

Here are some extracts of the court order:

(Orders No. 279)
Headquarters Camp at Buena Vista, April 26, 1847.

By a court of inquiry which convened at this camp in pursuance of Order No. 233, current series, and of which Brigadier-General Marshall is president, . . . the following have been announced as the facts of the case . . .

Facts: Through the exertions of General Lane and other officers, from one hundred and fifty to two hundred men of the Second Regiment of Indiana Volunteers were rallied, and attached to the Mississippi regiment and the Third Indiana, and remained with them on the field of battle during the remainder of the day.

By command of Brigadier-General Wool.

Irvin McDowell, A. A. General

General Taylor said the regiment could not be rallied, and after the retreat it took no further part in the action. Attention is directed to the squareness of denial with which the court meets the two assertions. General Lane then determined to put the blame for the retreat where it belonged; and with that in view he preferred charges against Colonel Bowles. General Taylor ignored these charges by declining to order a court. In a short time, however, public opinion—the term is as justly applicable to a camp as to a city—drove Colonel Bowles in turn to ask for a court of inquiry upon his conduct; and General Wool, who had succeeded to the command at Buena Vista, ordered a court with Colonel Bissell, of the Second Illinois Volunteers, for president, and from its report I submit extracts, not doubting that their pertinency will be instantly admitted.

(Orders No. 281)
Headquarters Camp at Buena Vista, April 27, 1847.

A court of inquiry, of which Colonel Bissell, Second Illinois Volunteers, was president, convened at this camp on the 12th instant, pursuant to Orders No. 267, current series, being instituted at the request of Colonel W. A. Bowles . . .

The court, after diligently and faithfully inquiring into the matter before it, report, from the evidence given, the following as the facts of the case, and its opinion thereon: Statement of facts:

In reference to the first charge, it appears from the evidence that Colonel Bowles is ignorant of the company, battalion, and brigade drills . . .

In relation to the second charge, it appears from the evidence . . . that Colonel Bowles gave the order, "cease firing, and retreat," that General Lane was present, and that he had no authority from General Lane to give such an order . . .

The court finds that the fact of Colonel Bowles having given the order above mentioned did induce the regiment to retreat in disorder, and that Colonel Bowles gave the order with the intention of making the regiment leave its position.

The court is of the opinion that at the time Colonel Bowles gave the order, "retreat," he was under the impression that the artillery had retreated, when, in fact, the battery at that time had gone to an advanced position under the order of General Lane, which order had not been communicated to Colonel Bowles.

And in conclusion, the court finds that throughout the engagement, and throughout the whole day, Colonel Bowles evinced no want of personal courage or bravery, but that he did manifest a want of capacity and judgment as a commander.

By command of Brigadier General Wool.

McDowell, A. A.-General.

The reader now has the evidence upon which I rely—viz., the findings and opinions of two military courts; not one, but two courts. To reach the full effect of the clash in simple truth, I will resort to the deadly parallel, the statements of General Taylor, on the one hand, and the findings of the courts, on the other.

General Taylor's Report	Court President	Finding
General Taylor imputed the falling back as attributed to cowardice.	Colonel Bissel	The regiment was ordered by its colonel to retreat; that the order "cease firing and retreat," was given by its colonel to induce the regiment to retreat, and that the colonel did induce it to leave its position.
General Taylor said that the regiment could not be rallied.	General Marshall	From 150 to 200 men of the regiment were rallied by General Lane and other officers.

General Taylor said that with the exception of a handful of men under its gallant Colonel Bowles, who joined the Mississippi regiment, the regiment took no further part in the action.	General Marshall	The 150 to 200 men who rallied remained on the field of battle during the rest of the day.
General Taylor said that the exceptional handful of men under Colonel Bowles joined the Mississippi regiment.	General Marshall	The 150 to 200 men who were rallied attached themselves to the Mississippi regiment *and the Third Indiana regiment.*

These differences are material; and, being cast into high relief, which is to be believed, General Taylor or the courts? The reports of General Taylor were forwarded before the trials took place. The records of the courts required General Taylor's signature so he *must* have seen them. Taking the finding of the court to be the truth, the small number found to have been rallied after the retreat—between 150 and 200 men—may cause a smile for *prima facie* it is a weakness in the argument.

Having reached the field shortly after the battle—only two days—I think my opportunities for information fit me to speak of the things then in controversy there. Colonel Bowles was a naturalist and a physician by profession. He was fairly brave, ambitious, pleasant-mouthed and easy-going. He did not master the basics of tactics in vogue at the time of his enlistment. To make the situation difficult for him an extreme attachment had arisen between the regiment and its late Colonel Joe Lane. The relation was precisely that which sprang up between General Taylor and the First Mississippi. In a practical sense Lane, when he became general, remained as a "colonel" to the suppression of Colonel Bowles. He looked after the discipline and personal welfare of the men. He drilled them and did a good job. To this Colonel Bowles made no objection. I have seen Colonel Bowles riding into camp bringing botanical specimens of the flora of the country while the regiment was on the parade ground under General Lane. He seemed incapable of jealousy. Certainly he had no sense of the awful responsibilities of command in battle. The men treated him good-naturedly. None of them dreamed that under his order the ultimate martial issue to which they looked forward so ardently would turn out to be a life-long provocation of tears and shame.

At roll call on the morning of February 23rd the total of muskets in the stacks of the Second Indiana did not exceed three hundred and sixty. Two companies (Walker's and Osborne's) had been drawn off the day before to form a provisional battalion under Major Gorman of the Third Indiana, leaving eight companies averaging 45 men each in the ranks.

The Third Indiana had been placed in reserve by General Wool. The actual command possessed by Brigadier General Lane was the Second Indiana and O'Brien's battery of three guns. We then have the anomaly, brought about by the relation Lane bore to the Second Indiana, of a regiment going into battle with practically two colonels in charge. One cannot help asking, what if in the turmoil and noise the orders of the two *colonels* should happen to conflict. To illustrate what if one ordered "Forward," and the other moved by a different inspiration should order "Retreat?"

It was extremely cold throughout the night of the 23rd. By 3:00 AM everybody was on the alert. As dawn approached the deadly business of the day was begun by the Mexicans. A swarm sprang out and spread darkly up and over the low foot-hills next to the plateau, going to the assistance of their balking skirmishers. Then on an elevation, advanced well towards the Second Indiana masses of men appeared dragging five field pieces into position.

On horseback and watchful General Lane was aware that it would never do for the fire of that battery (Ballarta's) to catch his companies unformed. He ordered the regiment to "Fall in." Just then the reports of the enemy artillery rolled over the plateau far and near. A few minutes later Colonel Churchill, of General Wool's staff, rode over to tell General Lane that the enemy was slowing down on the road in feint, while the real attack was coming against him up the first ravine at his front. Without informing Colonel Bowles, who was in the rear of the extreme right company, Lane galloped around the left flank of the regiment to a position in front of the colors. Then he ordered, "Forward—guide center—march!" At this point the double colonelcy was an established fact. Does the real colonel awake from his suppression and do some contrary thing which strikes him as the best? Promptly, as if on parade, the regiment stepped out, and O'Brien advanced his three guns.

Out of the first ravine, towards which Lane was heading a military band richly uniformed appeared and began playing the national air of Mexico. The regiment, observing it, cheered and took step from the inspiring music. Only for a moment, however, for the band, which did not halt, was succeeded by an interminable array of infantry in double columns, flag after flag. Suddenly the enemy became a line of battle. Two full divisions (Lombardini's and Pacheco's) moved forward, a splendid but terrible spectacle.

General Lane's object in advancing had been partly to reach a point from which to control the ravine before the enemy gained the plateau. Seeing that it was too late, he halted the regiment and sent his aide to order O'Brien into a battery formation; then, clearing the line of fire, he galloped to the rear by the left flank. Had he gone by the right flank, he could have spoken to the other colonel there and told him his wishes; as it was, he did all the commanding in solo fashion. At his word the men went to their knees, and at his word they began firing. Then O'Brien opened fire. Ballarta quickened all his guns, so that now, indeed, the battle for the plateau was joined.

Of the generalship I have nothing to say. My purpose is to help to an intelligent judgment of the conduct of the regiment in question.

There were only three hundred and sixty men in the ranks. Enfilading them from left to right, and within easy range, was a battery of five eight pounder guns. Advancing upon them in brigade front, thus overlapping their own front, were infantry columns of two divisions variously estimated, the most recent authority putting their strength at seven thousand—eighteen to one!

The regiment was nearly a quarter of a mile in advance of Bissell's Second Illinois. It was literally on the plateau alone, and unsupported, except if we reverse the order of things and call O'Brien's three guns a support. Lastly, this is the regiment's first battle, and I see no need of stopping to tell what all that means. Set upon by everything that makes battle terrible—overwhelming numbers in front, bullets *swishing* about them, shells bursting, comrades falling—if General Taylor was right, and that it was a band of cowards, it would certainly break now.

Did they break? In the supply box of every *man* were forty cartridges and three buckshot. Loading by rammer was a slow process; yet the Mexicans were brought to a halt, and their shooting grew wilder. The distance between them was about a hundred yards. Some of our men, to be sure, were white of face. A breeze blew fitfully lifting the smoke, so that now and then the very cool among them took deliberate aim, and that meant death, for at home they were woodsmen and hunters. The first chill went quickly—and then they were all steady.

Dante, in his *Inferno,* speaks of all horrible sounds, but nowhere of music; so in battle the noises are mostly explosive discordances; still one can become so intent upon his individual performance, whether with sword, musket, or great gun, that action becomes automatic. That was what now happened. The men loaded and fired, and heard nothing, neither whistle of bullet nor shriek of shell or stricken comrade. How full the air was of missiles may be judged. In the first position of the regiment twenty-one of the forty cartridges were fired. Of the three hundred and sixty combatants in the ranks ninety dropped dead or disabled by wounds. The color-sergeant fell. Seeing the flag go down and being near, paymaster Dix, a volunteer aide with General Lane ran over and picked it up, and kept it flying until Lieutenant Kunkel demanded it. Kunkel, a brave fellow, bore it the rest of the day, a mark for the enemy, a brave sight for fellow countrymen, if only they chose to see it. My poor friend and school-mate, Captain Kinder, was hit though not mortally wounded. The lancers overtook and killed him later in an ambulance. General Lane, in the act of cheering, was shot in the right arm; a hot canister cauterized his cheek; his horse's lower jaw was broken. And now, on account of Ballarta's gunners, it was necessary to shift the regiment. Forward or back? Just then General Lane saw the Mexicans at his front faltering, and he resolved to get closer to them. O'Brien must advance. Robinson, Lane's Adjutant-General, delivered the order, and it was instantly obeyed. From his place behind McRae's company, the last one on the left, Lane called out, "Forward"—when horror of horrors! The right was going to pieces, and streaming to the rear just as fast as its men could run.

The point of culminating interest in this most dismal episode at Buena Vista was now reached. In certain books, favorites of mine, the catastrophes cause me the keenest anguish. Such is the effect of the fall of Harold in Bulwer's novel of that name. Such, also, is the death of Uncas in Cooper's *The Last of the Mohicans.* So always, thinking of the break and flight of the Second Indiana in the midst of its well-doing, I have a return of the same pang sharper of a conviction that had the brave fellows been held to the attack three or four minutes longer, single-handed they would have routed the divisions before them. And then glory would have been theirs! And how the state would have shone in the reflected light!

Thanks now to the courts, there is no mystery about the cause of the break. We know it. It was by order. We know, too, by whose order. Wherefore the question—as the court says Colonel Bowles was not a coward, as General Taylor pronounced him *gallant,* how could he upon his own volition have done such a shameful thing?

The circumstance is one about which everybody can have a theory. I will give mine. The moment General Lane, at the left of the regiment, conceived the idea of shifting it closer to the enemy, Colonel Bowles, over on the right, dismounted, and, too far off for instant communication with his chief, was in a confusion of senses begotten, doubtless, of a consciousness of incapacity, not to speak of the sounds that assailed him, discordant, furious, and cyclonic. Old soldiers who have been in the heat of battles know how those sounds do actually buffet one as with blows, and how they are attended with stupefying sensations. Anyhow, holding his horse, if not behind it, he chanced to look through a rift in the smoke, and, not seeing O'Brien or his battery, was seized with an inspiration which was the opposite of General Lane's. He heard no voice of glory calling. If he saw an advantage, it was in getting the men and himself out of the tremendous broil; and not knowing how to do that by manoeuver, though there are a number of methods prescribed in the books; without thinking to send the flag back to indicate a place of rally; too much dazed, indeed, to remember that he himself was subject to order; too confused to consider anything but escape in the quickest possible time, he called out, "Cease firing, and—retreat," and in those words, doubtless, exhausting his slender store of tactical knowledge. Only the company nearest heard what he said, and they turned and gazed at him in wonder. A second time he raised his voice—"Cease firing, and—retreat."

Now no man shall say this was not an order. It was an order, and by one in authority. And at once all the shame of the flight that followed attaches to him who gave the order—*the gallant Colonel Bowles.*

In the next place there was a rally; and while in camp I myself heard the details of it, and am not permitted to doubt what I heard—else there is not honor among men.

General Lane, looking ahead, saw La Bosca forming a broad trench across the line of flight, and rode to it at full speed, taking Lieutenant-Colonel Haddon and Major Cravens with him. Wheeling his horse on the other side, he confronted the men. Fifteen of them in panic ran by him to the sheep-ranch nearly a mile away. There, with others from different commands, mostly riflemen dislodged, as we shall presently see, they did good service later in the forenoon. Quite one hundred and ninety of the regiment heard him and hastened to re-form; and when presently Lieutenant Kunkel overtook the body with the colors, an accounting for the absent was easy. This was the table generally agreed upon in the leisure following the fight:

Killed and wounded	90
Absent in care of the wounded	40
Rallied by Colonel Bowles	25
Rallied at the sheep-ranch	15
Rallied by General Lee and other officers	<u>190</u>
	360

Is it reasonable, now, asking more proof from me? Out of a total of three hundred and sixty men, two hundred and fifteen back under their own colors, ought, I insist, to be fact enough of itself, the question being whether there was a rally. Then, as to courage, ninety killed and wounded before the order to retreat—ninety out of three hundred and sixty—one-fourth of the entire firing line! How often has battle anywhere such a record of proportional loss?

We come next to the compliment to Colonel Bowles paid, as has been seen, by General Taylor. The colonel ordered the retreat; he rallied what his eulogist calls a handful of the men; then, rifle in hand, he spent the rest of the day as a private soldier, loading and firing in the front or rear rank of a strange regiment. What is gallantry in a private may be unqualified shame in an officer. This bit of military philosophy was never so pointedly illustrated as by Colonel Bowles when he stepped into the ranks of the Mississippians. The situation at the moment is worth an effort at appreciation. It is after the rally on the farther side of La Bosca. The one hundred and ninety of the Second Indiana are about to attach themselves to Colonel Davis's command. They are under their own colors. Lieutenant Colonel William R. Haddon is in command.

The crisis is terrible. Where is Colonel Bowles? I know nothing in war so strange as his conduct in that thrilling instant. With his rallied "handful" he approaches the Mississippians. First securing a rifle and cartridges—let us suppose from a wounded man or one dead—he takes his place in the ranks unobserved by the strangers. Near by is his own regiment. Their colors are his colors. He is entitled to command them. They are the men who voted him colonel, with whom he has tented and marched and lived the whole of his soldier life. He must have seen them—he must have seen the flag. Why did he turn away and abandon them to become for the time a Mississippian? Why prefer the strangers? Why? The question is beyond me. But—and this is the application—what of *gallantry* is there in his behavior?

Finally, on the point of cowardice. I am a dissenter to the opinion often urged that the sovereign test of the conduct of a corps in battle is the list of casualties; still, to apply that test in this instance, here is a table of the losses by commands at Buena Vista compiled from the official returns:

Corps	Killed	Wounded	Missing	Aggregate
General Staff	1	3	0	4
1st Dragoons	0	7	0	7
2nd Dragoons	0	2	0	2
3rd Artillery	1	22	2	25
4th Artillery	5	21	0	26
Mississippi Rifles	40	56	2	98
Kentucky Cavalry	27	37	0	61
Arkansas Cavalry	17	32	4	53
2nd Kentucky Cavalry	44	57	1	102
1st Illinois regiment	29	18	0	47
2nd Illinois regiment	48	75	3	116
2nd Indiana regiment	32	71	4	107
3rd Indiana regiment	9	56	0	65
Texas Volunteers	14	2	7	23
Total	267	459	23	746

When the intelligent reader, far removed from the petty jealousies of the men who fought at Buena Vista, examines this table, and sees, as he certainly will, that there was but one regiment with more casualties than the Second Indiana, he will wonder greatly, but at nothing so much as the general commanding. There may even come to him reading a realization of the lamentable fact that a man may have been a successful general and popular president of the United States, yet lack the elements without which no one can be truly great—**justice and truth!**

On May 24, 1847, the First Indiana left Walnut Springs going back to "the States" for mustering out. I left with them and I leave my pronouncements to your decision.

Chapter 7

Major General William Jenkins Worth

William Jenkins Worth was born at Hudson, New York on March 1, 1794, and received a good education, spending some time at the academy at Lennox, Massachusetts. The war of 1812 found him a clerk in a mercantile house located it Albany, New York. Somewhat later he accepted the post as private secretary to General Morgan Lewis, and on March 19, 1813, received a commission as a first lieutenant in the Twenty-third Infantry. He served as an aide-de-camp to General Lewis, and also to General Winfield Scott. He was brevetted a captain on July 5, 1814 for gallant and meritorious conduct at the battle of Chippewa, and was made a major for his services at the battle of Lundy's Lane, or Niagara, twenty days later.

In the latter action Worth was severely wounded. "I had the honor to receive a slight scratch—a fortune of war," he wrote to his sister. "The doctors have the modesty to tell me I shall be confined for some three or four months." But in another letter dated August 30, 1814, Worth acknowledged to his sister that his wound was "very severe," and, in fact, he suffered from it for the rest of his life.

"The battle of the 25th (Niagara) was, in my opinion," he wrote, "the fittest subject for the pen and pencil of the poet and artist that has occurred since the coming of Christ. The roar of twenty pieces of artillery and seven thousand small arms hushed the thundering Niagara to a murmuring rill, which only seemed to mourn the fallen brave, the heroes who had the noble daring to chastise an indolent and mercenary foe. Peace to their ashes, and glory to their memory!"

From 1820 to 1828 Worth was commandant of cadets at the West Point Military Academy, and in 1832 he saw service in the Black Hawk War. He was also instrumental in effecting an honorable settlement of the "Patriot War" on the Canadian border, and later was sent with his regiment to Florida, where, after several years of tedious and dangerous service, he brought about peace with the Seminole Indians. Many of his predecessors had failed in this object, and Worth's reward was to become a brevetted brigadier general. He was then a colonel of the Eighth Infantry.

When General Taylor was appointed to organize a corps of observation at Corpus Christi, Mexico, Worth received instructions to join him. He did so, and acted as second in his command. When Taylor pushed toward Point Isabel in order to establish a depot there, the army was left in Worth's hands. Single handedly, Worth planted the national colors on the river bank opposite Matamoros, Mexico.

Unfortunately, during the short season of inactivity that ensued immediately after his arrival at that station, a dispute arose between General Worth and Colonel Twiggs concerning military etiquette, in consequence of which Worth gave up his commission and set out for Washington in protest. This decision of Worth was out of a pure sense of justice and professional dignity, and not from any malice or envy. He assured his command at leaving, that could he at any time be of service to them, or if, contrary to the complexion of affairs at that time, war should ensue, he would waive all etiquette, and hasten to return. He had scarcely reached Washington, when news arrived that the Mexicans had crossed the river, surrounded both American stations, and placed Taylor in imminent danger. Worth immediately addressed the following note, dated May 9th, 1847 at 6:00 PM, to Adjutant General Jones, "Reliable information, which I have this moment received from the headquarters of the army in front of Matamoros, makes it not only my duty, but accords with my inclination, to request permission to withdraw my resignation, and that I be ordered or permitted forthwith to return to, and take command of the troops from which I was separated on the 7th of April . . ."

The answer from General Jones was as follows, "I have submitted your letter of this afternoon's date to the Secretary of War, in which, for reasons stated, you request that your resignation, recently tendered, may be recalled, and you may be ordered or permitted forthwith to return and take command of the troops from which you were separated. The motives which prompt this course on your part are fully appreciated, and I am directed to say that your request is complied with. You will, therefore, repair without delay to General Taylor's headquarters, and report to him accordingly."

Worth reached the Rio Grande in time to be present at the taking of Matamoros, and was appointed as the head of the delegation from the American army to negotiate the capitulation.

Worth was extremely mortified in having missed the battles of May 8th and 9th, in consequence of his voluntary absence. Appreciating this feeling, General Taylor gave a rare proof of his interest and sympathy with a brother officer, by entrusting him with an independent command during the storming of Monterey. A description of the defenses appertaining to this city was reported by General Taylor. Worth was sent with the 2nd division against a chain of fortified hills at that location. General Worth's operational report was as follows:

I have the honor to report that, in obedience to the verbal orders of the general-in-chief, the division under my command, composed of commands under Lieutenant Colonel Duncan, Lieutenant Colonel Childs, Captain Scriver, Captain Miles, Captain Blanchard, Lieutenant Mackall, General Persifer F. Smith, and Colonel Hays's regiment of Texan mounted riflemen, moved out from the main camp at Walnut Springs at 2:00 PM on September 20th, 1847.

My instructions were to *detour to* the right, to endeavor to find and reach the Saltillo road, carry out a thorough reconnaissance of the approaches to the city from that direction, cut off all supplies and reinforcements, and, if practicable, carry the heights.

Owing to the poor terrain after leaving the Marin road, and just before striking the Presquina Grande road, our division only went six miles. The men were involved in making the route suitable for the passage of artillery. They were under the command of Captain Sanders. Midway to the summit we passed the Bishop's Palace and at 6:00 PM we halted at the summit of an isolated mound called Independence Ridge. From there a reconnaissance of the Presquina Grande road was made by an undercover detachments of Hays's Texans.

This examination resulted in the conviction that the ground at our front and on our left constituted the weakest and the strongest points of the enemy's position. These points entered into the final equation for the defenses of the city. It was the enemy's weak point, because it commanded their only line of retreat and supply route to Saltillo, via the Presquina Grande road. It was the enemy's strong point, because of the peculiarly defensive character of the hills and gorges, and of the very careful and skillful manner with which they had been fortified and guarded. It was clearly indicated that our further advance would be strenuously resisted.

On the morning of the 21st, the division was put in motion. At 6:00 AM the advanced troops consisted of Hays's Texans supported by the 1st brigade under Captain C. F. Smith, and closely followed by Duncan's light artillery. When making a turn on the mountain at a hacienda called San Jeronimo, they came upon a strong force of enemy cavalry and infantry, mostly the former. A conflict immediately ensued.

The Texans received the heavy charge of enemy cavalry with their usual gallantry. The light companies opened a rapid and well-directed fire and Duncan's battery was in action in one minute, (promptly supported by a section under Mackall) delivering its fire over the heads of our men. Before the close of the combat, which lasted only fifteen minutes, the 1st brigade had formed to the front, on the right and left, and delivered its fire. The 2nd brigade was held in reserve, the ground not being suitable for their deployment. The enemy retreated in disorder upon the Saltillo road, leaving on the ground one hundred killed and wounded; among the former, Don Juan N. Najua, colonel of the permanent Mexican regiment of lancers. The enemy was closely pursued until we got possession of the gorge, where all the outlets from Monterey unite.

The defeated force, as well as their reinforcements and supplies were ex cluded from entering the city. At this important point the division was halted, and attention directed to the mountain forts which enveloped the city on its western and south-western faces. Discovering that our position brought us within effective range of the enemy batteries, the troops were advanced only some eight hundred yards further on the Saltillo road.

Besides the importance of our position, the examination thus far manifested the impracticability of any effective operation against the city, until we had possession of all the exterior forts and batteries. The occupation of these heights became indispensable to the restoration of our lines of communication with our head-quarters. These lines had been abandoned for the moment in order to secure the gorges along the Saltillo road. At twelve noon, a force was detached under Captain C. F. Smith, with orders to storm the batteries on the crest of the nearest hill, called Federation Hill and after taking that, to attack Fort Soldada, on the ridge of the same height. The two defenses effectually guarded the slopes and roads in either valley, and consequently the approaches to the city. Smith's command consisted of Green's, McGowan's, R. A. Gillespie's, Chandler's and Ballone's companies. It also included McCulloch's companies of Texan riflemen, under Major Chevalier, and four companies of artillery, amounting in all to about three hundred troops. It was impossible to mask the movement of the storming party. On approaching the base of the mountain, the guns of both batteries opened a withering fire, and numerous light troops were seen descending and arranging themselves at favorable points on the slopes.

In a short time the fire became general. The enemy gradually yielded and retired up the rugged slopes, with our men steadily pursuing. The appearance of heavy reinforcements on the summit, and the cardinal importance of the operation demanded further support, so Major Scott's, and Blanchard's companies of volunteers were immediately detached, accompanied by Brigadier General Smith, who was instructed to take direction in that quarter. The whole was now directed by General Smith who had been detached on special service, but who returned in time to share with fifty of his men in the first assault, and to take a prominent part in the second. On reaching the advance parties, General Smith discovered that he could, by directing a portion of his forces to the right, and moving it obliquely up the hill under ground-cover, carry Fort Soldada simultaneously with Federation Hill. He accordingly very judiciously directed and accompanied the 5th, 7th, and Blanchard's company in that direction. Having most gallantly carried the first object of attack, Captain C. F. Smith's command promptly turned the captured gun—a nine-pounder—upon the second object, and moved on with his main body to participate in the assault on Fort Soldada. This assault was carried in a gallant style by the forces under Scott, Miles, Blanchard, and Hays.

At this point we secured another nine-pounder, and immediately both pieces were brought to bear upon the Bishop's Palace, situated upon and midway up the southern slope of Independence Ridge, a valley of only six hundred yards intervening. We had now secured an important advantage, and yet only half the work was done. The possession of these heights only made the more apparent the controlling importance of those opposite, and the necessity of occupying the palace. A violent storm ensued, night closed in, and operations for the day ceased. The troops had now been thirty-six hours without food, and constantly were exposed to the most physical exertions. Such as could be permitted slept with arms in hand, subjected to a pelting storm, and without shelter until 3:00 AM, when they were aroused to take Independence Ridge.

Lieutenant Colonel Childs was assigned to lead the storming-parties. They consisted of three artillery battalion companies, three companies of the 8th infantry under Captain Scriven, and two hundred Texan riflemen, under Colonel Hays and Lieutenant-Colonel Walker, captain of rifles, all acting in concert. The command moved out shortly after 3:00 AM, conducted to its point of ascent by Captain Sanders, military engineer, and Lieutenant Meade, topographical engineer. Favored by the weather, the command reached within one hundred yards of the crest at dawn, where among the clefts of rocks a body of the enemy had been stationed the previous evening in apparent anticipation of the attack. The enemy's retreating fire was ineffectual,—and not returned until Colonel Child's and Colonel Hays's command had reached to within a few yards of the summit, when a well-directed and destructive fire, followed by the bayonet of the regulars and rush of the Texans, placed us in possession of the work. The cannon had been previously withdrawn, and no impression could be made upon the massive walls of the palace or its outworks, without artillery, except at an enormous sacrifice.

Lieutenant Rowland, of Duncan's battery, was ordered out from the main ranks with a twelve-pound howitzer. He was aided by Captain Sanders and fifty of his men from the line, whose job was to select the least difficult route. That enterprising and gallant officer had his guns in position, having ascended an acclivity as rugged as steep, between seven and eight hundred feet, in only two hours. A fire was immediately opened from the howitzer, covered by the epaulement of the captured battery, upon the palace and its outworks, four hundred yards distant, and soon produced a visible sensation. Meanwhile, to reinforce the position, the 5th, consisting of Major Scott's and Blanchard's volunteers, had been passed from the first heights, and reached the second in time to participate in the operations against the palace.

After many affairs of light troops and several feints, a heavy sortie was made, sustained by a strong corps of cavalry, with a desperate resolution to repossess the heights. Such a move had been anticipated and prepared for. Lieutenant Colonel Childs had advanced, under cover, two companies of light troops under the command of Captain Vinton, acting major, and judiciously drawn up the main body of his command, flanked on the right by Hays, and the left by Walker's Texans. The enemy advanced boldly, but were repulsed by a general discharge from all our arms. They fled in confusion, closely pressed by Childs and Hays, preceded by the light troops under Vinton; and while they fled, our troops entered the palace and fort. In a few moments the unpretending flag of our Union had replaced the gaudy standard of Mexico.

The captured guns included one six-inch howitzer, one twelve, and two nine-pounder brass guns, together with Duncan's and Mackall's field-batteries, which came up at a gallop, were used in full and effective play upon the retiring and confused masses that filled the street (of which we had the prolongation) leading to the Great Plaza or La Capella, also crowded with troops. At this moment the enemy's loss was heavy. The investment was now complete. Except for the forces necessary to hold the positions on Independence Ridge and serve the guns, (shifted to points where their shells would storm the Great Plaza) the division was now concentrated around the palace, and preparations were made to assault the city on the following day, or sooner, should the general-in-chief either so direct, or, before communication be bad, renew the assault from the opposite quarter. In the mean time attention was directed to every provision our circumstances permitted, to alleviate the condition of our wounded soldiers and officers; to the decent interment of the dead, not omitting in either respect all that was due to those of the enemy.

At about 10:00 AM on the 23rd, a heavy fire was heard in the opposite quarter. Its magnitude and continuance, as well as other circumstances, left us without any doubts that the general was conducting a main attack; and that his orders for my cooperation (having to travel a circuit of some six miles) had miscarried or failed to reach me. Under these convictions, the troops were instantly ordered to commence an operation, which, if not otherwise directed, I had designed to execute in part, under favor of the night. Two columns of attack were organized, to move along the two principal streets, leading from our position, in the direction of the Great Plaza, composed of light troops slightly extended, with orders to mask the men whenever practicable, avoid those points swept by the enemy's artillery, to press on to the Great Plaza, to get hold of the ends of streets beyond, then enter the buildings, and by means of picks and bars break through the longitudinal section of the walls, work from house to house, and ascending the roofs, to place themselves on the same breast-height with the enemy. Light artillery under Duncan, Roland, Mackall, Martin, Hays, Irons, Clarke, and Curd, followed at suitable intervals, covered by reserves to guard the pieces and the whole operation against the probable enterprises of cavalry upon our left.

This was effectually done by seizing and commanding the head of every cross street. The streets were, at different and well-chosen points, barricaded by heavy masonry walls, with embrasures for one or more guns, and in every instance well supported by cross batteries. These arrangements of defense gave to our operations at this moment a complicated character, demanding much care and precaution; but the work went on steadily, simultaneously, and successfully. About the time our assault commenced, the fire ceased from our force in the opposite quarter. Disengaged on the one side, the enemy was enabled to shift men and guns to our quarter, as was soon manifested by an accumulation of withering fire. At dark we worked through the walls and squares, and reached to within one block of the Great Plaza, leaving a covered path to our rear. We took a large building which towered over the principal defenses, and during the night and ensuing morning, crowned its roof with two howitzers and a six-pounder. All things were now prepared to renew the assault at dawn, when a flag was sent on, asking for a momentary suspension of fire, which led to the capitulation upon honorable terms to our arms.

As the columns of attack were moving from the palace hill, Major Munroe, chief of artillery, reached me with a ten-inch mortar, which was immediately advanced to the Great Plaza chapel, and put in position hidden by the church wall, its bed adjusted as rapidly as possible, and by sunset opened upon the great square. At this period, our troops had worked to within one square of the plaza; but the exact position of our comrades, on the opposite side, was not known, and the distance of the position to be assailed by the bomb battery, but conjecturing eight hundred yards was assumed, and out fuses and charges regulated accordingly. The first shell fell a little short of the point to which it was directed, but a slight increase of the projecting charge gave exact results. The whole service was managed by Major Munroe, most admirably, and, combined with other operations, exercised a decided influence upon the final results. Early on the morning of the 23rd, Major Brown's artillery battalion was dispatched with a select command, and one section of Mackall's battery, under Lieutenant Irons, to occupy the stone mill and adjacent grounds, constituting, one league in advance, the narrow gorge near St. Catarina. The major took possession, repulsed the enemy's pickets, and was preparing his command to resist any attack, when he received my orders to retrace his steps, enter the city, and form the main reserve to the assaulting columns. He came up in good time and in good order, and was at once under fire.

On the 25th, in conformity to the articles of capitulation, the Citadel, or "Black Fort" was taken possession of by a command consisting of two companies of each regiment, and one section of each battery, second division. General Smith was directed to take command of this corps, and conduct the ceremony; which duty he executed with delicacy to the unhappy and humiliated foe.

You will receive lists of captured munitions of war, lists of such as were surrendered having already been handed in. It is a source of high gratification that we have been able to accomplish such fortunate results with so moderate a sacrifice of gallant men. Annexed to my report is a return of killed and wounded, exhibiting dates, actions, and circumstances.

When every officer and every soldier, regular and volunteer, has, through a series of harassing and severe conflicts, in the valley and on the mountain, in the street and on the house-top, cheerfully, bravely, and successfully executed every service and complied with every exaction of valor and patriotism, the task is as difficult as delicate, to distinguish individuals; and yet it will always happen, as it has always happened in the varied scenes of battle and siege, that fortune presents to some those opportunities which all would have seized with gladness and avidity. It is my pleasing and grateful duty to present to the consideration of the general-in-chief, and through him to the government, the distinguished conduct of Brigadier-General Smith, Colonel of rifles, Brevet Lieutenant Colonel Childs, artillery battalion, Colonel Hays, Texan riflemen, Brevet Captain C. F. Smith, 2nd artillery, commanding light troops of the first brigade.

My attention was particularly directed by General Smith, to the gallant conduct of a number of my men during the assault upon the city. Particular attention has also been called to the two lieutenants, (the Nicholl brothers) Louisiana volunteers, as having highly distinguished themselves by personal daring and efficient service. The officers of brigade and regimental staff were conspicuous in the field, or in their particular departments. Lieutenants Hanson, (commanding) Vanhorn, aide-de-camp, 7th; Lieutenant Robison, 5th, (quartermaster's department) on the staff of General Smith; Lieutenant and Adjutant Clark, 8th infantry, staff 1st brigade; Lieutenant Benjamin, adjutant artillery battalion Peck, ordnance officer, artillery battalion; G. Deas, Adjutant 5th; and Page, Adjutant 7th infantry, are highly commended by their respective chiefs, to the justness of which I have the pleasure to add my personal observation. In common with the entire division, my particular thanks are tendered to Assistant Surgeons, Porter, (senior) Byrne, Conrad, De Leon, and Roberts, (medical department) who were ever at hand in the close fight, promptly administering to the wounded and suffering soldier.

To the officers of the staff, general and personal, more especially associated with myself—the Honorable Colonel Balie Peyton, Louisiana troops, who did me the honor to serve as aide-de-camp; Captain Sanders, military engineers; Lieutenant Meade, topographical engineers Lieutenants E. Deas, Daniels, and Ripley, quartermaster's and commissary's staff; and Lieutenants Pemberton, 4th artillery, and Wood, 8th infantry, my aides-de-camp—I have to express the greatest obligation. In such diversified operations during the three days and nights, they were constantly in motion, performing every executive duty, with zeal and intelligence and only surpassed by daring courage in conflict. I beg to commend each to special consideration.

We have to lament the death of the gallant Captains McKavett, 8th infantry, an officer of high merit, killed on the 21st, and Gillespie, Texas volunteers, on the 22nd. The latter eminently distinguished himself while leading his brave company at the storming of the first height, and perished in seeking similar distinction on a second occasion; Captain Gatlin and Lieutenant Potter, 7th, Lieutenant Rossell, 5th, and Wainwright, 8th infantry, and Lieutenant Reece, Texas riflemen, received honorable, but happily not mortal wounds.

In the several conflicts with the division, the enemy's loss is ascertained to exceed four hundred and fifty men, four nine-pounders, one twelve-pounder brass gun, one twenty-four-pounder howitzer, and two national (garrison) standards captured.

Samuel C. Reid Jr.[11] gave this vivid account of the street-fight in which Worth's men were engaged:

Every street was barricaded with works of masonry, the walls being some three or four feet thick, with embrasures for one or more guns, which raked the streets; the walls of the gardens and sides of the houses were all loop-holed for musketry; the tops of the houses were covered with troops, who were sheltered behind parapets some four feet high, upon which were piled sand-bags for their better protection, and from which they showered down a hurricane of balls.

Between three and four o'clock, from the cessation of the fire in the opposite direction, it was evident that the enemy had become disengaged, which enabled them to draw off men and guns to our side, as their fire had now become almost doubly increased. The street-fight became appalling—both columns were now closely engaged with the enemy, and steadily advanced inch by inch—our artillery was heard rumbling over the paved streets, galloping here and there as the emergency required, and pouring forth a blazing fire of grape and ball—volley after volley of musketry, and the continued peals of artillery became almost deafening. The artillery of both sides raked the streets, the balls striking the houses with a terrible crash, while amid the roar of battle were heard the battering instruments used by the Texans. Doors were forced open, walls were battered down, entrances made through the longitudinal walls, and the enemy driven from room to room, and from house to house, followed by the shrieks of women, and the sharp

---

[11]   In his excellent work, "The Scouting Expeditions of McCulloch's Texas Rangers," G. G. Evans & Co., Philadelphia, 1859.

crack of Texan rifles. Cheer after cheer was heard in proud and exulting defiance, as the Texans or regulars gained the house-tops by means of ladders, while they poured in a rain of bullets upon the enemy on the opposite houses.

Samuel C. Reid spoke of General Worth:

The position General Worth then occupied might have been considered as critical as it was dangerous. Separated from the main body of the army—his communication cut off, and no possible route less than eight miles to retain it—with but scanty supplies of provisions for four days, surrounded by gorges and passes of the mountains, from whose summits belched forth the destructive shot, shell, and grape, he was liable at any moment to be attacked by an overwhelming force in the direction of Saltillo, which had been reported to be daily expected, and which would have placed his command in the very jaws of the enemy. For although holding the gorges and passes of the Saltillo road, yet a superior force from the advance would certainly have forced him back to, and have turned upon him the very passes which he then held. It was feared too, from his impetuous nature, that he would rush his command into unnecessary danger by some rash and desperate attempt. But it was not so. He was collected, calm, and cool, and bore himself with that proud, resolute, and commanding mien, giving his orders with promptness and decision, which inspired men and officers alike with confidence.

He never appeared better than on that day; and all felt that with Worth they were sure of victory, he knew that General Taylor had staked the issue of the battle on him, and he felt the great and weighty responsibility that rested on the course he should pursue. As he surveyed the enemy's works before him with his glass, he seemed to feel that not a moment was to be lost. He saw at once that it would be necessary to carry by storm the battery on Federation Hill, situated on the right bank of the San Juan de Monterey, as well as Fort Soldada on the ridge of the same height, about six hundred yards from the battery on the crest of the hill, as these two batteries commanded the approaches from the Saltillo road, as well as the egress from the city. For this purpose, Captain C. F. Smith of the 2nd artillery was ordered to proceed with his own, and three companies of the artillery battalion, commanded by Lieutenants Shackelford, Van Vliet, and Phelps—accompanied by Lieutenant Edward Deas, of the Quartermaster's staff, and Lieutenant Gibson, together with two companies of the Texas Rangers (dismounted) under our brave and gallant Major Chevalier, commanded by Captains Gillespie, Ballowe, McCulloch, Chandler, Green, and McGowan. The whole command numbered in all three hundred men, more than half of whom were Rangers.

It was now about 12:00 noon, and the meridian sun poured down its hottest rays. Before us stood the steep and rugged hill, about three hundred and eighty feet high, whose slopes were covered with thick and thorny chaparral. The swarm of Mexicans that crowned the height could be seen with a glass, while its cannon that looked down in defiance at us, seemed to threaten with annihilation all who dared approach. The daring of the expedition was, thought to be one of the last hope; and men looked forward to meet death calmly in the face, as they felt that it was only by great sacrifice that they could gain a victory. General Worth rode up as the command moved off, and pointing to the height said—"*Men you are to take that hill and God knows that you will do it.*" With one response they shouted:—"*We will;*" and those who before had felt a doubt as to its practicability, now became reanimated and felt themselves invincible. The words of Worth had nerved every arm, and hearts swelled with that proud feeling of enthusiasm, which makes men indomitable before the foe.

The command took up its line of march along the Saltillo road, and then struck off to the right through fields of corn and sugar, in single file, in order to conceal, as far as possible, the movement from the enemy. On we hurried in double quick time, bristling through the rows of cane and corn towards the river bank. It was soon evident that we were discovered, and while yet in the fields, the batteries opened upon us a fierce and plunging fire, enveloping the crown of the hill with smoke, through which could be seen the blazing of the cannon, which seemed to vie with the sunbeams' glare. On we pressed toward their murderous artillery, until we gained the bank of the rapid stream, which we had to cross. Unprotected and exposed to the very face of the enemy, a terrific storm of shot and grape was now poured into our ranks. Nothing daunted the men rushed into the sweeping current, waist deep, while the enemy's shot, as it struck the water, sent forth a hissing sound, and made the river boil and foam with the whistling windage of their venomous copper balls. Bravely did our men stem the torrent amid the shower of galling grape, and soon we reached the opposite bank and clambered up the rocky steep without the loss of a man.

Worth was appointed the principal of the delegation to negotiate the capitulation, and contributed more than any other man to a final adjustment of the unfortunate issues which arose during the deliberations. While Taylor remained at Monterey, Worth marched against Saltillo with twelve hundred men and eight pieces of artillery, which he took possession of without the slightest opposition. Here he remained until the middle of January, when he was ordered to proceed with the regulars and volunteers of the army to join General Scott at Vera Cruz.

On arriving at the coast, General Worth soon convinced all around him that his part in the siege was going to be an active one. He was among the very few officers mentioned by Commodore Conner in his description of the landing. Commodore Conner described it thus:

The anchorage near this place was extremely narrow. In order to avoid crowding it with an undue number of vessels it became necessary to transfer most of the troops to the vessels of war for transportation to Sacrificios Island. Accordingly, at daylight on the morning of the 9th this transfer was commenced, all necessary preparations—such as launching and numbering the boats, detailing officers, etc.,—having been previously made. The frigates received on board between twenty-five and twenty-eight hundred men each, with their arms and accouterments, and the sloops and smaller vessels numbers in proportion. This part of the movement was completed very successfully at about 11:00 AM, and a few minutes thereafter the squadron under my command, accompanied by the commanding general, in the steamship *Massachusetts*, and such of the transports as had been selected for the purpose, got under way.

The weather was very fine—indeed we could not have been more favored in this particular than we were. We had a fresh and yet gentle breeze from the south-east, and a perfectly smooth sea. The passage to Sacrificios Island took between two and three hours. Each ship came in and anchored without the slightest disorder or confusion, in the small space allotted to her. The harbor was still very much crowded, notwithstanding the number of transports we had left behind. The disembarkation commenced immediately.

While we were transferring the troops from the ships to the surf-boats, (sixty-five in number) I directed the steamers *Spitfire* and *Vixen*, and the five gun-boats, to form a line parallel with and close in to the beach, to cover the landing. This order was promptly executed, and these small vessels, from the lightness of their drought, were enabled to take positions within grape-shot range of the shore. As the boats received their compliments of troops, they assembled in a line between the fleet and the gun-boats; and when all were ready, they pulled in together, under the guidance of a number of officers of the squadron, who had been detailed for this purpose. General Worth commanded this, the first line of the army, and had the satisfaction of forming his command on the beach and neighboring heights just before sunset. Four thousand five hundred men were thus landed on shore, almost simultaneously. No enemy appeared to offer us the slightest opposition. The first line being landed, the boats in successive trips relieved the men-of-war and transports of the remaining troops, by 10:00 PM. The whole army, (save a few straggling companies) consisting of upwards of ten thousand men, were thus safely deposited on shore, without the slightest accident of any kind.

An eye-witness of the same scene said:

General Worth, certainly the most useful man in command here, had a smart brush with a body of Mexicans last night (March 12th, 1847) and this morning, in which they were beaten. A cemetery was taken possession of about one mile from the city, and fortified by General Worth.

From the very nature of a siege, few individuals save the artillerists are able to distinguish themselves. Worth, however, received the commendations of General Scott, and was appointed to negotiate the terms of surrender. He also attended while the city was being evacuated by the Mexicans, and was subsequently appointed military governor. This office he held only for a short time, moving with the army in its march toward the Mexican capital. At Cerro Gordo, he marched with his whole division to support the left of General Twiggs, in the attack upon the main fort. During the whole time he was exposed to the full range of the enemy's fire, but in unison with his brother officer gallantly carried the redoubt, and completely routed the garrison.

On the 22d of April, 1847, Worth captured the town and the Castle of Perote, one of the strongest in Mexico. It contained immense quantities of ammunition, ordnance, small arms and other military stores. On the 15th of May he approached the city of Puebla. Here Santa Anna had a portion of his army, with which he was collecting provisions and other stores. As Worth approached, he was met by about fifteen hundred lancers, and a skirmish ensued on the plains of Amasoca, in which the enemy lost ten men, killed and wounded. They retreated, and were pursued over the plain, and through the streets of the city. Santa Anna fled at the same time, with the remaining portion of his troops.

The city of Puebla is located on a plain, and the main position of the place is nearly level, the streets a little wider than those of any Mexican towns I have seen—the style of building is nearly the same throughout the city; and taking it all through, is the best built town or city I have ever seen, and the people represent the worst population with which I have ever come in contact. The streets are daily more crowded than Chartres, Camp, or St. Charles Streets, in New Orleans, and depravity, vice and degradation are depicted in every expression of the great mass, from the infant to the aged and infirm. It seems utterly inconceivable that a population of this kind should inhabit such a beautiful and well built city. The population, I heard before my arrival, was about thirty thousand; but from all the information I can get I think it contains more than sixty thousand souls.

The people of this place are noted throughout the whole of Mexico for their villainy and their turbulent spirit. I am free to confess that I do not think there is as much religion, and as little morality, in any town on the continent of America, as can be found here. The mass of the people are very poor, while the rich are very rich—the poor are always ready to engage in crimes of every shape and hue, and prefer vice to labor for the purpose of procuring the necessary means of support. There are upwards of one hundred churches, seven hundred priests, and the value of the church property is a little over one hundred and forty-eight million dollars. The churches are all the very finest. It is impossible to convey an idea of the magnificence of the main cathedral. I have heard men who have seen every public building in the United States, and many of those in foreign countries, state that they have never seen any building that would, in the least degree, compare with the elegance and gorgeousness of this building and its decorations—the large paintings, solid massive gold and gilded carved work, are all of the finest style, and are so arranged as to present the appearance of sublimity. Although there are a great number of designs and paintings, there does not appear to be too many or too few, but just enough to show well.

Like all other places in this country, Puebla has its many places of amusement and resort. The Alameda[12] with its wide walks, blooming flowers, flowing fountains, and shade trees, all within a permanent and neat enclosure—theaters, an amphitheater for bull-fighting, cock fights, etc., to all of which the men, women and children flock in great crowds at certain seasons of the year, for the purpose of enjoying such festivities as may "be on hand." Bullfighting is their great national amusement, which usually takes place on Sundays and feast days, so that it may not interfere with their usual business. Church in the morning, and bull-fighting in the evening, and a fandango at night. Men, women and children, of all ages and conditions, visit the arena as their usual pastime and amusement. When the desperate conflict commences, they all, male and female, become excited alike. The men reward the victors with roars of applause, and the ladies with the waving of white handkerchiefs. The climate is a most pleasant one, the temperature varying but little between winter and summer. The nights are cool enough to make sleeping under a blanket comfortable, and the days warm enough to be agreeable. The heat is not oppressive, and mint juleps are available for those who wish to indulge in them. Snow and ice are daily brought down from the mountains, and hawked through the streets for sale.

From the peculiar adaptation of the climate and soil to the culture of all kinds of fruit, grain, and vegetables, this is one of the best supplied markets here I have ever seen—there is an abundance of all the fruits and vegetables of the northern parts of the United States, together with those of the South and West Indies. The meats and fowl are very fine, and the supply good, though, unlike our country, it is never offered for sale in the public marketplaces, but usually kept in private store-houses in different parts of the city. The rainy season has fairly commenced, but I cannot say it is at all unpleasant—the sun shines out fair and brilliant in the morning, and so continues until about two o'clock, when suddenly a dark heavy cloud makes its appearance on the mountain-side, and

---

[12] A large public garden.

soon passes over the valley, enveloping it in darkness, and pouring out its floods of water, which completely drenches the earth for about four hours. The rain usually ceases then and in half an hour the streets are as dry as if there had not been any rain for twelve months—all classes and conditions again sally out into the streets, and the city soon becomes the theater of a motley crowd; those who can lay any claim to decency are the more gay and lively, while vice and immorality, as if invigorated by a short respite, come out in all the gay and inviting dresses calculated to allure and deceive.

Puebla became the head-quarters of the army until the 8th of August, when General Scott commenced his march for the capital. He led the advance while marching around Lake Chalco, and was the first to reach the hacienda of San Gregoria, when a halt was ordered, in consequence of General Twiggs having met a large force of the enemy near Chalco.

On August 17th, General Worth renewed his march over a terribly rutted road, but by eight o'clock in the morning he was in sight of the domes and spires of the capital, without any opposition, except that rocks had been rolled into the road, and ditches dug, evidently showing that General Scott had stolen a march on Santa Anna. On reaching this point, however, a scattering fire was opened by a force stationed in an advantageous position, which was soon silenced by Colonel Smith's light battalion of the 2d artillery, under Major Galb. Another attack was shortly after made, but again the enemy's pickets were driven in without loss.

At seven o'clock on August 18th, General Scott arrived at San Augustine, and at ten o'clock General Worth was in full march for the City of Mexico by the main road. Majors Smith and Turnbull, Captain Mason and other engineer officers, were sent in advance, supported by Captain Blake's squadron of dragoons, to reconnoiter, when a masked battery was opened on them, and the first ball from an eighteen-pounder killed Captain Thornton of the 2nd dragoons, besides seriously wounding a guide.

Colonel Garland's brigade was ordered to occupy a position in plain sight of the enemy's batteries at San Antonio, while Colonel Stark's brigade and Duncan's battery took their station in the rear close by. A party was then sent out to reconnoiter to ascertain the practicability of finding a road by which the village of San Angel could be reached, and the stronghold of San Antonio thus turned; this party had a skirmish with the enemy, killing five or six, and taking as many prisoners, without losing a man.

The result of the reconnaissance was favorable, and it was ascertained that a road could be constructed. The Mexicans were plainly seen in force near Bronteras, and at a council held that night it was determined to attack them in the morning. While this reconnaissance was going on, General Worth had established himself at the hacienda of Buvera, from the windows of which countless numbers of the enemy could be seen at work upon the batteries of San Antonio. About noon they opened upon the hacienda with both round shot and shell. Nearly every shot took effect, but did no damage, except to the buildings. Late in the evening they ceased firing, and were silent during the remainder of the night. Had the fire been kept up, the hacienda might have been torn to pieces, and the entire command compelled to retire.

At eight o'clock on the morning of the 19th, the batteries again opened on General Worth's position. So hot was the fire that the troops were compelled to gain shelter behind the buildings, but did not give up their position. About 9:00 AM the divisions of Twiggs and Pillow were ordered to march in the direction of Bronteras, and by one o'clock in the afternoon were in plain sight of the enemy's batteries, and within range of the heavier guns. The brigade of Colonel P. F. Smith was ordered to advance directly towards the enemy's works, while that of Colonel Riley moved towards a small village at the right, and thus cut off reinforcements which might he sent to Valencia from the city. An incessant fire was opened on Colonel Smith's command, and soon the rifles were engaged with the pickets of the enemy, driving them in. The twelve-pounder battery of Captain Magruder, and the mountain howitzer batteries now commanded by Lieutenant Callender of the ordnance department, were pressed forward and opened on the enemy, but were so much exposed to a fire from heavier guns, that they were soon silenced. Lieutenants Johnson and Callender were seriously wounded.

At 3:00 PM, General Cadwalader was ordered out to support Colonel Riley—heavy reinforcements having been seen on their way out from the city, while General Pierce was sent to sustain General Smith. The firing from the enemy's batteries was incessant. At about 4:00 PM General Scott arrived, and seeing the immense strength of the Mexicans, at once ordered General Shields' brigade to support Riley and Cadwalader, and prevent, if possible, a junction of the forces coming out of the city, with those of Valencia. Few of the movements of our troops could be seen, but every motion of the enemy was visible. The order of battle at Valencia was most imposing. His infantry were seen drawn up to support the batteries, while long lines of the enemy's cavalry were stationed in the rear, as if awaiting the shock of the battle. Separate charges of the latter were distinctly seen to be repulsed by Colonel Riley. Until night had fairly closed in, the firing enemy's batteries had not slackened; it had been a continuous roar for nearly six hours.

General Scott returned to San Augustine st about 8:00 PM in the midst of a hard rain, and Generals Twiggs and Pillow came in at eleven o'clock, completely exhausted, not anticipating the great strength of the enemy.

It was thought that the batteries could he taken at a dash, and that the troops would be comfortably quartered at San Angel for the night; instead of this a large portion of them were compelled to bivouac, without blankets, in the midst of a pitiless storm. Early on the morning of August 20th, 1847 General Worth was ordered to move a part of his division (Garland's brigade) to aid in the attack on Valencia, for to force this position was deemed indispensable.

At 7:00 AM a few discharges of cannon were heard, and the rattling of musketry, and some even said, that in the distance horses of the enemy could be seen flying towards the city, yet few deemed that the batteries had been stormed and carried, yet it was so. General Scott, accompanied by General Worth, started for the scene of action, when they were met by Captain Mason, with the joyful intelligence that Valencia had been completely routed after a terrible struggle.

The attack upon his works was planned by General Smith, and resulted in the capture of fifteen pieces of artillery and some fifteen hundred prisoners, among them Mexican Generals Blanco, Garcia, Mendoza and the notorious Salas. Smith also captured all the ammunition and camp furniture, and the road over which those who escaped fled was strewed with muskets. No less than seven hundred of the enemy, among them many officers, were left dead upon the field, whilst the number of wounded was far greater.

The works of Bronteras were completely in the power of the American army. General Scott at once ordered General Worth to fall back to San Antonio, capture that work, and then push on towards the capital by the main road, while the main body of the army moved on towards San Angel and Cohoycam.

General Twiggs had scarcely moved a half a mile beyond the latter village, when a rattling fire of musketry announced that our forces was actively engaged with the outposts of the enemy, and the heavy booming of cannon now gave token that the noted second division had fallen on another strong work. A few minutes more and a tremendous firing from the right made it evident that General Worth's division was also actively engaged; he had completely turned the strong works of San Antonio, but while doing so, the enemy had abandoned the place with a loss of three heavy guns, and had fallen back on a second and stronger line of works.

It was now 1:00 PM on the 20th, and the time set for the commencement of the battle. Such a rattling of fire-arms has seldom or never been heard on the continent of America, accompanied with such booming of artillery. This was continued for over two hours, when the enemy was completely routed from every point, and until those who were not killed or taken prisoners were in full flight for the city. The strength of the enemy in this battle was known to have been fifteen or twenty thousand, all fresh troops, and occupying a position of uncommon strength. Opposed to them were about six thousand Americans, jaded and broken down by marches, counter-marches, and incessant toil.

After these brilliant victories the succeeding armistice delayed the operations of the army more than two weeks; but as all attempts to conclude a treaty had failed, both armies prepared for another desperate struggle. On September 7th, the American army commenced reconnaissance of the enemy's positions, with the purpose of making an immediate attack.

General Scott reported:

That same afternoon, a large body of the enemy was discovered hovering about El Molino del Rey, within a mile and a third of this village, where I am quartered with the general staff and Worth's division.

It might have been supposed that an attack upon us was intended; but knowing the great value to the enemy of those mills, containing a cannon foundry, with a large deposit of powder in Casa Mata near them;

and having heard, two days before, that many church bells had been sent out to be cast into guns, the enemy's movement was easily understood, and I resolved, at once, to drive him early the next morning, to seize the powder, and to destroy the foundry.

Another motive for this decision—leaving the general plan of attack upon the city for full reconnaissance—was, that we knew our recent captures had left the enemy not a fourth of the guns necessary to arm, all at the same time, the strong works at each of the eight city gates; and we could not cut the communication between the capital and the foundry without first taking the formidable castle on the heights of Chapultepec, which overlooked both and stood between.

For this difficult operation we were not entirely ready; and, moreover, we might altogether neglect the castle, if, as we then hoped, our reconnaissances should prove that the distant southern approaches to the city were more eligible than this south-western approach.

Hence the decision promptly taken, the execution of which was assigned to Brevet Major General Worth, whose division was reinforced with Cadwalader's brigade of Pillow's division, three squadrons of dragoons under Major Sumner, and some heavy guns of the siege-train under Captain Huger, of the ordnance, and Captain Drum, of the 4th artillery—two officers of the highest merit.

For the decisive and brilliant results, I beg to refer to the report of the immediate commander, Major General Worth, in whose commendations of the gallant officers and men, dead and living, I heartily concur; having witnessed, but with little interference, their noble devotion to fame and to country.

General Worth wrote the following graphic account of this battle:

Sir: Under the inconvenient circumstances incident to recent battle, and derangement from loss of commanders—staff, commissioned, and non-commissioned—and amid the active scenes resulting there from, I proceed to make a report, in obedience to the orders of the general-in-chief, of the battle of El Molino del Rey, fought and won on the 8th of September, 1847, by the first division, reinforced as follows:

1st. Three squadrons of dragoons and one company of mounted riflemen—two hundred and seventy men, under Major Sumner, 2nd dragoons.

2nd. Three pieces of field artillery, under Captain Drum.

3rd. Two battering guns, (twenty-four-pounders) under Captain Huger.

4th. Cadwalader's brigade, seven hundred and eighty-four strong, consisting of the Voltigeur regiment, the 11th and 14th regiments of infantry.

Having, in the course of the 7th, accompanied the general-in-chief on a reconnaissance of the formidable dispositions of the enemy near and around the castle of Chapultepec, they were found to exhibit an extended line of cavalry and infantry, sustained by a field-battery of four guns, occupying directly, or sustaining a system of defenses collateral to the castle and summit. This examination gave fair observation of the configuration of the grounds and the extent of the enemy's force; but, as appeared in the sequel, an inadequate idea of the nature of his defenses, they being skillfully masked.

The general-in-chief ordered that my division, reinforced as before mentioned, should attack and carry those lines and defenses, capture the enemy's artillery, destroy the machinery and material supposed to be in the foundry in El Molino del Rey, but limiting the operations to that extent; after which my command was to be immediately withdrawn to its position in the village of Tacubaya.

A close and daring reconnaissance, by Captain Mason, of the engineers, made on the morning of the 7th, represented the enemy's lines collateral to Chapultepec to be as follows: His left rested upon and occupied a group of strong stone buildings, called El Molino del Rey, adjoining the grove at the foot of the hill of Chapultepec, and directly under the guns of the castle which crowns its summit. The right of his line rested upon another stone building, called Casa Mata, situated at the foot of the ridge that slopes gradually from the heights above the village of Tacubaya to the plain below. Midway between these buildings was the enemy's field-battery, and his infantry forces were disposed on either side to support it. This reconnaissance was verified by Captain Mason and Colonel Duncan on the afternoon of the same day. The result indicated that the center was the weak point of the enemy's position, and that his flanks were the strong points, his left flank being the stronger.

Molino del Rey in the Foreground and Chapultepec Castle in the Background

As the enemy's system of defense was connected with the hill and castle of Chapultepec, and as my operations were limited to a specific object, it became necessary to isolate the work to be accomplished from the castle of Chapultepec and its immediate defenses. To bring about this object the following dispositions were ordered: Colonel Garland's brigade was to take a position on the right, strengthened by two pieces of Captain Drum's battery, to look to Molino del Rey as well as any support of this position from Chapultepec; and also within sustaining distance of the assaulting party and the battering guns, which, under Captain Huger, were placed on the ridge, five or six hundred yards from Molino del Rey, to batter and loosen this position from Chapultepec. An assaulting party of five hundred picked men and officers, under the command of Brevet-Major George Wright, 8th infantry, was also posted on the ridge to the left of the battering guns, to force the enemy's center. The 2nd (Clark's) brigade, the command of which devolved on Colonel McIntosh, (Colonel Clark being sick) with Duncan's battery, was to take post still further up the ridge, opposite the enemy's right, to look to our left flank and sustain the assaulting column if necessary, or to discomfit the enemy, (the ground being favorable) as circumstances might require. Cadwalader's brigade was held in reserve, in a position on the ridge, between the battering guns and McIntosh's brigade, and in easy support of either. The cavalry, under Major Sumner was to envelope our extreme left, and be governed by circumstances to repel or attack, as the commander's judgment might suggest.

The troops were to be put in position under the cover of night, and the work was to begin as soon as the heavy metal could be properly directed. Colonel Duncan was charged with the general disposition of the artillery. Accordingly, at 3:00 AM on the morning of September 8th, several columns were put in motion, on as many different routes; and, when the gray of the morning enabled them to be seen, they were as accurately in position as if posted in midday for review. The early dawn was the moment appointed for the attack, which was announced to our troops by the opening of Huger's guns on Molino del Rey, upon which they continued to play actively until this point of the enemy's line became sensibly shaken, when the assaulting party, commanded by Wright, and guided by that accomplished officer, Captain Mason, of the engineers, assisted by Lieutenant Foster, dashed gallantly forward to the assault.

Unshaken by the galling fire of musketry and canister that was showered upon them, on they rushed, driving infantry and artillery-men at the point of the bayonet. The enemy's field-battery was taken, and his own guns were trained upon his retreating masses; before, however, they could be discharged, perceiving that he had been dispossessed of this strong position by comparatively a handful of men, he made a desperate effort to regain it. Accordingly, his retiring forces rallied and formed with this object. Aided by the infantry, which covered the house-tops, (within reach of which the battery had been moved during the night) the enemy's whole line opened upon the assaulting party a terrific fire of musketry, which struck down *eleven* out of the *fourteen* officers that composed the command, and non-commissioned officers and men in proportion; including among the officers Brevet Major Wright, the commander; Captain Mason and Lieutenant Foster, engineers; all severely wounded.

For a moment this severe shock staggered that gallant band. The light battalion, held to cover Huger's battery, under Captain E. Kirby Smith, (Lieutenant Colonel Smith being sick) and the right wing of Cadwalader's brigade were promptly ordered forward to support them. This order was executed in the most gallant style; the enemy was again routed, and this point of his line carried, and fully possessed by our troops. In the mean time Garland's (1st) brigade, ably sustained by Captain Drum's artillery, assaulted the enemy's left, and, after an obstinate and very severe contest, drove him from this apparently impregnable position, immediately under the guns of the castle of Chapultepec. Drum's section, and the battering guns under Captain Huger, advanced to the enemy's position, and the captured guns of the enemy were now opened on his retreating forces, on which they continued to fire until beyond their reach. While this work was in progress of being accomplished by our center and right, our troops on the left were not idle. Up till this time engaged, Duncan's battery opened on the right of the enemy's line, and the 2nd brigade, under Colonel McIntosh, was now ordered to assault the extreme right of the enemy's line. The direction of this brigade soon caused it to mask Duncan's battery, the fire of which, for the moment, was discontinued; and the brigade moved steadily on to the assault of Casa Mata, which, instead of an ordinary field entrenchment, as was supposed, proved to be a strong stone citadel, surrounded with bastioned entrenchments and impassable ditches—an old Spanish work, recently repaired and enlarged. When within easy musket range, the enemy opened a most deadly fire upon our advancing troops, which was kept up, without intermission, until our gallant men reached the very slope of the parapet of the work that surrounded the citadel.

By this time a large proportion of the command was either killed or wounded, amongst whom were the three senior officers present, Brevet Colonel McIntosh, Brevet Lieutenant Colonel Scott, of the 5th infantry, and Major Waite, 8th infantry; the second killed, and the first and last desperately wounded. Still, the fire from the citadel was unabated. In this crisis of the attack, the command was momentarily thrown into disorder, and fell back on the left of Duncan's battery, where they rallied. As the 2nd brigade moved to the assault, a very large cavalry and infantry force was discovered approaching rapidly upon our left flank, to reinforce the enemy's right. As soon as Duncan's battery was masked, as before mentioned, supported by Andrews's Voltigeurs, of Cadwalader's brigade, it moved promptly to the extreme left of our line to check the threatened assault on this point. The enemy's cavalry rapidly came within canister range, when the whole battery opened most effective fire, which soon broke the squadrons and drove them back in disorder.

During this fire upon the enemy's cavalry, Major Sumners command moved to the front, and changed direction in admirable order, under a *most* appalling fire from the Casa Mata. This movement enabled his command to cross the ravine immediately on the left of Duncan's battery, where it remained, doing noble service until the close of the action. At the very moment the cavalry were driven beyond reach, our own troops drew back from before the Casa Mata, and enabled the guns of Duncan's battery to re-open upon this position, which, after a short and well-directed fire, the enemy abandoned. The guns of the battery were now turned upon his retreating columns, and continued to play upon them until beyond reach.

He was now driven from every point of the field, and his strong lines, which had certainly been defended well, were in our possession. In fulfillment of the instructions of the general-in-chief, the Casa Mata was blown up, and such of the captured ammunition as was useless to us, as well as the cannon-molds found in El Molino del Rey, were destroyed. After this my command, under the orders of the general-in-chief, returned to our quarters at Tacubaya, with three of the enemy's four guns, (the fourth, having been spiked, was rendered unserviceable) a large quantity of small-arms with gun and musket ammunition, and over eight hundred prisoners, including fifty-two commissioned officers.

The testimony of prisoners indicated that the enemy's force exceeded fourteen thousand men, commanded by General Santa Anna in person. His total loss, killed, (including the second and third in command, Generals Valdarez and Leon) wounded, and prisoners, amounts to three thousand, exclusive of some two thousand who deserted after the rout.

My command, reinforced as before stated, only reached three thousand one hundred men of all arms. The contest continued two hours, and its severity is painfully attested by our heavy loss of officers, non-commissioned officers, and privates, including in the first two classes some of the brightest ornaments of the service. It will be seen that subordinate commanders speak in the warmest terms of the conduct of their officers and men, to which I beg leave to add my cordial testimony. There can be no higher exhibition of courage, constancy, and devotion to duty and to country.

These operations, occurring under the observation of the general-in-chief, give assurance that justice will be done to the noble officers and soldiers whose valor achieved this glorious but dear-bought victory. Commending the gallant dead, the wounded, and the few unscathed, to the respectful memory of their countrymen, and the rewards due to valor and conduct, I present the names of those especially noticed by subordinate commanders, uniting in all they have said, and extending the same testimony to those not named.

(Here followed a catalogue of the officers who particularly distinguished themselves.)

The following more circumstantial sketch is given by a participant in the action:

I have just returned from another battlefield—one on which the victory of the American arms was complete, and on which our troops contended against an enemy immensely superior in number and strongly posted. General Worth commenced the attack at early daylight, and in less than two hours every point was carried, all the cannon of the enemy were in our possession, an immense quantity of ammunition captured, and nearly one thousand men, among them fifty-three officers, taken prisoners.

For more than an hour the battle raged with a violence not surpassed since the Mexican war commenced and so great was the odds opposed, that for some time the result was doubtful. The force of the enemy has been estimated at from twelve to fifteen thousand, strongly posted behind breastworks, and to attack them our small force of scarcely eight thousand was obliged to approach on an open plain and without the least cover; but their dauntless courage carried them over every obstacle, and notwithstanding the Mexicans fought with a valor rare for them, they were finally routed from one point or another until all were driven and dispersed. The defeat was total.

But to gain this victory our own loss has been uncommonly severe; it has been purchased with the blood of some of the most gallant spirits of the army. The 5th infantry suffered the most. This regiment, along with the 6th and 8th, was engaged in the attack upon a strong work on the enemy's right, and was opposed to such superior numbers, that it was compelled to retire along with the others. The celebrated Colonel Martin Scott was killed in this attack, along with Lieutenants Burwell and Strong, while Colonel Mcintosh and many other officers were badly wounded. After our men retired the worse than savage miscreants in the fort set up a yell, and came out and massacred such of our wounded as were unable to get off. In this way poor Burwell lost his life. Fully were they avenged, however; for within half an hour Duncan's battery, aided by the fall of another of their works, drove the dastardly wretches in full flight across the fields. No one knew or even surmised the strength of the place—it was an old fort, constructed long ago, and was one of the main defenses of the line of works.

On the enemy's left, and nearer Chapultepec, our loss was also great, although not as severe. It was here that Colonel William M. Graham, as brave a spirit as ever lived, was killed; Captains Merrill and Ayres also fell in this part of the field. The wonder now is how anyone could come out safely under such a terrible fire as the enemy poured from his entire line of works. Nothing but the daring and impetuosity of our men, who rushed onward while their comrades were falling thick around them, gained the victory. Had they once faltered all would have been lost.

The broken ground on the right of the enemy, cut up by deep ravines, saved many of Santa Anna's troops in their flight; yet as it was, our dragoons killed and captured many of the fugitives. Large bodies of Mexican cavalry approached the scene of strife several times, but they were driven like sheep by Duncan's battery.

The Mexican loss was even more severe than our own. General Balderas, General Leon, and many other officers were numbered among the dead, while the interior of their works, the tops of the houses from which they fought, and the ground over which they fled, were strewed with lifeless bodies. Such was the panic that many of our officers say that a few fresh troops might have taken Chapultepec itself almost without a struggle. Other than a few shots fired at that point from some of the captured cannon, no demonstration was made.

General Scott came out after the battle was over, accompanied by his staff, and also by Mr. Nicholas Trist. The Mexicans at the time were firing shells at some of the wagons that General Worth had sent out to pick up the dead and wounded. They had placed a howitzer in position aimed at Chapultepec at the close of the action. Now seeing the enemy within reach, the cowardly wretches opened upon the ambulances, and those who were gathering the bodies of their wounded and lifeless comrades. On seeing this worse than savage outrage, one of our officers, with a sarcastic expression of countenance, asked whether Mr. Trist had any new peace propositions in his pocket. Mackintosh did not come out after the battle to gain more time for his friend Santa

Anna, nor warm our fresh intelligence of the strength and movements of our army, in order that he might be of service to the Mexicans by communicating it.

The Mexican prisoners say that Santa Anna himself was on the ground in the rear of their works, but left at the commencement of the rout. They admit that their entire force was fifteen thousand, and it is certain that including killed, wounded, prisoners and dispersed, their loss has been near five thousand. Many of them were regulars, the 11th and 12th infantry regiments suffering most. The commander of the latter, Colonel Tenorio, is a prisoner in our hands; some fourteen officers belonging to the former are also prisoners, but the commander, General Perez, escaped. The foundry, in which several molds for casting cannon and other apparatus were found, was entirely demolished. After ascertaining this, General Scott ordered all his forces to retire, not wishing to hold the position.

The 13th was signalized by the storming of Chapultepec, of which Worth gives the following account, confined principally to his own operations:

On the evening of the 12th, having the verbal orders of the general-in-chief to designate a storming party, to aid in the assault upon the castle of Chapultepec, a command from my division, with scaling ladders, was organized. It consisted of ten officers—Captain McKenzie, 2nd artillery, commanding; and two hundred and sixty men, volunteers, drawn in due proportion from the several corps. At 5:00 AM, on the 13th, these detachments assembled at the appointed place, and proceeded to their duty. For the manner in which this was executed, I refer to the report, herewith, of the gallant commander.

At the same time, I had the orders of the general-in-chief to take position with the remainder of my division and support the operations of General Pillow. This position was taken at the time and place appointed, and that general informed of my preparations and of my readiness to support him. Lieutenant Raphael Semmes, (Navy) one of my aides-de-camp, whom I dispatched with this intelligence, found General Pillow, soon after the assault had commenced, wounded, at the foot of the hill. General Pillow desired him to return to me, with a request to bring up my whole division, and make great haste, or, he feared, I would be too late. Clark's 2nd brigade was ordered instantly to advance. It did so, passed on, mingled with the advancing forces, and entered *pellmell* with them into the assaulted work. At the same instant, Garland's 1st brigade, the light battalion, under Lieutenant Colonel C. F. Smith, and Duncan's battery, were put in motion, around the north-eastern base of the hill of Chapultepec, and moved, in operation, upon the San Cosme route and aqueduct. After advancing some four hundred yards, we came to a battery which had been assailed by a portion of Magruder's field guns—particularly the section under the gallant Lieutenant Jackson, who, although he had lost most of his horses, and many of his men, continued chivalrously at his post, combating with noble courage. A portion of Garland's brigade, which had been previously deployed in the field to the left, now came up and defeated the enemy's right; the enemy's left extending in the direction of the Tacubaya aqueduct, on which Quitman's division was *battling* and *advancing*.

Pursuing the San Cosme road, we discovered an arched passage through the aqueduct, and a cross route suitable for our artillery. It went for a considerable distance through the meadows, in the direction of the battery, and left of the enemy's line, which was endeavoring to check Quitman's advance. Lieutenant Colonel Duncan, with a section of his battery, covered by Lieutenant Colonel Smith's battalion, was turned off upon this route, and advanced to within four hundred yards of the enemy's lines. (which was as far as the nature of the ground would permit) They opened an effective fire—first upon the battery, and then upon the retreating troops, great numbers of whom were cut down. Having thus aided the advance, and cleared the front (being favorably situated) of my gallant friend Quitman, as far as it was in my power, this portion of the command was withdrawn. The 2nd brigade now came up and the advance upon the main road was continued. We soon came up with and carried a second battery, and afterwards a third, both of them strong works and enfilading the road. This brought us to the Campo Santo, or English burying-ground, near which the road and aqueduct bend to the right. At this point the general-in-chief came up, with his staff, and instructed me to press on, carrying the Garita[13] San Cosme, and, if possible, penetrate to the Alameda. Shortly afterwards Brigadier General Cadwalader reported to me, by order of the general-in-chief; and, later, between 8:00 and 9:00 PM, Colonel Riley, reported with the 2nd brigade, 2nd division. The former was left in position at Campo

---

[13]   Gate.

Santo, to hold that point, and look to the left and rear. The latter, coming up after the firing had ceased, was halted in the rear of the 1st division, and entered the city with it on the morning of the 14th.

Here we came in front of another battery, beyond which, distant some two hundred and fifty yards, and sustaining it, was the last defense, or the Garita of San Cosme. The approach to these two defenses was in a right line, and the whole space was literally swept by grape, canister, and shells, from a heavy gun and howitzer; added to which, severe fires of musketry were delivered from the tops of the adjacent houses and churches. It hence became necessary to vary our mode of operations. Garland's brigade was thrown to the right, within and masked by the aqueduct, and instructed to dislodge the enemy from the buildings in his front, and endeavor to reach and turn the left of the Garita, taking advantage of such cover as might offer, to enable him to carry out his objects. At the same time Clark's brigade was ordered to take the buildings on the left of the road, and, by the use of bars and picks, burrow through from house to house, and, in like manner, and carry the right of the Garita.

While these orders were being executed, a mountain howitzer was placed on the top of a commanding building on the left, and another on the church of San Cosme on the right, both of which opened fire with admirable effect. The work of the troops was tedious, and necessarily slow, but was greatly favored by the fire of the howitzers. Finally, at 5:00 PM both columns had reached their positions, and it then became necessary, at all hazards, to advance a piece of artillery to the evacuated battery of the enemy intermediate between us and the Garita. Lieutenant Hunt was ordered to execute this duty, which he did in the highest possible style of gallantry; equally sustained by his veteran troops, with the loss of one killed and four wounded, out of nine men, although the piece moved at full speed over a distance of only one hundred and fifty yards; reaching the breastwork, he came muzzle to muzzle with the enemy. It has never been my fortune to witness a more brilliant exhibition of courage and conduct. The moment had now arrived for the final and combined attack upon the last stronghold of the enemy in my quarter. It was made, by our men springing, as if by magic, to the tops of the houses into which they had patiently and quietly made their way by pick and bar, and to the utter surprise and consternation of the enemy, opening upon him, within easy range, a destructive fire of musketry. A single discharge, in which many of his gunners were killed at their pieces, was sufficient to drive him in confusion from the breastwork; when a prolonged shout from our brave fellows announced that we were in possession of the Garita of San Cosme, and already in the City of Mexico.

At this point we again had the pleasure to meet the Mexican presidente. We took one of his aides-de-camp, Captain Jóse M. Castanary, and several other superior officers, with many other equally unimportant prisoners; and one of my most gallant and leading subalterns had the gratification of eating his excellency's well-prepared supper.

The remainder of the division was now marched within the city gate, and Captain Huger, of the ordnance, who had been directed by the general-in-chief to report to me, with heavy guns, some time before, advanced a twenty-four-pounder and a ten-inch mortar, place them in position at the Garita, obtained the distance, and opened a few shot and shell upon the grand plaza and palace, assumed to be about sixteen hundred yards distant. This battery opened at 9:00 PM—three shots being fired from the gun and five from the mortar. They took with admirable effect, as at 1:00 AM in the morning a commission from the municipality came to my advanced post with a flag, announcing that immediately after the heavy guns opened fire, the government and army commenced evacuating the city, and that the commission was deputed to confer with the general-in-chief, to whose head-quarters it was passed under Assistant Adjutant General Mackall.

At 5:00 AM, on the 14th, my troops and heavy guns advanced into the city, and occupied the Alameda, to the point where it fronts the palace, and there halted at 6:00 AM, the general-in-chief having instructed me to take a position and await his further orders. Shortly after, a straggling assassin-like fire commenced from the house-tops, which continued, in various parts of the city, through the day, causing us some loss. The first shot fired at a group of officers at the head of my column, struck down Colonel Garland, badly wounded; and later in the day, Lieutenant Sydney Smith was shot down mortally wounded—since dead.

The free use of heavy battering guns upon every building from which fire proceeded, together with musketry from some of our men thrown out as skirmishers, soon quelled these hidden and dastardly enemies. About the time of our entrance into the city, the convicts in the different prisons, to the number of some thirty thousand men, were liberated by order of the flying government, armed and distributed in the most advantageous houses, including the churches, convents, and even the hospitals, for the purpose of exciting, if possible, the entire population of the city to revolt, and effect, by secret and dastardly means, what the whole Mexican army had been unable to accomplish. This was no time for half-way measures; and if many innocent persons suffered incidentally under the just infliction of punishment we found it necessary to bestow on these miscreants from the jails, the responsibility should rest upon the barbarous and vindictive chief who imposed upon us the necessity.

Officers and men of every corps carried themselves with wonted gallantry and conduct. Be pleased to refer to reports of subordinate commanders. Major Sumner had reported to me with his cavalry on the morning of the 13th, and was actively on service and under fire, and advanced upon the San Cosme road, to be at hand to pursue the enemy. Towards evening, the general-in-chief ordered his command to re-occupy Tacubaya. The commander and his excellent corps rendered every service which the incidents of the day offered to their ready acceptance.

I am most happy to have occasion to submit but a moderate list of casualties, compared with recent reports; two officers killed, ten wounded, and one hundred and twenty-nine rank and file killed, wounded and missing, of which full returns are forwarded herewith; as also a sketch of the ground, etc., covered by the operations of my command. All of which is respectfully submitted to the general-in-chief, himself a close observer of the incidents of the day.

Such has been the course of General Worth. He ranked among the best and most successful of all American officers.[14]

---

[14] After the war General Worth returned to the United States and was appointed as the administrator of the Texas and New Mexico military districts. He died of cholera in San Antonio on May 7, 1849. Eight years after his death New York City re-interred his remains in a monument and tomb fifty-one feet high, located at the corner of Broadway and Fifth Avenue.

Chapter 8

Brigadier General John Ellis Wool

Brigadier General John E. Wool was born in Orange County, New York in 1788. His family was Whigs of the Revolution. Losing his father at an early age, he was taken to be brought up by his grandfather, a farmer in Rensselaer County. Consulting the bent of his disposition, his grandfather placed him as a clerk in a store in the city of Troy. By attention, industry, and perseverance, John Wool became a merchant in a few years, and in due time he would have reached, in that capacity, the wealth and distinction that always follows energy, perseverance, and high honor; but a fire which caused a total loss of his property induced him to turn his attention to some other pursuit—one more congenial to his own desires. The war with England broke out about this time and Wool was offered, and accepted, a commission as a captain in the 13th regiment of United States Infantry. He immediately entered that career, in which he early on became very distinguished.

Wool was thrown upon his own resources early in his career, for the family from whence he sprung were poor but true and honest patriots of the Revolution. He was the founder of his own fortunes, and literally fought his way to military distinction. His commission as a captain bears the date of April 10, 1812. Immediately after its receipt, he commenced raising a company in Troy, New York, and having done so, he made his military debut at the battle of Queenstown Heights. Previous to this memorable action, our army had suffered so many reverses and defeats, as to cast the stigma of cowardice and misconduct upon our officers and troops. It was therefore necessary that some brilliant effort should be made, in order to redeem their character, and to raise throughout the United States a proper spirit for carrying on the war.

Queenstown Heights was a formidable post, fortified and held by a part of the British army. Major General Stephen Van Rensselaer commanded the militia of the State of New York on the Niagara frontier, and had established his military quarters at Lewistown. He determined to storm Queenstown Heights and accordingly a detachment of six hundred men under the command of General Van Rensselaer and Lieutenant Colonel Chrystie, were assigned to this hazardous service.

In this detachment were three companies of the 13th regiment and the command of these three companies fell on Captain Wool. The officers and men conducted themselves most gallantly under trying circumstances. An enemy position of extraordinary strength was about to be attacked by a band of less than three hundred men. The moment they reached the Canadian side of the river they encountered a tremendous fire from the enemy, so deadly in effect, that nearly every officer and most of the soldiers in Captain Wool's command were either killed or wounded. Colonel Van Rensselaer was badly wounded, and was dying from the loss of blood, when Captain Wool, although himself wounded in both thighs, sought him and requested permission to continue the assault. The colonel, at first unwilling to entrust the fate of the affair to so young an officer who was for the first time on the field, reluctantly consented. The assault was renewed with vigor by Wool and his gallant little band. They climbed the heights and drove the British from their batteries. The battle was renewed when the British received reinforcements from General Brock. Captain Wool, rallying his forces with a desperate effort, once more charged the British, reinforced though they were, and drove them a second time from the heights. General Brock was slain. Seeing this, the British abandoned their position in panic and fled, leaving the Americans as victors in the field.

For his gallant conduct at Queenstown Heights, Wool was promoted to the rank of major in the 29th regiment. He then volunteered his services wherever and whenever duty and danger called. After this engagement, Major Wool continued actively engaged with the army until the great battle of Plattsburg in September, 1814, in which he again distinguished himself. Wool received the rank of brevet lieutenant colonel on September 11th, 1814, after his gallant conduct at the battle of Plattsburg. Before the close of the war he was in several engagements of less magnitude, and in each displayed that coolness, intrepidity, and careful forethought, which have been his principal characteristics throughout.

At the expiration of the war, Lieutenant Colonel Wool continued in the army, and in 1816 he was commissioned an Inspector General, with the rank of colonel. In 1826 he was brevetted a brigadier general; and, on the 25th of June, 1841, he was promoted to the rank of full brigadier, and assigned to the command of the eastern division of the army, which had become vacant by the appointment of General Scott as general-in-chief, on the death of General Macomb. General Wool was an Inspector General for twenty-five years. His duties were connected with every department of the military establishment in the United States and her territories, extending from Eastport, in Maine, to the gulf of Mexico, and from the Atlantic to the Pacific Ocean. There were military posts established at Mackinac, Sault St. Marie, Chicago, Green Bay, Prairie du Chien, St. Peter's on the Upper Mississippi twenty-two hundred miles from its mouth, Council Bluffs, some eighteen hundred miles up the Missouri. There were also posts on the Arkansas River six hundred miles from its mouth, and on the Red River four hundred miles. All of these were within the limits of his tours of inspection, which annually embraced a distance of from seven to ten thousand miles. There were no means of reaching these several posts but by canoe and on horseback, with provisions packed for a journey of months through the wilderness.

The dangers, privations, and hardships, unavoidable in traversing lakes, rivers, and forests by such means, often with Indian guides, and always without a shelter, or any resting-place but the earth and a blanket, can hardly be realized by those who witness only the facilities and advantages of traveling in civilized communities. Such was the nature of the duties of an Inspector General prior to the settlement of the states west of the lakes and of the Mississippi River; yet, notwithstanding the many privations and hardships, Wool was at all times cheerful, prompt and energetic.

General Wool was also employed by the government in three special services, each of which required the skill, experience, and of an accomplished officer and gentleman. These were,

(1) The suppression of a Canadian outbreak, when the sympathy of our people for the struggles of the "Canadian Patriots" nearly blew the flame of disturbance into the conflagration of war. Its suppression was a delicate and hazardous service, but it was admirably conducted and completely accomplished by General Wool.

(2) A military visit to Europe. The object of this visit was to examine the state of military improvement abroad, for the purpose of engrafting on our own system and establishing any valuable changes. His reception abroad was as flattering to the object as he could wish.
And

(3) General Wool was placed in command of the Cherokee country, for the purpose of carrying out the treaty with those Indians, and extending the arm of the government for their protection until their transportation to the west. His conduct in this affair not only met with the approbation of the government, but with the gratitude of the Indians themselves.

After the war with Mexico was declared by Congress on May 11, 1846 General Wool has been occupied as follows: 1st, in the organization of Western volunteers, 2nd, in the buildup of a military division at San Antonio de Bexar, 3rd, in his march to Saltillo, and 4th, in the battle of Buena Vista.

Immediately after the war with Mexico was declared, General Wool volunteered to take part in the campaign, and a few days subsequent to the passing of the act by Congress, he was gratified by receiving orders to proceed forthwith to Washington. The very day he received these orders he was *en route* to the capital, and having obtained his instructions, he proceeded to the West to organize and muster into service the twelve months' volunteers of Ohio, Illinois, Indiana, Kentucky, Tennessee, and Mississippi. In six weeks he accomplished the task assigned him; raising in that short time fourteen and a half regiments, or over twelve thousand troops. Nearly ten thousand of these he sent to reinforce General Taylor;

the remainder, nearly three thousand, he concentrated at San Antonio de Bexar, as a separate division under his own command.

All these men were from the ranks of private life, and were without any experience in the art of war. When General Wool arrived they were all destitute of the means and supplies of a campaign, and all were anxious to push forward to their respective rendezvous to be inspected, mustered, organized, provided for, and sent off to the seat of war. General Wool found himself engaged in a novel, arduous, embarrassing, and unpleasant duty; in a situation involving all the details, great and small, unavoidable in mustering an army into service; in the heat of June and July, and amid the ten thousand questions, wants, and complaints of the volunteers.

It required patience, skill, and labor to prepare an army from six different states, and at the same time to conduct a correspondence with all governors, colonels, agents and other officers, as well as with the military authorities at Washington; to fly from state to state, rendezvous to rendezvous, and be almost simultaneously at them all, where volunteers were rushing forward in all the confusion incident to their first appearance, without even a tent or a camp-kettle. Notwithstanding all this, from the first week in June to the third in July of 1846 this perplexing and arduous, but most important service, was performed. He organized and prepared for service three regiments from Ohio, three from Indiana, four from Illinois, two from Kentucky; one of these a regiment of cavalry, and consequently requiring much more preparation than infantry; one of cavalry from Tennessee; and one and a half from Mississippi. How all this was done in so short a period, considering the various difficulties already mentioned, and the delays in procuring arias, camp-equipage, means of transportation and other necessaries, was a matter of surprise and admiration to military men and public authorities.

In six weeks after he had fulfilled his instructions in organizing the volunteers, and dispatched the required reinforcements to General Taylor, General Wool arrived at San Antonio de Bexar about the middle of August. There he commenced preparations for his own march through the province of Coahuila. This march terminated at Saltillo, and is one of the most remarkable and interesting of the war. Wool's army of about three thousand men had concentrated at this place. By the application of great exertion, and with the aid of indefatigable staff-officers, he was able to put about one-half of his army into a condition for marching, leaving the rear to be brought forward by the chief of his staff, Inspector-General Churchill, as soon as means of transportation, and indispensable supplies should arrive.

The following letter from a soldier in General Wool's army vividly describes the march of General Wool, and the battle of Buena Vista:

DEAR SIR: I seize the first opportunity afforded since the battle of Buena Vista, of writing to you from the field an account of the more recent operations of General Taylor's army, including that of General Wool's, heretofore known as the center division. The official details of the battle are, I suppose, already published in the states, and made familiar to you; but you must be ignorant of many occurrences of great interest precedent and subsequent to that memorable event.

General Wool landed from the Gulf on the 2nd of August, 1846, at Labaca, Texas, with the 1st and 2d Illinois regiments (infantry) commanded by Colonels Hardin and Bissell; and soon after took up the line of march to San Antonio de Bexar, one hundred and fifty miles to the north. There he was joined by Colonel Yell's mounted regiment from Arkansas, and Colonel Marshall's regiment from Kentucky. Captain Washington's well-drilled company of flying-artillery, eight pieces, from Carlisle, Pennsylvania, Major Bonneville's battalion of regular infantry, and Colonel Harney, with four companies of dragoons, were also attached to this division.

General Wool displayed great acclivity in organizing his army, and putting the commissariat in the finest possible condition. Sugar and coffee of the best quality have always been a part of his soldiers' daily diet. No army was ever better provided with these items.

The two months passed in this delightful region were well spent in drilling for active service. On the 26th of September, two days after the capitulation of Monterey, the advance, under Colonel Harney, marched for the Rio Grande, followed soon after by General Wool, who left Colonel Churchill, the Inspector, and Colonel Bissell, to bring up the rear, as they began to do on the 14th of October. The whole army at this time was two thousand six hundred strong. We, of the advance, marched to the Rio Grande, two hundred miles, in twelve days, resting on one day for General Wool to join us.

As I can only approximate its accuracy, I shall use round numbers in mentioning distances and the population of towns. Crossing the present boundary between our country and Mexico on the 12th day of October, we set foot upon the soil of the enemy. Then we marched a distance of four hundred miles to the city of Parras, on the south-western confines of this state, (Coahuila) and near a lake of the same name; passing through and taking peaceable possession, in our circuitous route, the cities of Presidio del Rio Grande, Nava, San Fernando, Santa Rosa, Monclova the ancient capital of this state, and Parras, which last we reached on the 6th of December, 1846.

These cities contained a population of from five to fifteen thousand souls, except Nava, which numbered about two thousand. Monclava and Parras are quite wealthy, and exhibit fine specimens of Spanish art and refinement. We spent some time in each of these cities with pleasure and profit, viewing much of Mexican manners and customs, and enjoying an apparently cordial intercourse with the citizens. Our line of march carried us through a great variety of scenery, marked, after three day's progress in Mexico, by high and barren mountains on the south and west, covered with traces of rich ores; by sterile plains and table-lands, scantily supplied, in the dry season, with water; and in the interior, by beautiful fertile valleys surrounding the quiet Mexican towns, and haciendas, and set off in the hazy distance by cloud-capped mountains covered with cedars. If you are acquainted with Illinois, you can form some idea of Mexico, as I saw it for six hundred miles, by imagining the Prairie State elevated a thousand feet, and made somewhat more broken and undulating, with craggy rocky mountains towering from one to two thousand feet above the plains, taking the place of the groves and interesting face of the country in all directions. But it is only by actual vision, that you can adequately estimate the grand, though uninviting picture of lonely desolation—the inhospitable sterility that met the eye of the wearied soldier, in his toilsome, thirsty marches, and often made him wish that an earthquake had sunk the country he was sent to conquer. The country bordering on the Rio Grande, where we crossed it, and for a considerable distance into Mexico, west and south, is low, level, very fertile, and well watered by streams or irrigating canals. It already supports a large population, and contains the cities of Presidio, Nava, and Fernando; the last two, situated forty and fifty miles west of the river, struck me as quite flourishing.

The land between the Nueces and the Rio Grande, for nearly a hundred miles, except a few fertile prairies, is divided into sandy deserts and marshy chaparrals, almost as difficult to access as the out-jungles of India. It will be the haunt only of savages and wild beasts for many generations, if not forever. Personal observation satisfied me that Senator Benton was right when he pronounced the Nueces "the most profitable western boundary of Texas." Of the country east of this river, of which I saw much, I must say as of Texas generally, her rolling and crystal streams, that here I beheld the future France of America, a land destined to bloom with "the olive and myrtle, the cedar and vine," and to flow, even in our own time, with milk and honey.

The effect of our long marching, the strict discipline enforced by our general, and the exercise taken in drill were most salutary upon the health of our army. After the professional and sedentary life in the bilious atmosphere of the Mississippi valley, the campaign had a most—renovating effect. The army lay encamped at Monclava three weeks, during which period our rear came up, and General Wool was ordered to co-operate with General Taylor at Monterey, instead of marching upon Chihuahua, which, up to this time, had been our destination. Eleven days brought us to Parras, two hundred miles farther into the country, where supplies were abundant. Here we lay in camp eleven days, in friendly intercourse with the people, of whom many were not destitute of moral worth and intelligence. The American sharpers among them—*soi-disant* gentlemen,—engaged in trade and marrying fortunes, struck me with more disgust than the most degraded Mexicans. Many of the better class of natives commanded my highest esteem. One Don Manuel Toarra, who was educated in the United States, found some old friends in the army, and treated us with hospitality commensurate with his great wealth. The position was fixed in neutrality by his intelligence and prudence; by his respect for the American character and institutions, sympathy for his country, and by an unfeigned aversion for his own rulers—the demagogues in the city of Mexico. Santa Anna had assessed his contribution for the army at sixty dollars per week. His reply to Santa Anna was, "Come with your army and take it."

But these halcyon days soon passed over our heads, and more stirring scenes were at hand. General Worth, who lay at Saltillo, one hundred and twenty miles north of east from us, with a thousand regulars, received intelligence (which he credited) on the 16th of December, that Santa Anna was within three days' march of him, with thirty thousand men, and was advancing. He dispatched expresses to Monterey and Parras for aid, promising to hold out one day against any force, and requesting us to reinforce him on the fourth day.

General Wool received this news on the evening of the 17th, and in less than two hours the whole of the army was on the march. On the 21st we reinforced Worth, but no enemy was to be seen. For three nights in succession on this march, which was accomplished in three days and a half, the army was aroused at 1:00 AM in the morning to resume the advance. The cavalry and artillery called us sleep-walkers, and complained that we were killing off their horses.

The spirit displayed by the men, their alacrity, cheerfulness and patience, were most admirable. Expecting as they did to meet the enemy every hour, their demeanor inspired the staff and all other officers with confidence in the result. Volunteers as they were, and, as compared with the regulars, hut imperfectly disciplined, they suddenly assumed a bearing, and readiness to obey orders, not altogether unworthy of the "Old Guard of Napoleon." This march was a fitting prelude to the battle of Buena Vista.

On December 21, 1846 we sat down at Agua Nueva, a small rancho or town, twenty-one miles south of Saltillo, and near the great pass in the mountains leading to San Luis Potosí, the seat of the Mexican power. Here we passed Christmas watching for the appearance of the enemy in this pass, and in two smaller ones, a few miles distant on each side of us. New Year's day was spent at La Encantada, nine miles nearer to Saltillo; we still watching, however, and enjoying the luxury of frequent false alarms. We soon after took up our fighting position at the Hacienda of Buena Vista, five miles from Saltillo, and prepared to defend the pass two miles in advance of our camp.

In the mean time, General Taylor was concentrating all his available forces at Monterey, either to receive the attack or to make it himself. General Scott, however, chose that he should receive it. Early in January, General Worth was detached with his division from General Taylor, and joined Scott at Tampico. Not content with taking this and General Patterson's command at Matamoros, Scott broke into our division (the marching column) and took for himself Colonel Harney with two companies of dragoons, and Major Bonneville's battalion of four companies, leaving General Wool an army of volunteers, if you except Captain Steen's squadron of dragoons, and Captain Washington's battery, which last even he (Scott) had the modesty to request for his own use.

Faithfully yours,
JAMES A. FLEMMING, Sergeant

The following valuable extracts from a letter of a commanding officer in General Wool's army, give accurate estimates of the force and condition of the division of the Center:

San Antonio de Bexar
October 14, 1846

DEAR SIR: It was the last of August before all the various detachments which had been ordered here to compose this division, arrived. As soon as they had done so, they were actively employed in organizing, drilling, maneuvering, etc., preparatory to taking the field. The stores, both of subsistence and ammunition, came in very slowly, as they had to be hauled in wagons from Port Laraca on the Gulf, a distance of one hundred and fifty miles; and sufficient means for transporting them were not supplied in season to bring them all on at once. It was the 25th of September before these stores had accumulated here to allow the general to commence his campaign. By that time a train of wagons large enough for the advance had been collected, and the 26th was appointed as the day on which that portion of the division should move. It was composed of 1171 troops and 66 officers under Colonel W. S. Harney in command.

Two boats had been constructed at this place by Captain Fraser of the engineers, by which the division was to cross the Rio Grande. They were taken apart and transported there in wagons. The general directed that all the men who were unable to march fifteen miles per day should be left behind, to come up with other troops, should they recover from sickness, and regain their strength.

Colonel Harney's force started out on the morning of the 26th of September. Every man was in fine spirits, and every company in the best possible fighting order. Captain Washington had a battery of six brass pieces—two twelve pounders and four six-pounders—and a good supply of ammunition for them. Two more brass six-pounders are to be forwarded from here. These are to be added to his battery, and will reach him at the Rio Grande.

On the morning of the 29th of September, General Wool, his staff, and escort (one squadron of the 1st regiment U. S. dragoons) left San Antonio for the Rio Grande. The squadron of the 1st dragoons was composed of the "A" and "E" companies and numbered one hundred and thirty-one soldiers. The aggregate of all forces which left on the 29th was 144.

Colonel Sylvester Churchill, Inspector General was left in command of the forces remaining at San Antonio de Bexar. These forces were to be forwarded on to join the general at the Presidio del Rio Grande just as fast as the means of transportation would allow.

On the 2nd of October eight companies of the 1st regiment Illinois volunteers took up their line of march. This force was commanded by Colonel John J. Hardin, 1st regiment, Illinois volunteers. The command totaled 574 including thirty-six officers. The command was in fine order, and not encumbered by any men unable to march fifteen miles a day.

The last intelligence received here from General Wool was dated at his headquarters on the evening of October 5th. He had overtaken Colonel Harney and the advance, and was then encamped twenty-five miles from the Presidio del Rio Grande. By his table of distances from one watering-place to another, for the whole route, (and giving an account of the grazing, etc., for the information of the forces to succeed him) including the Presidio was estimated to be one hundred and fifty-seven miles from San Antonio. The water abounded in sufficient quantities, and at intervals short enough to prevent the necessity of transporting it, except for a part of one day's march, for the whole trip. The grazing was also reported as being generally good, except at the Leona and Nueces rivers.

Since writing the foregoing, another express message has arrived from the general, with communications dated the 11th instant. He had arrived at the river on the 9th, and nearly the whole of the advance had crossed without opposition, and was already in Mexico. The following order was published to the troops on the 9th:

SOLDIERS!—After a long and tedious march, you have arrived on the bank of the Rio Grande. In the performance of this service the commanding general has witnessed with the greatest pleasure your patience, good order, and perseverance under many deprivations and hardships. All have done their duty, and in a manner that reflects the highest credit on both officers and men. From this remark he would not except his staff, who have actively and zealously devoted themselves to the service; while Captain Cross has been eminently successful in forwarding his long train of supplies, without delay or serious accident.

Tomorrow you will cross the Rio Grande, and occupy the territory of our enemies. We have not come to make war upon the people or peasantry of the country, but to compel the government of Mexico to render justice to the United States. The people, therefore, who do not take up arms against the United States, and remain quiet and peaceful at their homes, will not be molested or interfered with, either as regards their persons or property; and all those who furnish supplies will be treated kindly, and whatever is received from them will be liberally paid for.

It is expected of the troops that they will observe the most rigid discipline and subordination. All depredations on the persons or property of the people of the country are strictly forbidden; and any soldier or follower of the camp who may so far forget his duty as to violate this injunction, will be severely punished.

A report reached San Antonio last evening that the Mexicans had assembled a force of seven thousand at Monclava, to arrest General Wool's advance at that place; and it is also reported that Santa Anna has taken command of his army in person, and established his head-quarters at Saltillo.

The rear of the Central Division leaves here this day, to join General Wool. The officers include (1) Colonel Sylvester Churchill, Inspector-General U. S. A., commanding. (2) Captain George A. H. Blake, 2nd dragoons, commanding a detachment of artillery, dragoons and infantry. (3) Two companies of Arkansas mounted volunteers, commanded by Captain William G. Preston and Captain Hunter. (4) Colonel William H. Bissell, commanding the 2nd regiment of Illinois volunteers. (7 companies) and (5) One company of Texas volunteers, commanded by Captain Charles A. Seefeld. The whole of this command numbers seven hundred and twenty-four.

With the next train of wagons, Major Solon Borland, with the remaining two companies of Arkansas volunteers, is to come up. They

141

are commanded by Captain Moffitt and Captain Patrick, and will number 150. Then all the forces of this division will have left for the field, and will number all told, 2829 men.

The general will probably establish a depot for stores somewhere in the interior beyond Presidio—as when the rainy season commences, he no doubt desires to have the distance for immediate and frequent transportation as short as possible. It is thought by many here that we shall have a hard struggle before we capture Chihuahua. Let that be as it may, we will all try to render our country a good account of ourselves.

I shall write you again from the Presidio del Rio Grande. You have in this crude letter the different corps, and the strength of each; and when they are mentioned in future letters, you can refer to this for many data which will in them be necessarily suppressed.

The southwestern frontier of Texas, will be protected by a military police during our advance, composed of four or five companies of mounted rangers, three of which have already been mustered into the service of the United States for twelve months.

Fortunately for General Taylor, General Wool was not sent with the regular troops who had been called away from the Rio Grande to Vera Cruz. To him was entrusted the management of the battle of Buena Vista, and in all the extremities of that eventful field, the army leaned on him for advice and assistance. There the volunteers learned the use of that strict discipline which he had been so indefatigable to enforce; and his stern voice sounded along the gorges of Angostura like some mighty spirit, to whom was entrusted the chances of battle. His official report of the action, which we insert in its entirety, is the most scientific description of it ever published.

Agreeably to the orders from the commanding general, I have the honor to report that, on February 21, 1847 the troops at Agua Nueva broke up their encampment, and marched for Buena Vista and Saltillo. Colonel Yell's regiment of Arkansas volunteers remained to look out for the enemy reported to be advancing on Agua Nueva in great force. Colonel Yell was to guard the public stores left at the hacienda until transportation could be obtained to carry them to Buena Vista.

On the arrival of the commanding general at La Encantada, he directed that Colonel McKee's 2d Kentucky volunteers, and a section of Captain Washington's battery be kept at that place to give support to Colonel Yell in case he should be driven off by the enemy. Between La

Encantada and Buena Vista, at a place called the Pass of La Angostura, Colonel Hardin's regiment of 1st Illinois volunteers was stationed.

The rest of my command encamped near the Hacienda of Buena Vista. The major general commanding, accompanied by Lieutenant Colonel May's squadron, (2nd dragoons) Captains Sherman and Bragg's batteries, (3rd artillery) and the Mississippi regiment, commanded by Colonel Davis, proceeded to Saltillo, to provide against the attack meditated by Mexican General Minon, with a cavalry force reported to be three thousand strong. As many wagons as could be obtained were ordered to return forthwith to the town of Agua Nueva, and bring back what remained of the stores at that place.

In the course of the evening, agreeably to the instructions of the commanding general, transmitted from Saltillo, Colonel Marshall, with his regiment and the 1st dragoons, were ordered to Agua Nueva to reinforce Colonel Yell, who was directed in case be should be attacked to destroy everything at that place he could not bring off, and to retire before 12:00 noon. Colonel McKee, at La Encantada, with his artillery, was directed to join Colonel Yell on his retreat, and the whole to fall back to the Buena Vista Hacienda, should the enemy pursue them to that place. Before leaving Agua Nueva, Colonel Yell's pickets were driven in by the advanced parties of the Mexicans. He then retired with the reinforcements under the command of Colonel Marshall, after destroying a small quantity of corn yet remaining at the hacienda, and leaving a few wagons which had been precipitately abandoned by their teamsters.

All the advanced parties except Colonel Hardin's regiment came into Buena Vista before daylight on the morning of February 22nd. At 8:00 AM that day I received notice that the Mexican army was at Agua Nueva, and ordered a section of Captain Washington's artillery to move forward and join Colonel Hardin. Shortly afterwards I left for that position, where it was determined to attack the enemy. During the previous night, Colonel Hardin's regiment had thrown up a parapet on the heights, at the left of the road, and had dug a small ditch, and made a parapet extending from the road around the edge of the gully, on the right side of the road. They were then directed to dig a ditch, and make a parapet across the road for the protection of Captain Washington's artillery, leaving a narrow passage next to the hill, which was to be closed off by running two wagons loaded with stone into it.

About 9:00 AM, our pickets, stationed at La Encantada, three and a half miles distant, discovered the enemy advancing. Word was immediately dispatched to the commanding general at Saltillo; and I ordered the troops at Buena Vista forthwith to be brought forward. Captain Washington's battery was posted across the road, protected on its left by a commanding prominence, and on its right by deep gullies. The 2d Kentucky infantry, commanded by Colonel McKee, was stationed on a hill immediately in the rear of Washington's battery. The six companies of the 1st Illinois regiment, commanded by Colonel Hardin, took their post on the prominence at the left; and two companies, under Lieutenant Colonel Weatherford, occupied the breastwork on the right of Washington's battery.

The 2nd Illinois regiment was stationed on the left of the Kentucky regiment. The Indiana brigade, commanded by Brigadier General Lane, was posted on a ridge immediately in the rear of the front line, and Captain Stein's squadron was in reserve, in the rear of the Indiana brigade. The Kentucky regiment of cavalry, under the command of Colonel Marshall, and the Arkansas regiment, under the command of Colonel Yell, were stationed to the left of the second line of troops towards the mountains. Shortly afterwards the rifle companies of these two regiments were dismounted. With the cavalry company of the Kentucky regiment and a battalion of riflemen from the Indiana Brigade, both under the command of Colonel Marshall were ordered to take their position on the extreme left at the foot of the mountains.

These dispositions were approved by the major general commanding; who had now returned from Saltillo, bringing with him Lieutenant Colonel May's squadron of the 2nd dragoons, Captains Sherman and Bragg's batteries of artillery, and the Mississippi regiment of riflemen.

The enemy had halted just beyond cannon-shot, and could be seen on either side of the road, and commenced pushing his light infantry into the mountains on our left. At the same time, indications of an attempt on our right induced the Commanding General to order the 2nd Kentucky infantry and Captain Bragg's battery, with a detachment of mounted men, to take their post on the right of the gullies, and at some distance in advance of Captain Washington's battery, in the center.

Captain Sherman's battery was held in reserve in rear of the second line. The enemy was now seen pushing his infantry on his right towards the heights, showing evidently an intention to turn our left, in order to get possession of the key to our position—the prominence immediately on the left of Washington's artillery—and thus open a free passage to Saltillo.

Colonel Marshall, with his regiment, the Arkansas riflemen, under Lieutenant Colonel Roane, and the Indiana rifle battalion, under Major Gorman, was charged with meeting this party, and checking their movement on our left. Brigadier General Lane, with the 2nd Indiana regiment, and a section of Captain Washington's artillery, under Lieutenant O'Brien—since a captain in the quartermaster's department—was ordered to the extreme left and front of the plain, which was terminated by a deep ravine, extending from the mountain to the road, with orders to prevent the enemy from coming around by the base of the mountain.

At 2:00 PM, as the enemy's light infantry were moving up the side of the mountain and in the ravines, they opened a fire on our riflemen from a large howitzer posted in the road; and between 3 and 4 o'clock Colonel Marshall engaged the Mexican infantry on the side of the mountain, and the firing continued on both sides at intervals until dark. In this engagement our troops sustained no loss; while that of the enemy is known, by a subsequent inspection of the ground, to be considerable. After the firing had ceased, the major-general commanding again returned to Saltillo to see to matters at that place, and to guard against General Minon and his cavalry, taking with him the Mississippi regiment and squadron of the 24 dragoons.

The troops remained under arms during the night in the position they occupied at the close of the day. About 2:00 AM, on February 23rd, our pickets were driven off by the Mexicans, and at dawn the action was renewed by the Mexican light infantry and our riflemen on the side of the mountain. The enemy had succeeded during the night, and early in the morning, in gaining the top of the mountain, and in passing around to our left and rear. He had reinforced his extreme right by some fifteen hundred to two thousand infantry.

Major Prail, 2nd Illinois volunteers, was ordered to reinforce Colonel Marshall with his battalion of riflemen, who was presently engaged in holding the right of the enemy in check. The enemy now opened fire upon our left from a battery planted on the side of the mountain near where his light infantry had commenced ascending it—everything now indicating that the main attack would be against our left.

145

The 2nd Kentucky infantry and Bragg's battery of artillery were ordered from the extreme right under instructions given to Major Mansfield. Sherman's battery was ordered up from the rear to take its post with Colonel Bissell's regiment (2nd Illinois volunteers) on the plateau which extended from the center of the line to the foot of the mountain. The sides of the plateau were now filled with Mexican infantry and our riflemen, between whom the firing had become very brisk.

About this time the major general commanding was seen returning from Saltillo with the Mississippi regiment and the squadron of the 2nd dragoons. Shortly afterwards he arrived and took his position in the center of the field of battle, where he could see and direct the operations of the day. At 8:00 AM a large body of the enemy, composed of infantry, lancers, and three pieces of artillery, moved down the high road upon our center, held by Captain Washington's battery and the 1st Illinois volunteers, but were soon dispersed by the former. The rapidity and precision of the fire of the artillery scattered and dispersed this force in a few minutes with considerable loss on their side, and little or none on our own.

In connection with this movement, a heavy column of the enemy's infantry and cavalry moved against our left, which was held by Brigadier General Lane, with the 2nd Indiana regiment, and Lieutenant O'Brien's section of artillery. The enemy's fire was warmly returned, and, owing to the range, with great effect by Lieutenant O'Brien's artillery. General Lane, agreeable to my orders, and wishing to bring his infantry within striking distance, ordered his line to move forward. This order was duly obeyed by Lieutenant O'Brien. The infantry, however, instead of advancing, retired in disorder; and, in spite of the utmost efforts of their general and his officers, left the artillery unsupported, and fled the field of battle. Some of them were rallied by Colonel William Bowles, who fell in the ranks of the Mississippi riflemen, and during the day did good service with that gallant regiment. I deeply regret to say that most of them did not return to the field, and many of them continued their flight to Saltillo.

Lieutenant O'Brien was unsupported by any infantry. Not being able to make progress against the heavy column bearing down upon him with a destructive fire, he fell back, leaving one of his pieces in the hands of the enemy. Seeing themselves cut off from the center by the flight of the 2nd Indiana regiment, and the consequent advance of the Mexican infantry and cavalry upon the grounds previously occupied by it, the riflemen under the command of Colonel Marshall retreated from their positions in the mountain. There the riflemen had been successfully engaged with the enemy on the other side of the dry bed of a deep and broad torrent that was immediately to the rear of our position. Here many fled in disorder. Some of them were subsequently rallied and brought again into action, with their brave companions; others were stopped at the Hacienda of Buena Vista, and there re-formed by their officers.

The enemy immediately brought forward a battery of three pieces, and took a position on the extreme left of our line under the mountain. They commenced an enfilading fire on our center, which was returned with so much effect upon the advancing column of six thousand Mexican lancers and infantry, that it forced them to stay at the upper side of the plateau, close under the side of the mountain. Instead of turning to the left and advancing on our center, against the heavy fire of so much well-served artillery, they continued on their course perpendicular to our line on the extreme left, crossing over the bed of the dry torrent, in the direction taken by our retreating riflemen, keeping all the while close to the foot of the mountain. Colonel Marshall and Colonel Yell, with their cavalry companies, Colonel May, with the squadron of the 1st and 2d dragoons, and Captain Pike's squadron (Arkansas regiment) in connection with a brigade of infantry, formed of the Mississippi regiment, the 3d Indiana, (Colonel Jim Lane) and a fragment of the 2nd Indiana regiment, under Colonel William Bowles, and Braxton Bragg's artillery, and three pieces of Sherman's battery, succeeded in checking the march of this column.

The Mississippi regiment alone, with a howitzer under Captain Sherman, moved against some four thousand of the enemy, and stopped them in their march upon Saltillo. A large body of lancers from this body formed a column in one of the mountain gorges, and advanced through the Mexican infantry, to make a descent on the Hacienda of Buena Vista, near which our train of supplies and baggage had been packed. They were gallantly and successfully met by our mounted men, under Colonels Marshall and Yell, and the attacking column separated, part returning to the mountain under cover of their infantry, and a part through the hacienda. Here the latter were met by a destructive fire from those men who had left the field in the early part of the action, and had been rallied by their officers. Colonel May's dragoons and a section of artillery, under Lieutenant Reynolds, came up at this moment, and completed the rout of this portion of the enemy's cavalry. The column that had passed our left, and had gone some two miles to our rear, now faced about, and commenced retracing their steps, exposing their right flank to a very heavy and destructive fire from our infantry and artillery, who were drawn up in a line parallel to the march of the retreating column, of whom many were forced on and over the mountains, and many dispersed.

General Santa Anna, seeing the situation of this part of his army, and, no doubt, considering them as cut off, sent in a flag to the major general commanding to know what he desired. The general asked me to be the bearer of his answer, to which I cheerfully assented, and proceeded immediately to the enemy's battery under the mountains, to see the Mexican general-in-chief. But in consequence of a refusal to cease firing on our troops, to whom the news of the truce had not yet been communicated, and who were actively engaged with the Mexican infantry, I declared the parley at an end, and returned without seeing General Santa Anna, or communicating the answer of the general commanding.

The Mexican column was now in rapid retreat, pursued by our artillery, infantry, and cavalry; and, notwithstanding the effect of our fire, they succeeded for the greater part, favored by the configuration of the ground, in crossing the bed of the torrent, and regaining the plateau from which they had previously descended. While this was taking place on the left and rear of the line, our center, under the immediate eye of the commanding general, although it suffered much in killed and wounded, stood firm, and repelled every attempt to march upon it.

The Mexican forces being now concentrated on our left, made a bold move to carry our center, by advancing with his whole strength from the left and front. At this moment, Lieutenant O'Brien was ordered to advance his battery and check this movement. He did so in a bold and gallant manner, and maintained his position until his supporting force was completely routed by an immensely superior force. His men and horses were nearly all killed and wounded, and he found himself under the necessity of abandoning his pieces, and they fell into the hands of the enemy.

From this point the enemy marched upon our center, where the shock was met by Colonel McKee, of the 1st Illinois, under Colonel Hardin, and the 2nd Illinois under Colonel Bissell, all under the immediate eye of the commanding general. This was the hottest as well as the most critical part of the action; and at the moment when our troops were about giving way before the vastly superior force with which they were contending, the batteries of Captains Sherman and Bragg coming up most opportunely from the rear, and under the immediate direction of the commanding general, by a well-directed fire checked and drove back with great loss the enemy, who had come close upon the muzzles of their pieces. A part of the enemy's lancers took our infantry in flank, and drove them down the ravine in front of Captain Washington's battery, who saved them by a well-directed and well-timed fire from his pieces.

This was the last great effort of General Santa Anna. The firing continued well into the night. The troops lay on their arms in the position in which they were placed in the evening. Major Warren's command, consisting of four companies of Illinois infantry, and a detachment of Captain Webster's company, under Lieutenant Donaldson, were brought on the field from Saltillo. They had performed an important service during the day by repelling the attack of Mexican General Minon and his cavalry at that place. Every arrangement were made to engage the enemy early the next morning. At daybreak it was discovered that General Santa Anna had retreated under the cover of night, leaving about one thousand dead and several hundred wounded on the field of battle. The enemy left two hundred and ninety-four prisoners in our hands, one standard, and a large number of arms.

Our own loss was, I deeply regret to say, very great—equaling, if not exceeding, in proportion to the numbers engaged, that of the enemy. In killed, wounded, and missing, it amounted to over seven hundred. Among the dead, some of the most gallant of our officers fell while leading their men to the charge, and some who are well known to the country for distinguished services on other fields, among whom were Colonel A.Yell, of Arkansas, Colonel William McKee, Lieutenant Colonel Henry Clay, of Kentucky, and Colonel Hardin, of Illinois. I also lost my assistant adjutant-general, Captain Lincoln, who was as brave, gallant, and as accomplished an officer as I ever knew. He fell in the execution of my orders, and in the attempt to rally our men.

The troops posted in the center were constantly under the eye of the commanding general, and their movements and bearing during the battle are better known to him than myself. I think it proper, however, to bear witness with him to the particular good conduct of the 1st Illinois volunteers, under Colonel Hardin, and, after his death, under Colonel Weatherford; of the 2nd Illinois volunteers, under Colonel Bissell; and the 2nd Kentucky infantry, under Colonel McKee, Lieutenant Colonel Clay, and after their death, under Major Fry. These regiments suffered greatly in the contest, and were ably and gallantly led on by their officers, as their number, names, and rank of the killed will abundantly testify.

I also desire to express my high admiration, and to offer my warmest thanks to Captains Washington, Sherman and Bragg, and Lieutenants O'Brien and Thomas, and their batteries; to whose services at this point, and on every other part of the field, I think it but justice to say, we are mainly indebted for the great victory so successfully achieved by our arms over the great force opposed to us—more than twenty thousand men and seventeen pieces of artillery. Without our artillery we would not have maintained our position a single hour.

Brigadier General Joe Lane was very active and prompt in the discharge of his duty, and rendered good service throughout the day. He reports, among many others, Colonel Jim Lane and the 3rd Indiana regiment as having done themselves great credit. To Colonel Davis and the Mississippi regiment under his command, whose services were conspicuous in the open engagements on the rear of our left, great credit is due for the part they performed, and much praise for their conspicuous gallantry, which caused them to be a rallying point for the force that was driven in from the left, and who, in connection with the 3rd Indiana regiment, and a fragment of the 2nd Indiana, under its gallant colonel, constituted almost the only infantry opposed to the heavy column of the enemy.

Colonel Marshall rendered gallant and important services, both as the commander of the riflemen in the mountains, where he and his men were very effectual, and as the commander of the cavalry companies of his regiment, in connection with those of the Arkansas regiment, under Colonel Yell, and after his death, under Lieutenant Colonel Roane, (who commanded them in a gallant manner) in their operations against the enemy's lancers. Colonel Marshall reports that Lieutenant Colonel Field was everywhere during the battle, and equal entirely to his station, and rendered the most essential assistance.

Brevet Lieutenant Colonel May, 2nd dragoons, with the squadron of the 1st and 2nd dragoons, and Captain Pike's squadron of Arkansas cavalry, and a section of artillery, admirably served by Lieutenant Reynolds, 3rd artillery, played an important part in checking and dispersing the enemy in the rear of our left. They retired before him whenever he approached them. The gallant Captain Steen, whilst rallying, under the orders of the commanding general, some men running from the field of battle, was severely wounded in the thigh.

Major McCulloch, Quartermaster, in command of a Texas spy company, has, on the field, and in all the reconnaissances for several days previous to the contest, given me great assistance and valuable information.

Though belonging to the staff of the major general commanding, yet the very important and valuable services of Major Mansfield, to whom I am greatly indebted for the aid I received from his untiring exertions, activity, and extensive information, as well as for his gallant bearing during the days and nights of the 21st, 22nd, 23rd and 24th, give me the privilege of expressing to the commanding general my entire admiration of this accomplished officer's conduct.

My thanks are also due to Major Monroe, chief of artillery, for the services rendered by him on the field, as chief of artillery, and for his exertions in rallying the men at Buena Vista, and disposing of them at that place, to meet the attack of the enemy's lancers. Paymaster Dix and Captain Leonard rendered very valuable aid by their gallantry in rallying the troops. Lieutenant Renham, engineer, was very gallant, zealous, and efficient at all times, night and day, in the performance of the important duties with which ho was charged.

Of my staff I cannot speak in too high terms; their devotion to duty at all times, day and night, and their activity and gallant bearing on the 21st, 22nd, 23rd, and 24th, not only command my admiration, but is worthy of all praise.

I cannot close my report without expressing, officially and formally, as I have heretofore done personally to the major general commanding, the feelings of gratitude I have for the confidence and extreme consideration which have marked all his acts towards me; which have given me additional motives for exertion, and increased zeal in the execution of the responsible duties with which I have been charged.

Respectfully yours,
(Name deleted)

A writer, already quoted, gives the following account of Wool's conduct in the battle, together with many interesting incidents:

. . . Our general was encamped on the 5th of February with Colonel Bissell and Captain Washington, on the heights above and to the south of Saltillo, the rest of the army being distributed through the valley, still watching the passes to San Luis, when General Taylor who is called by his devoted soldiers "Old Rough and Ready", came up with Bragg's and Sherman's batteries and Colonel Jefferson Davis's Mississippi regiment. He expressed great satisfaction and pleasure with our discipline and the manner in which General Wool had "brought us up." By command of General Worth, General Lane, with his Indianians, and Lieutenant Kingsbury, had built a very good fort on the heights of Saltillo, and in it Captain Webster's two twenty-four-pound howitzers, with smaller pieces, were placed, and commanded every building in the city below, as well as the whole plain from mountain to mountain, east and west.

On the 8th of February General Taylor's whole army except for four Illinois companies, left to guard the town, lay in camp at Agua Nueva. Here our generals patiently awaited the arrival of new levies, which they hoped would make their forces ten thousand strong, and forty days' provisions, to enable them to march on Santa Anna's stronghold, San Lois Potosí, three hundred miles south of Saltillo. General Taylor expected to be ready for the march on the 1st of April. For a long time the signs had been thickening that the Mexican dictator was aiming a blow at us, the *Voluntarios,* as composed of more conquerable stuff than the regulars under Scott. Back on the 22d of January, Majors Borland and Gaines, Captain C. M. Clay, and Lieutenant Davidson, with eighty men, were at Incarnacion, sixty miles from Saltillo, on the San Lois road, scouting, when they were suddenly surrounded in the night by three thousand lancers under Mexican General Minon, taken prisoners in the morning, and marched off for the City of Mexico. Soon after this, Captain Eddy, of Kentucky, with seventeen men on picket guard, was captured in a similar manner—in a manner little creditable to the soldiers.

Our pickets were several times driven in, and the enemy's cavalry frequently hovered around us on the south and east, to cut off small parties. Many of the citizens suddenly became sullen towards the *Americanos,* who had scattered money among them with so lavish a hand. Three men were missing out of the Arkansas regiment, one of whom was found on the 9th of February, near the camp, dead, with a lasso around his neck, and presenting a horrid spectacle. For this act of an unknown criminal, a few comrades of the deceased, took a frantic and senseless revenge on the next day by shooting down about thirty unarmed Mexicans in cold blood, who, with their families, had abandoned the march, and were living in the mountains under cover of trees and bushes, to cut wood, as they said, for sale to our camp. Some Illinois infantry saved the greater part of these poor people from massacre. Generals Taylor and Wool were greatly enraged at the act, and branded it in general orders as a cruel and cowardly outrage.

Meanwhile a black cloud was gathering up from San Luis, soon to burst upon our heads in storm and thunder. On the 20th, Colonel May, Captain Howard, and Lieutenant O'Brien, with a scouting party at Idionda, twenty-five miles south-east, captured a Mexican, who said that Santa Anna was advancing upon us from Incarnacion. They came into camp early on the morning of the 21st, with this intelligence, which many things conspired to stamp with truth. Having breakfasted, the army leisurely retreated to Buena Vista, fourteen miles away, and there took up a position. All the infantry except Colonel Hardin, who remained in the center of our line at the pass of Buena Vista, encamped at the ranch, where our wagons, which had returned to Agua Nueva for the rest of our provisions in camp, came back that night in hot haste. Colonel Yell, by order of General Taylor, had remained there until near night, when he was attacked by the advanced guard of the enemy. Destroying such provisions and wagons as he could not carry off, he retired to our position.

On the next day, the morning of Washington's Birthday, Colonels Bissell and McKee, with their respective regiments, and General Lane with his brigade, marched out to meet the enemy. We left our tents standing, and our baggage and provisions, which were in the ranch, unguarded, except by teamsters, and one man more, Major Roman, commissary. Our force on the field varied little from four thousand men. That of Santa Anna was twenty-four thousand, as all concurred in stating. The mountains on each side of our position stand two miles apart, and were high and difficult to ascend. Our flanks rested upon them. The center occupied the road, with Washington's battery behind a slight breastwork of earth; above, a little on the left and in advance of which, Colonel Hardin was posted, on a high conical hill, behind a low breastwork of stone. His task was to guard this battery on the road below. On a level with this hill, to the left, was an elevated plain or table-land, terminating at the road in high bluffs, and cut up in front and rear of our line, as well as on its right, by very deep, wide ravines, dry, with sloping sides, and running for the most part at right angles with the mountain, and parallel with our line of battle. Here was our left wing. Our right wing was posted on a low alluvion, cut up in nearly all directions by deep precipitous ravines, now dry, which in the rainy season received and conveyed the mountain torrents. This low ground was commanded as far as the mountain, and could be swept by our cannon on the road. Near to and about parallel with the mountain on the right, a creek with high and perpendicular banks ran to the north, between which and the mountain the Kentuckians of Colonel McKee, with two of Bragg's cannon, were posted on the 22nd, and remained there till the morning of the 23rd, when, finding nothing to do on the right, they abandoned this position and rushed into the battle, then raging on our left.

It became evident on the 22nd, that the high plain was to be the principal field of battle. Most of that day was spent by Santa Anna in throwing a large force of infantry, under General Ampudia, into the mountain to our left, for the purpose of gaining our rear. At 4:05 PM on the 22nd, the battle began, with a cannonade on our right and center, followed soon after by a sharp engagement in the mountain to our left, between the Kentucky riflemen from Colonel Marshall's mounted regiment and the flankers of Ampudia, at least three thousand strong. The mountain sides to the top seemed alive with the enemy, whose bright English muskets glistened in the rays of the setting sun.

Night came, and all was still, save the hum of voices from the two opposing armies, bivouacked within musket-shot of each other. Had our forces been a little larger, that night would have seen the destruction of Santa Anna's army. But our only safety lay in an obstinate defense of our position. Early in the morning of the 23rd the ball opened. The 2nd Illinois, Colonel Bissell, occupied the right of the plain, his right resting on the head of a ravine, and well guarded by Bragg's and Sherman's artillery. On his left were O'Brien's three pieces, detached from Washington's battery; and still further to our left, next to the mountain, stood the 2nd Indiana, Colonel William Bowles, with General Joe Lane and his staff. The 3d Indiana, Colonel Lane, and Colonel Davis' well-tried Mississippians, were held in reserve. Behind our line, and sheltered by a ravine from the heavy artillery of the enemy, (much heavier than ours) was our cavalry. The battle today was opened by our riflemen in the mountains, who renewed the attack which they commenced the evening before. To their assistance was soon sent the rifle battalion of the 2nd Illinois, three companies under Major Trail. Here the blows of our men were soon felt by the enemy, who stood at bay, at a respectful distance from their rifles.

The main force of Santa Anna soon advanced against us on the plain, while their artillery played upon our ranks on the left. The infantry came on in admirable order, crossing one deep ravine after another in our front, and deploying out of them into line, with a regularity that excited our admiration, and must have struck the fancy of our two regular generals. Their eight columns of regiments, advancing in line, looked formidable indeed. As the enemy rose out of the first ravine in our front, they opened their fire upon us of the 2nd Illinois, which we received some time without returning, and advanced a short way in it; but which, when we did return it, quickly slackened. The ranks immediately before us soon staggered under our fire, and were ripe for a charge of bayonets by us, when the 2nd Indiana, on our left, was seen in base, inglorious flight. General Lane, and his aide, Mr. Robinson, strove in vain to rally them. The general had, just before this disgraceful rout, replied to an officer who suggested a retreat—"Retreat! Hell no; I'll charge them myself with my bayonet." Many of this "dying infantry" ran to the ranch, many to town, and some, the bearers of ill-tidings, may have run, for all I know, to the United States. The enemy now charged O'Brien's guns, of which they took one; and our left being turned, were concentrating their fire upon our single regiment with destructive effect. By command of Colonel Churchill, Colonel Bissell ordered his ranks to cease firing and retreat to the ravine in our rear; which order was several times repeated amidst the rattling volleys before it could be heard and obeyed. Rallying out of the ravine to the right behind the artillery, which was now ploughing through the advancing columns of the enemy, we quickly joined the Kentuckians under Colonel McKee, and with them drove back the enemy's left with slaughter into the ravines, where many of them were killed and wounded. But on our left the enemy were victorious, and were pushing into our rear. Their flankers in the mountains rushed forward to surround our riflemen, and the swarms of lancers driving before them the Arkansas cavalry, whom Colonel Yell in vain called upon and adjured to follow him to the charge.

Our brave skirmishers from the mountains were on the point of being exterminated, when Colonels Yell and Marshall, with a few companies and the dragoons of Captain Stern's squadron, slightly checked the career of the lancers, and enabled the greater part of our riflemen to retreat to the ranch. About this time, Captain Stern was struck with a grape-shot and compelled to retire. The gallant and good old captain was greatly missed throughout the day. Here, with many others, Lieutenant Price of Illinois fell, seventy-two years old. Captain Conner, of the rifles, was attacked by three lancers, and saved himself by his skill with the sword.

The lancers still made head against our cavalry, and drove them to Buena Vista, where they were finally repulsed, after charging and dispersing the Arkansas regiment, with the loss of its noble colonel. May, with the Dragoons, now came up, and with our riflemen and two pieces of artillery, soon drove back the main body of the lancers. But in the mean time, a large brigade of Mexican infantry had gained our rear, and a large force of lancers had cone by our left to attack Saltillo, in conjunction with General Minon on the north. These last were quickly repelled by our cannon in the front, and were chased a considerable distance back, by infantry from the town with a small cannon. The Mississippi infantry now marched to attack that of the enemy in our rear, drawn up along the base of the mountain, and gave them battle with a gallantry and steadiness worthy of veterans. They were soon joined by the 3rd of Indiana, and a large part of the tarnished 2nd, who had rallied and returned to the conflict. General Lane was in command here, though wounded early in the morning. The battle was bloody, obstinate, and long-continued. Two pieces of artillery, with our rallied riflemen under Major Wall, came up to the left, and attacked the right of the Mexican line with great effect.

General Wool was with this squad for a short time, cool and collected, directing the fire of the artillery and men, and placing them in the best positions. The battle on the plain, meanwhile, was confined to artillery, of which the enemy had planted a battery on our left, and alongside of which was the main body of the infantry. On the flanks of our artillery, opposed to that of the enemy, were Colonels Hardin, Bissell, and McKee, ready to repel an expected charge of the Mexican infantry, and in fall view of the splendid contest going on in our rear. Colonel Hardin, on finding that all the attacks by lancers on Washington's battery were feints, and that the stream of battle flowed only on our side of the field, left his hill and came with a portion of his regiment to the plain. With us was young Clay, whose firm set countenance and eye of fire, called up in memory his eloquent father in the height of an oratorical triumph.

At length, about 3:00 PM, we saw the Mexican force in our rear begin to falter and retrace their steps, under the well directed shot of our ranks of marksmen, and the artillery still pouring its iron death-bolts into their right. Their lancers, who had taken refuge behind their infantry, and there watched the progress of the fight, made one desperate charge to turn the fortune of the day by breaking the line of Indiana and Mississippi. But the cool, steady volunteers, sent them with carnage and confusion to Santa Anna, on the plain above, with the report that our reserve was five thousand strong, and filled all the ravines in our rear. The retreat of their infantry, which paused for a moment, was now hastened by the repulse of the lancers, but still under a galling fire. They marched back in excellent order. While making their toilsome and bloody way back, with their men falling at every step, Santa Anna practiced a ruse, to which any French or English officer would have scorned to resort. He exhibited a flag of truce, and sent it across the plain to our right, where stood our generals. The heralds first asked what troops we were; and one officer, a volunteer too, had the folly to say we were regulars, *"troupos de ligne."* They then asked General Taylor what terms he had to propose. "I demand that General Santa Anna surrender himself and his whole army prisoners of war; I wilt release them on parole"—was his reply.

In the morning Santa Anna had summoned Taylor to surrender, representing the folly of resistance with volunteers against his

157

overwhelming force of regulars. The old hero then replied, "we are here, come and get us." The tables were now turning. The bearers of the flag asked what time they could have to consider these terms—"An hour?" "Not half that time," exclaimed our second in command, who may be called Old Ready as well as our first; "not half that time." "Take thirty minutes," said our chief. The flag returned to the Mexican army, accompanied by General Wool. By this time the detachment in our rear, to save which the flag was exhibited, had nearly gained the plain, still, however, under the fire of General Lane, who did not intermit for a moment his terrible blows upon the retreating enemy. At length they joined the main army. The cannonade had recommenced on the side of the enemy against us, with the return of the flag, and was quickly answered by our "mortal engines." Soon afterwards their whole army commenced an orderly retreat along the base of the mountains.

Now came a disastrous movement. Colonel Hardin called his men to a charge on the retiring enemy. Colonels McKee and Bissell, under the influence of his example, and willing to share his fate, seconded the movement, and marched with their men against ten times our numbers. Our batteries took a nearer position and continued their fire. O'Brien, with his two remaining guns on our left, accompanied us to the middle of the plain, where he opened on the enemy. We continued to advance, when the Mexicans, wheeling into line, poured upon us, not yet formed into line, a fire such as no ranks ever withstood. At the same time their lancers, in immense squadrons, attacked our right, while their whole line of infantry advanced upon us in rapid, regular march.

Their discipline was wonderfully perfect. Had they been less eager to kill and plunder our wounded, and had their officers known the value of minutes, and how to improve them, the day had been lost to us in blood and horror; for they gave no quarter. Lieutenant Robbins surrendered, and was stabbed dead with his own sword. The same fate befell Lieutenant Leanhart in the morning and many others during the day. We retreated fighting to the head of a ravine far to right of our batteries, and in advance of our line in the morning. O'Brien's batteries and most of his gunners were gone. We made a short stand at the head of this ravine, where McKee, Hardin, and Clay fell, and then ran a gauntlet through it, of three—quarters of a mile, in the midst of shot from both sides, to the road where Washington's battery stopped the pursuit, and saved many.

I, with a few others, went down a short ravine, leading into the road near the battery, and climbed Hardin's hill. We were soon greeted with the appearance of Colonel Bissell, safe and unhurt. In the mean time, General Lane, with Colonels Davis and Jim Lane, and the Monterey heroes of Mississippi, the gallant Indianians, and the Illinois pioneers under their Sergeant McFarland, rose upon the plain, from their victory in the rear, and in full view of our rout, with their searching volleys called off the vultures from the massacre and plunder of the fallen. Following these up, with the American yell, so terrifying to Mexican hearts, they quickly put their discipline to a severe proof to save their own army from a total rout. They formed, however, rapidly, and renewed the battle. At this point General Lane fell off to our left to protect our artillery, whose thunders, above all other sounds, incessantly and without pause, continued to drown the groans of the wounded, and to chant the requiem of the dead, carrying death upon their bolts through the solid ranks of Santa Anna.

As soon as I had found a breathing place, I heard the shrill voice of General Wool, calling in trumpet tones, "Illinois, Illinois, to the rescue; go out, go out my brave boys, and defend our batteries." So complete had been our rout, and the dispersion of the 2nd of Illinois, which, with six companies, had in the morning kept her iron ranks against the whole Mexican line, that now only four men of the regiment were within hearing of this appeal, who answered it by rallying instantly, with a few Kentuckians and Illinoisans of the 1st, to repel, with General Lane, a threatened charge. These four men were Private Harman Busch, Corporal Charles Gooding, a lieutenant, and Colonel Bissell. I mention the last with greater pleasure, because he is a true man, a good officer, a native of your state, and my colonel. Our force augmented swiftly with the rallying fugitives; but Santa Anna judged it prudent not to make this charge, and thus to save a part of his army for other fields. Had he made it, I cannot bring myself to doubt as to the result, when I consider the exasperated mind of every survivor among us, inflamed to the highest and bitterest resentment for the wanton murders of the wounded and vanquished, committed under our eyes throughout the day. We had now determined to conquer them or die in the attempt.

Santa Anna resumed his retreat. Still under the fire of our artillery, and in good order, he re-crossed the ravines, out of which he had marched upon us in the morning. His bivouac was a little in advance

159

of our position till about midnight, when be retired to Agua Nueva, and thence, on the 26th, marched for San Luis Potosí. He admitted his loss to have been four thousand killed, wounded and missing, of whom, certainly, not half were deserters. We exchanged his prisoners for Cassius M. Clay and the others taken in January, whom he promised to send to Vera Cruz. Our killed and wounded were seven hundred. The dispatches have already informed you who they are. This letter is now so long that I must close with a brief notice of a few of the dead, reserving the most recent events for another epistle.

Captain Lincoln, so distinguished at Palo Alto and Resaca de la Palma, was shot through the head early in the day, while rallying us, and fell from his horse, near me, into the arms of Captain Raith. He was a gallant New Englander, and stood high in the esteem of all. He was the adjutant to General Wool. Colonel Hardin was slain by lancers, near where, and soon after McKee and Clay were shot. He was an excellent officer, a good lawyer, and a man of talent. His character and fate bear a strong similitude to that of Colonel Davies, who fell at Tippecanoe. Colonel McKee, whom I did not know, was much regarded in the army, and his character spoken of, universally, in the most exalted terms.

It was never my fortune to know a more kind-hearted, chivalric and accomplished gentleman, than Colonel Yell of Arkansas. He fell with Captain Porter, in a hand-to-hand conflict with Mexican lancers. He was but feebly supported by his regiment. None knew him but to love him; none named him but to praise. Lieutenant William Price, of our Illinois rifle battalion was slain by lancers while retreating from the mountains, after our left was turned in the morning. The frost of seventy-two winters had silvered his hairs, and he had left a home of affluence and ease, with the expressed wish to die in the service of his country, if need be, on the field of battle. "They cannot cheat me out of many years," he said. When ordered with the battalion, like a forlorn hope, to the trying contest in the mountains, he exclaimed with a look of joy, as he drew his sword, "Now boys, this looks like doing something." The enemy triumphed over his fall, supposing him to he General Wool; and some prisoners taken soon after said that General Taylor alone was left to save us. They judged erroneously of us from themselves, and would have found us an army still, though deprived of our three generals.

Lieutenant Colonel Henry Clay, Jr., was much lamented. His manners, voice, and features reminded the observer strongly of his father. You saw the suavity, ease, and dignity of his carriage and deportment in them both. The statesman of Kentucky will say with old Siward:

> My son has paid soldiers debt,
> in the unshrinking station where he fought.
> Had I as many sons as I have heirs,
> I would not wish them a fairer death:
> And so his knell is knotted.

In the same part of the field, and about the same time with Clay, McKee, and Hardin, another fell, pierced by a lance, whose name is worthy of a place in the rolls of fame—Private Alexander Konze, of Company H, 2nd regiment of Illinois. This writer was honored with his friendship, and had an opportunity of knowing him well, being a member of the same company and his tent-mate. His conduct on the field was most soldierly, cool, calm, deliberate, and prompt in obeying orders. His courage was conspicuous, even in the moment of his death, when he refused to surrender. Except a brother in South America, he left no relatives on this continent. His widowed mother lives in Bueckeburg, in Hanover, near to his native city, Hamburg, Germany. He received a splendid education at the Universities of Jena and Göttingen. He had been but a year in the United States when he joined our regiment in Alten, where he had come to volunteer, from Wisconsin. His motives in taking this step were that he might serve the country, whose constitution he respected before all other systems of government, and gratify his curiosity in a new mode of life, by seeing Mexico, and observing as he did with a philosophic eye, the character of her people and institutions. The writer promised much pleasure to himself in traveling with him through this country. Alexander was twenty-seven years of age, and probably the most learned man in the army. His knowledge of philology was accurate and profound. Such was his familiarity with Latin, that by one day's examination of a Spanish grammar, he was able to read this cognate language with facility. Many pleasant hours have we spent together in rambling over the plains and mountains of Mexico, while he filled his haversack with new plants to send to Germany, and which his knowledge of botany often enabled him to class in their several genera and species.

A better or a braver heart than his never beat its last on a field of battle. While awaiting upon the field, on the night of the 23rd of February, the renewal of the attack by Santa Anna, the thought was most consolatory to several of his comrades, that death on the next day, might make them companions of Miltiades, of Socrates, and of Alexander Konze. This man died for a country of which be was not a citizen; shall it be said that he, the republican son of Germany, was not a true American? May his example animate the hearts of those whom alone he would acknowledge as countrymen—the good and the true of every clime and country. General Taylor did not forget to accord due credit to the conduct of General Wool. In his first hasty dispatch to the department, he mentions him alone. These are his words: "I may be permitted here, however, to acknowledge my great obligations to General Wool, the second in command, to whom I feel particularly indebted for his valuable services on this occasion."

To Brigadier General Wool my obligations are especially due. The high state of discipline and instructions of several of the volunteer regiments was attained under his command, and to his vigilance and arduous service before the action, and his gallantry and activity on the field, a large share of our success may justly be attributed. During most of the engagement he was in immediate command of the troops thrown back on our left flank. I beg leave to recommend him to the favorable notice of the government.

Militarily Yours,
Amos T. Johnson

In addition to this high recommendation, a preamble and resolutions, passed at a mass meeting of the citizens of Troy, on the 10th of April, 1847 is hereby annexed:

Whereas, The Common Council of the city of Troy have (in common with their fellow-citizens) had the great gratification of hearing, from all quarters, of the courage and gallant bearing of our townsman, Brigadier General John E. Wool, during the hard-fought and nobly-won field of Buena Vista:

Therefore, *Resolved*, That General Wool has fully justified the high opinion always entertained among us, of his character as an accomplished soldier; and his courage and conduct at Buena Vista amply fulfil the bright promise of his first feat of arms at Queenstown.

Resolved, That feeling a just pride in his renown, and desiring to testify our high regard for both the citizen and soldier, we, in the name of the city of Troy, present to him a sword, as a testimonial of the place he occupies in the esteem of those who have known him so long and so well; and as a memorial, (though not a reward) of the distinguished services he has rendered to his country.

Resolved, That a committee of four persons be appointed by the mayor—two from the common council, and two from the citizens generally, to carry into effect the foregoing resolution.

The sword, made in accordance with a design from Brown, the sculptor, is thus described: "It is a Roman sword. The mountings—hilt and scabbard—are of gold. The blade is two-edged, broad and straight, about two feet four inches long. The hilt is surmounted with a Roman helmet. On its sides are figures of Hercules and Mars. The wings of the American eagle are outspread beneath the guard, and on the guard the following appropriate inscription appears:"

Presented by the Common Council and Citizens of Troy, N. Y., to their townsman, Brigadier General John E. Wool, as a token of their personal esteem, and of their high appreciation of his gallantry and military ability, as displayed on the bloody field of Buena Vista, on the 22d and 23d days of February, 1847. The scabbard is richly engraved with numerous battle scenes, arms, and banners, and other suitable devices, and bears the following inscription:

> *Queenstown*, Oct. 13, 1812
> *Plattsburg*, Sept. 11, 1814
> *Buena Vista*, Feb. 22 and 23, 1847

The following excerpts of a letter and accompanying remarks will be pleasing to every friend of General Wool. While it accords due justice to him, it also shows that his skill is as great in selecting an advantageous battleground, as in defending it when the enemy are upon him:

. . . So many persons have claimed the credit of saving the day at Buena Vista, and some in a most extraordinary manner, and so many claimants have appeared for praise for the honor of selecting the ground upon which the glorious battle of Buena Vista was fought, that it may not be improper, even at this late period, to "render unto Caesar the things that are Caesar's." As General Wool, in my opinion, is entitled to the credit of having selected the spot, the following letter, which incontestably establishes that fact, may not prove uninteresting. It is from the pen of Captain Carleton, of the United States Dragoons, a very gallant officer, and one whose pen has often enriched the columns of the New York *Times* and is addressed to General Wool.

Hacienda Buena Vista
July 27, 1847

DEAR SIR: By reference to my journal of the marches, etc., of your column, I find that on the 21st of December, 1846, you arrived in the valley of La Encantada with your whole force, consisting of cavalry, artillery, and infantry, with their complete trains, and encamped at Agua Nueva, situated at its southern terminator.

That point is twenty miles in advance of Saltillo, which city was then occupied by General Worth, to whose assistance you had marched from Parras, a distance of one hundred and fifteen miles, in less than three days. At that time the command of General Worth was only a brigade, and he had sent by express a request to you at Parras, to join him with your column as soon as possible, to assist in repelling an attack then daily expected from the enemy, in force under General Santa Anna.

About the same time, General Butler arrived at Saltillo from Monterey. On the evening of the 22d of December, you left your camp at Agua Nueva to visit both himself and General Worth; it being reported that they were confined to their beds in consequence of the wounds they had previously received. You were accompanied by Captains Lee, Hughes, and Chapman, United States Army, by your aid, Lieutenant McDowell, and by myself, then on duty as one of your aides-de-camp. It was quite dark when you left Agua Nueva, and when you arrived at that part of the pass of Buena Vista known as La Angostura, a heavy fog, accompanied by rain, had set in, rendering it so much more so that it was with the utmost difficulty the road could be kept. Indeed the officers who were with you were frequently obliged to dismount and seek for it on either hand. It was past 11:00 PM when you and your party reached Saltillo. The next day, when your interview with Generals Butler and Worth was concluded, you started on your return to your camp at Agua Nueva, accompanied only by myself, all the other officers who had gone to Saltillo with you being still detained there by official business. When you had proceeded as far as the Angostura Pass, one mile in advance of the Hacienda of San Juan de la Buena Vista, you halted, and, after having glanced over the ground on each side, you said to me "Mr. Carleton, this is the very spot of all others I have yet seen in Mexico which I should select for battle, were I obliged with a small army to fight a large one."

You then pointed out to me what you conceived were the great military advantages it possessed; and said that the net-work of deeply-worn channels on the right would completely protect that flank; that the heights on your left would command the road, while the ravines in front of them, and which extend back to the mountain on that side, would cripple the movements of the enemy should he attempt to turn that flank. You continued conversing with me on this subject until, as you may recollect, we met Lieutenant McCown, 4th artillery, a mile or more further on. So forcibly was I impressed with your choice, and all you had said in favor of it, that, immediately after my arrival at Agua Nueva, I described the place to some of the officers of your staff, (I think to Inspector General Churchill and his assistant, Captain Drum, United States Army) at the time saying that you had selected it for a battleground, and repeating all you had stated in relation to it.

It may not be improper likewise to add, that on the 26th of December General Butler visited you at Agua Nueva; and that on the 27th, before he returned to Saltillo, he gave you an order to move with your troops and select in the neighborhood of La Encantada or further down the stream towards Saltillo, a suitable place, and there encamp. As this order was entirely discretionary as to the precise locality for your proposed camp, you chose the plain between La Angostura and the hacienda before alluded to as the best, because it was not only less exposed to the bleak winds which continually swept through the pass at La Encantada, and which at that season of the year would cause the troops much suffering, as we were all in tents and fuel very scarce, but offered the additional advantage of an abundant supply of pure water, and besides was just in rear of what you had selected as the strong point of defense.

That evening, the 28th, General Butler sent you an order to return to La Eacantada and encamp there. You wrote a note to him, requesting, for reasons which you assigned, that he would permit you to remain where you were, and sent it by Colonel Hardin. Captain Drum and myself accompanied Colonel Hardin, and were present at the interview between General Butler and himself. During the conversation that ensued after your note had been delivered, Colonel Hardin, among other reasons which he gave why he hoped your request might be complied with, urged the fact that you were near a point which you believed you could maintain in case the enemy advanced upon you from the direction of San Luis Potosí. General Butler said he would not revoke his order, and remarked that if the Mexican army came he had already chosen a ground for battle, and even gone so far as to fix the points to be occupied by the several corps. That ground was the broad plain immediately in front of Saltillo, and I think he also said he had already prepared roads for the artillery, leading from the city up on to it. I have mentioned all these circumstances to show with what anxiety and exertion you endeavored to be permitted to occupy a point within striking distance of the one you had selected as the best for battle. On the 30th of December your whole command was obliged to retrace its steps to La Encantada, which it did with evident reluctance, as all the officers agreed entirely with you in opinion as to the disadvantages arising from such a change of position.

Previous to the time when you first went to Saltillo, on the 22nd, not one of your officers had ever gone through the pass of Buena Vista. All those who went with you on that occasion were prevented, as I have shown, by the extreme darkness even from seeing the great road on which they sought to travel, and could not therefore have had at that time a favorable opportunity for making military reconnaissances. You returned from the city and had pointed out the position to me, as I have stated, before they repassed over it. The choice and partialities of the officers in Saltillo, it is fair to presume, for many reasons, were coincident with those expressed by General Butler. When General Taylor came up from Monterey, he saw at a glance that your views were correct; and, although he moved the whole army forward to Agua Nueva, as there he could have an extensive plain for the drill and discipline of the troops, with wood and water convenient, and besides, by doing so, could take the initiatory step in one of the most beautiful pieces of strategy of modern times, still, when, by the advance of Santa Anna, the moment had ripened to gain the grand results by feigning a precipitate retreat, that retreat was but a rapid movement back to the *identical* spot you had chosen, and on to which the Mexican army was hurriedly drawn with all its fatigue and disarray consequent upon a forced march of upwards of forty miles; and where, on the 22nd and 23rd of February, 1847, was fought the battle of Buena Vista. The result of that conflict afforded conclusive evidence of the correctness of your first remark; for there four thousand six hundred and ten Americans contended successfully against upwards of twenty thousand Mexicans. This letter, general, is but a dry detail of facts, but I hope they are set forth with sufficient clearness to prevent their being misunderstood . . .

Respectfully yours,
John Carleton, Captain

Immediately after the battle, General Wool established his headquarters at Buena Vista. In the month of May following, he, on the occasion of taking leave of the 1st and 2nd Illinois regiments, whose term of service (one year) had nearly expired, issued the following orders, dated Buena Vista, May 28th, 1847:

GENERAL ORDER

The term of service for which the 1st and 2d Illinois regiments have engaged has nearly expired, and they are about to return to their homes. The general commanding takes this occasion to express his deep regret at the departure of those who have been so long under his immediate command, and who have served, and served so *well*, their country. Few can boast of longer marches, greater hardships, and none of greater gallantry in the field of Buena Vista. It was there that the general witnessed with infinite satisfaction their valor, which gave an additional luster to our arms, and increased glory to our country. To their steadiness and firmness, in connection with the 2nd Kentucky, Foot, in resisting the Mexicans at a critical moment, and where there were five to one against them—and, as General Santa Anna said, "when blood flowed in torrents, and the field of battle was strewed with the dead,"—we may justly ascribe a large share of the glorious victory over more than twenty thousand men.

A great victory, it is true, but attained at too great a sacrifice; Hardin, Zabriskie, Woodward, McKee, Yell, Clay, and many others fell leading their men to the charge. Their names and gallant deeds will ever be remembered by a grateful people.

In taking leave of these regiments, the general cannot omit to express his admiration of the conduct and gallant bearing of all, and especially of Colonels Bissell and Weatherford, and their officers, who have, on all occasions, done honor to themselves, and heroically sustained the cause of their country on the field of Buena Vista.

The wishes of the general will attend them to their homes, where they will be received with joy and gladness as the pride of their families and their state.

On the 23d of June, the following statement was made by the officers of these regiments:

BRIGADIER GENERAL WOOL: The officers and soldiers of the 1st regiment of Illinois volunteers, on the eve of leaving Mexico for their homes, would do violence to their own feelings did they not tender to their immediate commanding general a testimonial of their regard.

Upon entering the service a year since, they were not prepared to appreciate the importance of discipline and drill, and consequently complained of them as onerous and unnecessary. Complaints were loud and many. Their judgment convinced, their feelings have undergone a change, and they now thank you for your untiring exertions to make them useful to their country and a credit to their state.

Whatever, sir, of service we may have done our common country, or whatever honor we may have done the state of Illinois, to General John E. Wool is due the credit. You, sir, brought your column into the field, well provided for, and well disciplined, and fought them well when you got them there; and should our country ever again need our services in the field, it would be our proudest wish to again meet the enemy under the immediate command of one in whose energy, watchfulness and courage we, and the whole army, have the most unlimited confidence.

With the best wishes for your future fame and happiness, on the part of the regiment, we beg leave to subscribe ourselves your friends.

This letter was signed by W. Weatherford, Colonel of the 1st Illinois volunteer regiment, and by W. B. Waring, Lieutenant Colonel, and forty company and staff officers.

From the battle of Buena Vista, up to the last accounts from General Wool's command, we find that General Wool was stationed at Buena Vista, awaiting reinforcements to enable him and General Taylor to make a movement in the direction of San Luis Potosí, passing through and taking possession of Encarnacion along the route.

Chapter 9

COLONEL JEFFERSON DAVIS

I was born on June 3, 1808. The house in which I was born was very similar to the log cabin in which Abraham Lincoln was born a year later, less than a hundred miles away. When I was two years old my father took the family to Bayou Teche in Louisiana. Because of a plague of mosquitoes we moved again to a farm in southwest Mississippi. When I was eight years old my father sent me to Catholic school. After a few years of schooling I returned home. I attended Jefferson College near Natchez, and in the spring of 1823 I entered Transylvania University.

Three years after the death of my father, I sent Secretary of War John C. Calhoun an acceptance of my appointment as a cadet at West Point. When I graduated on June 30, 1828 I ranked 23rd out of a class of 32. I was commissioned brevet second lieutenant in the infantry in January 1829, and ordered to report to the Jefferson Barracks in St. Louis, Missouri for further training. I was granted a furlough and on August 26, 1828 I was given an extension of that furlough until December 31st.

On May 31, 1829 I was ordered to Fort Winnebago in Michigan Territory. West Point, I observed, rendered me unfit for civilian life. One of my earliest duties was to search for deserters in Illinois, and I also acted as a recruiting officer. I was transferred to Fort Crawford at Prairie du Chien, Michigan Territory, and remained there two years. In April 1832 Colonel Zachary Taylor took command of Fort Crawford. I fell in love with his daughter, and despite the opposition of Taylor to my courtship, we met secretly at the house of a friend.

On March 3, 1833 I was appointed as a second lieutenant of dragoons. In the summer of 1833 I was sent to Lexington, Kentucky on recruiting service. My tour was cut short due to a severe cholera epidemic which affected the town. When I returned in August 1833 to Jefferson Barracks I was appointed adjutant of my regiment. Then on May 10, 1834 I was commissioned first lieutenant of my dragoon regiment. On March 1, 1845 I applied for a leave of absence, and upon its expiration I resigned from the U. S. Army to take effect on June 30, 1835. The reason for my resignation was my intention to marry Sarah Knox Taylor.

After nearly two years of engagement Sarah Taylor and I were married on June 17, 1835 at the home of her aunt, three miles from Louisville, Kentucky. After the wedding Sarah and I look passage on a steamboat to "Hurricane," my brother's plantation. In late summer my bride and I visited my sister Anna who was married to a wealthy planter in Louisiana. At the home of my sister both Sarah and I came down with a serious attack of malaria. Sarah died on September 15, 1835 and she was buried in Anna's family graveyard in Louisiana. I was in serious danger for a month or so but I recovered. For a number of years afterward I continued to have recurring attacks of malaria.

In the winter of 1835-36 I made a trip to Havana, Cuba. From there I returned and went to Washington City where I observed and listened to the debates of Congressmen at the capital and met a number of prominent politicians. I then lived in seclusion on a plantation called "Brierfield" given to me by my brother Joseph. During the Christmas holidays of 1843 I met my future second wife, Varina Howell of Natchez, Mississippi. In January 1834 we became engaged. We were married at the bride's home in Natchez on February 26, 1845 in an Episcopal ceremony. None of my family attended the wedding. We took passage on a steamboat for New Orleans where they stayed six weeks at the swank St. Charles Hotel. After the honeymoon we proceeded to Brierfield.

I became involved in politics, and was elected a Congressman from Mississippi. Varina and I departed by the northern route for Washington in late 1845. I had planned to be in Washington for the opening of Congress, but arrived a week late. We found a nice boarding house and joined a "congenial mess" Varina enjoyed the social life in Washington.

I made my maiden speech in the House of Representatives two weeks after I took my seat. My most notable speech was delivered on the Oregon question on February 6, 1846. I favored the admission of not only Oregon as a state but California as well. I maintained that the country should not risk the danger of war by occupying all of Oregon, but should compromise by extending the 49th parallel to the Pacific. Congress adopted President Polk's proposal to extend the 49th parallel to Puget Sound.

I ardently supported the declaration of war against Mexico on May 13, 1846. Shortly afterwards the news arrived of the clash between Taylor's troops and the Mexican Army above the Rio Grande. On the day of the declaration of war I wrote to a friend in Mississippi that I expected a war over Oregon with England, but before this occurred the United States should quietly defeat Mexico, dictating a treaty of peace in the City of Mexico.

I volunteered my services and was elected a colonel of the First Mississippi Rifles at Camp Independence, near Vicksburg, on June 18, 1846. I gladly accepted a commission issued by Governor Brown, but I concealed this fact from Varina. She eventually found out and tried to dissuade me from going to war, but I prevailed in my resolution. I joined the Mississippi Regiment at New Orleans on July 21, 1846. Many Mississippi volunteers took their slaves, and they had to provide their own horses. I took along a black valet and a magnificent Arabian horse named Tartar.

In Mexico I sought some kind of glory. My success was partly owing to the generalship of the commander, my former father-in-law Zachary Taylor. Taylor looked and dressed the part of a farmer, and he was fond of talking about crops and his Mississippi cotton plantation tilled by many black slaves. After the declaration of war Taylor crossed the Rio Grande and began an invasion of Mexico. Establishing his base at Camargo, he advanced towards Monterey, the capital of Nuevo León. He had two divisions of troops commanded by General William J. Worth and General David Twiggs. The Mississippi Volunteers, which I commanded, marched with General Quitmann's brigade under General Worth.

During the three days-battle at Monterey, I won the highest applause for my fearlessness, both within the walls, and while employed to repel the charges of enemy cavalry. My riflemen were frequently in the thickest battle, between cross-fires, and exposed to the full action of the enemy's lancers. I was appointed by General Taylor as one of the commissioners to negotiate a capitulation, and subsequently became one of the warmest defenders of that measure. My fame as a soldier and as a leader was based upon my operations at Monterey.

After the battle of Monterey I obtained a sixty day furlough to return home. When I returned to my regiment on January 4, 1847 I found General Taylor's army at Saltillo, sixty miles south of Monterey. It was at this time that President Polk supported General Winfield Scott to command an expedition which was to land at Vera Cruz and then advance on the City of Mexico. On January 17th Scott ordered Taylor to turn over to him all his experienced troops and general officers. Among the troops that Taylor retained were my Mississippi Rifles and the battery of Braxton Bragg.

On February 8th, 1847 I wrote to Varina, AWe are here on the tablelands of Mexico, at the foot of the Sierra Madre. We came expecting a host and battle, but have found solitude and eternal peace. The daily alarms of this frontier have ceased and I believe the enemy has returned to San Luis de Potosi. We are waiting for reinforcements while General Scott is taking all who can be seized and incorporates them all in his division of the army. We have a beautiful and healthy position, and are waiting for some action or some such excitement.

After learning of the stripping of Taylor's army Santa Anna decided to attack. At the beginning of the battle fought at the Hacienda of Buena Vista on George Washington's birthday he sent a messenger to Taylor saying that with his numerical superiority of 20,000 men, the American army would inevitably have to surrender. Taylor wasn't about to surrender. He withdrew his troops to the Angostura Pass in the mountains, Aan ideal spot for a small army to fight a large one.

The battle was one in which each officer sustained the fortune of the day at intervals. This was my case, after the retirement of the 2nd Indiana regiment. The Mexican cavalry, elated by their success, rushed down in heavy columns, with shouts that rang above the din of battle, and in a direction which would bring them in direct contact with our Mississippians. Undaunted, however, by the formidable array, I threw

173

my command into the form of a V, with the opening toward the enemy, and firmly awaited their approach. They rushed at me at full gallop; but when near enough to render their features discernible, a sheet of fire was poured into their dense ranks, which mowed down their horses and riders, in a promiscuous slaughter. They rallied, and renewed the charge; but were driven back again and again, until perseverance became madness. Santa Anna would have been the hero of Angostura had he conquered in that charge. But, struck with dismay, his lacerated columns heaved back, and in mad confusion horses trod down horses, crushing wounded and dying beneath their hoofs, all in the reckless dash of retreat. It was a horrible moment; and when the pageant had passed away, heaps of mutilated beings were stretched along the ground, writhing in the extremity of agony. Those who only a moment before had been strong in life and hope, were now torn and trampled into the earth, while the blood was pouring from their wounds, and their hearts were hurrying on to their last shock. Early in the battle I was shot in my right foot, yet I remained on my horse until the battle was over.

Thus I became Athe hero of Buena Vista. President Polk appointed me a brigadier general of volunteers but I refused the commission. When the regiment returned to New Orleans on June 15, 1847, all our men were greeted with wild enthusiasm. Many brave soldiers and officers died at Buena Vista including Lieutenant Colonel Henry Clay. When the Mississippi Rifles returned to the United States there were only 376 men left of the 926 who so eagerly went off to war. My role in the victory at Buena Vista so advanced my popularity with the citizens of Mississippi that upon the sudden death of Senator Jesse Spreight in August 1847 Governor Brown appointed me to fill out the unexpired term. I returned to Washington with my wife Varina and took up residence. I was quickly chosen as chairman of the United States Senate Military Affairs Committee.

Chapter 10

Major Ringgold

A Tribute by his Peers

Major Samuel Ringgold was born in 1800 in Hagerstown, Maryland. He was the oldest son of General Samuel Ringgold, formerly a United States Senator from Maryland. His mother was the daughter of General John Cadwallader. In 1814 he entered West Point and graduated in 1818 with distinction at the head of his class. Not satisfied with his proficiency in military matters he visited various schools in Europe. He entered the Polytechnique, and afterwards the military institution at Woolwich, perfecting himself in the science of artillery.

Returning to this country Ringgold entered the United States army as a second lieutenant, and being recommended by General Scott, he was received as aide-de-camp into that officer's staff. In July 1822 he was promoted to first lieutenant; in which capacity he occupied Fort Moultrie in South Carolina until the settlement of the nullification difficulties of 1833. In 1836 he received the rank of captain.

His most arduous service was experienced in Florida. Rather delicate in health the diseases of that swampy country preyed upon his constitution. After the disbandment of his company in 1838 Ringgold went to Carlisle, Pennsylvania with instructions to organize and equip a company of light artillery. He was soon afterwards breveted a major for his meritorious services in Florida. He remained in Pennsylvania until the opening of war with Mexico.

Major Ringgold pressed for an efficient organization of artillery to complete our military establishment. He saw a branch of the military added to the army known as the "flying" artillery, which proved to be a resounding success during the Mexican war. He was with the "Corps of Observation" at the battle of Palo Alto. That engagement was commenced by Lieutenant Churchill with two eighteen-pound cannons. Ringgold stationed himself in front of these cannon, and at a distance of 700 yards from the enemy opened fire with withering effect.

Major Ringgold personally attended his guns and was very accurate in his management of them. For a while the battle was conducted with the artillery alone. The American infantry, drawn up as a support, stood watching with intense emotion the ravages of Ringgold's weapons, bursting forth into loud cheers at every discharge. While the battle was thus raging the Mexican lancers moved down towards the wagon train, and in consequence Lieutenant Ridgeley was detached with two pieces to protect it.

Notwithstanding this diminution of ranks, Ringgold still maintained the battle against fearful odds, and held the enemy at bay for three hours. He then received the wound which caused his death. A cannon ball passed through the middle of his right thigh and through the shoulders of his horse, and came out through his left thigh. Men and officers came to his assistance, but he waved them away, exclaiming, "don't stay with me—you have a battle to fight—go ahead and fight it!"

He was immediately carried from the field under the direction of Doctor Byrne, who dressed his wounds. He bore his pain well and up to the time of his death he conversed cheerfully with his attendants upon the incidents of the battle. He died at 1:00 AM on May 10, 1846. His burial took place the next day.

Even those who had known him only a short time partook the general sorrow; and when it was announced throughout the United

States that Ringgold had fallen, the shout of victory was dashed with a wail of sympathy. The feeling was especially manifested in his native state. On the 26th of May, 1846 the flags of all vessels and public buildings were half-masted and hung with crepe.

"His memory will be gratefully cherished so long as honorhas a victory, freedom a hero, or his country a name!"

Chapter 11

PROSECUTING THE MEXICAN WAR

Winfield Scott

As early as May, 1846 when it was known that the Mexicans had assumed a threatening attitude on the Rio Grande President Polk intimated to me that he would send me to that frontier. I replied that it was harsh and unusual for a senior, without reinforcements to supersede a meritorious junior. Furthermore I doubted whether it was the right season or that the Rio Grande was the right place for an *offensive* operation against Mexico. I said, however, that I had a plan for bringing about a peace which I would execute.

Leading Democrats took alarm at the appointment of a Whig to so high a trust. It caused Mr. Polk to doubt and reject my views. I said that without the approval of my campaign plan and the confidence and support of the government I would not be able to conduct any expedition to advantage; for soldiers had a far greater dread of a fire upon their rear, than of the most formidable enemy in front.

At this period of time I was spending from fifteen to eighteen hours a day in my office. One day, however, the Secretary of War called on me, and found me out of the office. In explanation I wrote a note to say that

I had only stepped out for a hasty bowl of soup. The private note found its way into the party newspapers.

Taylor's early successes on this side of the Rio Grande had won him great favor with the country. A resolution giving him a sword was promptly introduced. I myself produced a private circular to a dozen members of Congress—including the Kentucky Senators, and Mr. Jefferson Davis—arguing that a gold medal ought to be substituted for the sword—being the higher honor, and eminently Taylor's due. The suggestion was adopted and shows that I did not neglect the hero of the Rio Grande.

Before my written solicitude about the medal—in May 1846—the day on which the news of Taylor's first two victories arrived—a number of leading Whigs (not including Mr. Clay or Mr. Webster) in a panic, about the soup, called upon me to inquire whether Taylor was a Whig or not, and whether he might not advantageously be my substitute as their next presidential candidate?

Engraved by J.C.Buttre N.Y.

Winfield Scott

LIEUT. GEN. OF THE U.S.A.

General Winfield Scott

Taylor, highly stimulated and marching under the greatest difficulties upon the little village of Monterey, which he captured (cui bono?) and became *planted*, as it was impractical—no matter with what force, to reach any vital part of Mexico by that route. Accordingly, Taylor remained at Monterey and its neighborhood, with varying numbers down to the peace.

Reliable information was reaching Washington almost daily that the wild volunteers, as soon as they were beyond the Rio Grande, committed all sorts of atrocities on the persons and property of Mexicans. One of the volunteers even shot a Mexican from a concealed position as he marched out of Monterey, under the capitulation.[15]

American troops took with them beyond the limits of their own country, no law but the Constitution of the United States, and the rules and articles of war. These do not provide any court for the trial or punishment of murder, rape, theft, etc., etc.—no matter by whom, or on whom committed. To suppress these disgraceful acts abroad I drew up a *martial law order*—to be issued and enforced in Mexico, until Congress could be stimulated to legislate on the subject. My martial law order was published when I reached Tampico in Mexico. It was successfully republished at Vera Cruz, Puebla and the City of Mexico. Under it, all offenders, Americans and Mexicans alike, were punished with death for murder or rape, and for other crimes proportionately.

Several times in the summer and autumn of 1846 I requested my desire to be ordered to Mexico at the head of a competent force. At length my request was acceded to by Secretary of War Marcy on November 23, 1846. From an early day I believed that the Secretary of the Treasury, Mr. Walker and Secretary Marcy were in favor of giving me the substantial direction of the war on land—each having often done me the honor to express his fullest confidence in my zeal and capacity for the occasion.

For a week prior to Mr. Marcy's letter President Polk sent for me once or twice daily. He lavished kindness and confidence upon me. He fully won my confidence. When I was ready to embark on the expedition at New Orleans Mr. Hodge of that city communicated a letter to me from my dear friend Alexander Barrow, then a Senator from Louisiana,

---

[15]   General Taylor was advised to send the gangster home - that is, to reward him with a honorable discharge.

saying that the president had asked for the grade of lieutenant general in order to place Senator Benton over me in the Army of Mexico. I said that Barrow must be mistaken about Mr. Benton. Why? Because remembering Mr. Polk's assurance of his support and my reward—I am sure he intended that rank only <u>for me</u>. A grosser abuse of human confidence is nowhere recorded.

Mr. Polk's mode of viewing the case seems to have been this, "Scott is a Whig; therefore the Democracy is not bound to observe good faith with him. Scott is a Whig; therefore his successes may be turned to the prejudices of the Democratic Party. We must, however, profit by his military experience, and, if successful, by the force of patronage and other help, contrive to crown Benton with the victory, and thus triumph both in the field and at the polls."

This miserable treachery was planned during my very friendly interviews with Mr. Polk! The plan soon became fully developed, and, in all essentials, acknowledged before Congress. The lieutenant general position was rejected when Mr. Polk taxed his supporters to the utmost to procure for him authority to place a junior major general (Benton) over a senior (myself) and was again ignominiously defeated—aided by the manly spirit of the same small number of Democrats. This vile intrigue so disgusted Congress, and its defeat so depressed the zeal and influence of the Administration, that instead of authorizing the additional forces needed for the war at once, the augmentation was delayed until the end of the Congressional session.

I reached Brazos San Iago near the mouth of the Rio Grande on December 22, 1846 and proceeded up river to Camargo. Four days earlier I wrote Major General Taylor to set up a meeting with me, but by the gross neglect of the officer who bore it, it lost three days sitting at the mouth of the river. In the meantime Taylor took part of his troops to Tampico. I asked myself, "why did he divide his forces?" It was fully as difficult for an army to penetrate Mexico from that point as from Monterey.

I also made a blunder in my communication to Taylor. I sent a highly confidential sketch of my views and intentions. The letter was stamped "top secret" outside and inside. Yet at the volunteer headquarters at Monterey it was opened, freely read and discussed by the regulars. The package was resealed and forwarded to Taylor by a young officer with a few men who were inveigled by Mexicans into the Villa Gran and slain. The official dispatches were taken and received by Santa Anna long before Taylor saw the duplicate.

So the intended meeting with Taylor failed and it was a great disappointment to me. In the dispatches I had said that he should have his choice of the two armies, that is, either remain as the immediate commander in Northern Mexico, or accompany me in the command of a division to the capital, with every assurance, in either case, of my confidence and support.

I had now detached enough regular troops from the Army of the Rio Grande as I deemed indispensable for the descent on Vera Cruz and the conquest of the capital. I left Taylor a sufficient defensive force to maintain his position at Monterey. I should have ordered the contraction at once if Taylor had been present to support me. I also discovered at this time that my friend Alexander Barrow's message was fully founded—that is, instead of a friend in the president, I had, in him, an enemy none to be dreaded more than Santa Anna himself and all his cronies.

Taylor and the Secretary of War both concurred on a direct advance on the Mexican capital from the Rio Grande. Each had glanced at the Vera Cruz route, an idea always mine, but each favored the defensive line of Monterey or the Sierra Madre. Taylor seemed to favor starting on the defensive on the banks of the Rio Grande, which he had left against his best judgment.

The Mexicans had no apprehensions of an effective invasion from that quarter or from Tampico. In respect to either of these routes, they might have expressed what the Russians felt when Napoleon marched against Moscow, "come unto us with few, and we will overwhelm you; come unto us with many, and you shall overwhelm yourselves." As to holding the line of the Sierra Madre or another line of defense and standing fast, that would have been the worst possible state of things. It would have been "a little war," or a "war like a peace"—a perpetual condition—and Santa Anna would have regarded it as a mere scratch on the surface.

To compel an obstinate people to *sue for peace* it is absolutely necessary to strike fast and hard at the vitals of the nation. The order for the troops to descend from Monterey to the sea-coast was issued at Camargo on January 3, 1847 and I immediately returned to Brazos

San Iago. At a barbecue at Pascagoula, Mississippi, Taylor was quoted to say,

> You have alluded to my being stripped of *my* troops on the Rio Grande; and my being left, as it might seem, at the mercy of the enemy, just before the battle of Buena Vista, renders it proper that I should make a few remarks in relation to that matter. I received an order from the general-in-chief (Scott) while on my march to Tampico stripping me of the greater portion of my command, and particularly of my well trained regular troops and volunteers.

> The order was received by me with much surprise, and, I must confess, produced the strongest feelings of regret, mortification and disappointment, *as I knew that Santa Anna was in striking distance of my lines, with an army of 25,000—probably the best appointed men collected in Mexico.*

The nasty little errors quoted above, both of fact and opinion of a good man ought to be treated as a nurse treats a child—a little sick and a little spoiled—gently. However, if his errors, springing from vanity and self-love, wound another, the injury is deep and therefore should be dealt with unsparingly.

> Item 1. *He called the army of the Rio Grande "my troops!"*

> Item 2. *He knew that Santa Anna, with an overwhelming force, was in striking distance.*

> If so he withheld the fact from the War Department and the general-in-chief. Up to the last moment he gave the contrary assurance to both!

> Item 3. *He had been stripped, etc.—left at the mercy of the enemy!*

> I left Taylor a small fraction less than 7000 men with a reasonable portion of regulars, including batteries of field

artillery—and other regiments soon expected, with advice to stay behind the stone walls of Monterey, or to consider himself at liberty to take up the impregnable line of the Rio Grande. Taylor wrote from Monterey, January 27, 1847, "the force with which I am left, in this quarter, though greatly deficient in regular troops, will doubtless enable me to hold the position now occupied."

Item 4. *Santa Anna's 25,000 well appointed men at Buena Vista.*

It is true that Santa Anna in summoning Taylor to surrender intimated his strength at 25,000 men, but four days before the battle of Buena Vista Mexican officials put down his total force at 14,048 including some two thousand sick and lame and the remainder half famished with thirst and hunger.

General Taylor did not concentrate his army at Monterey as advised, but preferred the advanced position of Agua Nueva. He said it was in order "to fight the Mexican general immediately after he had crossed the desert country (about 150 miles in extent) which lay at my front, and before he could have time to refresh and recruit his army."

Actually if we assumed that the Americans had been concentrated within the walls of Monterey, the repulse of the enemy would have been more crippling, with less military loss on our part. It would have saved the battle of Buena Vista and Cerro Gordo, and by delaying Santa Anna, would have hastened the capture of "the Halls of Montezuma." Victory at Buena Vista was glorious but it did not advance the campaign one inch, nor quicken a treaty of peace an hour, as the Mexicans universally regarded it as a mere border affair. Back at the Brazos San Iago I had to wait for the troops coming from Monterey, and also for the means of transportation to Vera Cruz. Embarkation was therefore delayed until February 15, 1847.

While at New Orleans I heard from a few old ship-masters that some anchorage might be found in the vicinity of the Lobos Islands. These islands were a third of the distance from Tampico to Vera Cruz. Accordingly I appointed that location as the general rendezvous for all the troops and supply ships of the expedition—many of them being still due from New Orleans and points further North.

I remained at the Lobos Islands some one hundred and twenty miles from Vera Cruz for a few days till the greater part of my supplies had arrived. We next sailed a little past Vera Cruz and came to anchor on March 7, 1847 at Anton Lizardo where we would launch our boats and do some reconnaissance. We also had to take into consideration the surf for debarkation. Ignorant of Santa Anna's march over the desert upon Major General Taylor, we did not doubt meeting a formidable struggle when we landed and so all reasonable precautions were made.

On March 9th, a red letter day, the sun dawned propitiously on the expedition. It was the precise day when I had completed thirty years as a general officer. There was but little surf on the beach. This was a necessary condition for a landing from the open sea. The whole fleet of transports—some eighty vessels, in the presence of many foreign ships of war, stood off the coast, flanked by two naval steamers and five gunboats to cover the movement. I passed through them on board the large propeller *Massachusetts* and the shouts and cheers from every deck gave me assurance of victory, whatever might be the force prepared to receive us.

We anchored opposite a point a little beyond the range of the guns of the city and the castle. Some fifty-five hundred men filled up the sixty-seven surf boats which I had specially built. Each surf boat held from seventy to eighty men—besides a few cutters belonging to the larger war vessels. Commodore Conner supplied officers to steer and sailors as oarsmen. The first wave landed exactly as prescribed, at about 5:30 PM, without the loss of a boat or a man, and, to the astonishment of all, without opposition other than a few whizzing shells that did no harm. Another trip or two enabled the boats to put ashore the whole force.

The city of Vera Cruz, and the Castle San Juan de Ulúa were both strongly garrisoned. Santa Anna was relying on them to hold out until the *vomito* or yellow fever became rife. He had returned to the City of Mexico and was busy collecting additional troops in order to crush the invasion.

In 1847 the walls and forts of Vera Cruz were in top condition. Subsequent to its capture in the 1838 French war by Admiral Baudin and Prince de Joinville the castle was greatly enlarged—almost rebuilt, and its armament almost doubled. When we approached in 1847 the castle had the capacity to sink the entire American navy.

Immediately after landing I made a reconnaissance of the land side of the city with Colonel Totten and other staff officers. This was at once followed by stationing troops all around the city to cut off any communication between the garrison and the interior. The sea blockade, under Commodore Conner, had been completed earlier in time. I knew that grave deliberations were going on within the city. My first hope was to capture the castle under the shelter of the city, but I never submitted this plan for discussion. Several generals and colonels solicited the privilege of leading storming parties. I thanked them greatly but said nothing more. My military advisers consisted of Colonel Totten, chief engineer; Lieutenant Colonel Hitchcock, acting inspector general; and Lieutenant Henry L. Scott my acting adjutant general. We fully discussed the question of storming parties and siege approaches.

I was feeling President Polk's halter around my neck so I expressed myself quite strongly as follows:

> We, of course, gentlemen must take the city and the castle before the return of the *vomito*. We can use a slow scientific technique, or we can just storm the city. I am strongly inclined to attempt the former unless you can convince me that the other is preferable. Since our exhaustive reconnaissance I think the first suggestion practicable with only a moderate loss on our part.

> The second method, would, no doubt, be successful, but at the cost of an immense slaughter to both sides, including non-combatants—Mexican men, women and children—because the assaults would have to be made in the dark, and the assailants would dare not lose time in taking and guarding prisoners without incurring the certainty of becoming captives themselves, till all the strongholds of the place are occupied.

The horrors of such slaughter, with the usual terrible accompaniments are most revolting. Besides it is necessary to take into account the probable loss of some two or three thousand of our best men, and I have received but half of the numbers promised me. How then could we hope to penetrate the interior?

For these reasons, I added, I am strongly inclined to take the city with the least possible loss of life. In this determination I know as Dogberry says truly of himself, I "write myself down as an ass."

My decided bias in favor of a regulated siege was fully concurred to by my generals. Accordingly Colonel Totten, my able chief engineer and his accomplished assistants proceeded to dig the trenches and establish the gun emplacements deemed necessary. All sieges are much alike and as I do not wish to bore you with a treatise on engineering, I shall omit the scientific details. We took care in our approaches to keep the city as a shield between us and the terrible fire of the castle; but the forts in the walls of the city were formidable spit fires.

The arming of the advanced batteries had been retarded by a gale called a *norther* which cut off all communications with our vessels. Ground was, however broken on the 18th of March and by the 22nd heavy ordnance was in place. The governor of Vera Cruz, who was also the governor of the castle was duly summoned to surrender. The refusal was no sooner received than a fire on the walls and forts was opened. In the attempt to batter the walls and to silence the forts, a portion of our shots and shells, in the course of the siege, unavoidably penetrated the city and set fire to many houses. By the 24th of March the landing of additional heavy guns and mortars gave us all the battering power we needed. On the next day I reported to Washington that the whole was in "awful activity."

That same day we received a message from the foreign consuls in Vera Cruz, asking for a truce to enable them, and their women and children to withdraw in safety. They had been warned earlier of the impending danger and I instructed them to retire on March 22nd. This they sullenly neglected, and the consuls had also declined the written *safe-guards* I had pressed upon them. The season was advanced and I was fully aware of several cases of yellow fever in the city and neighborhoods. Detachments of the enemy were arriving at our rear, and rumors spread among them that a formidable army would soon approach and challenge our siege. Tenderness for the women and children—in the form of delay—might, in its consequences, have led to the loss of the campaign. Hence I promptly replied to the consuls that no truce could be allowed except on an application of the governor, and that with a pledge to surrender.

Accordingly the next morning General Landero who had been put in supreme command at Vera Cruz offered to entertain the question of submission. Commissioners were appointed on both sides, and on the 27th the terms of surrender, including both the city and the Castle of Ulúa agreed upon, the pact was signed and exchanged. The Mexican garrison marched out, laying down their arms, and were sent home as prisoners of war on parole.

The surrender of the Castle of San Juan de Ulúa was involved in the fate of the city because the enemy had expected the castle would be the first object of attack, and relying on its impregnable strength, had neglected to lay in a supply of fresh water and provisions—as these could be sent over daily from the city. The capture of the city, therefore, placed the castle entirely at our mercy.

So the city and the castle capitulated on March 29th and the Republic's principal point of foreign commerce, five thousand prisoners, small arms, four hundred pieces of ordnance and large stores of ammunition were ours twenty days after our landing. This was all done with a loss of sixty-four officers and men killed or wounded. My official report was taken to Washington by Colonel Totten, of the engineers, who was duly breveted a brigadier general for his gallant service in the siege.

Fortunately the frequency of the *northers* had kept off the *vomito* epidemic, though a few cases had occurred in the city; but unfortunately their lack of horses and mules for transportation detained the body of the army from March 29th till the middle of April.

On April 8th we hitched up a train sufficient to put Brigadier General Twigg's division on the march into the interior. Major General Patterson, commanding a division of three volunteer brigades under Generals Pillow, Quitman and Shields was next supported and followed Twiggs. Draft animals and wagons continued to arrive very slowly and so Worth's division of regulars was temporarily detained. Each division of troops had instructions to take subsistence for six days in their wagons; and oats for horses equal to three, besides the usual number of cooked rations for men in haversacks.

These supplies were deemed indispensable to take the corps to Jalapa. Jalapa was a productive region, however, abounding in many articles of food as well as in mules. We were able to purchase some hundreds of these animals there and sent them back to bring up ammunition, medicine, hospital stores, clothing and bacon. Fresh beef was not always to be had.

The Castle of San Juan de Ulúa

I received a message that Twiggs, supported by Patterson, found himself confronted by the enemy at the Plan del Rio, some fifty miles from Vera Cruz in the interior. Twiggs requested that I come to their assistance, so I left Vera Cruz on April 12th with a small escort of cavalry under Captain Phil Kearney. Major General Patterson, though quite sick had assumed the overall command on joining Twiggs. When Patterson arrived no commander was ever received with heartier cheers because the troops knew he would not allow any aggressive move before my arrival.

The two divisions lay in the valley of the Plan del Rio. The body of the enemy was about three miles off, in the heights of Cerro Gordo. Reconnaissances were made in search of some practical route, other than the winding zigzag main artery which ran through the mountains with heavy enemy batteries at every turn.

These reconnaissances were conducted with vigor under Captain Robert E. Lee at the head of a body of pioneers, and at the end of the third day a passage for light batteries had been marked out—without alarming the enemy. Captain Lee's route provided the possibility of capturing Santa Anna's whole army, except his reserve which lay a mile or two higher up the road. Sometime after the battle Santa Anna said he didn't believe a goat could have approached him in that direction.

The time for attack, being at hand, and in order to insure harmony by letting all commands know what each was expected to execute, I issued the following order:

GENERAL ORDERS No. 111
Headquarters of the Army,

Plan Del Rio, April 17, 1847

The enemy's whole line of entrenchments and batteries will be attacked in front, and at the same time turned, early in the day tomorrow—probably before 10:00 AM.

The second (Twiggs's) division of regulars is already advanced within easy turning distance toward the enemy's left. That division has instructions to move forward before daylight tomorrow, and take up a position across the national road in the enemy's rear, so as to cut off a retreat toward Jalapa. It may be reinforced today, if unexpectedly attacked in force, by regiments—one or two—taken from Shields's brigade of volunteers. If not, the two volunteer regiments will march for that purpose at daylight tomorrow morning, under Brigadier General Shields, who will report to Brigadier General Twiggs on getting up with him, or to the general-in-chief; if he be in advance.

The remaining regiment of that volunteer brigade will receive instructions in the course of this day.

191

The first division of regulars (Worth's) will follow the movement against the enemy's left at sunrise tomorrow morning.

As already arranged, Brigadier General Pillow's brigade will march at six o'clock tomorrow morning, along the route he has carefully reconnoitered, and stand ready, as soon as he hears the report of arms on our right, or sooner, if circumstances should favor him, to pierce the enemy's line of batteries at such point—the nearer to the river the better—as he may select. Once in the rear of that line, he will turn to the right or left, or both, and attack the batteries in reverse, or, if abandoned, he will pursue the enemy with vigor until further orders.

Wall's field battery and the cavalry will be held in reserve on the national road, a little out of view and range of the enemy's batteries. They will take up that position at nine o'clock in the morning.

The enemy's batteries being carried or abandoned, all our divisions and corps will pursue with vigor.

This pursuit may be continued many miles, until stopped by darkness or fortified positions, toward Jalapa. Consequently, the body of the army will not return to this encampment; but be followed, tomorrow afternoon or early the next morning, by the baggage trains of the several corps. For this purpose, the feebler officers and men of each corps will be left to guard its camp and effects, and to load up the latter in the wagons of the corps. A commander of the present encampment will be designated in the course of this day.

As soon as it shall be known that the enemy's works have been carried, or that the general pursuit has been commenced, one wagon for each regiment and battery, and one for the cavalry, will follow the movement, to receive, under the direction of medical officers, the wounded and disabled, who will be brought back to this place for treatment in general hospital.

The surgeon general will organize this important service, and designate that hospital as well as the medical officers to be left at it. Every man who marches out to attack or pursue the enemy will take the usual allowance of ammunition, and subsistence for at least two days.

By Command of Major General Scott,

H. L. SCOTT
Adjutant General

The plan of attack outlined in General Orders No. 111 was executed by the army before 2:00 PM on April 18, 1847. We were quite surprised by the results of the victory—the large numbers of ordnance, field batteries, small arms and accouterments captured as well as the large number of prisoners. About 3000 men laid down their arms with the usual proportion of field and company officers, besides five generals, several of them of great distinction. A sixth general, Vasquez, was killed in defending the tower in the rear of the line of defense, the capture of which gave us those glorious results.

Our loss, though small, was serious. Brigadier General Shields, a gallant commander was mortally wounded. Twigg's division, followed by Shield's (now Colonel Baker's) brigade are now at Jalapa, and Worth's division is also in route there, all pursuing, with good results that part of the Mexican army, perhaps six or seven thousand men, that fled before our right had captured the tower and gained the Jalapa road.

Pillow's brigade was near me at the depot of wounded, sick and prisoners. I estimated that our total lost, killed or wounded might be about two hundred and fifty, and that of the enemy three hundred and fifty. In the pursuit towards Jalapa (twenty five miles away) I learned that we had added much to the enemy's loss in prisoners, killed and wounded. His retreating army was almost completely disorganized, and hence I made haste to follow, in an hour or two, to profit by events.

General Gideon Pillow

I must not omit to say that Brigadier General Twiggs, in passing the tower in the mountains beyond Cerro Gordo, detached a strong force to carry that height, which commanded the Jalapa road at the fort, and could not fail, if taken, to cut off the whole or any part of the enemy's forces from a retreat in any direction. This detachment was under the temporary command of Colonel Harney, 2nd Dragoons, during the confinement of Brevet Brigadier General Persifer F. Smith to his bed. The execution of the maneuver was most brilliant and decisive. The brigade ascended the long and difficult slope of Cerro Gordo without shelter, and under the tremendous fire of artillery and musketry. With the utmost steadiness they reached the breastworks, drove the enemy from them, planted the colors of the 1st Artillery, 3rd and 7th infantry—the enemy's flag still flying—and after some minutes of sharp firing, finished the conquest with their bayonets.

Worth's division of regulars came up at this time. Worth reached the tower a few minutes before me, and observing a white flag displayed by the enemy he sent our Colonels Harney and Childs to hold a parley. The surrender followed in an hour or two.

President Santa Anna, with Generals Canalizo and Ampudia, and some seven thousand men escaped towards Jalapa just before Cerro Gordo was taken and before Twigg's division reached the National Road above. I determined to parole the prisoners, officers and men, as I did not have the means of feeding them beyond the present, and could not afford to detach a heavy body of horses and wagons to accompany them to Vera Cruz.

I ordered the small arms and their accouterments, being of no value to our army, to be destroyed. We did not have the means to transport them. I was also somewhat embarrassed by the number of bronze artillery pieces which we had captured. It would have taken a brigade and half the mules of my army to transport them fifty miles.

The Mexicans were on the run. They had abandoned Jalapa, and I pushed Worth's division forward to tread on the heels of the fugitives and increase the panic. Approaching Perote, its formidable castle also opened its gates without firing a gun, and Worth's division took quiet possession of the great city of Puebla. But here things were put on hold for a while.

I had been obliged to leave respectable garrisons of regulars in Vera Cruz and the Castle of San Juan de Ulúa. And now at Jalapa, without having received any reinforcements, it became necessary to discharge some four thousand volunteers whose respective terms of service were about to expire. They gave notice that they would remain with me till the last day, but would then certainly demand discharges and the means of transportation homeward. As any delay might expose them to yellow fever at Vera Cruz the discharges were given at once.

We were delayed nearly a month at Jalapa waiting for supplies and troops from Vera Cruz. Not a company came. At length, towards the end of May I marched to join Worth's advanced division at Puebla—leaving a strong garrison at Jalapa, under Colonel Childs, to keep the communication path open with Vera Cruz as long as possible.

Waiting for reinforcements the halt at Puebla was protracted and irksome. The Benton intrigue had so disgusted a majority of the two houses of Congress, that the bill authorizing ten new regiments of regulars lingered from the beginning of December 1846 to the 11th of February 1847.

In the meantime the army was not inactive at Puebla. All the corps, amounting to about five thousand men were put through training exercises every day. We were also kept on the alert by an enemy army sometimes of superior numbers, hovering about us, often assuming a menacing attitude; but always ready for flight the moment they saw that we were under arms. On those occasions it was painful to restrain the ardor of the troops. I steadily held to the policy not to wear out the patience and sole leather of my troops by running to the left or right in the pursuit of small game. I played for the big stakes. Keeping the army massed and our minds fixed upon the capital, I meant to content myself with beating whatever force that might stand directly in the way of that conquest—being morally sure that all smaller objects would soon follow that crowning event.

The city of Puebla, graced by a fine, flowing river, was near the center of a valley of uncommon fertility and beauty, producing, annually, two abundant crops for the subsistence of men and animals—one by rains, and the other by artificial irrigation. All the cereals—wheat, barley, maize and rye; all the grasses, including clover, lucerne, and timothy, and all the fruit-trees—the apple, peach, apricot and pear, grow here as well as in the region of Frederick, Maryland—the elevation (nearly seven thousand feet above ocean level) making a difference in climate, equal to eighteen or twenty degrees of latitude. Many objects within the horizon of Puebla are among the sublimest features of nature. The white peak of Orizaba, the most distant, may always be seen in bright weather. The Malinche mountain, near by, is generally capped with snow; Popocatapetl and his white sister, always, since the first snow fell after the creation. The city itself; with her hundred steeples and cathedral, in majestic repose—seen from a certain elevation, is itself a magnificent object in the general landscape.

During this halt, every corps of the army in succession, made a most interesting excursion of six miles, to the ruins of the ancient city of Cholula, long, in point of civilization and art, the Etruria of this continent, and in respect to religion, the Mecca of many of the earliest tribes known to tradition. Down to the time of Cortes, a little more than three hundred years before the Americans, Cholula, containing an ingenious and peaceable population of perhaps one hundred and fifty thousand souls, impressed with a *unique* type of civilization, had fallen off in 1847, to a miserable hamlet, its towers and dwellings of sun-baked bricks and stucco, in heaps of ruins. From these melancholy wrecks are yet disinterred productions of art of great beauty and delicacy, in metals and porcelain, both for ornament and use. The same people also manufactured cloths of cotton and the fibre of the agave plant.

One grand feature, denoting the ancient grandeur of Cholula, stands but little affected by the lapse of perhaps thousands of years—a pyramid built of alternate layers of brick and clay, some two hundred feet in height, with a square basis of more than forty acres, running up to a plateau of seventy yards square. There stood in the time of Cortes, the great pagan temple of the Cholulans, with a perpetual blazing fire on its altar, seen in the night many miles around. This the Spaniards soon replaced by a *bijou* of a church, something larger than the *Casa Santa* at Loretto, with a beautiful altar and many pictures. The ascent to this plateau is by a flight of some hundred and forty steps.

The prosperity of Cholula, in 1520, was already on the decline, having recently fallen under the harsh rule of the Montezumas, and it now sustained a heavy blow at the hands of Cortes, an invited guest, who, to punish a detected conspiracy, that was intended to compass the destruction of his entire army, massacred more than six thousand of the inhabitants, including most of the chiefs, besides destroying entire streets of houses.

One bright morning in June, as an admirer of scenery, and curious to view the ruins of Cholula, I suddenly determined to overtake a line brigade of regulars that had left for that excursion half an hour earlier. Even escorted by a squadron of cavalry this was an enterprise not without some danger, considering that I could make no movement without causing several citizens to fly off at full speed, on fine Andalusian horses, to report the fact to detachments of cavalry lurking in the vicinity.

Coming up with the brigade marching at ease,[16] all intoxicated with the fine air and splendid scenery, I was, as usual, received with hearty and protracted cheers. The group of officers who surrounded me, differed widely in the objects of their admiration—some preferring this or that snow-capped mountain, others the city, and several the pyramid of Cholula, that was now opening upon the view. An appeal from all was made to me as general-in-chief. I emphatically replied: "I differ from you all. My greatest delight is in this fine body of troops, without whom we can never sleep in the Halls of the Montezumas, or in our own homes." The word was caught up by some of the rank and file, marching abreast, and passed rapidly to the front and rear of the column, each platoon, in succession, rending the air with its acclamation.

Finally reinforcements began to arrive. Lieutenant Colonel McIntosh with some 800 men, escorting a large train was delayed by the enemy in his march near Jalapa. He was soon joined by Brigadier General Cadwallader with a portion of his brigade and a field battery. They swept away the enemy and the two detachments arrived safely at Puebla. Major General Pillow followed with another detachment of a thousand men; and finally Brigadier General Pierce arrived on August 6th with a brigade of 2500 men.

About this time when General Taylor had more troops than he could use and yet clamored bitterly for additional reinforcements—I was obliged, through paucity of numbers, to call out the garrison from Jalapa, under Colonel Childs, to make up my force at Puebla (including the late reinforcements) to about 14,000 men, of whom 2500 were sick (mostly diarrhea cases) and about 600 convalescents too feeble for a

---

16   Troops, marching at ease, bear their arms on either shoulder or in either hand, always keeping the muzzles of their arms up, and are at liberty to talk, laugh, sing or crack their jokes to their heart's content - only taking care not to confound their ranks.

day's march. We had to throw away the scabbard and to advance with the naked blade in hand.

The composition of my fighting corps was as follows:

Division	Brigade	Regiment
I. Brevet Major General Worth's Division.	1. Colonel Garland's Brigade.	2nd & 3rd of Artillery, serving as Infantry.
		4th of Infantry.
		Duncan's Field Battery.
	2. Colonel Clarke's Brigade.	5th, 6th and 8th Regiment of Infantry.
II. Brevet Major General Twigg's Division.	1. Brevet Brigadier General Persifer F. Smith's Brigade.	Rifle Regiment.
		1st Regiment of Artillery, serving as Infantry.
		3rd Regiment of Infantry.
		Taylor's Light Battery.
	2. Colonel Riley's Brigade	4th Regiment of Artillery, serving as Infantry.
		1st and 7th Regiment of Infantry.
III. Major General Pillow's Division.	Brigadier General G. Cadwallader's Brigade.	Voltigeurs.
		11th and 14th Infantry.
		A Light Battery.
	Brigadier General Pierce's Brigade.	9th, 12th and 15th Infantry.
IV. Major General Quitman's Division	Brigadier General Shield's Brigade.	New York Volunteers.
		South Carolina Volunteers.

	Lieutenant Colonel Watson's Brigade.	2nd Pennsylvania Volunteers.
		Detachment of U.S. Marines.
Detached	Colonel Harney's Brigade.	1st, 2nd and 3rd Light Dragoons.

On August 7, 1847 the first elements of this army marched out of Puebla led by Harney's Dragoons and followed by Twiggs's division. Quitman's Volunteers left on the 8th, Worth's division on the 9th and Pillow's Volunteers brought up the rear. I traveled with Quitman's division. On Tuesday, August 10th my lead division under Twiggs approached the Rio Frio mountain which I expected to find defended by Mexican troops, but there were none to be seen. We moved up to the crest of the mountain only a few hours away.

We were standing at a point 3000 feet above the floor of the valley which itself was 7000 feet above sea level. It afforded a spectacular view of the spires of the City of Mexico, some twenty-five miles distant. Two great volcanoes could be seen rising a full 7000 feet above the rim of the surrounding hills. As I sat astride my horse I saw not a panorama but a prize, "The object of all my dreams and hopes—toils and dangers. **This Splendid City Shall be Ours!**"

Meanwhile Santa Anna was feverishly preparing to defend the city against my advance. He brought General Valencia's Army of the North at San Luis Potosí down to a position just north of Lake Texcoco to guard the city from an attack from the North. To augment Valencia Santa Anna sent for the Army of the South and the garrison at the City of Mexico which each comprised some 10,000 men. His force was now something in excess of 25,000 men. He gambled that I would continue my approach along the National Road. He concentrated his main defense on a hill called El Peñon which dominated this route. Santa Anna and his staff came to El Peñon and personally climbed to the top amidst the cheers of his people.

On Wednesday, August 11th David Twiggs's division arrived at Buena Vista. I accompanied him so that I could make a final decision on the three routes I might take from Buena Vista to the City of Mexico. I had designated two officers, Major William Turnbull and Captain Robert E. Lee, to study the routes and report. Based on their studies I decided to turn south at Buena Vista. Twiggs was to continue westward to the small town of Ayotla and study the defenses of El Peñon. Once Twiggs had passed Buena Vista, heading for El Peñon, I sent Worth, who was following Twiggs, to reconnoiter the route that ran south of Lakes Chalco and Xochimilco.

On August 12th Worth was at the town of Chalco with Pillow's division behind him. I was still not sure that the southern route should be followed. I ordered Lee to confirm my conclusions. He immediately went out and returned late on the 13th convinced that the information he and Turnbull had put together was accurate. Lee estimated that Santa Anna had placed 7000 troops at El Peñon and 30 cannon; a force comparable in size to my entire army. Not willing to take the position I ordered Lee and his men to continue scouting for other routes.

By August 15th I decided that I would turn southward at Buena Vista and follow the secondary road which ran south of both Lake Xochimilco and Lake Chalco about seven miles south of Ayotla joining the Acapulco Road a major artery south of the capital. With this change of direction Worth's division was now leading, leaving Twiggs to create a diversion at El Peñon.

My scouting parties were hardly any secret to the Mexicans. On August 14th their spies indicated that I would by-pass El Peñon. Santa Anna didn't want to believe the news, his mind set to defend the National Road at that point. On August 16th, however, his force clashed with elements of Twiggs's division that was marching eastward, not westward, away from El Peñon. Santa Anna was whipped and he marched his badly demoralized men back into the City of Mexico.

The Churubusco River, really a canal, flowed from the west into the north end of Lake Xochimilco about five miles south of the City of Mexico. Its steep banks were almost impossible to cross except by a bridge. Only three such bridges crossed the Churubusco and they were all located within two miles of each other. Santa Anna and his men crossed the river to meet me on the south bank. Just a few miles south of the Churubusco Canal lays a fearsome volcanic lava bed known as the Pedregal, whose jagged lava surface renders it almost impossible to traverse. Infantry could cross with difficulty but supporting artillery and supplies could not. The Pedregal extended five miles in an east-west direction across which no road ran. Two roads run north and south around it. One, the Acapulco Road on the east, was the main artery. The

San Angel Road ran at the west end of the Pedregal, far out of the way, and beyond the sleepy hamlet of Contreras, otherwise known as San Geronimo. Santa Anna could block both roads by holding the town of San Antonio in the east and San Angel in the west.

Assuming that I would approach the capital via the Acapulco Road Santa Anna placed the bulk of his forces there. He also moved his single strongest force, the 5500 men of General Valencia to Coyoacán, a town halfway between the Acapulco and San Angel roads, where he would be able to reinforce Mexican forces holding either the east or west road. Santa Anna had a good plan but it fell through because General Valencia protested his orders to move to Coyoacán. He said the threat along the San Angel Road was a real one and that he should take a position further down that road at the town of San Angel. Santa Anna relented and gave his permission for Valencia to occupy San Angel. Even then Valencia wasn't satisfied. He moved his division another four miles down the San Angel Road to a hill in the vicinity of the Indian village of Padierna, north of the town of Contreras.

On Wednesday, August 18, Worth's division reached San Augustín Tlalpam on the Acapulco Road. At that point Worth turned north and headed towards San Antonio with the City of Mexico eight miles beyond. When Worth approached the town of San Antonio he found the only approach to the town consisted of a long narrow causeway with deep water on both sides. It looked like a dangerous situation so I decided to order Worth to halt in place and merely "threaten" San Antonio. By now the way to the capital was blocked and my army was running out of supplies. It was discouraging to see the road lined with men, horses, and wagons—the men without tents, the evenings cold, and everything menaced by heavy rain.

Even as Worth was probing San Antonio I sent an exploratory mission across the southern rim of the Pedregal to find a route that could carry my army from the Acapulco Road westward to the San Angel Road. For this mission I sent Lee, Beauregard, Tower and Major Larkin Smith, my chief engineer. My men brought back some encouraging news. At Peñe Pobre, a village 1.5 miles west of San Agustin Tlalpam they found a passable road. They followed the road for some time and reached a crest near a peak called Zacatapec. There Lee encountered a small group of Mexican cavalry and, after a brief skirmish, had deposed them. From that point Lee could see the village of Padierna on the San

Angel Road. Lee concluded that the Mexican cavalry came from the San Angel turnpike so that the road was probably passable all the way. I decided that this would be our viable travel route.

On Thursday, August 19th, I sent out a construction crew of 500 men from Pillow's division. Under the supervision of the engineers they were to build a road westward across the Pedregal. I did not intend this to be a fighting force. For this I sent Twiggs and his men. Pillow's men were to provide the work detail and Twiggs was "thrown farther out in front to cover the operation." This arrangement worked fairly well until about 1:00 PM in the afternoon when work was halted near the peak of Zacatapec due to heavy Mexican artillery fire. A strong enemy position—estimated at twenty-two heavy-caliber guns—was situated across a steep ravine, atop a hill near the obscure Indian village called Padierna and northeast of Contreras. We did not know it at the time but the position was occupied by some 7,000 men under the Mexican General Gabriel Valencia. We also did not know that another large force led by Santa Anna had followed Valencia down the San Angel Road to a position about four miles from him.

With this turn of events Lee returned to San Agustín Tlalpam to report to me. I sensed that something was wrong so I rode up to an observation point near Zacatapec. I arrived about 4:00 PM only to discover that a battle was underway. Since Lee had left the work party to report to me, Gideon Pillow committed troops without my authority at the first sign of hostile action. He ordered two artillery batteries under Captain John B. Magruder and Lieutenant F. D. Callender to haul their guns to a point where they could fire at the Mexican batteries. The exchange went on for about an hour before the heavier Mexican guns knocked them out of action. Pillow also sent two companies of mounted rifles for mop-up operations. He did not stop to think that such a formidable volume of Mexican artillery might be part of a major formation. The two companies were repulsed, not surprisingly, and they were unable to return from their exposed position. They therefore remained in position between Mexican General Gabriel Valencia at Padierna and Magruder's batteries.

Pillow then rode up to Colonel Bennet Riley, of Twiggs's division, and ordered him to cross the Pedregal. Riley, an experienced professional, asked the general if his own commander, Gwneral Twiggs, knew of the order. Pillow lied and said that he did, so Riley led his brigade across the lava beds of the Pedregal and down across the ravine, and seized the hamlet of Contreras at its base. He then continued to a spot between the two wings of the threatening Mexican army and reconnoitered the territory in order to send information back to Twiggs and Pillow.

In the meantime Pillow became aware of Riley's danger and when he realized that Riley was out of contact he attempted to reinforce him. He sent Cadwalader's brigade and Morgan's 15th Infantry in the direction Riley went, while he stayed at Zacatapec. Then Persifer Smith, sensing Pillow's indecision as to what to do next, took his brigade without orders across the Pedregal where he found the other brigade. He then assumed command of all the troops in the area.

By this time I became aware of the situation and sent Shield's brigade to join Persifer Smith. I also gave orders that Valentia's position must not be attacked during daylight hours. I returned to my headquarters at San Augustín Tlalpam. From here on Gideon Pillow was out of the picture. I communicated solely with Persifer Smith by personal messenger. Brigadier General Persifer Smith, now commanding nearly half of my army was a natural born soldier. He caught my eye some time back in Florida when he commanded the Louisiana Volunteers and lately when he distinguished himself at Monterey under Taylor.

When Smith arrived at Contreras and assumed command he had Cadwalader's brigade and Morgan's regiment, but he soon located Riley as well. Smith realized that his command was in peril facing General Gabriel Valencia on the south and a major buildup of Mexican troops threatening from a point less than a mile up the San Angel Road. Rather than wait for these forces to squeeze him, he planned to attack. He would assault the northern force leaving only a small force to guard against General Valencia in his rear. By the time he got into position it was too late in the day and darkness was falling. Smith therefore postponed the attack and consulted with Colonel Bennet Riley. The conversation was invaluable because Riley had found a way around to the rear of Valencia's position that had escaped the Mexican's notice. Smith decided to use this route and attack Valentia at daybreak.

General Smith ordered Lee to return to Zacatapec and inform me of his plans, and requesting a diversionary attack on Valentia's front. Lee, along with a few of his men, groped through the black night over the rocks of the Pedregal in a storm. Luckily the storm also provided intermittent lightning that illuminated the trail and Lee's main guidepost, the peak of Zacatapec. Finding me gone he continued on for three more miles to my headquarters at San Augustín Tlalpam arriving at 11:00 PM. I was delighted to receive Lee's news. Throughout the evening I had sent out messengers to find Smith but they all gave up in the darkness and peril of the Pedregal. I was enthusiastic about Smith's plans and held a council with Pillow, Twiggs, and Lee. I decided that the action near Padierna would be my main effort. I sent word to Worth to withdraw from San Antonio and follow Pillow's command to the west. On my invitation Pillow remained at my command post for the night. Twiggs, however, insisted on rejoining his division, so I sent Robert Lee with him. Twiggs and Pillow were to find troops to conduct the diversion that Smith had requested. Eventually Lee found Franklin Pierce's brigade near Zacatapec and after some difficulty got Pierce's men placed into position.

During the night Shields found Persifer Smith and though he was the senior officer he yielded to Smith's familiarity with the terrain. Smith posted Shields at Contreras to watch the Mexican forces to the north, while he and Riley made preparations for the early morning attack on General Valentia. At 3:00 AM the next morning Smith's force led by Riley's brigade began their march around to the rear of Valentia's position. Following Riley was part of Cadwalader's brigade followed by Morgan's regiment.

Valentia's men were in no condition to fight a major battle. Feeling the effects of a drunken brawl brought upon by Valentia's illusion that they had won a major battle the previous day. They were also suffering from the cold rain and frightened by the fact that the Mexican force they had seen coming to their rescue from the north had withdrawn. Some of the Mexican soldiers decided to desert before dawn broke. By dawn the rain had ceased and the sun was up and Smith's forces had not been detected.

At 6:00 AM the Americans struck. The slaughter lasted seventeen minutes. Valentia's men offered no resistance. They ran in every direction. Many of them were intercepted by Shields at Contreras. We pursued the fugitives all the way to San Angel. At that point the operation now known as the battle of Contreras was over. Pillow rode into San Angel to reassume command of his division. The battle of Contreras was a resounding victory for my army. Persifer Smith's 4500 men had shattered Valencia's 7000, all this going on with another 12,000 Mexicans under Santa Anna within easy striking distance.

One of Santa Anna's attributes was his ability to recover from devastating military defeats. He knew when his troops would fight and when they would not. After his defeat at Contreras he withdrew the bulk of his army to the City of Mexico, leaving only minimal forces at the Churubusco River crossings located at Coyoacán and at points north of San Angel. Any battle engagement at the bridges would only be a delaying tactic. As I rode through San Angel towards Coyoacán I had much to decide. I ordered Worth to recall whatever units he had sent behind Twiggs to turn once more to the north on the Acapulco Road towards San Antonio. Quitman was to follow him. I told Worth he was not to attack until Pillow's division, coming around the north end of the Pedregal from the west, should take the Mexican position at San Antonio in the rear.

When I reached Coyoacán I ordered attacks on two objectives, (1) the San Mateo convent and (2) the bridgehead over the Churubusco, about 300 yards apart. I gave priority to the convent and threw four brigades against that position. Two of them, Persifer Smith's and Riley's came from Twiggs's division. To surround the convent and cut off the garrison's retreat, I sent a mixed group under Shield's command to cross the Churubusco at Portales and then to turn southward to attack the convent in the rear. Since Pillow had been sent down the Acapulco Road to take San Antonio in the rear the bridgehead would have to be neglected in the early part of the operation. I followed Twiggs as he made the main effort.

The battle of Churubusco was vicious. The walls of the San Mateo Convent were solid and the defenders were determined. Over 200 men of the San Patricio Battalion, American soldiers mostly Irish, who had deserted the American Army and had joined to fight for Mexico faced us. After two hours of fighting the convent held firm. To the south of San Antonio Worth became tired of waiting for Pillow to arrive. He therefore sent one brigade under Colonel N. S. Clarke westward into the Pedregal around San Antonio. Clarke made good progress and soon returned to the Acapulco Road, to discover that the Mexican Garrison had departed leaving the way clear. This was reported to Worth who immediately started north with Cadwalader's brigade of Pillow's division and succeeded in taking the bridgehead within a half hour.

Shields and Pierce, attacking the convent from the north ran into a strong force at Portales, north of the river. I immediately sent a rifle regiment and some cavalry troops to Shield's support, as I was with General Twiggs at the time. That attack being successful, Shields was able to turn on the convent with his six brigades and Worth's division in support. The San Mateo convent surrendered, thus bringing the bloody battle to an end.

By the evening of August 20, 1847 I was satisfied that the battle of Churubusco was over. My men were utterly exhausted from almost two full days of battle, so I made no attempt to enter the City of Mexico at that time. I moved my headquarters from San Augustín Thalpam to the Bishop's Palace overlooking the town of Tacubaya. I sent a note to Santa Anna demanding that he surrender the capital without the need for a fight.

Santa Anna was aware that his disorganized army was incapable of repulsing an American assault, but he also realized that we were desperate to end the fighting in Mexico. He instructed his Minister of Foreign Relations Don Francisco Pacheco, to write a formal reply to Secretary of State James Buchanan's message of the previous April. Everybody realized that it would take weeks before an answer could arrive from Washington. Santa Anna also wrote a note to Nicholas Trist asking that my army be restrained from entering the City of Mexico. At the same time he informed the Spanish Minister of his actions and sought the support of Edward Thornton and Edward Mackintosh of the British legation.

Santa Anna chose General Ignacio Mora y Villamil to carry his dispatch to Trist. Mora rode out from the city on the 21st in a carriage. He encountered me with a flag of truce at Coyoacán south of the Churubusco River, as I was busily supervising the emplacement of an artillery position. I stopped my labors to examine the message, and rejected it out of hand. Pacheco was too arrogant in my mind. He had proposed a truce lasting a full year—absolutely out of the question. I knew Trist would agree with me.

General Mora intimated that Santa Anna would welcome my suspension of hostilities. I consulted with Trist and together we wrote a counterproposal calling for a much shorter truce. I appointed Quitman, Pierce and Persifer Smith as Commissioners to negotiate it, along with

Trist. Santa Anna seized the moment and by August 23rd an agreement was reached, to take effect on the 25th.

The provisions of the truce called for all hostilities to cease in a radius of 78 miles around the City of Mexico. Either side could terminate the truce with a notice of 48 hours. Neither side was to reinforce his position during the truce. We were to allow the passage of supplies through the gates into the city and American quartermasters were to be allowed to purchase provisions within the city. I agreed to release all Mexican prisoners-of-war. I don't think my men were happy with the truce. Most of them were anxious to destroy Santa Anna and enter the City of Mexico while he was still off balance. They were not aware of our low level of supply and my need to preserve a legitimate government in Mexico.

The Mexican civilians also resented the truce. On August 27th a convoy of supply wagons from my army was turned back at the gates to the city. Santa Anna quickly sent out a delegation to apologize and assure me that such an infraction would not occur again. On August 28th another encounter took place. An American convoy escorted by Mexican lancers entered the city only to be turned back by a mob of ugly Mexicans. Several American teamsters were wounded and two wagons were lost. The Mexican people vented their fury on Santa Anna as well. "Death to Santa Anna" was shouted as much as "Death to the Yankees."

Santa Anna arranged for supplies to be delivered to me by night with pack mules substituted for wagons, and escorted by Mexican troops. The new arrangement worked well as far as I could tell. But Santa Anna was up to no good. On August 31st Inspector General Ethan A. Hitchcock heard rumors that some 18,000 men had been assembled in the city which were reviewed by Santa Anna at the plaza. We took no action and supplies and specie continued to flow and the truce remained in effect.

During the lull I had to decide on the disposition of the 72 San Patricio deserters captured at Churubusco. The offense of desertion called for the death penalty by hanging. The prospect of hanging a man repulsed me. I placed all the prisoners before a court martial. One court sat at Tacubaya presided over by Colonel John Garland and the other presided over by Colonel Bennet Riley sat at San Angel. Seventy of the seventy-two were found guilty and sentenced to hang. I felt some pressure to evaluate the details of the case. I sat up late at night to find excuses to commute the death penalty. I finally approved the death penalty for 50 San Patricios. I pardoned five men and reduced the sentences of fifteen others, including John Riley who was considered the ringleader of the deserters. Riley had deserted from Zachary Taylor's army at Matamoros before war had been officially declared in May 1846. The sentences were scheduled to be carried out in early September.

On the evening of September 3rd, 1847 Hitchcock reported that Trist came out of his peace meeting looking dispirited and haggard. No meeting was held on the 4th. On the 5th I left my quarters at the Bishop's Palace at Tacubaya and on the 6th I concluded that all efforts to conclude peace had failed and I issued the forty-eight hour notice.

I now considered myself free to hold a council of war to discuss the routes the army might take in approaching the City of Mexico. I had been observing a set of flat roofed buildings located about a thousand yards to the east of Chapultepec. The cluster was called the Molino del Rey, or the King's Mill. Rumors had said it was a cannon foundry, and the Mexicans, I heard, were planning to use it to cast new artillery pieces. The mill was reported to be lightly defended, if at all. On the afternoon of the 7th I received word that Mexican troops had been spotted moving from Chapultepec to the mill. I decided it was time to attack. I sent for Worth, whose division was located at Tacubaya.

Worth agreed that he could take the Molino del Rey with no difficulty. He turned down my suggestion of making an attack at night. I conceded the point and attached Cadwalader's brigade, Sumner's dragoons and Duncan's field artillery batteries to him. Worth would attack in the morning. I remained at a vantage point near Tacubaya. We did not know that Santa Anna had reinforced the mill and its nearby outpost, the Casa Mata. He had brought up five infantry brigades, supported by artillery. He placed a cavalry force of 4000 men to cover the position to the west.

It took Worth two hours to take the mill and the nearby Casa Mata, but his losses were appalling. Worth lost 116 dead including Major Martin Scott and Captain Kerby Smith of the 5th Infantry. Colonel J. S. McIntosh, the 2nd Brigade Commander, and Major C. A. Waite, the Commander of the 8th Infantry fell seriously wounded. Worth's total losses came to 787 officers and men. No iron foundry was found at the Molino. The battle of Molino del Rey was, in my estimation, one of the great tragedies of the Mexican war.

I had to put aside my feelings and concentrate on capturing the capital. The lands south of the City of Mexico were swampy and Santa Anna had flooded them further. Any approach towards the City of Mexico would have to be made along one or more of the causeways that led out from the various city gates. The causeways consisted of stone aqueducts with double lane roads on each side and were defended at many points along their lengths. There were five serviceable causeways as follows:

Number	Causeway	Location	Gate
1	Belén	Runs northeast and then east from Chapultepec.	Garita de San Cosme.
2	La Verónica	Runs northeast from Chapultepec.	Garita de Belén.
3	Piedad	Runs north from San Piedad.	Runs into Belén Causeway.
4	Niño Perdido	Runs north a thousand yards east and parallel with the Piedad Causeway.	Garita de Niño Perdido.
5	San Antonio	Runs north from Cherubusco parallel with the Niño Perdido Causeway.	Garita de San Antonio.

My engineers favored using one of the three southern approaches in order to avoid having to take Chapultepec Castle. On September 9th, the day after the battle of Molino del Rey I took Captain Lee with me to the Niño Perdido Causeway. From there we could study the San Antonio Causeway. We could see the Mexicans hauling up artillery to protect the gates. It took me two days to reach a decision as what I would do. On the evening of September 11, 1857 I called my staff together in the small town of Piedad. I started the meeting by stating up front my feelings on the subject. I said the marshy conditions surrounding the causeways at the southern approaches to the city would preclude their choice. I thought it best to take Chapultepec and then follow the Belén and La Verónica Causeways into the City of Mexico from the west. I was supported by South Carolina Captain Benjamin Huger, who thought that Chapultepec would fall in the course of one day's bombardment.

Captain Lee disagreed with me and argued for the southern approach. I called for a vote. Only Twiggs and Lieutenant Beauregard sided with me. After the vote Beauregard rose to present his argument. So convincing was he in arguing for the Chapultepec route that General Pierce switched his vote. I was, however, not running an election so I stood up and declared, "Gentlemen, we will attack by the western gates. The general officers present here will remain for further orders—the meeting is dismissed!"

On September 12th I devoted my efforts to supervise the bombardment of Chapultepec, hoping to avoid the need for an assault. At the end of the day the castle was damaged but still capable of defense. I ordered my army to storm the castle on the next morning, September 13th. The Chapultepec position also included a large rectangular field surrounding it. The area was protected by high walls, three quarters of a mile long and a quarter mile wide. The Chapultepec hill occupied the eastern half of the rectangle and the western half between the hill and Molino del Rey was covered by a grove of ancient cyprus trees. The cyprus grove sheltered the source of water for the castle. The castle itself only held about three hundred defenders at most. When Santa Anna visited the castle on the 12th he even questioned the wisdom of holding the position. Its commander, General Nicholas Bravo, hero of the Mexican Revolution of 1821, was determined to defend Chapultepec to the death, however.

Two roads led to Chapultepec from the south, both starting out at Tacubaya. The secondary road ran from Tacubaya to the Molino del Rey and the main road ran past the southeast corner of the Chapultapec wall and connected with the Belén Causeway. Worth's division would ordinarily have received the honor for the main attack but because of the stress his men had undergone four days earlier I moved Pillow's division to Tacubaya during the evening of the 11th. The next morning Pillow moved forward on the secondary road and re-occupied the mill which Worth had evacuated after taking it on the 8th. When the attack on Chapultapec was launched on the 12th, Worth was ordered to follow Pillow as a reserve and support.

I assigned the main road to Quitman's division much of whom had seen no significant action. Quitman was brought up from San Augustín Tlalpam on the 11th. Thus on that night the bulk of my divisions were in the vicinity of Tacubaya. Twiggs's men were assigned the task of making a demonstration at the San Antonio gate during the morning of the attack so as to draw attention from the main thrust.

At 5:30 AM on September 13th my artillery opened fire on all parts of the Chapultapec compound. The bombardment was lifted at 8:00 AM to permit the movement of troops to begin. Pillow advanced with Cadwalader's brigade leading and Pierce's brigade falling behind. Cadwalader sent Colonel William Trousdale with two Infantry regiments and two field artillery batteries up the Belén Causeway to the northern edge of the Chapultapec confine. His mission was to prevent reinforcement of the position from the north and escape from the castle. At the same time the 9th and 15th Infantry (or Voltiguers as they were called) crossed the wall, going through the grove. Major T. P. Andrenos took one battalion inside the southern wall and Major Joseph Johnston took another to a point beyond the Cyprus grove. There, after destroying a Mexican redoubt, Johnston led his battalion through a gap at the foot of the Chapultapec hill. He quickly subdued two other redoubts inside the enclosure, leaving the winding road up to the summit of the hill open.

Early in the action Gideon Pillow sent a message back to me at Tacubaya that Worth's division should be brought forward to Molino del Rey to support him on short notice. I agreed and sent out a messenger only to learn that Worth had already left Tacubaya on his own volition.

Colonel T. B. Ransom commanding the 9th Infantry fell dead from a shot in the forehead while leading his troops forward. Pillow was hit in the ankle with a painful but not serious wound. Dragged to safety he called for Worth to make great haste or else it would be too late. Soon Pillow's troops were reinforced by Norman Clarke's brigade from Worth's division. On the Tacubaya road Quitman's assault party were held up about a hundred yards from the Mexican batteries guarding the southeastern gateway to Chapultapec. Quitman sent Persifer Smith's brigade to attack from the east but he was unable to do much except to brush aside a few skirmishers. Quitman finally sent the New York, Pennsylvania, and South Carolina regiments to the west where they passed through the gap in the wall opened earlier by Johnston. There they met with elements of Clarke's brigade.

The walls of the castle had been reached and the men were fairly safe. Mexican artillery could not hit the bottom of the walls. When the ladders arrived they were lined up fifty abreast. The assault troops scaled them. Two officers were killed but eventually Captain Joseph Howard, of the Voltiguers gained the parapet. Captain McKenzie followed soon after. By 9:30 AM, less than two hours after the assault began, the flag of Johnston's Voltiguers flew above Chapultepec Castle.

When I rode up the Tacubaya road toward the Belén Causeway my men pressed round. I told them how glad I was; how proud I was of them; and how proud their country, their wives, their sisters and their sweethearts would be; and it seemed if such cheering had never been heard anywhere in the world before.

There were a few tragic outcomes of the battle. We learned that fifty or so young Mexican cadets had insisted on remaining to defend Chapultepec Castle. Though most survived six did not. One young man jumped off the steep vertical east wall of the castle clutching a Mexican flag at his breast. On the same day the last of 30 of the San Patricio Battalion soldiers were scheduled for execution at the direction of Colonel William S. Harney. He placed each man with noose attached on a mule cart facing the Chapultepec Castle. When Harney and the men of the San Patricio saw the American flag rise above the walls of the castle the executioners were given the order to give the mules a whack. The prisoners screamed in horror as the noose took their lives.

It was still late morning and we had to advance. I sent orders to Worth at the northwest corner of the castle to get on the La Veronica Causeway and Quitman at the southeast corner to get on the Belén Causeway and start their advance toward the City of Mexico. I accompanied Worth as we marched toward the Garita de San Cosme. During the afternoon I sent Quitman several messages urging caution. Santa Anna had retreated to the Belén gate after the fall of Chapultepec, and conferred with General Andrés Terrés the local commander. While there Santa Anna brought up some artillery pieces up from the Piedad road and then headed for the San Cosmo gate without advising General Terrés what his responsibilities were.

Santa Anna, now stationed at the San Cosme gate, soon learned of the loss of the Belén gate. He hurried back with three Infantry battalions to face Quitman but he was unable to retake the gate. In his rage he relieved Terrés and placed him under court martial. It was now dark and both Worth and Quitman settled down for the night each in possession of a gate. Of the two Worth's prospects for taking the City of Mexico were better than Quitman's, because the Mexican Citadel did not lay in his path. I returned to my headquarters at Tacubaya for a good night's rest.

At 4:00 AM the next morning my slumber was interrupted by a delegation of Mexican officials who requested to see me under a white flag. They explained to me that earlier Santa Anna had called a meeting at the Citadel. In view of his weakened position he had decided to evacuate the city. By 1:00 AM on Tuesday, September 14th, Santa Anna's army was on its way to Guadalupe. I considered the delegation's request for surrender and specified that it be unconditional. I also levied a penalty of $150,000 to be paid in gold. (I was determined to recoup some of my money!) I joined Worth at the Alameda, ready for the triumphant entry into the Plaza of the City of Mexico. Harney's musicians played "Yankee Doodle." Even the Mexicans could not restrain themselves from a bit of applause. In the plaza we found Quitman's men who had arrived an hour earlier. I solemnly and formally reviewed all the troops of Worth and Quitman. I dismounted and entered the Plaza by the main doorway, and I announced, "Let me present to you the civil and military governor of the City of Mexico, Major General John A. Quitman. I appoint him this instant. He has earned the distinction and he shall have it."

The following order was published early for the army:

GENERAL ORDERS No. 286

Headquarters of the Army,
National Palace of Mexico.
September 1847

The general-in-chief calls upon his brethren in arms to return, both in public and private worship, thanks and gratitude to God for the signal triumphs which they have recently achieved for their country.

Beginning with the 19th of August, and ending on the 14th of September, this army has gallantly fought its way through the fields and forts of Contreras, San Antonio, Churubusco, Molino del Rey, Chapultepec, and the gates of San Cosme and Tacubaya or Belén, into the capital of Mexico.

When the very limited numbers who have performed those brilliant deeds shall have become known, the world will be astonished, and our own countrymen filled with joy and admiration.

But all is not yet done. The enemy, though scattered and dismayed, has still many fragments of his late army hovering about us, and, aided by an exasperated population, he may again reunite in treble our numbers, and fall upon us to advantage if we rest inactive on the security of our past victories.

Compactness, vigilance, and discipline are, therefore, our only securities. Let every good officer and man look to those cautions and enjoin them upon all others.

By command of Major General Scott

H. L. SCOTT
Adjutant General

The first task to pacify the streets of the city was more difficult than I anticipated. Santa Anna, had, before leaving, released thousands of prisoners and convicts from the city's prisons and a large number of them were armed. The city officials did their utmost to urge the people of the city to cease resistance. The church officials cooperated eagerly with the civilian authorities. By October 1st, two weeks after I had entered the city, a reasonable degree of peace was restored.

Though Santa Anna had fled the City of Mexico I did not regard his flight as signaling the end of the war. Santa Anna was still up to his tricks and took a force of 5,700 men to Puebla, intent on destroying the American garrison there. On September 21, having surrounded the city, he issued an ultimatum to Colonel C. F. Childs. Childs stood firm and Santa Anna, unable to make his dispirited men attack settled for a siege which eventually evaporated. The temporary Mexican President Manuel Peña y Peña ordered Santa Anna to abandon his command and face a court martial. For a while Santa Anna considered rebelling against the government, but when he found no support for such an undertaking he went into hiding at a small spa some 70 miles southwest of Puebla. He later escaped to Jamaica.

A temporary government of Mexico was set up at Toluca, west of the City of Mexico, on September 22nd. It moved to more comfortable surroundings at Querétaro in early October, but was not sufficiently organized to do business until November 11th, when a formal election named General P. M. Anaya president and Peña y Peña minister of foreign affairs. Peña y Peña and Nicholas Trist had been working for five days when word arrived from Washington that Trist was recalled and I was to prosecute the war anew. Both Trist and I were aghast.

The reason for this stupid reversal was caused by slow communications and natural distrust between President Polk and his two subordinates in the field. Lacking direct intelligence from me the only source of information available to Polk, Macy, and Buchanan was grossly distorted. Letters from Gideon Pillow and newspaper reports were often slanted, and Polk himself was biased in his opinions. Polk's decision was made on October 5, based upon receiving word of Santa Anna's refusal to negotiate even after having received a substantial bribe.

Polk had been informed that Trist was considering a treaty that would grant to Mexico the territory of Texas between the Nueces and the Rio Grande. On October 23, Polk raged that Trist had bungled his negotiations. He had exceeded his instructions and had invited proposals from the Mexican government that the United States could never accept. Polk directed Mr. Buchanan "to prepare a dispatch expressing in strong terms my disapprobation and to repeat my order of the 6th instant for his immediate recall." Due to the infrequency of the convoys running from Vera Cruz to the City of Mexico the two messages arrived together on November 16th.

Fortunately Trist was under no pressure to leave immediately. I could not provide him an escort to Vera Cruz before December 4th so he had two weeks to consider his options. At first he considered obeying orders and depart, but on November 24 he received a note from Peña y Peña advising him that President Anaya had appointed commissioners to negotiate the peace with the United States. A chorus of persons advised Trist to stay on to complete his negotiations. Most influential among those was Bernardo Couto, one of the new commissioners, and who had served on the commission of the previous September. By December 3rd Trist decided to stay on. He passed the word on to Couto who transmitted it to Edward Thornton of the British Legation. Two days later he sent a long and elaborate letter to the State Department explaining his actions.

On December 8, I hosted an elaborate dinner in honor of General David Twiggs who was leaving to take command at Vera Cruz. The bulk of the junior officers including Robert E. Lee, Pierre Beauregard, Zealous Tower, and Ulysses S. Grant were too low-ranking to be included in the guest list.

I complied with President Polk's demands that the Mexicans be forced to pay for the American occupation. At the end of 1847 I announced an annual assessment of $3,000,000 on the nineteen states of Mexico. The Federal District of Mexico, in which the capital stood was assessed $668,000. On December 29, 1847 Trist wrote President Buchanan that he expected to sign a treaty within a week, and I said on January 7th of 1848 that I expected a treaty within three days. By the end of January the Mexicans were ready to sign, but they demanded $30,000,000 for the territories the United States was assuming, a figure Trist had never been authorized to meet. Trist, unhappily, declared the negotiations at an end!

On January 30, 1848 I was invited to a visit of the nuns of a Carmelite convent about 15 miles outside the City of Mexico. I made some general remarks to the effect that I desired a lasting peace. Two days after that outing I learned that Trist was joining the Mexican commissioners at Guadulupe Hidalgo, just north of the City of Mexico, for the purpose of signing an agreement. On that evening, February 1, 1848, copies of the text arrived at my headquarters. The next morning Trist and the Mexican commissioners signed the treaty. Upon receiving notification I pledged to suspend all hostilities.

In the past President Polk always seized upon a chance to humiliate me. His main tool was my friend Gideon Johnson Pillow. Pillow was not malicious. He was enthusiastic about the tasks which the army faced, but only for his own personal ends. Law required that his commission as a major general would expire as soon as the peace treaty was signed. His every act was directed toward reaping glory from his military service so that it would serve as an asset for a future career in public life. He was bound to create trouble in my army.

My army had barely entered the City of Mexico when Pillow ran into trouble. One of the two Mexican howitzers taken at the storming of Chapultepec was found to be missing from my inventory of captured weapons. One of Pillow's subordinates found it in Pillow's baggage wagon. Pillow attempted to get rid of the weapon, but one of the officers proffered court martial charges against him. Pillow, realizing that he was trapped tried to throw the blame on two of his younger lieutenants, but was unsuccessful. He was duly reprimanded on October 27, 1847. The court found that Pillow only returned his war trophy when caught. The ruling was, however, countermanded in Washington by President Polk.

In Pillow's official report of the battle of Contreras he portrayed himself as in command over my whole army without mentioning my name. He also claimed to have given the order to Quitman and Worth to advance to the City of Mexico after Chapultapec had fallen. I was inclined to brush off Pillow's exuberance and falsehoods. On October 2nd I invited Pillow's attention to several pages in his report of August 24th and September 18th, pointing out glaring misrepresentations. I called them "inadvertent" and I presumed they had been "silently corrected." Pillow came to me the next day gushing over my kindness and expressed "no hesitation" in correcting the reports.

Late in October the *American Star* reprinted an article in the New Orleans *Delta* of September 10, 1847 just before the attack. The article was signed by a person who called himself "Leonidas" and concluded that Pillow's plan of battle at Contreras was most judicious and successful, showing a masterly military genius and a profound knowledge of the science of war. One sentence really caught my eye however,

During the great battle, which lasted two days, General Pillow was in command of all the forces engaged, except General Worth's division, and this was not engaged . . .

There was little doubt who the author of the *Delta* article was. At about the same time another one carried in the *American Star* which originated in the *Pittsburgh Star* and later reprinted at Tampico, Mexico, added to my annoyance. It involved my decision of August 15th to turn south from the National Road to avoid the risk of attacking Santa Anna's position on El Peñon. The wise move, the article stated, was not mine at all. It gave full credit to Worth. It was followed by another article praising Pillow, and it was signed "Veritas."

On November 12, 1847 I published General Order #349 which called the attention of certain officers to an 1825 regulation which forbade them from writing for a civilian publication on military operations. General Worth demanded to know whether I applied the epithets in the order to him. I brushed him off with a noncommittal answer, so a frustrated Worth sent a letter to President Polk, and provided me with a copy. In it he appealed for redress and accused me of acting in a manner "unbecoming an officer and a gentleman," and enumerated his complaints in detail.

I couldn't take much more of this pettiness. I placed Worth in arrest and preferred court martial charges against him for "behaving with contempt and disrespect toward his superior and commanding officer." Worth's artillery man Colonel James Duncan promptly wrote a letter to the *North American* in support of Worth admitting that he had written the so called "Tampico" letter. I therefore preferred charges against Duncan as well. When I learned that Pillow had written Secretary Marcy in connection with his alleged theft of a howitzer at Chapultepec, I preferred charges against him as well. Two of my division commanders plus my most noted artillery man were now in arrest.

On New Years Eve, 1847, President Polk conferred with two influential Democratic Senators, Lewis Cass and Jefferson Davis. Both were loud in condemning my conduct and recommending my recall from Mexico. On New Year's Day Secretary Marcy finally decided that I should be replaced by General William O. Butler. That evening Postmaster General Cave Johnson and Attorney General Nathan Clifford concurred in a Cabinet meeting. Polk was now reinforced with support from his Cabinet so he nullified my court martial charges against Worth and directed that all three officers should be released from arrest. He reduced the investigation of Pillow and Duncan to a court of inquiry, a watered down hearing that bore no criminal implications.

On January 13, 1848 Secretary Marcy sent me three communications:

1. Nullification of my charges against Worth for insubordination.
2. Instructions for me to set up a court of Inquiry to meet at the Castle of Perote on February 18th.
3. A stiffly written message stating that the president was determined to release me from further duty as commanding general in Mexico.

I was advised to turn over my command to Major General Butler, or "in his absence to the officer highest in rank with the column under you." I was prepared for this and the official orders arrived on February

18, 1848. My farewell message was generous towards General Butler calling him "a general of established merit and distinction in the service of his country." I then returned from my "ex" military headquarters to prepare for the forthcoming court of inquiry which was scheduled to meet at the Castle of Perote, but switched at the last minute to the City of Mexico.

On February 19th at a dinner given to me by the British Legation, Senior British foreign officers deplored the order relieving me and observed that "it would be bitterly condemned in Europe as the result of low and vulgar intrigue by inferior men." By the time the court of inquiry convened in the City of Mexico in mid-March 1848 I was ready to forget and drop the whole thing. The authorities in Washington had so couched the terms of the trial that I became a defendant in the trial as well. Pillow saw an overpowering advantage over me and refused to let the charges be dropped. I assented, wearily, to go ahead with the trial. Testimony began on March 21st.

Nicholas Trist appeared as one of my effective witnesses. Trist held Pillow responsible for <u>poisoning</u> the president's mind against me. His venom toward Polk's old law partner exceeded even his rage over the intensity of Pillow's cross-examination when Trist's testimony was finished. Nicholas Trist left for home on April 8, 1848. There was no friendly send-off for him.

By April 21st, the court of inquiry decided it had taken all the testimony necessary in Mexico, and would reconvene at Frederick, Maryland where such trials are usually held. On April 22nd I departed from the City of Mexico by mule train accompanied by a disabled soldier as an aide. I tried to slip away without any fanfare but a crowd of officers surrounded my wagon and many brought their horses so that they could follow me out of the city. At one point there was a cry, "**God Bless You General**!"

I arrived back at Vera Cruz on May 1st and called on Commodore Matthew Perry. He offered me use of a new steamer to take me back to the United States, but I declined saying the steamer could be put to better use carrying wounded and sick soldiers. I took passage with the old sailing vessel *Petersburg* and landed in New York City on May 20, 1848. I procured a rowboat to take me home to Elizabethtown, New Jersey, where my wife and three daughters awaited me. I felt like a king. I was "overpowered" by newspaper men and delegations from New York and I was invited to a dinner given me by the city in my honor. It was a magnificent reception both militarily and civil. I learned that Congress had requested a medal to be struck in my honor.

The court of inquiry reconvened on June 5th. It was more of an ordeal at Frederick than it had been in the City of Mexico. I was feeling sick from a touch of the *vomito* I had contracted at Vera Cruz and Pillow was in fine fettle. The attitude of the court was outright hostile towards me. I had few allies among the high-ranking officers present. Quitman, while friendly, was a Polk man through-and-through so my greatest support came from David E. Twiggs. He was questioned on June 9th and testified as to the truth of the matter. A parade of other witnesses did my case no good. Finally on July 1, the court martial found Pillow's conduct at Contreras on August 17th as "meritorious" and said it was emphatically approved by General Scott at the time. Finally the court expressed its opinion that no further proceedings against General Pillow were called for. Pillow was triumphant. He returned to Washington to celebrate his acquittal at a White House dinner with his buddy James K. Polk, president of the United States.

As the court of inquiry wound down the Whig Presidential Convention met and nominated Zachary Taylor for president of the United States. I resumed my administrative duties as general-in-chief of the Army but moved my headquarters to New York City in July 1848. Back in November Zachary Taylor was elected president of the United States by a small majority over the Democratic candidate, Lewis Cass. On March 6, 1848 I went to Washington and called on General Taylor at the White House. In a cordial meeting I secured permission to keep my headquarters of the Army in New York City, and Taylor accepted that arrangement. I found an excuse to avoid going to General Taylor's Inauguration ceremony.

The treaty of Guadalupe Hidalgo became truly a historic document. The treaty spelled out the border between the two countries. The United States would assume the debt owed by Mexico to American citizens and pay $15,000,000 for the territory transferred. The treaty was duly ratified on March 10, 1848 and on June 12, 1848 the last American troops sailed from Vera Cruz bound for home. I dropped out of sight to ponder the future.

Chapter 12

MY CONFLICT WITH GENERAL SCOTT

William Selby Harney

A t the end of 1846 General Winfield Scott determined to take the field himself and formed his plans for an advance on The City of Mexico from Vera Cruz. He planned his campaign irresponsibly so as to leave General Taylor in the lurch, depriving him of the troops he had in the field. Major General Zachary Taylor wrote a letter to General Scott on January 15th, 1847 from a camp near Victoria, Mexico in which he complained vigorously to the General.

I had grown up under the shadows of the Hermitage. I enjoyed the confidence and esteem of General Jackson, who never gave his confidence lightly and never wavered in his friendship for anyone who once gained it. General Scott disliked General Jackson. Jackson had reached the presidency by the will of the people. Scott was also ambitious to reach it and hoped this campaign in Mexico would bring him closer to that goal. He had always been envious of Jackson, and was then fearful that Taylor's well-earned laurels would raise up another rival.

While Scott was quietly avenging himself on his immediate rival he took occasion to take vengeance upon me as a friend of General Jackson. His attack on me took the shape of depriving me of the command of my 2nd Dragoons, and placing that regiment in the command of Major Sumner. Scott gave the reason that "Major Sumner, of the Second Dragoons," was "a much safer and more efficient commander than Colonel Harney of the Second." He added, "that particular command is entirely too important to the success of my expedition to allow me to leave anything to hazard which it is in my power to control in advance."

The following letter was issued by General Scott,

> Headquarters of the Army
> Brazos Santiago, January 22, 1847
>
> SIR: Major General Scott desires me to say, that upon your receipt of this communication, you will turn over your command to the next senior officer, and proceed yourself, personally, to Major General Taylor's headquarters, to whom you will report for duty with the Dragoons that remain under his command.
>
> I am, very respectfully, your obedient servant,
>
> > H. L. SCOTT
> > Adjutant General
> > Colonel W. S. Harney
> > 2nd Dragoons, Matamoros

William Selby Harney

On January 23rd I replied to H. L. Scott's order by saying that I was very surprised at the unexpected nature of his order, and I wrote, "I had fully hoped to share the dangers and privations of my regiment . . . I shall not speak of the injustice which I consider to be done in separating me from seven companies of my regiment, and ordering me on duty with the remaining two." I ended my letter by saying that I turned over my command to Major Sumner "and should it not be deemed expedient to change the order under consideration, I have to request that I may be informed at what point I may find the headquarters of Major General Taylor."

General Winfield Scott replied through his adjutant general on the 24th. H. L. Scott wrote me that General Scott had made his arrangements and they could not be changed. Upon the receipt of this letter I immediately resumed command and sent off the following letter to Major General Scott:

Matamoros, Mexico
January 25, 1847

SIR: Your communication of the 24th instant was received last night, and I hasten to return a reply.

In my letter of the 23rd I endeavored to explain my position, and to disabuse the mind of Major General Scott, in relation to any preconceived views he may have formed in my prejudice. It was humiliating to do so, but I deemed it my duty, in the present state of affairs, to make any reasonable sacrifice to preserve harmony, and to enable me to accompany this portion of my regiment into the field. Your reply has disappointed me; if not a revocation of your order, I at least expected that some good and sufficient reason would be given for depriving me of my regiment, or that reparation would be made to me for it in another quarter; and with this view I relinquished my command.

By your letter referred to, you have not only deprived me of my regiment, but you have placed my junior, the major of my own regiment, in command of it; and the imaginary command, to which you have been pleased to allude, I consider as entirely inadequate to the one you would force me to relinquish, even should it ever be brought into existence. If General Scott does not deem me capable of discharging my appropriate duties, he may arrest, but he shall not unresistingly degrade me. It is painful to be driven to this alternative. I have endeavored to avoid the issue; it has been forced on me, and I must abide by the judgment of my peers.

As long as I am a colonel I shall claim the command of my regiment; it is a right which I hold by my commission and the laws of the land, and no authority short of the president of the United States can legally deprive me of it. In adopting this course, I feel that I am not only defending my own, but the rights of every officer of the army. It is true, another course is open to me, but it is well known by your presence with the army that an important expedition against the enemy is at hand, and my desire to participate in it will not allow me to await redress by an appeal to higher authority. It is in full view of all the consequences in which I may be involved, that I have taken this step. I do it with no desire to show a spirit of insubordination, but because I believe my honor and my character as a soldier is involved in the issue. I have no hope that anything that I may say will alter your determination; to discuss the subject further would be useless, and I have only to add, that I have assumed the command of my regiment, and will accompany it to the mouth of the river.

I am, sir, very respectfully, your obedient servant,

WM. S. HARNEY
Colonel, 2nd Dragoons
Major General Winfield Scott,
Commander-in-Chief U. S. Army

Charges were preferred by General Worth, and I was placed in arrest and a court-martial ordered. The charges were disobedience of orders and insubordinate conduct. On January 28th 1847 I had a follow-up letter from General Scott's adjutant This letter said, in part,

. . . Considering your well known and long continued personal hostility to Major General Scott, and that it may, however erroneously, be supposed that a reciprocal feeling has been generated on his part; and considering the perfect confidence that all may entertain in the honor and impartiality of our officers generally, and almost universally, I am instructed by Major General Scott to say, you may, if done promptly, select yourself, from the officers near at hand, any seven, nine, eleven, or thirteen, to compose the court for your trial on that charge and its specifications, and that he, Major General Scott, will immediately order them to assemble accordingly . . .

On the same day I wrote back from Camp Page in Texas as follows:

January 28, 1847

SIR: I feel deeply indebted to Major General Scott, for his magnanimity in allowing me to select the members of my court, but there are many reasons why I should decline this privilege. It is sufficient that I regard the charge on which I am to be tried as involving a general principle, which shall not be decided by a court of my friends, or persons from whom I should look for favor, but by impartial judges who are to render judgment in a case where the rights of all are concerned.

Wholly concurring in the views entertained by Major General Scott, "in the honor of our officers generally and almost universally," I leave with him the entire selection of the court, requesting to be excluded the first and third officers named on the list which you inclosed. In regard to the feelings of personal hostility alluded to by Major General Scott, I am not aware that any act of mine can indicate such a feeling towards General Scott, so clearly as his own attempt to remove me from my proper command will evince in the estimation of all.

I am, sir, very respectfully, your obedient servant,
WILLIAM S. HARNEY
Colonel, 2nd Dragoons
Lieutenant H. L. Scott, Adjutant General

227

Philip F. Rose

A court-martial was convened at Headquarters, Brazos, Santiago, near the mouth of the Rio Grande with Colonel Clark as Judge Advocate. The charge was disobedience of orders and insubordinate conduct. The first specification was that I failed as ordered to set out for Major General Taylor's headquarters, and the second specification was that after I relinquished my command I illegally resumed command.

To which I pleaded as follows:

> To the first specification, "GUILTY.
> To the second specification, "GUILTY."
> To the charge, "GUILTY," except the words "*and insubordinate conduct.*"

> The court found the accused as follows:
> Of the first specification, confirm his plea, *guilty.*
> Of the second specification, confirm his plea, *guilty.*
> Of the charge, confirm his plea, *guilty* of disobedience of orders, *not guilty* of insubordinate conduct.

SENTENCE: The court does therefore, sentence the said Colonel W. S. Harney, 2nd regiment of Dragoons, "*to be reprimanded in general orders.*"

STATEMENT OF THE COURT:

> The court, in awarding this mild sentence, is moved by the belief that the accused has acted under the impression that he could not legally be ordered, against his consent, to separate himself from the principle portion of his regiment; and while he has, in the belief of the court, been influenced by a laudable desire to lead his regiment into battle, he has overlooked the paramount importance, especially with an army in the field, of an immediate and an unhesitating obedience to orders.

The papers and documents were transmitted to the Secretary of War who sent a letter of rebuke to the commander-in-chief, Major General

228

Winfield Scott. In part he said that the president of the United States regretted the occurrence. Furthermore he said:

> In the case as you have presented it, he does not discover a sufficient cause for the order depriving Colonel Harney of the command which appropriately belonged to him, and devolving it upon his inferior in rank. Without intending to approve of the conduct of Colonel Harney in disobeying your orders, the president deems it proper to apprize you of his opinion that Colonel Harney had good cause to complain of that order, as derogatory to his rights, and he hopes that the matter has been reconsidered by you, and that the colonel has been restored by you, and that the colonel has been restored to his appropriate command.

On February 24th, 1847 General Scott wrote to the Secretary of War of his complaints about the affair. This letter deserves to be analyzed, as an instance of how childish a great soldier can become, when he gives way to a pedantic vanity for writing, and combines it with an unrestrained political ambition, unworthy of his great office. In regards to his complaints in my case of which the very sentence of the whole court martial, his own remission of the sentence, and his restoration of my command which he had compelled to turn over to a junior officer, had of itself condemned him and vindicated me.

Chapter 13

VICTORY AT CERRO GORDO

William Selby Harney

After being court-martialed and returned to my proper command on February 3rd, 1847 I marched with parts of the First and Second Dragoons to report to General Twiggs for active duty in the field. We embarked on transports at the mouth of the Rio Grande River in Texas, and proceeded to the island of Lobos where we joined the other fleet of transports carrying the main body of General Scott's army, who had rendezvoused there. On our way the transport *Yazoo* was stranded at San Lizardo. It resulted in the loss of ten horses, but no men. Among the horses on board were those belonging to me. One of them, Buncombe, my favorite horse was in the sea twenty-four hours, but he finally swam safely ashore.

On March 7th, 1847 General Scott reconnoitered the city of Vera Cruz for the purpose of finding a convenient spot for landing his army. Vera Cruz is the seaport for The City of Mexico. It is situated on the Gulf of Mexico and is well fortified and protected by the castle of San Juan de Ulúa, a strong fortification situated on an island just off the coast. Also at the southwest extremity of the city is another small fortification known as Fort Santiago, and another small island called Sacrificios lies southwest of the castle. There was no anchorage for a large fleet in the harbor, so on the 9th of March the troops were landed near Sacrificios. The enemy, not anticipating a landing at that point, had not made the proper precautions to prevent it. Five thousand five hundred men embarked in surf boats and safely reached the shore.

The Americans planted the Stars & Stripes on the soil of the Aztecs in full view of the city. The first division of troops landed at sunset and the two other divisions followed after nightfall. Although the landing was not opposed by any troops, the guns from the castle and the city pounded our men with a constant broadside of shot and shell. By the 12th of March the city of Vera Cruz was in a state of siege. It was not until the 17th that ten mortars and four twenty-four pound guns were landed, and on the night of the 18th the engineers with sappers and miners began the approach to the city. On March 22nd the city was requested to surrender. The governor, construing the summons to mean the surrender of the castle, as well as the city, refused. The American mortar battery then opened fire on the city.

While the siege was progressing the men in the trenches were fed with provisions from the country in the rear. There were some French gardeners on the Medellin River, some nine miles southwest of Vera Cruz. A detachment of Mexican troops were successful in intercepting the supplies which the people were willing to sell to the American troops.

At that time I was in command of the 1st and 2nd Dragoons belonging to General Twigg's division at Camp Washington. General Scott ordered me to make a reconnaissance to ascertain the position of the enemy on the Medellin. I was ordered only to evaluate the strength of the enemy and by no means to engage them. I proceeded on the morning of March 25th towards the Medellin River. It was reported that a considerable mounted force was in that direction. I moved without opposition until I came near the stone bridge of the Morena, which was skirted by a dense chaparral. I learned that it was fortified by 2000 Mexican troops and artillery. The enemy was prepared, and when I came within 60 yards of the bridge they attacked fiercely.

I fell back and sent a request for two pieces of cannon. With the aid of this artillery I felt convinced that I could drive the enemy from the bridge and put him to rout. We were reinforced by Captain Hardee's foot soldiers, companies of the First and Second Tennessee Regiment. A little later Lieutenant Judd arrived with two pieces of artillery and I decided to act. Lieutenant Judd opened fire upon the fortification, and after six or seven well directed rounds the heads of the enemy were no longer seen above the parapet. At this moment I ordered a charge upon the bridge. The fortification opposed no obstacle and the enemy fell back and reformed well behind the bridge. The pursuit was continued to the village of Medellin, six miles from the bridge. We routed the enemy, but with night coming on I was reluctantly compelled to desist. I returned to camp with my command, which I reached at 3:00 AM in the morning. In the day's action I lost two men killed and nine wounded.

When I reported to Scott after this action I said to the General, "Damn it, sir, I did violate your orders, but I attacked the enemy, and drove them back to Medellin."

General Scott then said, "why did you violate my orders?"

I replied, "General, I have done exactly what you would have done under the circumstances; I believed Vera Cruz got all her supplies from the gardens at Medellin through Spanish vessels."

General Scott sighed, "well, colonel, we will let it pass."

The affair at Medellin was not mentioned in the commanding general's reports to Washington. The consequent occupation of the country hastened the fall of Vera Cruz, for it cut off the supplies of the beleaguered enemy. On the same day that I had my victory at the Medellin, General Taylor met and signally defeated General Santa Anna at Buena Vista.

More ordnance arrived for our troops on the 24th and fire was extremely heavy on the 25th. That evening the foreign consuls residing at Vera Cruz sent a note to General Scott for a flag of truce to enable them to retire from the city with the women and children. General Scott told them that a truce could only be granted on application of the Mexican governor, General Morales.

It was plain to the besieged that the city must surrender or be destroyed. General Landero, in command of the city made overtures of surrendering. General Worth, General Pillow and Colonel Totten met with the Mexican commissioners and the articles of capitulation were signed on March 27th. The Stars & Stripes flew over both castle and city two days later after a siege of fifteen days. General Worth was placed in command of Vera Cruz and General Scott prepared to march upon the capital. Four thousand prisoners were paroled, and five hundred pieces of artillery, with munitions, arms and stores were the spoils of victory.

The battle of Buena Vista had defeated General Santa Anna but he fell back with his scattered forces, recalled his troops, reorganized his army and seized the important mountain passes, through which an invading army must penetrate in marching from Vera Cruz to the City of Mexico.

General Scott was delayed by the slow arrival of wagons without which he could not carry his stores, arms or ammunition. On April 8th he had enouh transportation to push forward General Twiggs' division which included my Dragoons, to the Jalapa Road. The other divisions soon followed, and at the end of three days we were at the foot of the magnificent mountains leading to the City of Mexico. General Santa Anna had strongly fortified Cerro Gordo,[17] a mountain outpost guarding the Jalapa Road. On the 12th of April General Twiggs' men made a reconnaissance of the lofty Cerro Gordo outpost. I soon discovered that a main route attack would be dangerous. Engineers in the Mexican army had cut down all the trees and bushes and sharpened all the stumps.

I had found an old stage driver by the name of Jonathan Fitzwater who was very familiar with the country between Vera Cruz and the City of Mexico. Fitzwater suggested an obscure approach which might be what we were looking for. I soon made a reconnaissance of the route suggested by Fitzwater, and became elated because I believed we could take Cerro Gordo. I reported all my findings to General Twiggs and insisted on attacking the enemy.

General Scott was not far distant with the main army. I felt that if I did not attack immediately the victory that would belong to me by right of discovery would be divided between me and the whole army. When the general sent out engineers commanded by Robert E. Lee and G. T. Beauregard they reported as their selection *the very same route* I had fixed upon. General Scott ordered a road to be cut to the right of Cerro Gordo, which would enable them to wind around the base of the mountain and ascend the peaks in the rear of the Mexican batteries so as to reach the Jalapa Road behind the Mexican position. For the next few days the Mexicans did not discover our advance by this route. It was

---

[17] Literally fat hill.

nearly completed by April 17th, when the Mexicans finally opened fire on the working parties.

On the evening of April 16th, owing to the illness of Brevet Brigadier General Persifer F. Smith, I was placed in command of the 1st brigade of the 2nd division. Our encampment at Plan del Rio enabled the engineering officers to make frequent observations of the enemy's position. It was ascertained that they had fortified themselves on a range of hills for two miles in a mountain pass, and that the last of their works was on Cerro Gordo, which from its position and defenses, was considered almost impregnable.

On the morning of the 17th the 2nd division under the command of Brigadier General Twiggs was directed to turn the enemy by the right flank, and I was ordered by that officer to seize and maintain all the heights in the neighborhood of the Cerro Gordo Hacienda, which, from their proximity and position, might be an advantage in an attack on that fortress. Shortly after the column turned off to the right from the main road, Lieutenant F. Gardner of the 7th Infantry was directed with his company to move to the crest of the hill on the left, and to watch the enemy's movements. While doing so he was attacked by the enemy, but he maintained his position against fearful odds, until he was reinforced by the riflemen of Major Sumner and the artillery under Lieutenant Colonel Childs. La Atalaya, the adjacent steep hill, was then stormed and held, even though the enemy made three successive charges to regain it. A portion of the troops under Lieutenant Colonel Childs, led on by their zeal and desire to attack, rushed down the hill to the ascent of the Cerro Gordo; but as an attack was not intended at that time; they were recalled to rejoin General Twiggs.

Throughout the night there were 8,000 Mexicans lying upon and around the various heights, protected by breastworks and fortifications, and further secured from direct assault by deep ravines and almost precipitous rocks, up whose steep sides they imagined a man would scarcely dare to climb. In addition to the forces thus formidably posted, there was a reserve of 6,000 men, encamped upon the plain in the rear of Cerro Gordo, and close to the Jalapa road.

The riflemen and infantry troops slept on the hill, and to that point were brought that night a 24-pounder cannon and two 24 pound howitzers under a corps of engineers commanded by Lieutenant Wagner. They were placed in position and the engineers on the hill cut away the light brush in front of the guns. At 7:00 AM a cannonade commenced aimed at the enemy's fortification on the Cerro Gordo. The cannon's roar echoed from the mountain sides, and were returned from the guns of the enemy.

Early that morning I was reinforced by the four companies of the 1st Artillery under Lieutenant Colonel Childs, and six companies of the 3rd Infantry under Captain Alexander. I immediately gave orders to the different commanders to prepare their troops for storming the heights. The riflemen were directed to move to the left in the ravine and to engage the enemy; and I instructed Major Loring that as soon as he commenced the attack I would move forward with my troops. The 7th Infantry was formed on the right and the 3rd Infantry on the left, and the artillery was placed in the rear to support the Infantry. General Shields pressed forward to take possession of the Jalapa road in the rear of Cerro Gordo.

Observing that a large force was moving from the left on the main road, towards the Cerro Gordo, I deemed it prudent to advance at once, and immediately ordered the charge to be sounded without waiting for the fire of the riflemen. The enemy fired at us from many positions around the hill, but my troops made a steady advance. Around the hill, about sixty yards from its foot there was a breastwork constructed of stone which was filled with Mexican troops who offered a stubborn resistance. They continued to fire until our troops reached the breastwork, at which point the fight continued with fixed bayonets. Beyond this point there was another breastwork which opposed our progress, but the men immediately surmounted it. We climbed the rocky, steep ascent towards the telegraph tower[18] under heavy fire. I was a full fifty yards in advance of my column and waved my sword to encourage my troops to follow and do battle. As soon as one comrade fell his spot was filled with another. We gained the top at 10:45 AM and dashed toward the fortification with loud epithets and spirited shouts. The Mexican Commander, General Vasquez was found dead within the walls. The American flag was raised over Cerro Gordo and the Mexican colors pulled down, amidst the proud rejoicing of our troops.

The riflemen moved to the left where they again became engaged with the enemy which they held in check, notwithstanding a most

---

[18] Called by the Mexicans, El Télégrafo.

galling fire from the enemy's entrenchments and from the musketry in front. After the enemy's cannon had been captured, I directed Captain Magruder to take charge of the pieces and to direct their fire upon the enemy, which he executed with zeal and ability. I also directed Lieutenant Colonel Plympton to move with his regiment at the same time down to the Jalapa road and cut off the enemy's retreat, which he promptly executed, and maintained his position until the forts and forces of the enemy had surrendered.

General Shields, in the meantime, moved upon the Jalapa road, storming a fort in their front, which was carried by their valor, but the brave General was shot through the lungs. The road was taken, and General Santa Anna's 8000 men were fugitives, while General La Vega and three other general officers, with three thousand men were prisoners. When Santa Anna observed the fall of Cerro Gordo he hastily mounted his horse and made good his escape, leaving in our hands his carriage riddled with bullets, containing an extra cork leg, his private and public papers, and his baggage. A wagon was also captured containing $16,000 received the day before for the pay of the troops. The Americans were victorious at every point, except for Pillow's division, which, retreating under an enfilading fire, was held at bay until the storming of Cerro Gordo and the threatened capture of the Jalapa road put Santa Anna to flight. In the two days of fighting I had two officers killed, and nine wounded; 29 non-commissioned officers and privates were killed, and 175 wounded. The officers killed were Lieutenants Ewell and Davis of the rifles. Major Sumner was one of the officers wounded.

When the contest was ended the general-in-chief was overflowing with joy and rushed over to me, and with tears in his eyes embraced me with great emotion. The battle, I knew it had been won, seemed like a dream. I could not shake off the feelings as I rode along the enemy's lines of entrenchments, entered his dismantled forts and magazines, and looked from the heights upon the paths in which our troops rushed into the jaws of death. When the battle was over a Mexican officer was seen slowly riding along the road at the foot of the hill and in reach of American fire. My troops, without orders, commenced firing at him, until I gave the order to cease fire. Before the order could be transmitted, some one thousand shots had been fired at him. The Mexican never altered his pace, but as soon as the firing ceased he raised his hand to his head and gracefully saluted the Americans.

On May 15th when the news had reached New Orleans and Lafayette of what I am told was my gallant conduct at Cerro Gordo, the citizens made me a present of a horse, which was shipped to me here in Mexico, with the accompanying letter:

> New Orleans
> 15th of May, 1847
> Colonel Wm. S. Harney:
>
> SIR: The undersigned, in behalf of the citizens of New Orleans and LaFayette, have purchased a horse, which they beg you to accept as a token of the esteem and adoration in which you are held by them for your gallant conduct, but more especially for the important services you have rendered our glorious republic in the late battle of Cerro Gordo.
>
> W. B. HIGDON,
> JOHN M. CARRIGAN

On the 18th of April, 1847, for gallant and meritorious conduct at Cerro Gordo, I was breveted brigadier general in the United States army. This complement came to me as a prompt recognition of my services to the country. The victorious army then moved immediately upon Jalapa, after caring for their wounded and prisoners.

The victorious Americans took possession of Jalapa on April 19th, 1847. On April 22nd General Worth occupied the castle of Perote, and on May 15th the ancient Puebla los Angeles[19] was captured by General Worth. The Mexicans had been able to make but little resistance after their signal defeat at Cerro Gordo, and but feeble resistance was offered the American army, reduced in numbers by the casualties of battle and disease.

Puebla is a city of 80,000 inhabitants and is 90 miles from the City of Mexico and 200 miles from Vera Cruz at an altitude of 7000 feet. General Scott's army of 14,000 men had been reduced to less than 5000 due to the discharge of volunteers, sickness, death and disability. For this reason he delayed his march on the City of Mexico. The government was anxious for peace and the president and Cabinet sent

---

[19]   City of the Angels.

an agent, Mr. Nicholas P. Trist, Chief Clerk in the State Department to negotiate. He arrived at Jalapa just before the occupation of Puebla. Mr. Trist's negotiations as well as Scott's waiting for reinforcements from the United States, necessitated a cessation of active hostilities. In about two months the army at Puebla grew to about 11,000 men.

A council of war was held on August 5th, 1847 and the plans of the commander-in-chief for the advance on the capital were submitted and explained. General Scott placed a brigade of cavalry under my command. We moved out of Puebla as the advanced guard, followed by the second division under General Twiggs. On the 8th of August the division of General Quitman followed, Worth's division moved on the 9th and Pillow's on the 10th. The route was the stage road from Vera Cruz, by way of Puebla, to the City of Mexico. The route was very mountainous and the volcanic peak of Popocatapetl loomed over the smaller ranges on the left.

On the third day of March we reached the Rio Frio and the Anahuac range, some 45 miles from the capital. Beyond this location the enemy had prepared for resistance, but they had abandoned their intention of offering battle at this point. After passing the Anahuac range several miles and turning suddenly to the right we came in sight of the vast plain in which is situated the City of Mexico. On August 10th General Twiggs camped at the base of the mountains. He could see Lake Texcoco to his front and a fortified mountain called El Peñon. Before approaching the enemy's abandoned fortifications General Scott sent for me and said, "Look Harney I have information from General Worth of enemy activities in our front and I want your most vigilant attention to their movements and approach."

I replied, "General, whatever force of the enemy there be, I may not be able to defeat them, but I promise you I can hold them at bay." General Scott boldly grabbed my hand and said, "By God Harney I have every confidence in you."

There are three great roads which enter the City of Mexico; the National Road, on which General Twiggs was encamped at Ayotla which he reahed on August 11th, the Acapulco Road fortified by the Churubusco post, and the Tacubaya Road. On August 12th my cavalry brigade reconnoitered El Peñon, the strongly fortified mountain on the National Road about half way between Ayotla and the City of Mexico. They reported the route to the city by that road impracticable.

I cautioned General Scott not to advance by the National Road so he decided to make the approach by the Acapulco Road and the Tacubaya Road. On August 17th we reached San Augustin.

On the 18th Worth's division advanced towards San Antonio, a fortified place on the Acapulco Road and in a skirmish with the enemy Captain Thornton of my regiment was killed. He was the first to die in the operations which resulted in the capture of the City of Mexico.

The Mexican forces made their strongest dispositions for defense at the new points of attack. General Rincon took command at Churubusco and strengthened the fortifications there. Santa Anna was rapidly strengthening General Valencia, who with 6000 men advanced to the fortified hill of Contreras. On August 20th I attempted to take the Contreras hill. At 6:00 AM our men rushed over the hill and dashed into the enemy entrenchments. The batteries were taken, and General Valencia's army was driven out. The battle ended almost before it started. I charged down the road towards the City of Mexico after the retreating enemy. They were overtaken within a mile of the city and there suffered their final defeat.

About 8:00 AM on the same day Churubusco was marched on. At San Pablo, which is the citadel of Churubusco a company of about 100 Irish-American deserters, the so called San Patricios, were posted under the command of John Riley, late sergeant of Company "K", U. S. Fifth Infantry. They fought desperately and created great havoc for our troops. They would not surrender, and when the Mexicans hung out their white flag Riley pulled it down. San Pablo was finally taken and the deserters taken at their guns.

On the next day preparations were made for peace; Mexican commissioners were appointed, and ineffectual efforts were made by Mr. Trist for a treaty of peace. The war was now in remission. On September 7th General Scott made a reconnaissance of the enemy's defenses at Tacubaya, about 2.5 miles from the city. Directly ahead of him lay the formidable fortifications at Chapultepec. It was now necessary to take this fortified hill of porphyritic rock on which stood a castle which served as a military school. At the base of the hill were two strong works; Molino del Rey and the Casa de Mata. Molino del Rey was targeted for the first attack. I began the assault at 3:00 AM and while advancing could not see any indications of the enemy. I decided to ride forward alone and reconnoiter. The enemy allowed me to approach within 120 yards and then laid down a withering fire. I wheeled my horse around and galloped off in a hurry. They did not, as in the case of the Mexican officer at Cerro Gordo, give me the opportunity of saluting them.

Both Casa de Mata and Moleno del Rey were taken by assault, leaving the Castle of Chapultepec alone standing between the American army and the City of Mexico. I was on the sidelines while General Scott prepared for the storming of this bastion. Major Sumner was commanding the six companies of the 2nd Dragoons which belonged to my regiment.

In the mean time pending the negotiations, inefficient as they proved, between Mr. Trist and the Mexican commissioners, the deserters captured at San Pablo were tried by court-martial. General Scott, in examining the proceedings of the court, appears to have released every man from the penalty of death, in whose favor any reason or mitigation could be pleaded. Among the three whom he found who were not legally subject to the penalty of death, because they had deserted previous to the commencement of war was the notorious Riley, the commander of the deserter's company. He was lashed and branded with the letter D on his cheeks—a pretty harsh punishment—but one, unfortunately, which war carries with it.

The unpleasant duty of hanging twenty of the doomed men fell on me while I was detached from my brigade. The hour appointed for their execution was during the last day's struggle for the possession of Chapultepec. The place of execution was in sight of the castle where all could see and hear the terrible struggle. Seeing that the place would soon fall I ordered the execution delayed until the condemned deserters could see the Mexican flag come down and the American flag run up. The prisoners hearing me give this order raised a cheer, because they believed Chapultepec was impregnable. I had but a few minutes to wait for the firing to cease, and the Stars & Stripes run up the pole by First Lieutenant George Pickett of the Eighth Infantry. With a long drum roll, the whips snapped and the mules lurched forward. The prisoners met their death in horror.

On September 18th the American army entered the City of Mexico, and, although not relieved from the command that exiled me from the storming of Chapultepec, I placed my next senior officer in command and entered the city with the victorious army. Shortly after the capture of Mexico I was ordered in October 1847 to return to Washington with dispatches. On the way to Vera Cruz I was given the duty of conveying a train filled with gold and other valuables. Captain Cassius M. Clay who had been a prisoner of the Mexicans since the battle of Buena Vista accompanied me. Captain Clay had been released along with Major John P. Gaines by an enemy exchange. It was a long tedious trip, but the friendship of Captain Clay made it memorable.

On the way to Washington I was the victim of an ovation at New Orleans where the citizens cheered me lustily, and at St. Louis, where my family and friends lived. At St. Louis a coach and six white horses drew up to my residence where I was captured and carried in State to the People's Theater where I had a tremendous ovation. Reaching Washington I witnessed the restoration of peace in Mexico and was ordered to the command of my regiment; the Second Dragoons, on the frontier of the Eighth Department headquartered at San Antonio, Texas.

Chapter 14

My Brother Levi

David E. Twiggs

I am the fifth son of Major General John Twiggs of Revolutionary War memory and my brother Levi was the sixth son and was born in Georgia on May 21, 1793. At the declaration of war against Great Britain in 1812 Levi was nineteen years of age and wanted to enter the service. Failing to obtain the approval of our parents he continued his studies at Athens College in Georgia for several months longer.

On learning of the capture of the *Macedonia* under Commodore Decatur Levi immediately left college and begged consent of our parents to apply for an appointment in the Marine Corps which was granted. He entered the corps as a second lieutenant on November 10, 1813 and was stationed on the *Pataxent*, to oppose the passage of the British fleet which was hovering along the coasts of the Chesapeake. Next Levi was ordered to join the frigate *President* commanded by Commodore Decatur on her last memorable cruise under our flag. She sailed from New York on January 14, 1815 and soon after encountering the British fleet she was captured.

The officers of the *President* were detained as prisoners-of-war in Bermuda until news of the peace reached there, when they returned to their country. Levi was then attached to the New York station, and in 1822 he married the daughter of the deceased Captain McKnight, of the Marine Corps, and niece of Commodore Decatur. In 1823 Levi was sent to Philadelphia and in 1824 he was ordered to the frigate *Constellation* under Commodore Warrington to cruise among the West India Islands, in which service he was absent nearly two years, returning then to Philadelphia.

In November 1825 Levi was placed in command of the marines at the Norfolk Navy Yard. In June 1826 Levi, now a captain, was ordered to Florida where he engaged in the Seminole war. From his return from Florida until 1843, having attained the rank of major on November 15, 1840, he commanded marine posts at Philadelphia, New York and Washington. In 1843 he assumed command of the Philadelphia Navy Yard where he proved himself worthy of his rank and station.

On June 2nd 1847 Levi departed for Mexico having solicited active service. On June 29th he arrived at Vera Cruz and on the 16th of July he left for the interior with General Pierce's brigade. He reached Puebla on the 6th of August and then left with Major General Quitman's division. A few days later, on September 13th and at the head of his command, he fell leading them to the assault and storming of Chapultepec, pierced by a bullet through his heart!

On the way to join me as an aide on the 12th of August, Levi's gallant son, George Decatur Twiggs, died as a volunteer in Major Lally's command at the National bridge. Having just entered his twentieth year, a youth of the first rank, and with the brightest prospects, pursuing his legal studies with zeal, he was poised for national fame. In one action he had already gained the applause of his commander; but in the last, while actively pursuing the enemy, a fatal missile cut him down in the flower of his youth!

Of the many brave men who laid down their lives for their country's honor during the war, none fought more gallantly, nor died more nobly than did those kindred spirits, the father and the son. Levi was a tender and affectionate husband, a most kind and indulgent parent, leaving a wife and three daughters to lament his loss; alas!

Among the testimonials was the following order dated at Washington, November 20, 1847 and addressed to Captain J. G. Williams, commanding marines at Philadelphia:

> The commandant of the corps with profound and cordial sorrow announces to the officers and soldiers the death of Major Levi Twiggs, while leading his command to victory and glory, on the 13th of September, under the walls of the City of Mexico. In his loss the corps has to mourn for a gallant officer, who has passed all of his youth in its ranks, and his country for an estimable and patriotic citizen, and those who knew him most intimately, for a valued friend and a high minded gentleman.
>
> The usual badge of mourning will be worn for him by the officers of the corps for one month, and the flag at headquarters will be half masted tomorrow.

By order of the Brevet Brigadier General

Chapter 15

Negotiating a Peace

Nicholas P. Trist

The unpopularity of the Mexican War caused President Polk to make a major effort to effect a peace. A plan was evolved to send a commissioner to Mexico in 1847 with broad powers of negotiation. The president wanted a man who would not make waves in a political sense. Mr. Buchanan suggested me, the Chief Clerk of the State Department, and knowledgeable about international affairs. I was apprized of the post and Polk's Cabinet gave unanimous approval.

I was born in Virginia in 1800 and received a broad but good education. I became proficient in the French and Spanish languages, married a member of the Thomas Jefferson family, and was a staunch member of the Democratic party. I supported Andrew Jackson vigorously. Henry Clay, then John Quincy Adam's Secretary of State, gave me a job in the State Department. Later I served as Jackson's private secretary, and in 1833 I was appointed Consul to Havana. I was made chief clerk of the State Department by a fellow Virginian, Abel Upshur, after Daniel Webster resigned as Secretary of State to be replaced by James Buchanan. I served as acting Secretary of State whenever Buchanan was absent from Washington.

I was thrilled when I was selected to negotiate a peace with Mexico. I had an excellent knowledge of Spanish and the Spanish tradition. I was a party man without strong political ambitions, but most importantly I was privy to the entire background of the war. I was furnished my instructions and the proposals for a treaty on April 15, 1847. I was empowered to negotiate and I could offer up to $30 million in indemnities if Mexico would cede California, New Mexico, and the right of transit across the Isthmus of Tehuántepec. I was also given dispatches for General Scott, but the entire project was to be kept secret.

I slipped out of Washington quietly and traveled overland to New Orleans where I registered as a Mr. Prescot. However there had been a leak, and news of my journey filtered into the newspapers. Of course nobody knew the details of my instructions. I arrived in Vera Cruz on May 6th and waited there for an escort to General Scott's headquarters in Jalapa. I forwarded a personal letter to General Scott by courier along with a dispatch from the War Department and the sealed April 15th proposal for the treaty.

Secretary of War Marcy's instructions included a statement that if I notified Scott that a certain "contingency" had occurred, Scott was to cease all military operations. To Scott this was tantamount to placing him under the command of a State Department clerk. If I had presented these instructions verbally, I could have explained that the "contingency" was nothing more or less than the ratification of the treaty which I was to negotiate. Scott sent a nasty note to me, acknowledging receipt of the material and giving notice that he would refuse to obey any armistice instructions. I sent back a letter, the tone of which angered the general, in which I informed him that the order regarding the armistice came directly from the *president*.

When I finally arrived at Jalapa General Scott had quarters provided for me, but he refused to call on me. Consequently I refused to call on the general. More letters flew back and forth Meanwhile the dispatch of April 15th from the State Department had been placed in the hands of Mexican Foreign Minister Jóse R. Pacheco, but not answered. The entire effort of the United States government in Mexico ground to a screeching halt.

Eventually the general made an overture of peace. I became ill eating the local food and General Scott sent me a jar of marmalade. I accepted the peace offering graciously, and by the end of July the quarrel was over. Actually we became the best of friends. But the president wrote, "because of the personal controversy between these two self-important personages, the golden moment for concluding a peace with Mexico may have passed."

There never was a "golden moment" for negotiating with Mexico because of the instability of their government. Santa Anna marched from Puebla to the Capital on May 15, 1847, and seized the presidency from Pedro María Anaya. Santa Anna now called himself El Presidente, but was trusted by no one and held the office only because he held the army. On June 15th the Mexican Congress assembled but failed to obtain a quorum. Thus Santa Anna became a virtual dictator and ruthlessly prepared the defense of the City of Mexico.

Scott's army began its advance on August 7th and Churubusco fell on August 20th. That night Señor Pacheco, the Mexican Foreign Minister, requested the British Minister to ask for a truce for the purpose of answering the sealed dispatch of April 15th which he had received weeks earlier. Scott agreed to a truce and sent a note to Santa Anna the next morning. Santa Anna ignored the note. I then bumbled into Santa Anna's hands by entering into negotiations with the Mexican commissioners, who at the time had no instructions from their government. The Mexican Congress passed an arrogant resolution that no peace would be considered until the American armies were withdrawn from Mexico, and Mexico was indemnified for the cost of the war. I held meetings with the commissioners from August 27th through September 2nd, but the discussions were futile. Essentially the Mexicans were willing to abandon Texas provided that the United States would pay for it. But this was ridiculous since a victorious American army was encamped just outside the capital and the Mexican nation was in a state of anarchy, with an illegal government in power.

I could not make a peace if I refused to negotiate over this absurd Mexican position. I therefore entered into discussions, and before the meetings were over I had violated and exceeded my instructions. Yes, I was out-talked by the Mexicans. On September 6th the commissioners submitted another proposal. Mexico would accept the annexation of Texas if the United States paid for the territory. The Nueces River would be its boundary. Mexico would part with Upper California provided the United States grant concessions including the assumption of all claims.

Santa Anna used the truce to gather his forces and bolster the defenses of the city. Aware that negotiations had broken down Scott canceled the truce on September 6th. Fighting began again at Molino del Rey two days later and on September 14th American forces took possession of the capital. Santa Anna slipped away and resigned as president on September 22nd. Manuel de la Peña y Peña, who was serving as Chief Justice, assumed the acting presidency. He moved the seat of government to Querétero in early October. The Mexican Congress assembled and on November 11th named Pedro María Anaya president again. Peña y Peña became Foreign Minister. Perhaps peace negotiations could now be renewed.

President Polk said that I had managed the negotiations in a most bungling manner. He remarked, "I thought you had more sagacity and common sense . . ." On October 6th orders were issued in no uncertain terms recalling me back to Washington and stating that Mexico must sue for peace before further negotiations would be considered. On October 21st my recall order was sent out to Mexico for a second time.

I offered to reopen peace negotiations on October 20th. Peña y Peña assured me that new commissioners would soon be appointed. Four commissioners were appointed on November 15, including Manuel Rincón and Luís Gonzaga Cuevas. On November 16th I received Washington's recall message of October 6th and the rebuke letter of October 21st. A few days later Foreign Minister Peña y Peña also received the news of my recall and assured me that it was a blow to peace in Mexico. Polk's demand that Mexico must sue for peace might prove more than the national vanity could stomach. I pondered over the impossible position I found myself in. A treaty of peace based on my original instructions was definitely possible if I ignored the recall. If I did not negotiate the war might go on much longer. There would be guerilla uprisings and the new moderate government at Querétero would probably fail. Right or wrong I reached a momentous decision on December 4th.

On that day I notified the British Minister that I proposed to enter into negotiations with the new Mexican commission. On December 6th I set the government in Washington straight on the situation here in Mexico. Without doubt I disobeyed orders and then proceeded to negotiate a treaty contrary to my government's position and even contravened my original instructions. Nobody would know what might have happened had I not "grasped time by the forelock." As I explained it to Mr. Buchanan, "if the present opportunity be not seized at *once*, all chances of making a treaty *at all* will be lost for an indefinite period—probably forever." My detractors complained that I was out-maneuvered by the Mexican peace commissioners, and that I gave away all that had been won at the treaty table at an enormous expenditure of money and a frightful cost of human lives.

Peña y Peña

Sixty days would pass between the time I made my decision not to leave Mexico and the completion of the treaty negotiations. My sole communication in that period was a letter to my wife telling her that I was well and that I missed her.

The treaty stipulated that the United States would rescue any Mexican citizen held by our Western Indians, and we would restrain such tribes from entering Mexico. I overlooked my instructions to obtain a favorable railroad route to the West Coast in the Gila Valley and instead agreed that no railroad should be built without the mutual consent of both nations. I ignored my orders to obtain an outlet on the Gulf of California and accepted the Gila and Colorado rivers as the boundary. I ignored my orders not to recognize land grants made in the ceded territory after the declaration of war. I not only agreed to an indemnity of $15 million but also agreed to assume the payment of claims owed by Mexico to American citizens. I did, however, negotiate a treaty which met the major demands; the Rio Grande boundary, New Mexico and Upper California, and the settlement of the claims question.

The stipulations of the treaty of Guadalupe Hidalgo are well known and the United States honored all land grants in the ceded area, including some rather questionable last-minute alienations. The commissioners and I signed the treaty on February 2nd, 1848, and it arrived speedily in Washington on February 19th. The president's Cabinet argued the merits of the treaty and did not consider my malfeasance. They embraced it and submitted it to the United States Congress. In the midst of the debate the venerable John Quincy Adams fell unconscious at his desk in the House. He died two days later, and a somber influence pervaded the final days of the debate. On March 10th, however, the treaty secured the two-thirds majority needed for ratification. It was now a done deal!

On March 17th, 1848 I was placed under arrest and escorted out of Mexico. I lost my job at the State Department, but I was never put on trial. I was <u>never</u> offered a government job again, and I was <u>never</u> compensated for my expenses in Mexico. I am just another ordinary citizen now anticipating that *another* terrible war will break out. I keep asking myself, "Have I grown any older and wiser, or just <u>older</u>?"

Chapter 16

Treaty of Guadalupe—Hidalgo

Ratified March 10, 1848
Copy Received, July 5, 1848

Although strongly disapproving of the independent role played by Nicholas Trist in making the peace treaty with Mexico, Polk nonetheless felt it would be wise to accept it. He knew the political passions of the day would only be further aroused, and a treaty on broader terms would probably not be passed in the long run. The treaty of Guadalupe-Hidalgo, signed in Mexico on February 2, was ratified by the Senate, 38-14, on March 10, 1848, and by the Mexican Congress on May 25. Ratifications were exchanged on May 30, and the treaty proclaimed in effect by President Polk on July 4, 1848.

ARTICLE I.

There shall be firm and universal peace between the United States of America and the Mexican Republic, and between their respective countries, territories, cities, towns and people, without exception of places or persons.

ARTICLE II.

Immediately upon the signature of this treaty, a convention shall be entered into between a commissioner or commissioners appointed by the general in chief of the forces of the United States, and such as may be appointed by the Mexican government, to the end that a provisional suspension of hostilities shall take place, and that, in the places occupied by the said forces, constitutional order may be reestablished, as regards the political, administrative, and judicial branches, so far as this shall be permitted by the circumstances of military occupation.

ARTICLE III.

Immediately upon the ratification of the present treaty by the government of the United States, orders shall be transmitted to the commanders of their land and naval forces, requiring the latter (provided this treaty shall then have been ratified by the government of the Mexican Republic, and the ratifications exchanged) immediately to desist from blockading any Mexican ports and requiring the former (under the same condition) to commence, at the earliest moment practicable, withdrawing all troops of the United State then in the interior of the Mexican Republic, to points that shall be selected by common agreement, at a distance from the seaports not exceeding thirty leagues; and such evacuation of the interior of the Republic shall be completed with the least possible delay; the Mexican government hereby binding itself to afford every facility in its power for rendering the same convenient to the troops, on their march and in their new positions, and for promoting a good understanding between them and the inhabitants. In like manner orders shall be dispatched to the persons in charge of the custom houses at all ports occupied by the forces of the United States, requiring them (under the same condition) immediately to deliver possession of the same to the persons authorized by the Mexican government to receive it, together with all bonds and evidences of debt for duties on importations and on exportations, not yet fallen due. Moreover, a faithful and exact account shall be made out, showing the entire amount of all duties on imports and on exports, collected at such custom-houses, or elsewhere in Mexico, by authority of the United States, from and after the day of ratification of this treaty by the government of the Mexican Republic; and also an account of the cost of collection; and such entire amount, deducting only the cost of collection, shall be delivered to the Mexican government, at the City of Mexico, within three months after the exchange of ratifications.

The evacuation of the capital of the Mexican Republic by the troops of the United States, in virtue of the above stipulation, shall be completed in one month after the orders there stipulated for shall have been received by the commander of said troops, or sooner if possible.

ARTICLE IV

Immediately after the exchange of ratifications of the present treaty all castles, forts, territories, places, and possessions, which have been taken or occupied by the forces of the United States during the present war, within the limits of the Mexican Republic, as about to be established by the following article, shall be definitely restored to the said Republic, together with all the artillery, arms, apparatus of war, munitions, and other public property, which were in the said castles and forts when captured, and which shall remain there at the time when this treaty shall be duly ratified by the government of the Mexican Republic. To this end, immediately upon the signature of this treaty, orders shall be dispatched to the American officers commanding such castles and forts, securing against the removal or destruction of any such artillery, arms, apparatus of war, munitions, or other public property. The City of Mexico, within the inner line of entrenchments surrounding the said city, is comprehended in the above stipulation, as regards the restoration of artillery, apparatus of war, etc.

The final evacuation of the territory of the Mexican Republic, by the forces of the United States, shall be completed in three months from the said exchange of ratifications, or sooner if possible; the Mexican government hereby engaging, as in the foregoing article to use all means in its power for facilitating such evacuation, and rendering it convenient to the troops, and for promoting a good understanding between them and the inhabitants.

If, however, the ratification of this treaty by both parties should not take place in time to allow the embarkation of the troops of the United States to be completed before the commencement of the sickly season, at the Mexican ports on the Gulf of Mexico, in such case a friendly arrangement shall be entered into between the general-in-chief of the said troops and the Mexican government, whereby healthy and otherwise suitable places, at a distance from the ports not exceeding thirty leagues, shall be designated for the residence of such troops as may not yet have embarked, until the return of the healthy season. And the space of time here referred to as, comprehending the sickly season shall be understood to extend from the first day of May to the first day of November.

All prisoners of war taken on either side, on land or on sea, shall be restored as soon as practicable after the exchange of ratifications of this treaty. It is also agreed that if any Mexicans should now be held as captives by any savage tribe within the limits of the United States, as about to be established by the following article, the government of the said United States will exact the release of such captives and cause them to be restored to their country.

ARTICLE V

The boundary line between the two Republics shall commence in the Gulf of Mexico, three leagues from land, opposite the mouth of the Rio Grande, otherwise called Rio Bravo del Norte, or opposite the mouth of its deepest branch, if it should have more than one branch emptying directly into the sea; from thence up the middle of that river, following the deepest channel, where it has more than one, to the point where it strikes the southern boundary of New Mexico; thence, westwardly, along the whole southern boundary of New Mexico (which runs north of the town called Paso) to its western termination; thence, northward, along the western line of New Mexico, until it intersects the first branch of the river Gila; (or if it should not intersect any branch of that river, then to the point on the said line nearest to such branch, and thence in a direct line to the same) thence down the middle of the said branch and of the said river, until it empties into the Rio Colorado; thence across the Rio Colorado, following the division line between Upper and Lower California, to the Pacific Ocean. The southern and western limits of New Mexico, mentioned in the article, are those laid down in the map entitled "Map of the United Mexican States, as organized and defined by various acts of the Congress of said Republic, and constructed according to the best authorities, Revised edition, published at New York in 1847, by J. Disturnell," of which map a copy is added to this treaty, bearing the signatures and seals of the undersigned Plenipotentiaries. And, in order to preclude all difficulty in tracing upon the ground the limit separating Upper from Lower California, it is agreed that the said limit shall consist of a straight line drawn from the middle of the Rio Gila, where it unites with the Colorado, to a point on the coast of the Pacific Ocean, distant one marine league due south of the southernmost point of the port of San Diego, according to the plan of said port made in the year 1782 by Don Juan Pantoja, second sailing-master of the Spanish fleet, and published at Madrid in the year 1802, in the atlas to the voyage of the schooners *Sutil* and *Mexicana*; of which plan a copy is hereunto added, signed and sealed by the respective Plenipotentiaries.

In order to designate the boundary line with due precision, upon authoritative maps, and to establish upon the ground land-marks which shall show the limits of both republics, as described in the present article, the two governments shall each appoint a commissioner and a surveyor, who, before the expiration of one year from the date of the exchange of ratifications of this treaty, shall meet at the port of San Diego, and proceed to run and mark the said boundary in its whole course to the mouth of the Rio Bravo del Norte. They shall keep journals and make out plans of their operations; and the result agreed upon by them shall be deemed a part of this treaty, and shall have the same force as if it were inserted therein. The two governments will amicably agree regarding what may be necessary to these persons, and also as to their respective escorts, should such be necessary.

The boundary line established by this article shall be religiously respected by each of the two republics, and no change shall ever be made therein, except by the express and free consent of both nations, lawfully given by the general government of each, in conformity with its own constitution.

ARTICLE VI

The vessels and citizens of the United States shall, in all time, have a free and uninterrupted passage by the Gulf of California, and by the river Colorado below its confluence with the Gila, to and from their possessions situated north of the boundary line defined in the preceding article; it being understood that this passage is to be by navigating the Gulf of California and the river Colorado, and not by land, without the express consent of the Mexican government.

If, by the examinations which may be made, it should be ascertained to be practicable and advantageous to construct a road, canal, or railway, which should in whole or in part run upon the river Gila, or upon its right or its left bank, within the space of one marine league from either margin of the river, the governments of both republics will form an agreement regarding its construction, in order that it may serve equally for the use and advantage of both countries.

ARTICLE VII

The river Gila, and the part of the Rio Bravo del Norte lying below the southern boundary of New Mexico, being, agreeably to the fifth article, divided in the middle between the two republics, the navigation of the Gila and of the Bravo below said boundary shall be free and common to the vessels and citizens of both countries; and neither shall, without the consent of the other, construct any work that may impede or interrupt, in whole or in part, the exercise of this right; not even for the purpose of favoring new methods of navigation. Nor shall any tax or contribution, under any denomination or title, be levied upon vessels or persons navigating the same or upon merchandise or effects transported thereon, except in the case of landing upon one of their shores. If, for the purpose of making the said rivers navigable, or for maintaining them in such state, it should be necessary or advantageous to establish any tax or contribution, this shall not be done without the consent of both governments.

The stipulations contained in the present article shall not impair the territorial rights of either republic within its established limits.

ARTICLE VIII

Mexicans now established in territories previously belonging to Mexico, and which remain for the future within the limits of the United States, as defined by the present treaty, shall be free to continue where they now reside, or to remove at any time to the Mexican Republic, retaining the property which they possess in the said territories, or disposing thereof, and removing the proceeds wherever they please, without their being subjected, on this account, to any contribution, tax, or charge whatever.

Those who shall prefer to remain in the said territories may either retain the title and rights of Mexican citizens, or acquire those of citizens of the United States. But they shall be under the obligation to make their election within one year from the date of the exchange of ratifications of this treaty; and those who shall remain in the said territories after the expiration of that year, without having declared their intention to retain the character of Mexicans, shall be considered to have elected to become citizens of the United States.

In the said territories, property of every kind, now belonging to Mexicans not established there, shall be inviolably respected. The present owners, the heirs of these, and all Mexicans who may hereafter acquire said property by contract, shall enjoy with respect to it guarantees equally ample as if the same belonged to citizens of the United States.

ARTICLE IX[20]

The Mexicans who, in the territories aforesaid, shall not preserve the character of citizens of the Mexican Republic, conformably with what is stipulated in the preceding article, shall be incorporated into the Union

---

[20] Somewhat modified at a later date.

of the United States, and admitted as soon as possible, according to the principles of the Federal Constitution, to the enjoyment of all the rights of citizens of the United States. In the mean time, shall be maintained and protected in the free enjoyment of their liberty, their property, and the civil rights now vested in them according to the Mexican laws. With respect to political rights, their condition shall be on an equality with that of the inhabitants of the other territories of the United States; and at least equally good as that of the inhabitants of Louisiana and the Floridas, when these provinces, by transfer from the French Republic and the Crown of Spain, became territories of the United States.

The same most ample guaranty shall be enjoyed by all ecclesiastics and religious corporations or communities, as well in the discharge of the offices of their ministry, as in the enjoyment of their property of every kind, whether individual or corporate. This guaranty shall embrace all temples, houses and edifices dedicated to the Roman Catholic worship; as well as all property destined to its support, or to that of schools, hospitals and other foundations for charitable or beneficent purposes. No property of this nature shall be considered as having become the property of the American government, or as subject to be, by it, disposed of or diverted to other uses.

Finally, the relations and communication between the Catholics living in the territories aforesaid, and their respective ecclesiastical authorities, shall be open, free and exempt from all hindrance whatever, even although such authorities should reside within the limits of the Mexican Republic, as defined by this treaty; and this freedom shall continue, so long as a new demarcation of ecclesiastical districts shall not have been made, conformably with the laws of the Roman Catholic Church.

ARTICLE X (no text)[21]

ARTICLE XI

Considering that a great part of the territories, which, by the present treaty, are to be comprehended for the future within the limits of the

---

[21]   Stricken out by the United States Congress.

United States, is now occupied by savage tribes, who will hereafter be under the exclusive control of the government of the United States, and whose incursions within the territory of Mexico would be prejudicial in the extreme, it is solemnly agreed that all such incursions shall be forcibly restrained by the Government of the United States whensoever this may be necessary; and that when they cannot be prevented, they shall be punished by the said government, and satisfaction for the same shall be exacted by all in the same way, and with equal diligence and energy, as if the same incursions were meditated or committed within its own territory, against its own citizens.

It shall not be lawful, under any pretext whatever, for any inhabitant of the United States to purchase or acquire any Mexican, or any foreigner residing in Mexico, who may have been captured by Indians inhabiting the territory of either of the two republics; nor to purchase or acquire horses, mules, cattle, or property of any kind, stolen within Mexican territory by such Indians.

And in the event of any person or persons, captured within Mexican territory by Indians, being carried into the territory of the United States, the government of the latter engages and binds itself, in the most solemn manner, so soon as it shall know of such captives being within its territory, and shall be able so to do, through the faithful exercise of its influence and power, to rescue them and return them to their country. or deliver them to the agent or representative of the Mexican government. The Mexican authorities will, as far as practicable, give to the government of the United States notice of such captures; and its agents shall pay the expenses incurred in the maintenance and transmission of the rescued captives; who, in the mean time, shall be treated with the utmost hospitality by the American authorities at the place where they may be. But if the government of the United States, before receiving such notice from Mexico, should obtain intelligence, through any other channel, of the existence of Mexican captives within its territory, it will proceed forthwith to effect their release and delivery to the Mexican agent, as above stipulated.

For the purpose of giving to these stipulations the fullest possible efficacy, thereby affording the security and redress demanded by their true spirit and intent, the government of the United States will now and hereafter pass, without unnecessary delay, and always vigilantly enforce, such laws as the nature of the subject may require. And, finally, the sacredness of this obligation shall never be lost sight of by the said government, when providing for the removal of the Indians from any portion of the said territories, or for its being settled by citizens of the United States; but, on the contrary, special care shall then be taken not to place its Indian occupants under the necessity of seeking new homes, by committing those invasions which the United States have solemnly obliged themselves to restrain.

ARTICLE XII

In consideration of the extension acquired by the boundaries of the United States, as defined in the fifth article of the present treaty, the government of the United States engages to pay to that of the Mexican Republic the sum of fifteen millions of dollars.

Immediately after the treaty shall have been duly ratified by the government of the Mexican Republic, the sum of three millions of dollars shall be paid to the said government by that of the United States, at the City of Mexico, in the gold or silver coin of Mexico. The remaining twelve millions of dollars shall be paid at the same place, and in the same coin, in annual installments of three millions of dollars each, together with interest on the same at the rate of six per cent per annum. This interest shall begin to run upon the whole sum of twelve millions from the day of the ratification of the present treaty by the Mexican government, and the first of the installments shall be paid at the expiration of one year from the same day. Together with each annual installment, as it falls due, the whole interest accruing on such installment from the beginning shall also be paid.

ARTICLE XIII

The United States engage, moreover, to assume and pay to the claimants all the amounts now due them, and those hereafter to become due, by reason of the claims already liquidated and decided against the Mexican Republic, under the conventions between the two republics severally concluded on the eleventh day of April, eighteen hundred and thirty-nine, and on the thirtieth day of January, eighteen hundred and forty-three; so that the Mexican Republic shall be absolutely exempt, for the future, from all expense whatever on account of the said claims.

ARTICLE XIV

The United States do furthermore discharge the Mexican Republic from all claims of citizens of the United States, not heretofore decided against the Mexican government, which may have arisen previously to the date of the signature of this treaty; which discharge shall be final and perpetual, whether the said claims be rejected or be allowed by the board of commissioners provided for in the following article, and whatever shall be the total amount of those allowed.

ARTICLE XV

The United States, exonerating Mexico from all demands on account of the claims of their citizens mentioned in the preceding article, and considering them entirely and forever canceled, whatever their amount may be, undertake to make satisfaction for the same, to an amount not exceeding three and one-quarter millions of dollars. To ascertain the validity and amount of those claims, a board of commissioners shall be established by the government of the United States, whose awards shall be final and conclusive; provided that, in deciding upon the validity of each claim, the board shall be guided and governed by the principles and rules of decision prescribed by the first and fifth articles of the unratified convention, concluded at the City of Mexico on the twentieth day of November, one thousand eight hundred and forty-three; and in no case shall an award be made in favor of any claim not embraced by these principles and rules.

If, in the opinion of the said board of commissioners or of the claimants, any books, records, or documents, in the possession or power of the government of the Mexican Republic, shall be deemed necessary to the just decision of any claim, the commissioners, or the claimants through them, shall, within such period as Congress may designate, make an application in writing for the same, addressed to the Mexican

Minister of Foreign Affairs, to be transmitted by the Secretary of State of the United States; and the Mexican government engages, at the earliest possible moment after the receipt of such demand, to cause any of the books, records, or documents so specified, which shall be in their possession or power, (or authenticated copies or extracts of the same) to be transmitted to the said Secretary of State, who shall immediately deliver them over to the said board of commissioners; provided that no such application shall be made by or at the instance of any claimant, until the facts which it is expected to prove by such books, records, or documents, shall have been stated under oath or affirmation.

ARTICLE XVI

Each of the contracting parties reserves to itself the entire right to fortify whatever point within its territory it may judge proper so to fortify for its security.

ARTICLE XVII

The treaty of amity, commerce, and navigation, concluded at the City of Mexico, on the fifth day of April, A. D. 1831, between the United States of America and the United Mexican States, except the additional article, and except so far as the stipulations of the said treaty may be incompatible with any stipulation contained in the present treaty, is hereby revived for the period of eight years from the day of the exchange of ratifications of this treaty, with the same force and virtue as if incorporated therein; it being understood that each of the contracting parties reserves to itself the right, at any time after the said period of eight years shall have expired, to terminate the same by giving one year's notice of such intention to the other party.

ARTICLE XVIII

All supplies whatever for troops of the United States in Mexico, arriving at ports in the occupation of such troops previous to the final evacuation thereof, although subsequently to the restoration of the custom-houses at such ports, shall be entirely exempt from duties and charges of any kind; the government of the United States hereby engaging and pledging its faith to establish and vigilantly to enforce, all possible guards for securing the revenue of Mexico, by preventing the importation, under cover of this stipulation, of any articles other than such, both in kind and in quantity, as shall really be wanted for the use and consumption of the forces of the United States during the time they may remain in Mexico. To this end it shall be the duty of all officers and agents of the United States to denounce to the Mexican authorities at the respective ports any attempts at a fraudulent abuse of this stipulation, which they may know of, or may have reason to suspect, and to give to such authorities all the aid in their power with regard thereto; and every such attempt, when duly proved and established by sentence of a competent tribunal. They shall be punished by the confiscation of the property so attempted to be fraudulently introduced.

ARTICLE XIX

With respect to all merchandise, effects, and property whatsoever, imported into ports of Mexico, whilst in the occupation of the forces of the United States, whether by citizens of either republic, or by citizens or subjects of any neutral nation, the following rules shall be observed:

(1) All such merchandise, effects, and property, if imported previously to the restoration of the customhouses to the Mexican authorities, as stipulated for in the third article of this treaty, shall be exempt from confiscation, although the importation of the same be prohibited by the Mexican tariff.

(2) The same perfect exemption shall be enjoyed by all such merchandise, effects, and property, imported subsequently to the restoration of the custom-houses, and previously to the sixty days fixed in the following article for the coming into force of the Mexican tariff at such ports respectively; the said merchandise, effects, and property being, however, at the time of

their importation, subject to the payment of duties, as provided for in the said following article.

(3) All merchandise, effects, and property described in the two rules foregoing shall, during their continuance at the place of importation, and upon their leaving such place for the interior, be exempt from all duty, tax, or imposts of every kind, under whatsoever title or denomination. Nor shall they be there subject to any charge whatsoever upon the sale thereof.

(4) All merchandise, effects, and property, described in the first and second rules, which shall have been removed to any place in the interior, whilst such place was in the occupation of the forces of the United States, shall, during their continuance therein, be exempt from all tax upon the sale or consumption thereof, and from every kind of impost or contribution, under whatsoever title or denomination.

(5) But if any merchandise, effects, or property, described in the first and second rules, shall be removed to any place not occupied at the time by the forces of the United States, they shall, upon their introduction into such place, or upon their sale or consumption there, be subject to the same duties which, under the Mexican laws, they would be required to pay in such cases if they had been imported in time of peace, through the maritime custom-houses, and had there paid the duties conformably with the Mexican tariff.

(6) The owners of all merchandise, effects, or property, described in the first and second rules, and existing in any port of Mexico, shall have the right to re-ship the same, exempt from all tax, impost, or contribution whatever.

With respect to the metals, or other property, exported from any Mexican port while in the occupation of the forces of the United States, and previously to the restoration of the custom-house at such port, no person shall be required by the Mexican authorities, whether general or state, to pay any tax, duty, or contribution upon any such exportation, or in any manner to account for the same to the said authorities.

ARTICLE XX

Through consideration for the interests of commerce generally, it is agreed, that if less than sixty days should elapse between the date of the signature of this treaty and the restoration of the custom houses, conformably with the stipulation in the third article, in such case all merchandise, effects and property whatsoever, arriving at the Mexican ports after the restoration of the said custom-houses, and previously to the expiration of sixty days after the day of signature of this treaty, shall be admitted to entry; and no other duties shall be levied thereon than the duties established by the tariff found in force at such custom-houses at the time of the restoration of the same. And to all such merchandise, effects, and property, the rules established by the preceding article shall apply.

ARTICLE XXI

If unhappily any disagreement should hereafter arise between the governments of the two republics, whether with respect to the interpretation of any stipulation in this treaty, or with respect to any other particular concerning the political or commercial relations of the two nations, the said governments, in the name of those nations, do promise to each other that they will endeavor, in the most sincere and earnest manner, to settle the differences so arising, and to preserve the state of peace and friendship in which the two countries are now placing themselves, using, for this end, mutual representations and pacific negotiations. And if, by these means, they should not be enabled to come to an agreement, a resort shall not, on this account, be had to reprisals, aggression, or hostility of any kind, by the one shall be allowed to keep a commissary of prisoners, appointed by itself, with every cantonment of prisoners, in possession of the other; which commissary shall see the prisoners as often as he pleases; shall be allowed to receive, exempt from all duties a taxes, and to distribute, whatever comforts maybe sent to them by their friends; and shall be free to transmit his reports in open letters to the party by whom he is employed.

And it is declared that neither the pretense that war dissolves all treaties, nor any other whatever, shall be considered as annulling or suspending the solemn covenant contained in this article. On the contrary, the state of war is precisely that for which it is provided; and, during which, its stipulations are to be as sacredly observed as the most acknowledged obligations under the law of nature or nations.

ARTICLE XXII

This treaty shall be ratified by the president of the United States of America, by and with the advice and consent of the Senate thereof; and by the president of the Mexican Republic, with the previous approbation of its general Congress; and the ratifications shall be exchanged in the City of Washington, or at the seat of government of Mexico, in four months from the date of the signature hereof, or sooner if practicable.

In faith whereof we, the respective Plenipotentiaries, have signed this treaty of peace, friendship, limits, and settlement, and have hereunto affixed our seals respectively. Done in quintuplicate, at the city of Guadalupe Hidalgo, on the second day of February, in the year of our Lord one thousand eight hundred and forty-eight.

N. P. TRIST
LUIS P. CUEVAS
BERNARDO COUTO
MIGL. ATRISTAIN

Chapter 17

St. Patrick's Battalion

John O. Riley

I was born in 1817, the year of the famine which ravaged Ireland for the first seven years of my life. I lived in Galway County and embraced the struggle of Catholic Ireland. I developed anti-authority convictions differing little from many of the Irish who would flee their homeland.

In my teens I walked into a British army garrison in Galway and signed up. I told them that I was married and had a baby son. I joined the 89th Regiment and received my stripes in September 1839. I was noted in 1841 as a regimental pioneer, a man who acted under engineering orders to scout and prepare lines of march. Winning my stripes was a source of pride to me, but I realized I would rise no higher in Britain's Army.

I was mustered out in 1843 with the memory of a job well done. Leaving my family behind in Galway I crossed the Atlantic Ocean to start over, joining the flow of Irish immigrants yearning to pass through the "Golden Door," a term applied by refugees to describe hopes for prosperity and happiness in America, our promised land.

I soon boarded a Great Lakes skiff and headed to Mackinac, Michigan where I hoped to build my new life. This place housed a growing Irish-Catholic colony. I had already met Charles O'Malley, Pat McNally, Helen Kelly and others. O'Malley's group gathered together on Saturday evening to eat, drink, sing and dance; but most of all we reminisced about the good old days back in Ireland. I soon became bored with the monotonous routines of dockside labor at Mackinac. I started looking for other opportunities because I was bubbling over with ability and ambition.

In February, 1845 a joint resolution of the United States Congress endorsed the annexation of the Republic of Texas. In July 1845 I met Captain Moses E. Merrill who was trying to enlist men for a possible war with Mexico. I remarked that if I were to join up, I would do so only if it afforded me the chance "to obtain my former rank." On September 4, 1845 I went to the recruiting station, where Captain Merrill and Sergeant James Everstine greeted me. After obtaining my vital statistics I signed the enlistment form for Company "K" of the 5th U.S. Infantry. Company K's marching orders came only two days after I signed my enlistment papers.

I boarded a transport bound for Detroit, Michigan. There the 5th Infantry was assembled for the long journey to Texas. Fully half of us were either Irish or German. We finally arrived at New Orleans. We had traveled from Mackinac there in less than a month. We then went on to Texas. At Corpus Christi we marched and drilled for hours on end at the Kinney Ranch training station. Scores of men collapsed and fell on the drill field. Officer's kicks or their blows with their swords forced some of the men to stagger back into line. Epithets punctuated every order despite General Zachary Taylor's well deserved reputation as a leader who judged soldiers not by their accents but by their merit.

My ruddy complexion darkened as I trampled and trudged across the dusty parade ground in the Texas sunshine. As I noted, like British cavalrymen, the U.S. cavalry were also trained to fight on foot, but hated to do so. I would use that knowledge at a later date. I also saw a new kind of artillery group known as a "flying battery." It was the brainchild of Major Samuel Ringgold. It featured six-pound bronze field pieces which were hitched and unhitched from their team of horses very rapidly. They would deploy very fast when enemy infantry or cavalry threatened to pierce our formations. Major Ringgold oversaw our drill at Corpus

Christi. After days of infantry drills I could do little but hide my envy of the Irishmen who were in command of the field pieces. Handsome Lieutenant Braxton Bragg also drilled his gun crews incessantly, and his diligence paid off. But he hated the Irish and Germans and he enjoyed having us flogged for the least unintentional breach of drill.

This would lead to two assassination attempts by us later in the war. Most young officers, however, complained for lack of battlefield experience with harsh and instantaneous discipline. A traditional punishment inflicted upon us was "riding the horse." For trivial offenses officers would set us up on a high wooden sawhorse where we would sit for hours with our hands bound behind our backs and with iron weights anchored to our feet.

By mid October 1845 we were deemed ready for war. While officers and men alike languished in camp, November approached, heralding the storms of the Gulf winter. We were already questioning our impending roles. I was mulling over the religious and ethnic contradictions in camp. My ego was smashed with the realization that my dreams of rank and honor were futile. We languished in gauze-thin tents that the army had used during the Seminole campaign. Sleet froze the canvas and water turned into ice inside the tents. As the winter advanced, military exercises were suspended, and we passed our days in inactivity and disgust. With the erratic weather and hard discipline disease swept through the camp. At one time one-sixth of the entire encampment was on sick-report and unfit for duty.

We Irish discovered one welcome solace at Kinney's Ranch. Sometimes an itinerant Mexican priest would hold Catholic Mass. When the service ended tortillas and generous amounts of whiskey were served. I abstained from the alcohol but others gambled that they could return to their frozen tents before an officer detected spirits on their breath.

Travel orders secretly arrived at Corpus Christi on February 4, 1846. General Taylor replied that he would lose no time in marching to Point Isabel and then on to Matamoros on Mexican soil. The ill-kept secret evaporated on February 24th when General Taylor assembled us on the parade ground and told us to be prepared for a field movement at short notice to the Rio Grande, 150 miles across territory claimed by both Texas and Mexico.

On March 8th, 1846 Ringgold's flying batteries assembled, and at dawn on March 10th Company K led by Captain Merrill departed. The march was difficult and we often went for days without water. At night we slept on the bare ground invaded with rattlesnakes and tarantulas. When we finally reached Point Isabel it was on fire. General Taylor sent us on to the outskirts of Matamoros where we cleared a field of six-inch high corn stalks, in preparation for a fortification. We pitched our tents along the Rio Grande. Bathing in the river became a preoccupation with us because we could view Mexican peasant girls gathered on the opposite bank washing clothes. Many of them would slip naked into the water and laugh at us.

To assess Mexican General Mejia's strength General Taylor turned to General Worth for help. Worth selected a soldier from the 8th Infantry to be a spy. On March 29th Paul Standish swam across the Rio Grande, "surrendered" to Mexican troops, and announced himself a deserter. His captors led him to General Mejia who offered him a captain's commission to persuade other Americans to join him. Free to wander about Matamoros and study the Mexican fortifications Standish "served" his new army for one day and then stole back across the river back to Taylor's camp. Standish recounted an alarming development for the U.S. Army. Mejia's offer to commission him to raise a company of deserters heralded a Mexican strategy aimed at Taylor's men by the tolling of Church bells, the sounds of Latin prayers, and by the priests who sprinkled holy water upon the cannons and fortifications. Mexican generals knew of the rancor between Nativist officers and immigrants in Taylor's ranks. On March 31st an American officer noted that "two men, both foreigners, swam the river and deserted." In response to this General Taylor issued orders that all men seen swimming across the river should be ordered to immediately return, and in case they did not turn around they should be shot. Taylor had taken the illegal step of ordering that deserters be shot while no state of war existed, a blatant violation of the Articles of War.

On the morning of April 4th Private Carl Gross, a Frenchman serving in Company I of the 7th Infantry decided to desert. He plunged into the Rio Grande. Pickets spotted him and ordered him to stop. He kept swimming and several musketeers shot him dead. That evening as the men gathered at their evening mess to discussed Gross's death, two Irishmen, both of Company H in the 3rd Infantry sneaked down to the riverbank, eluded the pickets, and reached the Mexican lines. On the following evening another attempt at desertion ended in death for a Swiss national, a private who had also attempted to flee by swimming the river.

Mexican reinforcements began to stream in. Intelligence that General Ampudia was nearing Matamoros to take command from Mejia convinced most of us that he carried orders from the City of Mexico to start the war. Taylor ordered a round-the-clock work on our fortification called Fort Texas. Captain Mansfield ensured that all men off-duty would be constantly employed until the fort was finished. Company officers also scrutinized workmen who were liable to desert and swim the river.

On the evening of April 7, 1846 several deserters, standing on the Mexican bank, called over to their former tent-mates by name. They urged them to leave the U.S. Army and sample the "wine, women and song" across the Rio Grande. The next day four or five men jumped into the water in broad daylight. A bead was drawn on them, but the Rio Grande, flowing fast that day, took them all to the river bottom before the sentries could squeeze their triggers.

On April 10, 1846 Church bells tolled loudly in Matamoros, and a twenty gun salute was fired. Mexican troops marched into the town plaza to welcome General Pedro de Ampudia who had just ridden in from Monterey with about two hundred cavalrymen.

That night I pondered over the prejudice I had encountered in the American Army. I had three years to go before becoming a naturalized citizen. I had no family in America and I was a strict Catholic. Mexico certainly had its merits. On Sunday morning I requested a signed pass to attend a Catholic mass at a farm building just north of Fort Texas. It was granted and signed by my commanding officer Moses E. Merrill. I walked out of camp and at some point out of the pickets sight I edged close to the river, waiting for the right moment to slip in and swim to the opposite bank. The U.S. War Department would record, "He failed to return to duty at the expiration of a pass, and was recorded as having deserted on April 12, 1846."

Shortly after climbing out of the water I was captured by the Mexicans and brought back as a prisoner to Matamoros. I was led across the plaza to Ampudia's headquarters and had an audience with the general himself. Through an interpreter the general asked me several questions concerning the camp of General Taylor and his men. I told Ampudia that I was just the man to deliver a company of fellow deserters. I sold him on that premise and he tendered me a first lieutenant's commission on the spot. I said, "Thank you, I accept it!"

The next day I donned the dark cloth coat and white canvas pants of a Mexican officer. I was to receive a pay of 67 pesos, equivalent to $57.00. My monthly wages as a U.S. private had been only $7.00. I was accepted with kindness. From my first days in a Mexican uniform I cultivated friendships with my superiors and some prominent citizens of Matamoros.

I soon learned the Mexican drill protocols and the issuance of military orders. I also learned some Spanish. I adjusted from hardtack to tortillas, chile, tacos, enchiladas and the tamales of Mexico. I perceived some glaring problems, however. Many companies were filled with Indians, Mexico's lowest class. With 32,000 troops available Mexico believed that, despite the Army's flaws, it could handily defeat the invaders. Officers at Matamoros derided seedy old Zachary Taylor. They declared that the American dragoons shot poorly and rode even worse.

As I watched the Mexican Cavalry charging and the Infantry marching I knew I wanted no part of either military branch. I convinced my superiors to let me serve in the Artillery. When I broached the notion of forming deserters into a company of gunners the Mexicans eagerly consented. Foreign military experts believed that the Mexican Army had long ignored the use of modern field pieces and tactics. I gathered John Little, James Mills, John Murphy and Thomas Riley and convinced them to become gunners. In full sight of the Americans I put my men through the traditional paces of the artilleryman. Other deserters signed on, and in fact I formed a company of 48 Irishmen at Matamoros.

At 10:00 AM on April 24, 1846 cheers burst out from the plaza. As regimental bands played the Mexican troops paraded in review for their newly arrived leader Major General Mariano Arista. Ampudia was furious at his removal from command, but could do nothing but salute. Arista, an enemy of Santa Anna, inspected the troops. He had spent several years in exile in Florida and Cincinnati to escape Santa Anna. He had developed a liking for Americans and respected their actions. Arista was spoiling for a fight, however. Along with Arista's promise of land to deserters, his assurance of immediate citizenship, and "friendship" for Europeans he targeted Taylor's immigrant soldiers, that is men like me.

At reveille on April 25th Captain Seth Thornton's scout rode into Taylor's camp and delivered news of Thornton's ambush, and the death of fourteen of his dragoons at the hands of the Mexicans. It was the first blood shed in the Mexican war and it created an immense sensation in the United States. On April 26th Taylor sent a terse communiqué to Washington, "Hostilities may now be considered as commenced."

I was determined to attack Fort Texas. On the morning of May 3, 1846 we rammed round shot down our muzzle loaders. The firing lanyards were ready. With the command *"Fuego"* 30 cannons belched and recoiled as we jumped aside. Shot screeched across the Rio Grande and slammed against the walls and bomb shelters of the American fort.

After several hours of our bombardment on Fort Texas, Major Brown ordered his artillerymen to set Matamoros ablaze. They heated their balls in a furnace and the "hot shot" was hurled until 11:00 PM that night, three and a half hours after our guns ceased fire. Casualties in Matamoros proved light, as most of the townspeople had fled. Worried about Major Brown's plight, General Taylor decided to send Captain Samuel Walker and his Texas Rangers toward the besieged fort.

At 5:00 AM the next morning we started firing at Fort Texas again. As Major Brown's gunners loaded their 18-pounders to return the fire, they discovered the source of the previous night's barrage; the fact that we had thrown up a redoubt on the American side of the river. A battery of 12-pounders now hammered away just several hundred yards to the northwest.

The news that men who had eaten, drilled, laughed and suffered with them at Kinney's Ranch now manned Mexican guns spread quickly in the American camp. I stated later, "I participated in the action at Matamoros with 48 Irishmen." By 10:00 AM on May 6th we had been pounding the fort since dawn. One of our shells tore into Major Brown who I was told died three days later. At 4:30 PM we went to the Americans under a white flag and demanded that the garrison surrender. They refused and we started firing again.

On May 8th, while we were bombarding the fort, General Arista started the march of 2100 infantry and 1600 cavalry at 2:30 PM towards Palo Alto to face Taylor's anticipated line of march. He exhorted his men to hurl back the "gringos." I anticipated a Mexican victory—a short war with rank and land awaiting me for my part in Arista's triumph. The battle of Palo Alto was fought that afternoon. Late in the afternoon a grass fire ignited by a flaming wad from one of the field pieces forced the armies to disengage. As the smoke lifted Taylor's flying batteries shattered our infantry. Mexican retaliation was fruitless because of their inferior ammunition. At 7:00 PM the firing ceased and the Mexicans fell back

Early on May 9th Arista withdrew from Palo Alto and moved five miles up stream to Resaca de la Palma, still between Taylor's army and Fort Texas. Arista deployed his infantry in a river bed lined with shrubs, small trees, pools of water and numerous rocks. Arista's artillery started firing at the advancing Americans. Captain Charles May, a Kentuckian, charged our batteries but our gunners kept firing. Captain May and his men, however, captured General Rómolo Díaz de la Vega, Arista's chief of battlefield operations.

Taylor's men swarmed over our men bayoneting them all over the *resaca*. Arista's army which had fought so bravely throughout the afternoon buckled. From the ramparts of Fort Texas cheers arose. My artillerymen and I could only gape as thousands of soldiers surged down the road. They fled past the redoubt where my men and I stood and clogged the riverbank. At the first glimpse of Yankees up the road my men and I abandoned our cannons and bolted into the chaos on the riverbank.

On May 13, 1846 the United States Congress declared war on Mexico. We staggered southwest on dirt trails overgrown with cactus and mesquite. We struggled to keep up with the Mexican soldiers who were capable of making up to thirty miles in a day. A sudden downpour brought some relief. With food gone the men shot their packhorses and ate them. The citizens of Linares awakened on May 28th to find us staggering into the main plaza where hundreds fell to their knees at a large fountain and gulped down the spring water. We had tramped some 200 miles.

U.S. President Polk had sent a message to General Taylor to use priests to keep Catholic immigrants in the ranks. He sent the Reverend John McElroy and Father Anthony Rey of the Roman Catholic Church. On June 2nd the priests departed for the Rio Grande. Taylor had orders to show deference to McElroy and Rey—like it or not. The priests landed at Fort Polk on July 2nd, opened a mission, and made a visit to a base hospital. They then boarded a small steamer and reached Taylor's headquarters four days later.

In the meantime we marched northwest from Linares with the Army of the North towards the city of Monterey. Meija was now in command, because Arista was the designated scapegoat for the disaster at Palto Alto and Reseca de la Palma. Arista and his key officers were court-martialed and dismissed from the army. Most of the men grew to dislike Meija as a commander.

In late July we ascended into the Sierra mountains. Along the upper ridge we could look down and see Monterey, a vista of haciendas, spacious plazas and the Santa Catarina River. I, of course, looked for all the threats posed by any attacker. The Bishop's palace Obispado loomed above the city's western edge. Troops could easily protect the Saltillo road from this vantage point. On the southern bank of the river Federacion Hill, with it's escarpments, faced the Bishop's palace. Taylor's likeliest route would be from the north. This was protected by the Citadel which contained embrasures for 22 cannons. I noticed that the stone homes of Monterey with their flat roofs offered ideal spots for snipers to protect the cobblestone streets. We attended Mass, went to bullfights, and flirted with the local lassies at numerous fiestas and fandangoes.

At the end of August General Meija decided he needed more troops. On August 29th we received infantry reinforcements followed on September 6th with an infantry brigade and another brigade on September 8th. General Ampudia rode at the head of the third brigade. He held an order naming him as Meija's successor as the Army of the North's commander.

General Ampudia drafted workmen from Monterey to construct two bastions, the Teneria and El Diablo at the east end of Monterey near the main road. Priests allowed Ampudia to use the Cathedral as his main magazine. He crammed the interior with cases of shot and kegs of gunpowder. My men and I were under the direction of General Thomas Requena, Ampudias's second-in-command. He worked us hard dividing us among several batteries. I was creating the nucleus of my future foreign legion by adding another group of deserters to the forty-eight I had already formed at Matamoros.

On September 3rd a Mexican commission unveiled a program of land grants for American soldiers "who, not having been born in the United States, would abandon the North American lines and pass over to ours." As a lieutenant I could claim 200 acres after my military service was completed.

Taylor, accompanied by the two priests reached Camargo in early August and over the following few weeks assembled the men he would use to march to Monterey. From August 19th until September 6th, 1846 columns marched out of Camargo and headed towards Monterey. Father's McElroy and Rey accompanied them. Taylor had left behind 4700 volunteers to guard his 400 mile supply line to Point Isabel. Taylor's troops pitched tents at the Bosque de San Domingo which the Americans dubbed Walnut Springs, though Pecan Springs would have been a more descriptive name.

At 11:00 AM on September 20th we spotted Taylor's 5th and 7th Infantry and two flying batteries under Worth's command moving towards the city from the west. We opened fire without much effect. Worth's men got to the Saltillo Road and out of range. Also on the morning of September 21st Lieutenant Colonel John Garland's 1st and 3rd Infantry and John Quitman's volunteers pushed toward's the eastern end of Monterey. As the gunfire waned on the evening of September 21st the church bells at Monterey tolled evening vespers. I was soaked with sweat and covered with black gunpowder as a soothing rain began to fall. Taylor had lost 400 men—nearly 10% of all Americans in action on this first day of battle, including 34 officers.

On September 22nd, soggy as hell, we mounted the city's eastern rooftops waiting for Taylor's advance. My gun crews dueled with the American's heavy batteries throughout the day, but neither side's cannonade inflicted any telling damage. The day's real action was at the western end of Monterey. Worth's men had crept up Independencia Hill in the rain. They took the western redoubt with few casualties. By 4:00 PM Worth's infantry climbed from their earthen works and poured into the palace's courtyard. They hauled down the Mexican banner from the palace's flagstaff and hoisted Old Glory above Independencia Hill. Ampudia ordered his men to abandon all their positions, including El Diablo, and to join the defenders of the city closest to the main plaza. The rain stopped before dawn on September 23rd and Taylor sent Quitman's brigade to probe the city's eastern defenses as the cannons of the Citadel opened fire again.

The Americans had a tactic to advance in the city. They battered holes in the sides of the houses, hurled shells with timed fuses inside, and poured through after the explosion to batter through the next house. They left sharpshooters to blaze away in rooftop duels with the Mexicans on top of the buildings. By nightfall the firing let up, but Taylor's massive 24-pounder howitzers kept firing at the plaza. Ampudia, holed up in a private home at the far end of the square from the cathedral had had enough.

Ampudia called for a parley with the Americans the next morning, September 25th. After several sessions of negotiations Ampudia surrendered the city to Taylor. Taylor allowed the Mexican troops to withdraw from the city if they would not pursue the Americans for eight weeks. Of all the combatants the only ones who had anything to fear about were my deserters. Early on the 26th I buttoned my blue tunic with the insignia of the Mexican artillery and joined 211 artillerymen at the rear of Ampudia's 1st Brigade. The Americans recognized some of their old deserter friends, including myself. Father's McElroy and Rey were about to encounter more deserters. Granting me and my gunners safe passage would prove to be a bloody mistake for General Zachary Taylor.

Ampudia's army marched southwest down the Saltillo road to the city of Saltillo. After loading supplies there we continued on towards San Luis Potosi. In three weeks we reached that town which was about 300 miles from the City of Mexico. Santa Anna was there and he was anxious to talk to me. He said he had a plan for me which I would welcome. He summoned me on October 25th. He was revered by many Mexicans as "the soldier of the people," that he was a fighter, peg leg and all. His ability to raise and equip an army was legendary, and as he interrogated me Santa Anna saw an experienced soldier whom he could use in his plan to pry at least 2,000 foreigners from Taylor's army.

Santa Anna believed that a unit in which the deserters would serve as a body, rather than scattered through various Mexican units, would prove a powerful attraction to immigrants. Since I had proven my talents with gun crews Santa Anna picked me. To placate any Mexican officer's anger Santa Anna designated Captain Francisco Rosendo as the deserter's nominal commander. He allowed me free rein to organize and train the unit and he worked with me to welcome new deserters to the Irish volunteers, and persuade recruits to man the cannons and equipment belonging to the unit. Santa Anna turned over his 16 and 24 pounder guns to us. I drilled my men on the parade ground of San Luis Potosi. On Sundays we could attend Mass at Our Lady of Carmen Cathedral. We attended bullfights, fandangos, and strolled the streets, enjoying everything that was happening. I sketched a design for my unit's flag and had the nuns of the San Luis Potosi convent to sew the banner. It was of green silk and had a harp on one side surmounted by the Mexican coat of arms. The other side had a picture of St. Patrick with the words "*San Patricio*" painted below.

By December 1846 the unit strength was 125 men with Irishmen dominating the muster rolls. Once Ampudia's army had marched south and Taylor had occupied Monterey the old problem between immigrants and officers in the camps appeared. Just three weeks after the battle Taylor reported that several Monterey priests had persuaded some fifty more men to desert. Many turned up at Santa Anna's camp in late 1846.

On January 3rd, 1847 General Winfield Scott and his staff arrived at Camargo. He had arrived as Polk's new commander-in-chief of the U.S. Army of Occupation, and with the authority to strike at the City of Mexico with the president's authority. Scott envisioned an amphibious assault on Vera Cruz and a westbound strike at Mexico's capital. With Taylor to the south at Victoria, Scott ordered General William O. Butler to start the bulk of Taylor's army towards Tampico on Mexico's eastern coast and 225 miles from San Luis Potosi.

To the north of Monterey Father Rey rode out into the countryside on a trip to Matamoros. He encountered a party of rancheros who brutally murdered him and took all his clerical vestments. His body was never found. On January 26th our Volunteer Company at San Luis Potosi received its marching orders. We were told to pack extra shirts, forty rounds of ammunition and cooking utensils. We were now called the "San Patricios" and were ordered to head north.

For the first thirty miles we marched across cultivated country, but then we started up into the mountains where we encountered cold icy winds and sleet. When we reached Matahuela, an ice storm descended down upon us, and a number of our party froze to death. After leaving Matahuela we had another hundred miles of desert marching. We arrived at La Encarnacion on February 5, 1847. Santa Anna held a review of his army on the 20th and the 15,000 or so who had survived the death march greeted him with cheers. Santa Anna informed us that Taylor was waiting 35 miles to the north at Agua Nueva.

We started out at 11:00 AM on February 21st. The cold was intense, but we marched till late night and reached the pass. Santa Anna halted the army for a short rest before dawn. We saw some smoke rising to the north and an hour later cavalrymen dashed in from that direction to report to the general. The Americans had abandoned Agua Nueva and had burned everything in sight, including their food supply. We were counting on Taylor's victuals as our victory banquet. Santa Anna drove us onward as Taylor's men were reportedly retreating to the north. We were fifteen miles behind them.

We halted near a ranch called La Encantada. Santa Anna galloped ahead to view the American positions and found Taylor's men defending a bottleneck in the road called La Angostura or the "Narrows." The Narrows was a passage way only forty feet wide flanked by the mountains. To the east of the road there was a broad flat expanse or plateau which could be used to deploy heavy weapons. With a few generals I went up to the Narrows on horseback and saw that from the top our heavy cannons could sweep the road and the plateau. I dismounted and yelled to the men below to drag up the guns. By 3:00 PM we had placed our field pieces and began to haul cases of shot, grape and canisters. The San Patricios anticipated the moment to avenge our humility at Monterey. We outnumbered Taylor three to one.

Santa Anna sent a note to Taylor giving him one hour to surrender. Old Rough and Ready declined. At 3:10 PM Santa Anna sent General Santiago Blanco's division forward into the Narrows. They halted and exchanged musket fire with the 1st Illinois. This was merely a feint to cover a move by Ampudia's 2,000 infantry into the mountain at Taylor's left flank. Taylor ordered the Arkansas and Kentucky cavalry regiments, and a battalion of Indiana infantry to intercept Ampudia. After dusk the gunfire ceased. We had not fired a shot all day long and we cooked up the last of our rations. A cold drizzle began to fall as darkness approached.

We awoke at dawn the next morning. Mexican bugles sounded and to our right the 7,400 infantrymen of General's Manuel Lombardini and Francesco Pacheco plunged into the ravine in front of the plateau and advanced slowly. From the ridge I shouted orders to load our guns with canisters. I estimated the range to the plateau at 250 yards and adjusted our muzzles. I trained my guns on the 2nd Indiana Volunteers and gave the command to fire "in battery." The Indianans, ravaged by the bursts from our cannons, edged backwards. At 9:00 AM Lombardini and Pachecho assembled for an assault against the plateau. At about the same time Taylor returned from Saltillo and rode onto the plateau in full view of both armies. As Pacheco's division pummeled the 2nd Indiana, Colonel William Bowles ordered his regiment to retreat. They broke and fled towards Buena Vista. By noon we had littered the plateau with dead and wounded volunteers.

Taylor decided after seeing our distant green banner that he had to take our battery, come what may. He ordered Lieutenant John Paul Jones O'Brien to accomplish the task. I waved my sword and shouted orders to my gunners. I had spotted the riders in the haze and I realized that I couldn't lower my muzzles enough to fire at them. Our muskets blazed, but again our shots went high. Each time we fired we moved backwards, reloaded, and fired again. Our musketry pounded O'Brien's men. A bullet tore into O'Brien's leg and the Mexicans swarmed over his four-pounder and bayoneted its few remaining gunners. A ball from one of our guns damaged the barrel of one of O'Brien's six-pounders. His horses all dead or wounded, O'Brien ordered several men to drag the crippled gun away.

At this point Davis's Rifles and the Illinois and Indiana infantry formed into lines and poured flank fire into our ranks. Our advance slowed up. Braxton Bragg's battery let go a deafening barrage. Taylor reportedly ordered Bragg, "Double-shot your guns, and give em hell!" Bragg did so eagerly. He elevated his muzzles at the ridge in front of the plateau and opened fire upon us. Soon Sherman's and Washington's flying batteries pumped double loads of shot into us. All around us lead balls sliced into my gun crews. At dusk nearly one-third of my men lay wounded or dead around our guns. Our attack had failed.

At daybreak on February 24th the Mexican Army and our San Patricios retreated. On the ridge where our green silk banner had fluttered, Taylor's men would find at least 22 dead deserters. My men and I had carried off our wounded, saving them from American nooses. Santa Anna rushed towards the City of Mexico well ahead of his men.

What I did not know yet was that my performance at Buena Vista had won the respect of the Mexican generals. We would never face Taylor again, for the war in northern Mexico was over. On February 25th General Francesco Mejia lauded the San Patricios as "worthy of the most consummate praise because the men fought with such daring bravery."

When we struggled back to San Luis Potosi in the second week of March 1847 I found a Captain's commission and a hike in pay awaiting me. I also learned that Winfield Scott had landed 8,600 troops two and a half miles south of Vera Cruz and was bombarding the city. I was able to replenish my unit with several dozen Irish residents of Mexico. We refurbished our heavy guns. In the third week of March we left San Luis Potosi and turned southward to join the Army of the East.

Vera Cruz was ravaged by bombardment and suffered over 200 civilians dead from American shells, which forced the garrison to surrender on March 29, 1847. It was at this time that the deadly *vomito* appeared in Scott's ranks. On April 8th Scott started General David Twiggs up the sandy National Highway at the head of 2600 infantry troops, two flying batteries, six 24-pounders, two 8-inch howitzers and a company of dragoons. Scott, along with Worth's regulars and General Robert Patterson's Volunteers headed for Jalapa between April 9th and April 14th, seventy-four miles up the highway and 4700 feet above the yellow fever belt. With over a 1,000 men left behind with the *vomito* sickness in Vera Cruz, the Americans could not afford any delay in reaching the healthier mountains.

Twiggs's vanguard halted in front of a gorge at the Rio del Plan, twenty miles east of Jalapa. Two mountains loomed above the highway, El Télégrafo and La Atalaya. Santa Anna's Army of the East was situated between the gorge and the mountains. With about 165 deserters I planted our flag and dug in south of the National Highway which led to the town of Cerro Gordo. Scott ordered his best engineers, Robert Lee, Pierre Beauregard, Joseph Johnston and Zealous Tower on a night reconnaissance to find a route to flank the Mexicans towards Cerro Gordo. Beauregard determined that a route could be hacked out of the brush to the west of La Atalaya, but he fell sick. On the night of April 15th Lee scouted the suggested route and he agreed with Beauregard's assessment.

Robert E. Lee and his men reported back to Scott on the 16th and Scott ordered Lee to form a construction party and cut a road along and past El Télégrafo. That night they hacked a trail wide enough for artillery to pass. Our Mexican pickets never detected the American work crews. At 4:00 AM on the morning of April 17th Twiggs's division and a brigade of Illinois and New York Volunteers had a hasty breakfast and formed into formation to traverse Lee's narrow trail.

They reached the base of La Atalaya four hours later. Twiggs ordered his 3rd and 7th Infantry to engage the enemy. They swarmed up the southwestern slope and drove off the Mexicans towards El Télégrafo.

Our batteries south of the highway opened up on them with our 16-pounders. These weapons cut down scores of Americans and sent hundreds diving behind rocks and trees. At sunset we ceased firing but Mexican bugles blared across El Télégrafo and they formed their men into an attack line. On La Atalaya Twiggs's artillerymen had dragged a small howitzer to the crest and loaded it with grapeshot. The Mexican column swept the hill and advanced within two hundred yards of the Americans. At this point the American howitzer boomed and sprayed grape shot into the Mexicans.

A veteran Mexican soldier said he never saw such sudden havoc and confusion caused by a single shot. As the Mexicans retreated down the hill with their wounded an Irishman of the 1st Artillery remarked that the howitzer "knew how to pay the piper." Twiggs's men carried their wounded soldiers to medical tents and on La Atalaya the men had a few mouth fulls of biscuit and a smoke before trying to sleep.

Shortly after dawn on April 18th grapeshot was directed into the Mexican battery. Americans had lugged two 24-pounders up La Atalaya during the night. Colonel Harney, in command there, then ordered a charge. At the sounds of the bugles and with "an excited hurrah," the infantry descended the slopes. Mexican musket fire peppered the Americans, but slowly as the 24-pounders did their dirty work the return fire slackened. Harney's men reached the lower breastworks of El Télégrafo and overran the Mexican troops with point-blank fire and bayonets. The Mexicans tossed their muskets aside and ran down the rest of the hill in confusion.

Soon after Harney's men secured El Télégrafo the entire Mexican line disintegrated. We abandoned our guns and fled with them. By 10:00 AM on April 18th the battle was over. Scott's army captured over 3000 Mexicans and 40 cannons including all our heavy pieces. They also "captured" Santa Anna's spare cork leg at his Cerro Gordo camp. We headed towards the City of Mexico about 200 miles up the National Highway. Actually Santa Anna was far from being defeated. Reaching the City of Mexico I welcomed more Irishmen and other foreign nationals living in the city into the ranks of the San Patricios. Once new recruits had signed on we found life in the city easier. After daily drill the new men were free to roam the capital with the other San Patricios. Few of our men had ever strolled through a park so lovely as the Alameda, with its giant trees, tropical mountain flowers and magnificent fountains.

In late May 1847 Scott departed Jalapa leaving a thousand man garrison and marched the bulk of his army to join General Worth at Puebla, arriving on May 28th. Everyone had thought that Scott had made a big mistake. U.S. President Polk sent Nicholas P. Trist to negotiate with the Mexican government for peace. Trist arrived at Jalapa on May 14th. Scott was furious at Polk's lack of confidence in him. Scott arranged his army into four divisions and planned a campaign to take the City of Mexico.

At the new San Patricio's barracks, an abandoned monastery near the Alameda, we met some new deserters from "the ould sod." I explained carefully to all the newcomers how they could be influential landowners at the end of the war. To handle all the new cannons and wagons I added German dragoons. I reported to Santa Anna that over 200 deserters were now billeted at the San Patricio's barracks. Santa Anna ordered us into a new unit on July 1st named the "Foreign Legion of San Patricio." Along with the directive I received a promotion to the rank of major. I was equally delighted that my friend Dalton had been promoted to first lieutenant.

We were now a foot artillery outfit. Some of us still manned four heavy pieces but the rest of us would act as infantry to protect the guns or serve as assault troops. At 2:00 PM on the afternoon of August 9, 1847 the sound of cannons were heard in the distance. The alarm was sounded that Scott's army had entered the Valley of Mexico. Negotiations had failed and soldiers were being ordered to their posts.

As I reviewed my 204 men marching beneath their green flag I counted 142 Irishmen all gathered by me. The noncoms and privates had new headgear consisting of jaunty red-tasseled caps. A new officer of the battalion rode next to me. Patrick Maloney, an Irish immigrant and a member of the 5th Infantry had deserted just three days earlier. He turned up at our barracks, signed his contract, and was immediately commissioned a lieutenant.

At El Penõn peak, crowned by a fortress and 30 cannons Santa Anna gathered 15,000 troops to block Scott's line of march up the National Highway. For the moment all we could do was wait. Scott never came near El Penõn. He marched south past Lake Chalco and Lake Xochilco and headed for the town of San Augustin. General Scott sent Lee to reconnoiter the volcanic lava fields or Pedregal which blocked his advance on August 18th. Lee returned and informed him that a rough path across the southern edge could be widened for artillery to pass. On August 19th Lee started work on the path through the Pedregal.

On the same day Santa Anna ordered us to take up positions at the Franciscan monastery of Santa Maria de Los Angeles at Churubusco. We were camped in the open fieldwork and all we saw that night was rain. General Valencia defied an order from Santa Anna to pull back to the town of San Angel and planned to meet the Americans with his 4000 troops and 23 cannons the next morning. In the morning Valencia spotted Lee's work crews and started his bombardment. He sent a message assuring Santa Anna that his assault would finish off the Americans on August 20th.

Valencia and his men proclaimed a victory that night, and they all got drunk. The next morning the Americans poured into Valencia's camp from behind and killed several hundred Mexicans with one volley. Then they fixed bayonets and charged. Valencia's troops crumbled in seventeen minutes. Over three thousand scared men dashed up the road towards San Geronimo, where Shield's brigade captured hundreds more. Some 2500 Mexicans fled toward the Rio Churubusco. Santa Anna, on horseback, met Valencia's fleeing troops and lashed at them with his riding crop.

Scott caught up with his men at San Angel. As 4,000 Americans pursued Valencia's men General William Worth marched his divisions toward Churubusco. Twiggs's division came forward from the left less than a thousand yards from the monastery where we were located. All morning the San Patricios watched as the American regiments drew closer. I knew that we had to hold the monastery to the death, buying time for the army to flee across the Rio Churubusco's main bridge.

At noon cries of "here they come" echoed across our battalion's defenses. Twiggs's division was headed directly towards us and Worth's men had rushed the bridgehead. I ran up our green flag in plain view of the on-rushing Americans. When the enemy was within sixty yards of us I gave the order to fire. Grapeshot tore Twiggs's column apart. His soldiers dove into the surrounding cornfields and the firing became intense. Worth's charge wilted in similar fashion at the bridgehead. His men were forced into the muddy cornfields, marshes and dikes.

One hour later Twiggs's men were still pinned down, their losses piling up with each volley fired at them. My gunners, covered with sweat and black from gunpowder, fired their cannon with unerring precision. In front of the monastery at about 2:15 PM Twiggs's men crawled forward toward us. I was told that our flag incensed the men who were writhing and crawling in the cornfields. By 3:15 PM the Americans had realized that our men were singling out "the Yankee disciplinarians whom they hated so bitterly."

To the left of our defenses Scott sent Shields's and Pierce's brigades against 2200 Mexican infantry deployed in the ditches behind the road. Santa Anna, fearing that Shields and Pierce would eventually break through along the highway and cross the river, sent a large detachment to his right flank. Santa Anna also rushed 200 infantry and a wagon of ammunition to the monastery at 2:45 PM. Soldiers quickly unloaded the wagon and doled out the powder and musket balls. Shortly after 3:00 PM the Americans led an assault with loud shouts. They splashed across the chest-high waters of the Rio Churubusco and charged to cut the road behind the bridgehead. James Longstreet of the American 8th Infantry planted the Stars and Stripes on the bridge. In front Captain James Duncan's flying battery pounded the Mexicans. He turned his guns on the monastery and blasted the walls and field works.

Twiggs's and Worth's infantry closed in on us from two sides. In the breastworks I exhorted my gunners to keep firing as Duncan's shells shattered three of my four cannons and scores of my gunners. I ordered the sole cannon to be loaded with grape. Down to their last few rounds they reached for the powder supply. Somehow, however, a spark ignited the last keg of powder and the flames enveloped Captain O'Leary and three other gunners. We put out the fire and carried the four wounded men into the monastery. I poured a round of grape into the Americans and then ordered my men into the monastery for a last stand. They carried their bullet-torn green banner with them.

The enemy surrounded the courtyard and clubbed open the door of the monastery with their musket butts. Others poured shot into the windows. We heaped furniture in front of the doors. Cries, curses, and gunfire were heard as Twiggs's and Worth's men drove us into a narrow corridor on the top floor. A Mexican man tried to raise a white flag, but a deserter tore it down. Some of our men slipped down a back staircase and made a dash for the river.

It was now over. Eighty-four men and myself sat or lay on the floor waiting for the Americans to do what they planned to do. We had bought Santa Anna time, but now what loomed, in the words of an American captain, "was the eventful and deserved fate of traitors to their adopted country."

Sixty percent of our men were killed or made prisoner at Churubusco. About one hundred had escaped. Twiggs and Worth rode up to us and swore at us loudly. The troops of the 14th Infantry which had seized our green flag waved it contemptuously as they marched out of the courtyard past us. In the City of Mexico Santa Anna lamented, "Give me a few hundred men like Riley and I would have won the victory."

We were kept in the courtyard that night, and of course it rained all night. The sentries hoped that some of us would try to escape so they could shoot us. Lightning showed glimpses of the City of Mexico's spires only four miles away. Santa Anna sent Scott a request for a truce on August 21st. Scott agreed to a temporary cease-fire, in large part to let his army recover from the battles of August 20th, dubbed "Bloody Friday."

Four days later, at the order of Captain George Davis we were removed from the monastery and ordered to march. One column went northwest to the town of Tacubaya and the other southwest to San Angel. I was taken to San Angel with 28 of my men on August 27th. At every step of the march we were cursed and catcalls were shouted as the Americans recognized their former comrades who had poured grape and musket balls at them from Fort Texas to Churubusco.

On August 25th Captain George Davis reported that he had turned over all the San Patricios for trial as deserters. Up north at Tacubaya 43 deserters sat in a warehouse as Colonel John Garland received General Order No. 259 with a message to convene a General Court Martial. General Scott later issued General Order No. 263 to Colonel Bennet Riley who was to serve as President of the General Court Martial to convene at San Angel at noon on August 26th.

The trial of the 43 men at Tacubaya began at the specified time on August 23, 1847. The first man tried was Frederich Fogel who pleaded guilty. The verdict of guilty came quickly and Fogel was sentenced to be hanged by the neck until he was dead. Over the next two weeks the other 42 men were tried. Thirty-seven pleaded not guilty. Twenty-seven offered a defense of being drunk when they were impressed into the St. Patrick's Battalion. Thirty-two of the defendants claimed that despite Mexican coercion they had never fired a shot against the Americans, or else had shot too high to hit anyone. The court sentenced 41 of the 43 prisoners to be hanged. Only Edward Ellis who had neglected to sign his enlistment papers and Lewis Pieper, "a perfect simpleton" were spared.

At San Angel I had seen my men hauled out of prison and tossed back in jail an hour or so later with a death sentence. On September 5th it was my turn. I stood staunchly before the judges. Dried blood, encrusted dirt and sweat did not hide the gilded epaulets and yellow insignia of my Mexican major's dark-blue suit. I was determined to infuriate my judges by dragging out my case as long as possible and insult the commission's intelligence. I, of course, pleaded "Not Guilty." I was portrayed by the prosecutors as the force behind the St. Patrick's Battalion. To gall the court I summoned a prominent English businessman from the City of Mexico to testify that he had seen me providing food and clothing to American prisoners, and that any talk that he had coerced any men into the St. Patrick's Battalion was a damned lie.

I said that General Ampudia had given me three choices:

1. Face an American firing squad.
2. Face a Mexican firing squad.
   Or
3. Join the Mexican Army.

Throughout my testimony I reiterated that I was <u>not</u> an American. I thought I had presented a rather effective defense. After a short deliberation the court found me guilty of the specification and sentenced me to be hung by the neck until I was dead.

On September 8, 1847 Scott's regiments stormed Molino del Rey about three miles from the gates to the City of Mexico. By 1:00 PM the battle was over. Scott had killed or wounded some 2,000 Mexicans and captured nearly 700. The formidable bulk of Chapultepec Castle still guarded the city. Rumors emerged that General Scott was going to spare my life. Earlier that week he had been sent the transcripts of the trials for the General's "approval, modification, or rejection." He noted carefully that the Articles of War said that <u>only</u> a soldier who deserted in a declared war could be executed for the crime.

Word spread quickly on September 9th that Scott had upheld the death sentence of 50 of my men, pardoned five, and had reduced fifteen execution orders. Scott ordered that the 15 who had reduced sentences should be stripped and receive fifty lashes and be branded with the letter "D" high up on the cheek-bone near the eye, but not close enough to jeopardize his sight.

Scott's enraged officers could only hope that the fifty lashes, well laid, would "kill the notorious Riley." Scott ordered that the executions and the lashings and branding be carried out between 6:00 AM and 7:00 AM on the morning of September 10th. Scott handed General David E. Twiggs the task.

It rained at San Angel on the evening of September 9th. Twenty-seven of us were in chains inside the prison. Shortly before dawn the showers ended. Another hour or two went by as we waited for the American soldiers to come. They arrived at 6:00 AM and removed our chains and ordered us to stand. We were herded into two groups. I said my final good-byes to those who were to be hanged. As we neared the plaza several hundred soldiers filled the square. Hundreds of Mexican civilians stood behind the soldiers. Women were weeping and many held rosaries and crucifixes aloft as the guards marched the prisoners into the square. The scaffold was about 40 feet in length, consisting of heavy pieces of timber supported by large square uprights. It was fourteen feet high and sixteen nooses dangled from the top timber.

General David Twiggs, on horseback, ordered the guards to march the sixteen condemned men to the gallows and the rest of us to a stand of trees in front of the church. Because the gallows had no platform eight mule drawn wagons and a teamster in each were parked below the ropes. American officers held white caps to be pulled over the heads of the condemned. But first, they would watch me and the others receive our lesser punishment. Twiggs read the orders for our punishment. Mexican muleteers drew back their whips containing eighteen-inch long knotted rawhide tails—and waited for Twiggs to begin the count. Twiggs counted slowly, increasing the chances that we would bleed to death or slip into shock. About halfway through the fifty lashes, the general "lost count," and before he "remembered" the correct number, nine extra strokes had ripped into me and the others. I did not cry out or faint.

Finally Twiggs shouted for the muleteers to stop. As we sagged to the ground seven soldiers approached with red hot cattle brands and held the smoking irons inches from our faces. Twiggs ordered the branders to proceed. They pressed the "D" into our right cheekbone just under the eye. Several screamed, but not me. Twiggs looked at me and noted that the D had been burned in upside down on my cheek. Twiggs ordered the soldier to brand an upright D on my other cheekbone. I passed out, but soldiers tossed a pail of water over me to revive me.

Meanwhile the drumbeats suddenly stopped. The driver's whips cracked, the carts lurched forward and the fifteen others were "swung off without a struggle." Guards thrust shovels in our hands and we buried out comrades below the gallows. When we had tossed the last shovel full of dirt upon our men, Twiggs issued one other order. Seven American soldiers crudely shaved our heads leaving each scalp a bloody mess. We were then dragged back to the jail. On September 11th the four men for whom there had been no room on the San Angel gallows were hung in the village of Mixcoac. On September 13th twenty-nine more men with nooses around their neck stood on wagons beneath the gallows at Mixcoac. They faced the walls of the Chapultepec Castle.

The Hanging of the San Patricio's at San Angel

The Americans were firing solid shot at the castle. They had pounded the position, the site of Mexico's Military College, most of the previous day. Scores of teenage Mexican cadets had endured their baptism of fire. At 6:30 AM Colonel William Selby Harney rode out to inspect the gallows. None of Scott's officers relished a hanging more than William S. Harney. Scott loathed Harney, having court-martialed him for insubordination in early 1847.

Harney read General Order No. 283 and then pointed at Chapultepec and the Mexican flag hanging above a parapet nearly shrouded by white smoke. The deserters, he cried, would stand under the gallows with the ropes in place and would remain until the American flag was deployed from the walls of Chapultepec. Harney then raved that he would then swing them "into eternity."

Scott's batteries hammered the lower defenses of the castle. At 8:00 AM the American regiments poured from Molino del Rey toward the western flank of Chapultepec. One of the doomed Irishmen addressed Harney, "If we won't be hung until your dirty old flag flies from the castle, we just might live to eat the goose that will fatten on the grass above your grave, Colonel." Hundreds of American troops scaled the stone walls of the fortress, as Worth's division breached the gates. Six young cadets, one clutching a Mexican flag, leaped from the ramparts to their death, rather than surrender or die from Yankee bayonets. Mexico would revere these youths as the "Los Ninōs Heroicos."

The din from the fortress reached a crescendo and suddenly died out. On a staff visible through the smoke above the parapets the Mexican flag disappeared. At 9:30 AM a rumbling cheer arose from the throats of the American soldiers. Harney sat rigidly in his saddle viewing the Stars and Stripes. The whips snapped and then thirty bodies dangled and swung under the gallows. A soldier asked Harney whether the bodies should be cut down. Harney replied, "No, I was ordered to have them hanged, and I have no orders to *unhang* them."

On Scott's order a few days after his triumphal entry into the City of Mexico some generals hauled me and the other branded prisoners into the city, and put us in cells in the Acordada prison. Mexican luminaries and journalists condemned the hangings and the whippings and the branding as "an atrocious act." In late November 1847 Scott ordered that all the San Patricios be moved to Chapultepec Castle where visits to the prisoners were restricted. In a letter to the British Consul I sought my release. On February 2, 1848 Nicholas Trist and the Mexican negotiators signed the treaty of Guadalupe Hidalgo. Mexico did not ratify the treaty until May 25, 1848 because many of the Mexican leaders wanted to keep on fighting, even though Santa Anna had been exiled.

Rumors that we would be shipped to New Orleans reached my cell at Chapultepec. On June 1, 1848 General William O. Butler succeeded General Scott in command. Butler issued General Order No. 116, and the order was given to Lieutenant Gileson to execute. At the prison he read aloud the generals "disposition" of the deserters, "The prisoners in confinement known as the San Patricios, will be immediately discharged." We were unchained and dragged out of the building.

While waiting for my orders to report back to the Mexican army I spent many hours of frustration at Tlalnepantla, a northern suburb of the City of Mexico. In late June 1848 my orders arrived, and I took command of the revamped St. Patrick's Battalion. Along with the directive came a promotion to colonel for me. At about this time General Mariano Parades was involved in an abortive rebellion to take over the Mexican government. Because of the involvement of one of my captains all of the San Patricios fell under suspicion. I was now arrested again, this time by the Mexicans, and escorted to a cell at Santiago Tlateloco, a military prison.

General Jose Joaquin Herrera crushed the coup by General Parades in July 1848. General Herrera ordered that the San Patricio Battalion be disbanded and its men given honorable discharges with all back pay and reassignment to new Mexican units. A military judge exonerated me on September 5th and ordered me to report back to the army, and I was reassigned to the regular infantry at Vera Cruz. In the spring of 1849 after contracting the *vomito* I was sent to a garrison at Puebla "on account of health." Soon thereafter I was medically discharged.

In February 1849 U.S. Navy Lieutenant John Perry spotted me on the streets of Puebla. Perry described me as having a "miserable dissipated look." What Perry thought as "dissipated" was actually the features of a man recovering from yellow fever. I soon headed back to Vera Cruz—Mexico's chief Atlantic seaport. Counting my back pay of $1224 I could live comfortably for a time. I planned to depart Vera Cruz for Havana, where ships stopped before crossing the Atlantic, and head home to Galway.[22]

---

[22]   *Recently discovered death records state in translation, "In the heroic city of Vera Cruz on August 31, 1850, I Don Ignacio Jose Jimenez, curate of the parish church of the Assumption of Our Lady, buried in the general cemetery the body of John Riley, 45 years old, a native of Ireland, unmarried, parents unknown. He died as a consequence of drunkenness, without the sacrament of the last rites."*

Chapter 18

LESSONS LEARNED IN THE MEXICAN WAR

Ulysses S. Grant

In taking military possession of Texas after annexation, the army of occupation, under General Zachary Taylor, was directed to occupy the disputed territory. The army did not stop at the Nueces River and offer to negotiate for a settlement of the boundary question, but went beyond, apparently in order to force Mexico to initiate war.

The present Southern rebellion (1860) is largely the outgrowth of the Mexican war. Nations, like individuals, are punished for their transgressions. I believe our punishment is yet to come.

I n May 1844 we went into camp at a place called Salubrity near the Red River on a high, sandy, pine ridge with springs of cool pure water. Fort Jesup was twenty-five miles away and we were near the old towns of Natchitoches and Grand Ecore in Louisiana. Our 4th Infantry Division was commanded by Colonel Vose, an old and venerable gentleman.

The summer was wiled away in social enjoyments between the officers and the inhabitants of the area. With a war with Mexico in prospect my hopes of being ordered to West Point as an instructor vanished. In the fall men were put to work building barracks and in a short period of time all were comfortably housed. The winter was spent more agreeably than the summer, and the winter climate was delightful.

During the short session of Congress in the winter of 1844-45 the bill for the annexation of Texas to the United States was passed. It reached President Tyler on March 1st, 1845 and promptly received his approval. We were expecting "further orders," but none arrived so I asked for, and received, a twenty days leave of absence to visit St. Louis and see my family.

Early in July 1845 we were transferred to the New Orleans Barracks. The yellow fever was raging in New Orleans *so* we stayed mainly on the post. In September our regiment left New Orleans for Corpus Christi, now in Texas. After reaching Shell Island by boat the labor of getting to Corpus Christi some 17 miles away was slow and tedious. The channel to the bay was so shallow that the steamer, small as it was, had to be dragged over the bottom when loaded. Not more than one trip a day could be effected. Later this was remedied by deepening the channel and increasing the number of vessels suitable to its navigation.

Corpus Christi is near the head of the bay formed by the entrance of the Nueces River. There was a small Mexican hamlet there and a small American trading post, at which goods were sold to Mexican smugglers. The bulk of the trade in this area was in leaf tobacco. Almost every Mexican, above the age of ten years, and many much younger, smoked hand rolled cigarettes. The price of tobacco was enormously high, and made successful smuggling very profitable at the time.

All laws for the Mexican government were enacted for many years in Spain. The Mexicans had been brought up ignorant of how to legislate or how to rule themselves. When they gained their independence after many years of war, it was the most natural thing that they adopted as their own the laws then in existence, including the tobacco tax.

Gradually the "Army of Occupation" assembled at Corpus Christi. It then consisted of seven companies of dragoons, four companies of light artillery, five regiments of infantry and one regiment of artillery acting as infantry—about three thousand men in all under the command of General Zachary Taylor.

We were sent to provoke a fight, but it was essential that Mexico should commence it. It was doubtful that Congress would declare a war, but if Mexico should attack our troops the Chief Executive could then prosecute the contest with vigor.

Mexico showed no willingness to come to the Nueces River to drive the invaders from their soil so we approached a little closer. Preparations were made to move the army to the Rio Grande at a point near Matamoros. The distance from Corpus Christi to Matamoros is 150 miles. There was no haste, and some months were consumed in the necessary preparations for the move. General Taylor encouraged officers to accompany expeditions to pay off small detachments located at Austin and San Antonio. I accompanied one of them in December 1845. San Antonio was equally divided in population between Americans and Mexicans. From there to Austin there was not a single residence except at New Braunfels, on the Guadalupe River. From Austin to Corpus Christi there was only a small settlement at Bastrop, with a few farms along the Colorado River.

I had never been interested in hunting, but many officers carried a shot gun, and every evening, after going into camp, some would go out and soon return with venison and wild turkeys, enough for the entire camp. I never went out and came to the conclusion that as a sportsman I was a complete failure.

I arrived back at Corpus Christi just in time to avoid being away without official leave. Soon afterwards I was promoted from brevet second lieutenant of the 4th Infantry to a full second lieutenant of the 7th Infantry. Our principal activity consisted in securing mules and getting them broken to harness. The process was slow, but amusing. Our soldiers came mostly from the larger cities and had never driven a mule-team in their life. They had to learn fast! Five mules were allotted to each wagon. In two's the men would approach each animal selected, avoiding as far as possible his sharp heels. Two ropes would be put about the neck of each animal with a slip noose, so that they could be choked if they became too unruly. They were then led out, harnessed by force, and hitched to the wagon in the position they had to keep ever after. In time all were broken in to do their duty submissively, if not cheerfully, but there never was a time during the campaign when it was safe to let a Mexican mule get loose. Their drivers were all professional teamsters by the time they got through.

While at Corpus Christi all the officers who had a fancy for riding kept horses. I soon had three of them which were cared for by a young colored boy who also looked after a few of our tents and cooked for the same group. I paid him $8.00 per month. One day he let my horses wander off and they were lost forever. I was quite upset at the time.

Orders to advance came on March 8th, 1846. We were divided into three brigades, with the cavalry being independent. Colonel Twiggs with his dragoons and a battery of light artillery moved on the same day. He was followed by the other two sections with a day's interval between the commands. Thus the rear brigade moved on the 11th.

General Taylor's orders to the troops were for us to make the highest payment for supplies, and to respect the rights of the peaceful people along the way. Having lost my horses I went on foot, but my company commander purchased another and I was induced to take the horse. I was sorry to do so because I felt that, belonging to a foot regiment, it was my duty to march with the men.

At the point where we struck the Colorado River the stream was quite wide and of sufficient depth for navigation. We all bunched up there since the troops were not instructed in bridge or raft construction. To add to the embarrassment there was a great deal of Mexican opposition on the far bank. A few of our cavalry dashed into the water and forded the stream where all opposition was soon dispersed. I do not remember a single shot being fired. We eventually waded the stream with our teams. The water was deep enough that the mules had to swim for a short distance, and that was a sight to see!

At about the middle of March the advance of our army reached the Rio Grande and went into camp opposite the city of Matamoros, and almost under the guns of a Mexican fort at the lower end of the town. The engineers laid out a fortification and construction commenced. The Mexicans were incensed at the near proximity of our troops and it was unsafe for our men to go beyond the limits of camp.

General Ulysses S. Grant

At the time I was with General Taylor at Point Isabel on the coast. It was the base of our supplies, and was about twenty-five miles from the garrison at Matamoros. As we lay in our tents upon the sea-shore the artillery near the fort on the Rio Grande could be distinctly heard. The war had begun. For myself, a young second lieutenant who had never heard a hostile gun before, I seriously wondered why I had enlisted.

By the latter part of April the works were in a partially defensible condition, and the 7th Infantry, Major Jacob Brown commanding, was marched in to garrison it. The little garrison was being continually besieged by the Mexicans on the Rio Grande.

On the evening of May 7th General Taylor started on his return from Point Isabel to relieve the post. After marching for about seven miles we halted and passed the night. On the next day as Palo Alto was approached at about noon an army outranking our small force was seen drawn up in a line of battle just in front of the timber. General Taylor halted his army before the head of the column came in range of the Mexican artillery. As I looked down that long line of about twenty-three hundred armed men, advancing towards a larger force also armed, I thought what a fearful responsibility General Taylor must be feeling.

The Mexicans opened fire upon us, first with artillery and then with his infantry. Their cannon balls struck the ground and ricocheted through the tall grass such that we could see them and step aside. When we got to a point where the artillery could be used with effect, a halt was called, and the battle opened up on both sides. General Taylor had three or four twelve-pounder howitzers with him which fired explosive shells, besides his eighteen-pounders which had a large range. The Mexicans only had artillery that fired solid shot. We greatly had the advantage in this respect.

Our artillery was advanced in front of the line and opened fire. On our side there was little loss while we occupied the position. During the day several advances were made, and just at dusk it became evident that the Mexicans were falling back. Our casualties for the day were nine killed and forty-seven wounded.

On the morning of May 9th we were ready to renew the battle but the enemy had left our front during the night. General Taylor selected Captain C. F. Smith of the artillery and Captain McCall of my company to take one hundred and fifty selected men each and find where the enemy had gone. This left me behind in command of the company, an honor and responsibility I thought great. Smith and McCall found the enemy at Resaca de la Palma and sent back for the rest of the army to advance. There seemed to be a few of the enemy out front and at one point I chanced upon them with my company. We captured a Mexican colonel, who had been wounded, and a few men. There was no further resistance. On the evening of the 9th the army returned and was encamped on its old ground near the fort, and the garrison was relieved. Major Jacob Brown of the 7th Infantry, the commanding officer, had been killed in the fighting on May 6th, and in his honor the new fort was named Fort Brown.

At about this time we learned that war officially existed between the United States and Mexico. On learning this fact General Taylor transferred our camps to the south or west bank of the river, and Matamoros was occupied. We then became the "Army of Invasion."

Up to this time General Taylor had regular troops in his command, but now that the invasion had taken place volunteers for one year commenced arriving. We remained there until sufficiently reinforced to warrant a movement into the interior. At this time Colonel Twiggs was second in command and Colonel or Brevet Brigadier General Worth was next to Twiggs in rank but claimed superiority by virtue of his brevet rank, and the question was submitted to Washington. It was decided against General Worth, who at once tendered his resignation and headed towards the capital. His resignation was not accepted and he was ordered back. He thus missed the battle of Palo Alto and Resaca de la Palma. In any events he returned to the army in time to command his division at the battle of Monterey.

We spent the summer pleasantly enough at Matamoros while waiting for volunteers. On the 19th of August the army started out for Monterey, leaving behind a small garrison at Matamoros. We were moved up river to Camargo on steamers. Some of us marched at night (because of the heat) on the south side of the river. When we reached Camargo I was detailed to act as quartermaster and commissary to the regiment. The advance from Camargo was commenced on the 5th of September. The army was divided into four columns separated from each other by one's day march. The advance troops reached Cerralvo in four days and halted for the remainder of the troops to catch up. By the 13th of September the rear guard arrived, and on the same day the advance resumed its march, followed as before, with a day separating the divisions. The forward division halted again at Marin, twenty-four miles from Monterey. From Marin the movement was in mass. By September 19th General Taylor was encamped at Walnut Springs, north and within three miles of Monterey. In front of us stretched an extensive plain on which stood a strong fort, enclosed on all sides, to which our army gave the name "The Black Fort." Its guns commanded the approaches to the city of Monterey. There were two hills north of the city which were also fortified. On one of these stood the Bishop's Palace at the west end of the city. The road to Saltillo left from the western end of the city under the protection of the palace's guns.

Just to the south of the city the Santa Catarina River flowed towards the east. Beyond the river there was a range of foot-hills and wilderness. There was a plaza in the center of the city. All the roads leading from it were swept by artillery. The house-tops near the plaza were converted into infantry fortifications by the use of sand-bags for parapets. General Ampudia, with a force of 10,000 men was then in command there. I remained at Walnut Springs in charge of the camp and the public property when the troops moved out.

General Taylor's force was about 6500 men strong. It was divided into three divisions under Generals Butler, Twiggs, and Worth. (now back in command) Major Mansfield, of the engineering office, determined that it would be practical to get troops around the Black Fort and the works on the detached hills to the northwest of the city, to the Saltillo Road. With this road in our possession the enemy would be cut off from receiving further supplies, if not from all communication with the interior.

General Worth was given the task of taking possession of this road. In selecting Worth for this role, critical for the success of the campaign, Taylor was pointedly ignoring the fact that Twiggs, not Worth, was the senior regular subordinate. Worth was the best soldier in Taylor's army and Taylor could not afford to take any unnecessary risks. Twiggs apparently raised no protest. Worth started on his march at 2:00 PM on the afternoon of the 20th. I was there to wish the troops success in their mission. I was very excited about their prospects. The divisions under General Butler and General Twiggs were drawn up to threaten the east and north side of the city and the works on these fronts.

General Worth's march that day was uninterrupted, but the enemy was seen to reinforce the Bishop's Palace. The general bivouacked for the night just outside of the range of the enemy's guns. Captain Saunders and Lieutenant George G. Meade made a reconnaissance to the Saltillo Road under the protective cover of night. At the same time General Taylor established a battery of his two twenty-four pounder howitzers and a ten-inch mortar, at a point from which he could threaten the Black Fort. The 4th Infantry was ordered to support the artillery while they were entrenching themselves and their guns.

At daylight the next morning fire opened on both sides and continued with, what seemed to me on that day, great fury. My curiosity got the better of me, and I mounted my horse and rode to the front to see what was going on. I had been there but a short time when the order to charge was given, and lacking the moral conviction to return to camp—where I had been ordered to stay—I charged with the regiment. At first we were under the fire of the Black Fort. As we advanced we came under the fire from batteries guarding the east, or lower, end of the city, and of musketry. About one-third of our men engaged in the charge were killed or wounded in the space of just a few minutes.

We retreated to get out of the barrage in an easterly direction perpendicular to the direct road running into the city from Walnut Springs. I was, I believe, the only person in the 4th Infantry in that charge who was on horseback. When we got to a place of safety the regiment halted and regrouped—what was left of it. Lieutenant Hawkins, the adjutant of the regiment, who was not in robust health was huffing and puffing from the charge and retreat, and seeing me on horseback, asked me if he could ride. I offered him my horse and he accepted immediately. A few minutes later I saw another soldier, a quartermaster's man, mounted, not far away. I ran to him, took his horse, and was back with the regiment in a few minutes. In a short time we were off again; and the next place of safety was a corn field to the northeast of the lower batteries. Lieutenant Haskins was killed in that last movement and I was designated to act in his place.

This charge on the 21st was ill-conceived and badly executed. We belonged to the brigade commanded by Lieutenant Colonel Garland who had received orders to charge the lower batteries of the city and carry them if he could without too much loss of life, for the purpose of creating a diversion in favor of Worth, who was conducting the movement which was intended to be decisive. There was no undue loss of life in reaching the lower end of Monterey, except that sustained by Garland's command.

Meanwhile Quitman's brigade, conducted by an officer of engineers, had reached the eastern end of the city and was placed under cover of the houses without much loss. Colonel Garland's brigade also arrived at the suburbs, and with the assistance of some of our troops who had reached house-tops from which they could fire into the battery covering the approaches to the lower end of the city, the battery was speedily captured, and its guns were turned upon another work of the enemy.

The entrance to the east end of the city was now secured, and the houses protected our troops located there. On the west General Worth reached the Saltillo Road after some fighting but without heavy loss. He turned from his new position and captured the forts on both heights in that quarter. This gave him possession at the upper or west end of Monterey. The Black Fort and the plaza in the center of the city were still in the possession of the enemy. Our camp at Walnut Springs was guarded by a company from each regiment.

The 22nd day of September was quiet for the United States troops, but the enemy kept up a harmless fire upon us from the Black Fort and the batteries still in their possession at the east end of the city. During the night they evacuated the eastern batteries and so on the morning of the 23rd we held undisputed possession of the east end of Monterey. Twiggs's division was well covered from the fire of the enemy. But the streets leading to the plaza were commanded from all directions by artillery. The houses were all flat roofed and one or two stories high, and about the plaza the roofs were manned with infantry, their troops being protected from our fire by parapets made of sand-bags. All advances into the city proper were thus fraught with much danger.

While moving through the streets which did not lead to the plaza, our men were protected from fire, and from the view of the enemy, except at the cross streets, where a volley of musketry and the discharge of grape-shot were invariably encountered. The 3rd and 4th Infantry regiments made an advance nearly to the plaza with heavy loss. The loss of 3rd Infantry in commissioned officers was especially severe. When the small command (ten companies in all) was within a block of the plaza it halted and regrouped. Our men spent the time during this exercise watching for an enemy to appear above the sand-bags on the neighboring houses. The exposure of a single head would bring a volley from our soldiers.

We had not occupied this position very long when it was discovered that our ammunition was growing low. General Garland wanted to get a message back to General Taylor to this effect. Deeming this mission dangerous he did not want to order any one to do it and asked for a volunteer. I immediately raised my hand and General Garland said, "go with God's speed, Lieutenant Grant, and good luck!"

My ride back was fearsome. I hung on to my horse on the side furthest from the enemy and with my exposed arm over his neck. I started out at full run. It was only at street crossings that my horse was under fire, but these I crossed at such a flying rate that generally I was past and under cover of the next block of houses before the enemy fired. I got out safely without a scratch. What luck!

At one point during my ride I saw an American sentry walking in front of a house, and I stopped to inquire what he was doing there. Finding that the house was full of wounded American officers and soldiers, I dismounted and went in. I found Captain Williams, of the engineer corps, fatally wounded in the head, and Lieutenant Terrett, also badly wounded, his guts protruding from his wounds. There were quite a number of badly bleeding soldiers also. Promising to report their situation, I left, readjusted myself on my horse, recommenced the run, and was soon with the troops at the east end. Before the ammunition could be collected, the two regiments I had been with also returned, running the same gauntlet I did, and with comparatively little loss. The main movement was countermanded and the troops were withdrawn. The poor wounded officers and men I had found, fell into the hands of the enemy during the night, and all died.

While all this was occurring in the east General Worth, with a small division of troops, was advancing towards the plaza from the opposite side of the city. He resorted to a better expedient for getting there than we did. Instead of moving through the open streets he advanced through the middle of the houses, cutting passageways from one to another. Without much loss of life he ended up in view of the plaza during the night. General Ampudia, viewing his precarious position made overtures for the surrender of the city and garrison. This brought a cease fire and the terms of the surrender were soon agreed upon. The prisoners were paroled and permitted to take their horses and personal property with them.

I was overwhelmed with pity seeing the large garrison of Mexicans marching out of town as prisoners, and no doubt the same feeling was expressed by most of our army who witnessed it. I thought how little interest the men before me had in the result of the war, and how little knowledge they had of "what it was all about."

After the surrender of Monterey we led a quiet camp life until midwinter. The locals fraternized with the "Yankees" in the most pleasant manner. Their property and person were thoroughly protected; and a market was opened up for all the products of the country such as the people had never enjoyed before. The wealthy portion of the population, however, abandoned their homes and remained away as long as they were in the possession of the invaders; but this class formed but a small percentage of the whole population.

The Mexican war was a political war. President Polk and his Secretary of War desired to make party capital out of it. General Scott was the indisputable commander of the military and he was a Whig. The Administration was Democratic. Scott had political aspirations and nothing so popularizes a candidate for high civil positions as military victories. It would not do to give him command of an "army of conquest."

The plans submitted by Scott for the Mexican campaign were disapproved and he replied in a tone somewhat disrespectful, "if a commander's plans are not to be supported by the Administration, success can not be expected."

That interchange occurred on May 27th, 1846. Four days later General Scott was notified that he need not go to Mexico. General Gaines was next in rank but he was old and feeble. Colonel Zachary Taylor was next, and he too was a Whig. But he was not supposed to entertain any political ambitions; nor did he while in battle. After the fall of Monterey and his third complete victory the Whig papers at home began to speak of him as *the* candidate of their party for the president.

Something had to be done. Taylor could not be relieved of duty in the field where all his battles had been victories. It was finally decided to send General Scott to Mexico as commander-in-chief and authorize him to capture Vera Cruz and march upon the capital of the country. The Administration had the problem of winning a war of conquest which had to be won to attain all the promised political benefits. It was no doubt supposed that Scott's ambition would lead him to destroy the chances for Taylor's presidency, and yet it was hoped that he would not make sufficient capital himself to secure the prize. The solution was to destroy Scott's chances without the loss of conquest and without permitting another general of the same political party to acquire like popularity. In blunt terms the Administration wanted Scott to disgrace himself!

Now that Scott was in command of all the forces in Mexico, he withdrew most of Taylor's troops and left him only enough volunteer troops to hold the line of the invading army. General Taylor protested against this depletion of his army, and his subsequent movement against Buena Vista indicated that he did not share the views of his chief in regard to the unimportance of conquest beyond the Rio Grande. General Scott estimated the men and material needed to capture Vera Cruz and to march to the City of Mexico, two hundred and sixty miles into the interior. He was promised all he asked for and seemed to have the confidence of the president. *The promises were all broken!*

Only half the troops he requested were sent, war material was withheld, and Scott had scarcely left for Mexico before the president undertook to supersede him by appointing Senator Thomas H. Benton as a lieutenant general. The whole idea was refused by Congress and General Scott remained in command; but every general appointed to serve under him was politically opposed to the chief, and several were downright hostile.

General Scott reached Point Isabel, at the mouth of the Rio Grande, late in December, 1846 and proceeded up river to Camargo, where he had written General Taylor to meet him. Taylor, however, was on his way to Tampico for the purpose of establishing a post there and had started his march before he was aware of General Scott being in the country. Under these circumstances Scott issued orders designating troops to be detached from Taylor, without the personal consultation he had expected to hold with his subordinate.

General Taylor's outstanding victory at Buena Vista on February 24th 1847 with a volunteer army over a vastly superior force made his nomination for the presidency by the Whigs a foregone conclusion. When Scott assumed command of the army of invasion I was in General David Twiggs' division under Taylor; but under the new orders my regiment was transferred to the division of General William Worth, under Scott. The troops withdrawn from Taylor to form part of the forces to attack Vera Cruz were assembled at the mouth of the Rio Grande preparatory to embarkation for their destination.

I found General Worth quite different from any other officer I had served under. He was nervous, impatient, and restless and was decidedly uptight when any responsible or important duty confronted him. He enjoyed, however, a fine reputation for his fighting qualities, and thus his officers and men were loyal to him.

Our army lay in camp on the beach near the mouth of the Rio Grande for several weeks, awaiting the arrival of transorts to carry it to its new field of operations. The passage was a tedious one; and many of the troops were on shipboard for over thirty days before they debarked south of Vera Cruz. The hot weather added to the discomfort of all. The transports assembled in the harbor of Anton Lizardo, sixteen miles south of Vera Cruz, where we waited for the remainder of the fleet bringing artillery, ammunition, and supplies from the North.

Finally on March 7th, 1847 the army of ten or twelve thousand men, given Scott to invade a country with a population of seven or eight millions in a mountainous country affording a natural advantage for defense was all assembled and ready to commence the perilous task of landing from vessels lying in the open sea. The main debarkation took place by the little island of Sacrificios, some three miles south of Vera Cruz. The vessels could not approach shore, so everything had to be landed in surf-boats. General Scott was aware of the situation and provided for the crafts before leaving the North. The men all jumped into the water when they came to the shallows, but the camp and garrison equipage, provisions, ammunition and all stores had to be protected from the salt water, and therefore their landing took several days. The Mexicans did not seem to mind our landing except for an occasional shot from the nearest fort. On the 9th of March the troops were all landed and a few days later the stores were on shore.

Vera Cruz at this time was a walled city. There were strong fortifications at regular intervals along the line. In front of the city and on an island half a mile out in the Gulf, stood San Juan de Ulúa, an inclosed fortification of great strength. Batteries were established, under cover of night, far to the front where the troops lay. These batteries were well protected, but no serious attempt was made by the Mexicans to capture any of them or drive our troops away. The siege continued with brisk firing until March 27th when a considerable breach had been made in the wall about the city. General Morales who was both governor of Vera Cruz and San Juan de Ulúa, commenced communication with General Scott proposing surrender of the town, forts and garrison. On March 29th Vera Cruz and San Juan de Ulúa were occupied by Scott's army. About five thousand prisoners and four hundred pieces of artillery were taken. The casualties on our side during the siege amounted to sixty-four officers and men, killed or wounded.

As I stated earlier General Scott had less than twelve thousand men at Vera Cruz. This was a small army with which to penetrate two hundred and seventy miles to besiege a capital of over one hundred thousand inhabitants. The line of march led through mountain passes easily defended, and in fact there were only two roads from Vera Cruz to the City of Mexico that could be taken by an army; one by Jalapa and the other by Cordova, the two coming together on the great plain extending to the City of Mexico.

Another major problem at the time was disease. It was important to get away from Vera Cruz as soon as possible, in order to avoid the *vomito* which visits that city early in the year and is in many cases fatal. It was absolutely necessary to have enough supplies for the army to proceed to Jalapa, 65 miles in the interior, and above the fevers of the coast. Not counting the sick and weak, the moving column was now less than 10,000 strong. It was composed of three divisions under Generals Twiggs, Worth and Patterson. The importance of escaping the *vomito* was so great that as soon as we had enough transportation to make a division the advance towards Jalapa was commenced by General Twiggs' division on April 8th. He was followed very soon by Patterson and General Worth who brought up the rear. Worth left on April 13th.

The leading division ran up against the enemy at Cerro Gordo, some fifty miles west, and went into camp at Plan del Rio, about three miles from the fortifications. General Patterson reached Plan del Rio soon after Twiggs arrived. General Scott remained at Vera Cruz to hasten preparations for the field; but on April 12th, receiving word of the situation at the front, he hastened to take command.

Santa Anna had selected Cerro Gordo some thirteen miles east of Jalapa as the easiest to defend against an invading army. The road, said to have been built by Cortez, zig-zags around the mountain-side and was defended at every turn by artillery. On either side of the road were deep chasms or mountain walls. After the arrival of the General-in-Chief upon the scene, reconnaissances were sent out to find or construct a road by which the rear of the enemy's position might be reached without a frontal attack. The reconnaissance was made under the supervision of Captain Robert E. Lee, assisted by Lieutenant P. G. T. Beauregard, Lieutenant George B. McClellan and others. The reconnaissance was completed and the labor of constructing a road to the rear of the enemy was practically completed by the 17th of April. General Scott issued his order for the attack on the 18th.

The attack was made as planned. Under the supervision of the engineers roadways had been opened over chasms to the right where the walls were so steep that we could barely climb them. Animals could not. The engineers, who had directed the opening, led the way and the troops followed. Artillery was let down the steep slopes by hand. The men engaged in this activity attached a strong rope to the rear axle and let the guns down, a piece at a time, while the men at the ropes kept their ground on top, and directed the course of the piece. In like manner the guns were drawn by hand up the opposite slopes. In this way Scott's troops reached their assigned positions unobserved at the rear of the enemy entrenchments.

The attack was completed, the Mexican reserves behind the works beat a hasty retreat, and those occupying them surrendered. On the left General Pillow's command made a magnificent demonstration, which doubtless contributed to the victory. The surprise of the enemy was complete, the victory overwhelming, and some 3000 prisoners fell into Scott's hands along with ordnance and ordnance stores. The prisoners were paroled, the artillery parked, and the small arms and ammunition destroyed.

When Taylor moved to Saltillo and then advanced on to Buena Vista, Santa Anna crossed the desert confronting the invading army, hoping to crush it and get back in time to meet General Scott in the mountain passes west of Vera Cruz. His attack on Taylor was disastrous to the Mexican army, but notwithstanding this, he marched his army to Cerro Gordo, a distance not much short of a thousand miles by the line he had to travel, in time to entrench himself well before Scott got there. If he had been successful at Buena Vista his troops would no doubt have made a more stubborn resistance at Cerro Gordo.

After the battle the victorious army moved on to Jalapa, far above the fevers of the coast. Jalapa, however, was still in the mountains, and between there and the great plain leading to the City of Mexico the whole line of the road was easy to defend. It was important, therefore, to get possession of the great highway between the sea-coast and the capital up to the point where it leaves the mountains, before the enemy could have time to reorganize and fortify his defenses. Worth's division was selected to go forward and secure that result. The division marched to Perote on the great plain, not far from where the road emerges from the mountains. The Castle of Perote offered no resistance and fell into our hands with all its armament.

General Scott had now only nine thousand men or so and with the enlistment time for four thousand of them about to expire, a long delay ensued. The troops were in a healthy climate so General Scott determined to discharge them immediately, because a delay until the expiration of their time would have compelled them to pass through Vera Cruz during the season of the *vomito*. This left Scott with about five thousand men in the field.

Early in May, Worth, with his division, left Perote and marched on to Puebla, and we arrived there on May 15th. General Worth was in command at Puebla until the end of May, when Scott arrived. Here, as well as on the march up, General Worth's restfulness, particularly under pressure, showed itself. The brigade to which I was attached changed quarters three different times in about a week, occupying at first quarters near the plaza in the heart of the city; then at the western entrance; and finally at the extreme east. On one of those latter days General Worth had all his troops at attention in line, under arms, all day, with three days' cooked rations in their rucksacks. He galloped from one command to another proclaiming the proximity of Santa Anna with a horde of armed troops poised to attack. When General Scott arrived we heard nothing more of Santa Anna and his myriads, and after his arrival I was sent, as quartermaster, with a large train of wagons, to procure forage for the animals. We had less than a thousand men as escort, and never thought of danger. After a two days march we procured full loads for our entire train at two large Mexican plantations, which easily could have furnished more.

There had been a great delay in obtaining the authority of Congress to raise the troops asked for by the Administration. There was a bill to create ten additional regiments to be attached to the regular army, but it was the middle of February 1847 before it became law. Appointments of officers had to be made; men had to be enlisted; the regiments equipped and the whole transported to Mexico. It was not until August before General Scott received reinforcements sufficient to resume his advance again. He now had about 10,000 troops again in four divisions commanded by General Twiggs, Worth, Pillow and Quitman. There was also a cavalry corps under General William S. Harney, composed of detachments of the 1st, 2nd, and 3rd dragoons. The advance commenced on August 7th with Twiggs's division in front. The remaining three divisions followed, with an interval of a day between.

I now had been in battle with the two leading generals in a foreign land. General Taylor never wore a uniform, and dressed comfortably. He moved with the troops to observe the situation for himself. Often he would be without any of his staff officers. His style of riding was quite unique. He was very much given to sit on his horse side-ways with both feet on one side—particularly on the battlefield.

General Scott was the exact opposite. He always wore the uniform prescribed when he inspected his lines and word would be sent to all commanders in advance notifying them of the hour when the commanding general might be expected. On these occasions he wore his dress uniform, cocked hat, aiguillettes, saber and spurs. His staff also followed in uniform and in the prescribed order. Orders were prepared with great pains and evidently with the view that they would be in the history books which would follow. General Scott was very precise in his language. He was proud of his rhetoric and would speak about himself in the third person, and he could bestow praise upon that person without the least embarrassment. Taylor was not a conversationalist but on paper he could put his meaning down so plainly that there could be no mistaking it. He knew how to express what he wanted to say in the fewest well chosen words.

Both were great generals; both were true, patriotic and upright. Both were pleasant to serve under—Taylor was pleasant to serve with. Scott saw things through his staff officers while Taylor saw for himself; and gave orders to meet the situation without reference to how they would read in a history book.

The route followed by the army from Puebla to the City of Mexico was over the Rio Frio mountain, the road leading over which, at the highest point, is about 11,000 feet above sea level. The pass through this mountain was not defended, and the advance division reached the summit in three days after leaving Puebla. The City of Mexico lies west of the Rio Frio mountain, on a plain backed by another mountain six miles further west, with others on the north and south. Between the Rio Frio mountain and the City of Mexico there are three large lakes, Chalco and Xochimilco on the left and Texcoco on the right extending to the east end of the City of Mexico. Lakes Chalco and Texcoco are divided by a strip of land over which the main road to the capital runs. Xochimilco lies to the left of the road but at a considerable distance south of it, and is connected with Lake Chalco by a narrow channel. There is a high rocky crag called El Peñón on the right of the road springing up from the low flat ground dividing the lakes. This hill was strengthened by entrenchments at its base and summit, and rendered a direct attack impracticable.

Scott's army was concentrated about Ayotla and other points near the eastern end of Lake Chalco. Reconnaissances were made up to El Peñón, while engineers were seeking a route by the south side of lake Chalco to flank the city, and come upon it from the south and southwest. A way was found around the lake and by August 18th the troops were in St. Augustin Tlalpam, a town about 11 miles due south from the plaza of the capital. Between St. Augustin Tlalpam and the city lies the hacienda of San Antonio and the village of Churubusco, and southwest of them is Contreras. Contreras is situated on the side of a mountain, near its base, where volcanic rocks are piled up reaching nearly to San Antonio. This made the approach to the city from the south very difficult.

I was attached to General Garland of Worth's division. We were sent to confront San Antonio, two or three miles from St. Augustin Tlalpam, on the road to Churubusco and the City of Mexico. San Antonio is in the valley and the elevation is only a few feet above the level of the lakes, and is cut up by deep ditches filled with water. To the southwest was the Pedregal—the volcanic rocks just mentioned—over which the cavalry or artillery could not pass, and infantry could make but poor progress if confronted by an enemy.

If Contreras, some three miles west and south should fall into our hands, troops from there could move to the right flank of all the positions held by the enemy between us and the city. Under these circumstances

General Scott directed holding the front which faced the enemy without making an attack until further orders.

On August 18th we reached San Augustin Tlalpam and Garlands's brigade secured a position within range of the advanced entrenchments of San Antonio, but where his troops were protected by some embankment that had been thrown up for other purposes. General Scott sent his engineers to reconnoiter the works about Contreras, and on the 19th movements were commenced to get troops into position from which an assault could be made upon the force occupying that place. A road was completed during the day and night of the 19th and troops were dispatched to the north and west of the enemy.

All the troops with General Scott in the Valley of Mexico, except a part of the division of General Quitman at St. Augustin Tlalpam and the brigade of Garland (Worth's division) at San Antonio, were engaged at the battle of Contreras, or were on their way, in obedience to orders of their chief, to reinforce those who were engaged. The assault was made on the morning of the 20th and the battle was won in less than one-half hour, with a large quantity of ordnance and other goods in our possession. The brigade commanded by General Riley was the most conspicuous in the final assault.

In Garland's brigade we could see the progress made at Contreras and the movement of troops toward the rear of the enemy opposing us. San Antonio was found evacuated, the evacuation having probably taken place immediately when the enemy saw the Stars & Stripes waving over Contreras.

Churubusco proved to be the severest battle fought in the valley of Mexico. General Scott ordered two brigades, under Shields, to move north and turn to the right of the enemy. This Shields did without difficulty. The enemy gave way leaving in our hands prisoners, artillery and small arms.

General Franklin Pierce joined the army at Puebla, a short time before the advance on the capital commenced. By an unfortunate fall of his horse on the afternoon of the 19th he was painfully injured. On the 20th his brigade was ordered against the flanks and rear of the enemy guarding the different points of the road from San Augustin Tlalpam to the City of Mexico. General Pierce attempted to accompany them. He was not sufficiently recovered to do so, and fainted. This circumstance gave rise to unjust criticism of him when he became a candidate for the

Presidency in 1853. He was a gentleman and a man of courage. I was not a supporter of him politically, but I knew him more intimately than I did any of the other volunteer generals.

General Scott did not enter the city because Mr. Nicholas Trist, the commissioner from the United States, who came to negotiate a treaty of peace with Mexico was with the army; and either he or General Scott thought—probably both of them—that a treaty would be more possible while the Mexican government was in possession of the capital than if it were scattered and the capital was in the hands of an invader.

Be this as it may, we did not enter the capital at that time. Negotiations were at once entered into with Santa Anna, who was then practically *the Government* and the immediate commander of all troops engaged in defense of the country. A truce was signed which denied either party the right to strengthen its position, or to receive reinforcements during the armistice, but authorized General Scott to draw supplies for his army. Negotiations were continued between Mr. Trist and the Mexican commissioners until September 2, 1847, at which time Mr. Trist gave his ultimatum in which he said that Texas was to be given up absolutely by Mexico, and New Mexico and California ceded to the United States for a stipulated sum to be determined at a later date.

The Mexicans were outraged at the proposed terms and they commenced preparations for their defense without giving notice of the termination of the armistice. General Scott wrote a vigorous note to President Santa Anna on September 4th calling attention to the violation. He received an unsatisfactory reply and declared the armistice at an end.

Worth's division was now occupying Tacubaya, a village four miles southwest of the City of Mexico. Molino del Rey[23] stood more than a mile west, and also a little above the plain. The mill was a long store-like structure, one story high and several hundred feet in length. Our intelligence reported that a portion of the mill was being used as a foundry for the casting of cannon barrels. This, however, proved to be a mistake. The mill was valuable to the Mexicans because of the huge amount of grain it contained. The building was flat roofed, and a line of sand-bags over the outer walls rendered the top a formidable defense for their infantry. A short distance from Molino del Rey stood Chapaltepec which was a mound springing from the plain to a height

---

[23]   The King's Mill

of three hundred feet and in direct line between Molino del Rey and the western part of the City. It was fortified both on the top and on the rocky and precipitous sides.

The City of Mexico received its water via two aqueducts. One of the aqueducts drew its water from a mountain stream coming into it at or near the Molino del Rey, and ran north close to the west base of Chapultepec; then along the center of a wide road running east into the city by the Garita San Cosme[24]; from which point the aqueduct and road both ran east to the City of Mexico. The second aqueduct started from the east base of Chapultepec, where it was fed by a spring, and ran northeast to the city. This aqueduct, like the other, ran down the middle of a broad road. The arches supporting the aqueduct afforded protection for the advancing troops as well as for those engaged defensively. At points on the San Cosme road parapets were thrown across, with an embrasure for a single piece of artillery in each. At the point where the road and aqueduct turned at right angles from north to east there was a gun parapet and the houses to the north of the San Cosme road, facing south and commanding a view of the road back to Chapultepec, were protected by parapets made of sand bags and were heavily manned with artillery. Deep ditches, filled with water, lined the sides of both roads.

Prior to the war General Scott had been very partial and friendly towards General Worth—and he continued to be so up to the close of hostilities—but for some reason, Worth estranged himself from his chief. I never knew why. Scott evidently took the coldness somewhat to heart. He did not retaliate, however, but on the contrary showed every opportunity to appease his subordinate. It was understood that he gave Worth authority to plan and execute the attack on Molino del Rey with no strings attached for the purpose of restoring their former relations. The effort failed, and the two generals remained thereafter cold and indifferent towards each other, if not actually hostile.

The battle of Molino del Rey was fought on September 8th. On the previous night Worth assembled his commanders and their staff to issue the battle plans. These orders contemplated a movement up to within striking distance of the mill before daylight. The engineers had reconnoitered the grounds as well as possible, and had determined the best approach for the attack. Before daylight on the 8th the troops

---

[24]   The gates of San Cosme.

were at their designated places. The grounds in front of the mill to the south was commanded by the artillery from Chapultepec, as well as by the lighter batteries at the mill. A charge was ordered and soon it was all over. Worth's troops entered the mill by every door, and the enemy beat a hasty retreat to Chapultepec. Had this victory been followed up with an immediate attack on Chapultepec the place would have fallen into our hands without further loss. The defenders of the works could not have fired upon us without endangering their own men. This was not done and five days later more valuable time was sacrificed to take Chapultepec which was so nearly in our possession on the 8th. But I cannot criticize Worth for his failure to capture Chapultepec at this time. The result that followed the first assault could not possibly have been foreseen to profit from the unexpected advantage, the general would have had to give the necessary orders at that moment. The loss on our side at Molino del Rey was severe for the numbers engaged. It was especially so among the commissioned officers.

I was with the first wave of troops to enter the mill. I passed quickly through to the north side looking towards Chapultepec and happened to notice that there were a number of armed Mexicans still on the roof and only a few feet from our men. Not seeing any stairway or ladder reaching the top of the building, I took a few soldiers and brought a cart that was standing nearby up against the wall. By climbing on the cart we were able to make our way up to the roof of the building. We could see that there were still quite a number of Mexicans on the roof, who had not succeeded in getting away before our troops occupied the building. What surprised me was that they were being guarded by a Yankee soldier who had managed to get on the roof by some other route. I relieved the soldier and received the swords from the commissioned officers, and proceeded, with the help of the soldiers with me to disable their muskets by bashing them against the edge of the wall, and then throwing them to the ground below.

Molino del Rey was now captured and most of our troops were marched back to their quarters at Tacubaya. The whole engagement lasted only a short period of time, but the killed and wounded were numerous for the number of troops engaged. During the night of the 11th batteries were established which could play upon the fortifications of Chapultepec. The bombardment commenced on the morning of the 12th, but there was no further engagement during the day other than the artillery barrage. General Scott assigned the capture of Chapultepec to General Pillow and gave his specific orders on how to accomplish it. Two assaulting columns of 250 volunteers each were formed and they successfully stormed Chapultepec, but it was a very bloody attack.

The causeways or major arteries into the city were flanked by ditches filled with water, each ended in a massive Garita, more than just a gate, the Garita included a large paved space and strongly built buildings where taxes were collected on goods entering the city. The assaults upon the gates of San Cosme and Belen along the aqueduct roads were determined upon after Chapultepec fell. General Quitman, a volunteer from the State of Mississippi, commanded the column acting against Belen. General Worth commanded the column against San Cosme.

I was on the La Veronica Causeway heading north towards San Cosme and I can tell you about that action. When opposition was encountered our troops sheltered themselves by keeping close to the arches supporting the aqueduct, advancing one arch at a time. We encountered our first serious enemy action when we were close to the point where the road we were on intersected with the road running east to the city, the point where the aqueduct turned at a right angle. There were but three commissioned officers there beside myself. These were Lieutenant Raphael Semmes of the Marine Corps, and Captain Lane and Lieutenant Judah, of the 4th Infantry. Our progress was halted at the intersection by a single piece of artillery and an infantry company occupying house-tops back from the artillery piece.

West of the road at this point stood a house occupying the southwest corner of La Veronica Causeway and the San Cosme road. A stone wall ran from the house along each of the roads for a considerable distance. At the cross roads the wall enclosed a large yard around the house. I skipped behind the south wall and proceeded cautiously to the corner of the enclosure. I peeked around, and seeing nobody, continued until I reached the crossroad. I then returned to the troops and called for volunteers. About a dozen offered their services. Commanding them to carry their arms at a trail, I watched for an opportunity and got them across the road and under the cover of the wall behind, before the enemy had a shot at us. When we reached a safe position I instructed my little command again to carry their arms at a trail, and not to fire at the enemy until ordered. I told them to move very cautiously behind me until the San Cosme road intersection was reached.

When we reached the southwest corner of the yard enclosure I saw some friendly troops pushing north through a shallow ditch near by. This was the company of Captain Horace Brooks, of the artillery, acting as infantry. I told Brooks about my reconnaissance and what I planned to do. He told me he would follow us with his men. We moved up to the intersection and got on the road leading to the city. The Mexican troops on the parapet retreated, and those on the house tops followed. Our men went after them in close pursuit—the troops we had left under the arches joining us. No reinforcements had yet come up except Brook's men, and the position we had taken on the San Cosme road was too advanced to be held by so small a force. We retreated, but we retook our position later in the day, with some loss.

Worth's command now gradually advanced to the front now open to it. In the late afternoon I found a church south of the road which looked to me as if the belfry would command the San Cosme road near the gate. I got an artillery officer with a mountain howitzer and men to work it, to go with me. The road in front of us was in the possession of the enemy and so we took the fields south of the road to reach the church. This took us over several ten-foot wide ditches breast deep in water and grown up with water plants. The howitzer was carried by the men in pieces to its destination. When we got to the church I knocked for admission and a priest came to the door, who, while being very polite, refused to let us in. With my limited Spanish I explained to him that by letting us in he might save lives and property. I told him that otherwise he would become a prisoner and I intended to go in whether he consented or not. He reluctantly opened the door and we carried our gun parts to the belfry and put it together. We were not more than two or three hundred yards from San Cosme. The shots from our little gun dropped in upon the enemy and created great confusion. Why they did not send out a party to capture us I will never know.

The effect of this gun upon the troops near the gate of the city was so pronounced that General Worth saw it from his rear position. He was so pleased that he sent his staff officer, Lieutenant Pemberton, to bring me to him. General Worth told me he had ordered a captain of the voltigeurs to report to me with another howitzer to be placed next to the one already operational. I didn't have the heart to tell him that there wasn't enough room in the steeple for another gun. I took the captain with me, but I did not use his gun.

The night of September 13th was spent by General Worth's troops in the houses near San Cosme. My troops were in the houses north of the road and we were engaged during the night in cutting passage ways from one house to the next towards town. During the night Santa Anna, with his army—except for the deserters—left the city. He liberated all the convicts in the prisons, hoping, no doubt, that they would inflict some injury upon us before daylight; but several hours after Santa Anna left the city, authorities sent a delegation to General Scott at 4:00 AM to demand an armistice, respecting church property, the rights of citizens, and permitting the city authorities to remain and manage affairs. General Scott declined the armistice but told the city officers that he would not bother the inhabitants if they behaved themselves.

General Quitman had also advanced successfully and on the night of the 13th his command occupied nearly the same position at Belen that Worth's troops did at San Cosme. After the interchange with the city officials, orders were issued for the cautious entry of both columns into the city the next morning. The troops under Worth were to stop at the Alameda, a park near the west end of the city. Quitman was to go directly to the Plaza, and take possession of the Palace. These buildings were generally designated as the "Halls of the Montezumas."

On entering the city the troops were fired upon by the released convicts, deserters, and hostile citizens. The streets, however, were deserted. Firing from house-tops and windows did their deadly business. Lieutenant Colonel Garland of my regiment was badly wounded and Lieutenant Sidney Smith of the 4th infantry was killed. Because of this tragedy I was promoted to a first lieutenant. General Scott soon followed the troops into the city. He took up quarters at the "Halls of the Montezumas," and from there issued his wise and discreet orders for the government of a conquered city. The city soon settled into a quiet, law-abiding place. The people began to make their appearance upon the streets without fear of our troops.

It has always seemed to me that the northern route to the City of Mexico would have been the better one to have taken. My later experiences taught me a few important things, however, and they are:

(1) Things are seen much clearer after the events have occurred.
(2) The most confident critics are generally those who know the least about the matter criticized.

General Scott's successes were the answer to his criticizers. He invaded a populous country, penetrated two hundred and sixty miles into the interior, with a force at no time equal to one-half of that opposed to him; he was without a base, the enemy was always entrenched, always on the defensive, yet he won every battle, he captured the capital, and conquered the government.

The victories in Mexico were over vastly superior numbers. Both General Scott and General Taylor had special armies. At the battle of Palo Alto and Resaca de la Palma, General Taylor had a small army, but it was composed exclusively of regular troops, under the best of drill and discipline. Every officer from the highest to the lowest was educated in his profession, and many graduated from West Point. The volunteers who followed were of good material, but without drill and discipline at the start. They learned rapidly, however. The Mexican army of that day, on the other hand, was hardly an organization. The private soldier was picked from a low class, his consent was not asked, he was poorly clothed, worse fed, and seldom paid. He was turned adrift when no longer wanted.

After the fall of the capital and the break up of the government it looked very much as if military occupation of the country might be necessary for a long period of time. General Scott acted accordingly. He contemplated making Mexico pay all the expenses of the occupation. His plan was to levy a tax upon the separate states, and collect at the ports left open to trade, a duty on all imports. In this war private property had not been appropriated, either for the use of the army or of individuals, without full compensation. This policy was to be pursued. Military possession was taken of Cuervenaca, fifty miles south of the City of Mexico; of Toluca, nearly as far west, and of Pachuca, a mining town of great importance, some sixty miles to the northeast. Vera Cruz, Jalapa, Orizaba and Puebla were already in our possession.

Meanwhile the Mexican government in the person of Santa Anna, had flown the coop and it looked doubtful for a time whether the United States Commissioner, Mr. Trist, would find anybody to negotiate with. A temporary government was established at Quéretero, and Trist began negotiations for a conclusion of the war. Before concluding his negotiations he was ordered back to Washington, but General Scott prevailed upon him to remain, as things were so close to an agreement. The treaty was signed on February 2nd, 1848, and accepted by the government at Washington. It was called the "Treaty of Guadalupe Hidalgo," and secured to the United States the Rio Grande as the boundary of Texas, and the whole territory then included in New Mexico and Upper California, for the sum of $15,000,000.

Soon after entering the City of Mexico the dislike of General Pillow, Worth and Colonel Duncan to General Scott became very marked. Scott claimed that they had demanded of the president his removal. I don't know if this was true, but I do know of their unconcealed hostility to their chief. At last Scott placed them in arrest, and preferred charges against them of insubordination and disrespect. About the middle of February orders came convening a court of inquiry. Shortly afterwards orders were received from Washington, relieving Scott of the command of the army in the field and assigning Major General William O. Butler of Kentucky to his place. This order also released Pillow, Worth and Duncan from arrest. It is interesting to note that in 1840 General Worth named his only son Winfield Scott Worth, in admiration, but after the Mexican war he changed his son's name to William Worth, leaving out the middle name Scott.

There were many who regarded the treatment of General Scott as harsh and unjust. It is quite possible that the vanity of the general clashed with the president and afforded a plausible pretext to the Administration for doing just what it did. General Scott left the country, and ever since has had no more than nominal command of the army. The selection of General Butler was agreeable to everyone concerned.

The efforts to politically kill off the two successful generals, made them both candidates for the presidency. General Taylor was nominated in 1848 and was elected. Four years later General Scott received the nomination but was badly beaten, and the party nominating him died with his defeat.

I was with the occupation troops and we passed the time as best we could. Every Sunday there was a bull fight for the amusement of those who would pay the price of admission—fifty cents. I attended one of them—just one—not wishing to leave the country without having witnessed the national sport. The sight was sickening. I couldn't see how human beings could enjoy the suffering of beasts, and often the peons, as they seemed to do on these occasions.

There are usually from four to six bulls sacrificed. The audience sits around the ring and has a good view of the massacre. When all is ready a bull is released into the ring. Three or four men come in mounted on old horses that are either blind or blind-folded. The men are armed with sharp spears. Other men enter the arena on foot armed with red capes and explosive charges like a musket cartridge. To each of these explosives a barbed needle is attached which serves the purpose as an anchoring device. Before the bull is turned loose a bunch of these explosive barbs are attached to him. When the explosions of the cartridges commence the animal becomes frantic. As he makes a lunge towards one horseman, another runs a spear into him. When the bull turns towards the last tormenter a man with a red cape waves it in his face. Back and forth the bull lunges until he is worked into an uncontrollable furore. The horsemen withdraw, and the matadors—literally murderers—enter armed with sharp blades some twelve to eighteen inches long under their cape. The trick is to dodge an attack from the animal and stab him in the heart as he passes. He is then dragged off and another is let into the ring.

Another amusement of the people of Mexico, and one in which nearly all indulge in, male and female, old and young, priest and layman, was Monte playing. Regular fairs were held every year at St. Augustin Tlalpam, eleven miles out of town. There were Monte dealers for every sort of customer. In many of the booths *clakos*—the copper coin of the country were piled up with the silver to accommodate the people who could not bet more than a few pennies at a time. In some of the booths only gold coins were to be seen. Here the rich could bet away their entire fortunes in a single day.

I was kept busy during the winter of 1847-48. My regiment was stationed at Tacubaya. I was still regimental quartermaster and commissary. General Scott had been unable to get clothing for the troops from the North. The men badly needed clothing. Material was purchased and the local women employed to make up "Yankee uniforms." The regimental bands of that day were kept up partly by government pay and partly by pay from the regimental fund. A band leader could receive non-commissioned officer pay and the remainder the pay of privates. The best way we had of supplying the fund was to save money from our bread allowance. I rented a bakery in the city, hired Mexican bakers, bought supplies, and made large amounts of hard bread. In two months I made more money for the fund than my pay amounted to during the entire war!

In the spring of 1848 a group of us obtained leave to visit Popocatapetl, the highest volcano in America. Near the base of the volcano, at a town called Ozumba, we procured guides and two pack mules with forage for our horses. High up on the mountain there was a solitary log house consisting of one room, called the Vaqueria, which had been occupied in the past by cattle men. The pasturage up there was fine and there were still some cattle, descendants of the former domestic herd, which had now become wild. We were able to go to the Vaqueria on horseback.

The night at the Vaqueria was one of the most unpleasant I ever experienced. It was cold and the rain came down in torrents. The wind blew with great velocity. There was little sleep that night. As soon as it was light on the next morning we started out on foot to make the ascent to the summit. The weather was still cloudy but the rain and snow had stopped. The wind was still wild and carried the loose snow around the mountain sides in such volumes as to make it almost impossible to advance against. We labored on and on, until it became evident that the top could not be reached before night, and we concluded to return. At the cabin we mounted our horses, and by night-fall we were back at Ozumba. The next day we went to the village of Ameca, where we stopped again for the night. The next morning we were all recovered from our adventure and could see Popocatapetl in all its beauty. This invited us to return for another try for the top. Half of our party went back and the rest of us decided to visit the great caves of Mexico, ninety miles away on the road to Acapulco.

The cave party which I was with moved south down the valley to the town of Cuantla. Soon after the armistice had been agreed to limits were designated beyond which troops of the respective armies were not to go during its continuance. We knew nothing about these limits. As we approached Cuantla bugles sounded and soldiers rushed from the guard-house on the edge of town towards us. Our party halted, and I tied a white handkerchief to a stick, and, using it as a flag of truce, proceeded on to town. We were delayed at the guard-house until a messenger could be dispatched to the commanding general who authorized that I should be conducted to him. The Mexican general reminded me that it was a violation of the truce for us to be there. When I told him that we knew nothing about the terms of the truce he relented and permitted us to occupy a vacant house near the guard-house for the night, with the promise of a guide to put us on the road to Cuernavaca the next morning.

Cuernavaca is west of Cuantla. The mountains between the two towns were occupied by full-blooded Indians, very few of whom spoke Spanish. We had with us a cart which was probably the first wheeled vehicle that had ever passed through that region. After a day's rest at Cuernavaca we set out again for the great caves of Mexico. We had proceeded a few miles when we were stopped again by a guard who notified us that we could go no further. We convinced the guard that we were only tourists and he said he would confer with the commanding general that afternoon. By night time there was no response from the general, but the guard was sure he would have a reply by morning. Again in the morning there was no reply. The second evening the same thing happened, and finally we learned that the guard had sent no message to the department commander. We determined to go on unless stopped by a force sufficient to compel obedience.

After a few hours' travel we came to a town where a scene similar to the one at Cuantla occurred. This was the last interruption; that night we rested at a large coffee plantation, some eight miles from the cave. The natives were all playing Monte. I recollect one poor slob, who had lost his last *clacko*, and literally bet the shirt off his back at the next game. The next morning we were at the cave, provided with guides, candles and rockets. We explored in to a distance of three miles where we found a succession of chambers of great dimension and of enormous beauty when lit up with our rockets. Stalagmites and stalactites of all sizes were discovered. The stalagmites were all a little concave and the cavities were filled with water. Some of the immense columns, many of them thousands of tons in weight, served to support the roofs over the vast chambers.

Some of our party decided to go back before we had reached the point to which the guides were accustomed to take explorers, and started back without guides. They got confused and got turned around in their direction. When the rest of us had completed our explorations, we started back with our guides, but had not gone far before we saw the torches of an approaching party. Very soon we found it was our friends. It took them some time to conceive how they had gone where they were.

My experience in the Mexican war was invaluable. The war brought nearly all the officers of the regular army together so as to make them personally acquainted. I graduated from West Point in 1843 and knew all the cadets who graduated between 1840 and 1846—seven classes. These classes embraced more than 50 officers who afterwards became generals on one side of the fence or the other.

The treaty of peace was at last ratified and the evacuation of Mexico by United States troops was ordered. Early in June the troops in the City of Mexico began to move out. Many of them, including the brigade to which I belonged, were assembled at Jalapa, above the elevation for the vomito, to await the arrival of transports at Vera Cruz. But with all the precautions that we knew about my regiment was in camp on the sand beach in the hot July sun for a full week before embarking, while the fever raged with great virulence only two miles away. We embarked for Pascagoula, Mississippi to spend the rest of the summer of 1848. As soon as I was settled in camp I obtained a leave of absence for four months, and proceeded to St. Louis. Everything that could be nice happened there and on August 22nd, 1848 I married Miss Julia Dent. We visited my parents and relatives in Ohio, and at the end of my leave, I proceeded to my new post at Sackett's Harbor, New York.

Chapter 19

ON THE RUN

Antonio López de Santa Anna

After the end of the Mexican War in 1848 I requested permission of the United States Occupying Forces for safe conduct to go into exile. Colonel George W. Hughes, United States military governor of the department of Jalapa granted this request, allowing me to proceed to my hacienda of El Encero, and from there I left on April 5, 1848 on the Spanish brig *Pepita* for exile to Jamaica. Thus ended a period of less than two years during which I was back in my native country.

I left my homeland in a chaotic state, filled with internal dissent, the presence of foreign troops and financial disorder. Once again the newly framed Mexican Congress decided to banish me permanently by official resolution, this being considered the ultimate degree of punishment for their despised former leader.

I arrived at the lonely British colony at Jamaica and lived there with my family for about two years. None of us were happy living among the British subjects. Their customs seemed strange and I never did learn English. As a result we left in early April 1850 for New Granada. I purchased a large hacienda in Turbaco which was in a state of disrepair, and I began the life of a retired gentleman. I resolved to spend the "rest of my days" in Turbaco, because I was relatively happy there and my family loved the place. I began the cultivation of sugar cane and tobacco, and bred cattle, all of this providing employment for the poor people of the district. I had the resources to maintain my family and some of my followers in great comfort throughout this period of my exile.

The war with the United States had ended, but the strife in Mexico had not subsided. The Federalists emerged triumphant at the war's end, but Mexico's instability resulted in a succession of five presidents from 1848 to 1853. As early as June 1851 Elgio Ortiz made a pronouncement that I should return and run the country. Midway through 1852 a revolt occurred when José Maria Blancorte denounced President Arista and stated that he favored my return to guide the nation. Arista was forced to resign on January 5, 1853, leaving the presidency in the hands of the Chief Justice of the Supreme Court of Mexico, Juan B. Ceballos.

General Manuel M. Lombardini seized control of the government and ordered elections held to determine who should be president. On March 17, 1853 the newly assembled Congress opened the ballots submitted by the states. I received 18 of the 23 votes cast and Lombardini sent a Commission to visit me in New Granada and advise me of my election to the presidency, and to invite me to return.

I reached Vera Cruz on April 1, 1853 and received a rather cool reception. I did, however, receive the keys to the city from the authorities. Upon leaving Vera Cruz I spent nearly ten days at El Encero before continuing via Puebla to the village of Guadalupe on the outskirts of the City of Mexico. There I visited the famous shrine in honor of the patron Saint of Mexico, the Virgin of Guadalupe. In three more days I entered the capital and took the oath of office for the fifth time on April 20, 1853.

I began my Administration with great vigor. Within a week I stated that I would oppose anyone who expressed a desire to have Mexico annexed by the United States. On April 22nd I published a decree establishing a Centralist Administration until a new Constitution could be drawn up. I appointed a very conservative Cabinet led by Lucas Alamán. During the next month I dissolved the old Congress and formed a Council of States to assist in governing the nation. I also changed the tax system so that the central government rather than the states would administer taxes.

I knew I would have to deal with political foes. I sent my son to Oaxaca to put Benito Juárez and others in prison. I justified this step on the grounds that the public welfare demanded unity. In June 1853 the offenders were allowed to go into exile. These individuals, however, banded together in a movement that would soon give me trouble. They called themselves *La Reforma*.

I supported the army to the extent of my financial resources as president. I reinstated the Order of Guadalupe and other medals to reward individuals for outstanding military service. An unfortunate event occurred only 43 days after my inauguration on June 2, 1853—Lucas Alamán suddenly died of natural causes. The Cabinet, now without its revered leader, virtually fell apart. Resignations followed which I filled with loyal handpicked *Santanistas*. Gradually the Mexican nation moved toward a monarchy.

I encouraged the building of roads, the extension of telegraph lines, and provided for a survey leading to the construction of Mexico's first railroad. But the main thing was that I established order by insuring that the nation was well policed.

Of those who had invited me to return, the *agiotistas*, or financiers, headed by Manuel Escandón wanted me to pay back some 4 million pesos in debts from previous Administrations. They hoped to control the Custom Houses, establish a monopoly over the tobacco industry, and build a railroad from Vera Cruz to the City of Mexico. I had to favor this group over others.

I continued to stress that I didn't want foreign interference in Mexico. In September 1853 I announced that the states would again be officially known as departments. Even though my treasury suffered deficits I created a huge infrastructure providing many jobs for military officers and I distributed commissions liberally. We had magnificent parades, celebrations, and galas. Titles were granted through the Order of Guadalupe; and resplendent uniforms, trimmed in gold, became the order of the day.

As the deficit mounted I resorted to very inventive measures to raise money. I placed taxes on taverns, factories, horses, dogs, and even the drain gutters on houses. I also entered into a negotiation to sell some desert land known as the Mesilla Valley to the United States. I concluded the treaty with James Gadsden, the United States Minister to Mexico, on December 30, 1853 by which Mexico sold the area south of the Gila River to the United States for ten million dollars. I told my people that the United States would have "seized" the land if I had not sold it to them.

I made an agreement when I returned that my term of office would only be for one year. I now sought to alter this condition on December 16, 1853. As a consequence I became absolute ruler of Mexico. I refused the title of emperor, but I accepted "His Most Serene Highness." This gave me indefinite power and the right to name my successor. By the end of December I finally was able to emulate my old boyhood hero, Louis Napoleon Bonaparte.

A new revolt occurred in the early months of 1854. Juan Âlvarez and other rebels proclaimed the Plan of Ayutla on March 1, 1854. By its terms I was to cease exercising political authority and a Congress was established to write a Federally oriented Constitution. I was undecided on my course of action, but on March 16th I led an army in person to burn towns that had rebelled against the supreme government. I moved slowly to Chilpancingo where I visited Nicholás Bravo and his wife, and then moved on to make an assault on Acapulco. There I failed miserably and retreated to the capital, but I bombarded the citizens along the way with handbills announcing my "victories" over the rebels.

I could see difficulties on the horizon, so I decided to move on a more modest course. I even feigned sickness as a excuse for not attending a military ball in my honor. I called for a national plebiscite on December 1, 1854, and asked for a vote of confidence. The voting in the City of Mexico resulted in 12,452 votes in my favor and only one vote in opposition. In fact the nation cast 435,000 votes, all in my favor during the plebiscite.

But the revolution of Ayutla continued to grow. I felt threatened and made plans to leave the capital if necessary, placing cash reserves abroad should the necessity arise. I sent my family ahead to El Encero and stationed loyal troops along the Vera Cruz road to provide a future escape route. When news reached the City of Mexico that my home province of Vera Cruz had revolted against me, I realized the situation was desperate. I departed at 3:00 AM on the morning of August 9, 1855, appointing three men to take temporary charge of the government. When I reached El Encero I issued a public statement of my abdication.

On August 16th my family and I boarded a Mexican vessel appropriately named *Iturbide* near Vera Cruz, and for the third time sailed off into exile.

I proceeded to the Caribbean again to begin a new period of exile. I did not perceive the significance of the movement that had disposed me. The Liberal revolt won out and principles predominated over personalities—and *La Reforma* insured that conservatism was not to dominate my native land. I just could not understand the principles of the Liberals.

After a short stay in Havana I proceeded back to my hacienda at Turbaco which I found in a state of deterioration. Here I spent the next two years and six months of my life. I left for St. Thomas, in the West Indies in 1858. I was well informed of all the events that occurred in Mexico during this period, and still had friends there whom I corresponded with. The conservative faction initiated violent civil strife in 1858 and along with early conservative victories I felt encouraged.

My property in Mexico was confiscated to make up for my sale of the Mesilla Valley to the United States. El Encero passed on to an Agricultural society and Manga de Clavo was purchased by private individuals. At St. Thomas I settled down and resumed my customary issuance of public proclamations. In 1859 I began a correspondence with José María Gutiérrez de Estrada. This intrigue was designed to promote intervention by Napoleon III of France into Mexican affairs to establish an empire. I must say, *"Things are looking bright again—I feel it in my bones!"*

Chapter 20

LETTERS OF GENERAL WORTH

O ne of the American commanders to distinguish himself in the Mexican war of 1846-1848 was General William Jenkins Worth, a soldier who had in previous campaigns acquired the habit of making a careful record of his experiences in active service. His personal recollections of the fighting in Mexico were set forth in letters to various members of his family, and from a descendant of General Worth the *Times Magazine* has received the most important of these documents, none of which have heretofore been published.

Aside from their literary quality and their characteristic military flavor, General Worth's letters are highly valuable from a historic standpoint. They present glimpses of the political motives which influenced President Polk and his Secretary of War, William L. Marcy; they reveal the jealousy that existed between the regular army and the volunteers; they point out military blunders and inefficiency, reveal the danger of using in Mexico troops not properly seasoned, and contain more than one lesson for the nation of today.

Moreover, the general's letters show that the Mexican problem had not changed in seventy years. "Cursed with a bad government and a vile despotism," he said, "they (the Mexicans) know not their rights, and a siesta reconciles them to their deep and damning degradation. However unrighteous this war, good will come from evil in the ways of Providence. An infusion of Saxon energy, enterprise, and perhaps of blood, with the schoolmaster, will a quarter of a century hence show its fruits, regenerating, I hope, this favored land."

Opinions expressed by General Worth in regard to the attitude of the United States toward Mexico are surprisingly like some of those heard at this moment of controversy between the two governments. He was convinced that North Americans were destined to overrun the whole continent. "It being then a part of our destiny to overrun the country," he wrote, "a destiny which we can no more avoid, despite all the struggles of short-sighted politicians, than we can change the order of nature, the question is whether we shall complete the work we have already so nearly accomplished, or leave it to be undertaken de novo by our children." These words were written after the capture of Mexico City in 1847, and the Mexican question is still unsettled.

The general took part in the battles of Monterey, Vera Cruz, Puebla, Churubusco, Chapultapec, and Molino del Rey, and although he was assailed for political reasons by partisans of his superior officers in the Mexican campaign, he received the thanks of Congress and the states of New York, Louisiana, Texas, and Florida, and also four swords of honor. Although the general died of cholera in San Antonio, he was buried in Madison Square Garden, New York City, beneath a granite shaft which has long been a famous landmark.

In 1845 General Worth joined the United States Army assembled at Corpus Christi, near the mouth of the Nueces, in Texas. He received command of a brigade, and was eventually to lead the advance of General Zachary Taylor's army to the Rio Grande, and take part in many battles, including the capture of Monterey and Mexico City.

A variety of causes led to the war with Mexico. Texas had seceded from Mexico, and in 1837 the United States recognized her independence. This did not please the Mexicans, and their resentment was further increased when Texas was annexed to the United States in 1845. Immediately there was a dispute over the boundary line. The United States claimed the Rio Grande as the proper boundary, while Mexico held that Texas did not extend further south than the Nueces. There were other causes of friction, including border outrages, and the press of both countries was inflamed to a degree.

This was the situation when General Worth arrived at Corpus Christi in September 1845. In a letter written to his son-in-law, Captain John T. Sprague, the general speaks of having established his camp. "The Eighth is in order," he says, "and an example of order: the influences whereof has already been manifest by a changed and changing state of things in neighboring camps. On my left are the Second Dragoons, an Augean stable; but I fear no Hercules to cleanse it. One Captain Frank resigned a few days ago under charges of drunkenness, etc. A court martial now in session for the trial of Kent and Rogers, drunkenness, fighting, and still grosser immoralities. Amid all this there are some noble fellows in it." He continues:

> General Taylor construes his orders and instructions as inhibiting a forward movement. He has invited me to a perusal, and my careful reading conducts to a directly opposite construction. They most plainly and distinctly indicate that he is at once to occupy to the Rio Grande, which it is manifest is to be our western boundary *nolens volens*.

Apparently General Worth has some misgivings about the justice of the boundary dispute, for under the date of October 3, 1845 he writes to his old commander, General Winfield Scott, that "beyond doubt or peradventure it is decided that the Rio Grande shall be our border; whether right or wrong is a question of political ethics to be settled by statesmen."

In other letters to his daughter and to Captain Sprague, the general speaks of whipping his brigade into shape, and there is some advice for the Captain, who is stationed in Florida, and having his troubles with the politicians. The general also speaks of his own troubles in a letter written in November:

> I told you there was tone here, and so there was, that discipline was improving, and so it was, that instruction was being inculcated and well received, and so it was; but the enthusiasm is persisting under disappointment and inaction, the zeal abated, indolence follows, idleness next, then dissipation and then—what? We shall see. On the extreme left of the camp fifty houses have been put up of every size, kind and description, of brick, wood and gauze,

in which I hear everything is going on from the gambling table to throat cutting, stabbing, and gouging. There are probably one hundred gamblers on the ground, and a due proportion of the ministers and notaries of every other vice. A theater is going up—'My Lord, the players have arrived,' quoth a Hamlet. A racecourse is being laid out, and what next, heaven only knows!

Then the general expresses the opinion that the American people are anxious for a war of some sort, and that the "speculators" are fostering it:

By the last paper it appears our affairs with Great Britain are assuming a more serious aspect. If this be really so, our government will press a settlement of our difficulties with Mexico, so as to prepare to meet the foeman with undivided front, and we hope soon to be recalled from inaction here. The message will doubtless give us an insight into coming events. Our people will not rest satisfied without a war with some power. All the bad elements combine in that direction. The speculators in land, stocks and politics, composing three-fifths of the whole, I am reconciled to it in the belief that it may bring demagogues into disrepute and disaffect the political atmosphere.

War with England was averted, however, and early in March 1846, General Worth received orders to begin the advance toward the Rio Grande. On April 2nd he wrote to his daughter Maria, from a camp opposite Matamoros, Rio Grande that he had just heard of the President's decision on the subject of brevet rank:

I have this moment sent in the resignation of my commission, and shall, I trust, in six weeks cease to belong to that beloved service and profession which I have idolized for thirty-three years. I can no longer remain in it with honor or self-respect. I led the advance of the army across the desert from Corpus Christi, and four days later planted the first American standard on the left bank of the Rio Grande within 600 yards of the bristling cannon of Matamoros. There may

it ever wave until further advanced in glory. The enemy don't
mean to fight, so I have felt at liberty to demand permission
to retire.

Worth's professional pride had been wounded in the controversy
over precedence in rank which involved himself, a Colonel and Brevet
Brigadier General, and Colonel Twiggs. President Polk decided in favor
of the latter, and Worth's resignation followed. He went to Washington,
and there heard the news of the battles of Palo Alto and Resaca de la
Palma. His soldierly spirit was so stirred that he forgot his grievance
and withdrew his resignation. The first of June found him again in
Matamoros. Writing about himself to Captain Sprague, he said:

> Amid all my anguish and wreck of heart I find some
> consolation in what I hear all around me, that if he were not
> here in person he was in spirit. His discipline and inculcations
> were everywhere manifest.

In another letter dated June 13th, he speaks of the crimination and
recrimination which had followed the recent battles and says that "those
least active and really conspicuous in the presence of the enemy are loudest
in talk and most covetous to appropriate all the credit and rewards."

General Worth also complains that the inefficiency of the
quartermaster's department has become "a proverb," and tells of
preparations for the coming campaign. His comment on the volunteer
forces is far from complimentary. "Every regiment of volunteers," he
says, "costs equal to three of regulars, plus loss of arms, accouterments,
and equipage. Thirty-three per cent are sick and the remaining sixty-six
not worth a straw, but they offer a beautiful commentary upon executive
action recently, to wit—while the president is officering new regiments
with the scum of civil life, hardly one of these volunteer regiments has
failed to elect, and governors to appoint, retired regular officers."

From Ceralvo, Mexico, General Worth wrote to his daughter on
September 11, 1846, saying that he had orders to march three days later
and must overcome the enemy. "We must be victorious," he said, "for
our failure would be most disastrous. We are working for Mr. Polk,
Marcy & Co., and playing a bold and hazardous game in which the
country at large has little interest."

By September 16th the American Army was in sight of Monterey and faced by an enemy estimated to be from eight to ten thousand strong. "We shall not exceed 5,000," said General Worth, "if reaching that point, which I doubt. Two-fifths are volunteers, leaving 8000 of the latter and 700 or 800 regulars some ten marches in the rear. We have but ten days' subsistence. No prospect of getting any from our distant depot or other supplies than we can forage from the country."

In several of his letters General Worth speaks of his self-esteem, and it is obvious that he held an excellent opinion of his abilities as a soldier. His letter describing the capture of Monterey is filled with exultation:

Headquarters, Second Division
Monterey, October 2, 1846

MY DEAR RYAN: Ere this reaches you, you will have heard the good news from this quarter. My cup of distinction and happiness is full. My duty, my whole duty, and more has been done. In respect to my operations and the brilliant results, there is but one voice, and that a loud and stunning acclaim. If not well poised my head would be turned. I am satisfied with myself. The most vindictive foes crouch at my feet, and my enemies choke with joy and delight. I have earned the triumph and bear and wear it with modesty and humility. My soldiers and volunteers throng my quarters and huzza me in the streets.

Thank God, I have escaped. In a long service I have never been under such a dreadful fire. I have almost lost my hearing on one side, caused by several consecutive shots that passed so near as to stagger me almost out of my saddle. In the street fight I was in uniform and the malignant scoundrels frequently brought their volleys to bear upon me, but all is safe.

I send you a copy of the official report and my pencil notes written to Taylor during a three day period, frequently under fire. Poor McKerett was knocked all to pieces. The blow made you a captain. The first division and volunteers were taken into action without order, direction, support or command; in fact murdered. The miserable devil Twiggs stands disgraced before the army. He did not see his division, nor it him during the day. Lieutenant Garland presided at the slaughter. I am afraid you will hear too much of myself for taste, but revived malignity will neutralize all that.

I bowed to the Mexican troops, four brigades 8500 out of town gracefully, kindly, etc. We have taken immense magazines, principally munitions of war. My division, being in charge of the city, my time is incessantly occupied, aided by six or eight staff officers in regulating affairs, civil and military. I am playing the part of a governor, etc., and besides, from the force of circumstances, exercising most of the qualities of general-in-chief.

General Worth refers to the prospect of peace in a letter to Captain Sprague, dated November 2nd, and gives a picture of troubled Mexico that might well serve today:

I confess great impatience to hear from you after getting the news. I had concluded that peace would follow, arguing from the known wishes of our government, the obvious policy of Mexico, and the anticipated wishes of the European powers. Mexico is as obstinate, as corrupt and cowardly; overrode by a miserable army, the people have no voice. They are merely used for insurrectionary and revolutionary purposes by any military upstart who may figure for the day. Santa Anna, the most enlightened man among them, doubtless desires peace, and will make it if assured of the support of the army.

In this and other letters General Worth referred to political interference with those in high command in the army. "Deep intrigues," he said, "are going on looking to the removal of Taylor and the substitution of Butler. These plans, it is believed, are favored in Washington. Let them touch a hair of Taylor's head and 18 to 20 of the 20,000,000 will bear him by force to the presidential chair, whether he will or no. We shall see fine work in a few weeks. Volunteer corps are already quarreling about the division of glory, and some regulars cutting in. These are all on one side of the town. On our side, nothing was inconclusive; of course, nothing to dispute about."

The day after this was written General Taylor received dispatches giving notice of the termination of the armistice. Written from Saltillo on November 20th, Worth tells how he had entered the city three days before without opposition. He had with him only 1,000 effectives of all arms, and the march was hard and harassing.

Another part of this letter reveals General Worth as a chivalrous soldier who believed in making war against soldiers and not against civilians:

> In the states I perceive they talk of foraging off the enemy in order to make the people feel the war. There are no people in the sense in which we use the phrase. There is no public opinion to be brought to bear upon the government. As I said before, they only know they have a government through its oppressions. Again, if not conciliated, the means of our subsistence would be concealed, or, if foraged for, an army would have to be kept in constant operation for that object alone of sufficient size to consume what it secured. We must pay for what we get and have luck at that; it is not only just and proper, it is necessary.

Here the general speaks of his promotion—the reward for his services at Monterey:

> I told you or Maria in my last letter that I had received a most kind message from Mr. Polk. He was more than kind, and expressed his gratitude, adding that the moment Congress met he would make a more signal manifestation of his appreciation—the brevet of major general, with assignment accordingly. It will be gall and wormwood in certain quarters.

One of General Worth's duties at Saltillo was to "hold all sorts of courts and do justice in any and all events." To his daughter, Mrs. Sprague, he made serious charges against the volunteer soldiers:

> Our people, the lawless volunteers, stop at no outrage, he wrote, and but for the regulars, to whom in noble confidence

they (the Mexicans) fly for refuge and protection, it were a charity to slay them outright. The innocent blood that has been basely, cowardly and barbarously shed in cold blood, aside from other and deeper crimes will appeal to Heaven for, and, I trust, receive just retribution, and God's mercy alone will forbear involving the innocent with the guilty.

Referring to rumors that General Scott was coming, Worth said that the event might call him to the coast and on a service which he did not relish. He had no illusions regarding the difficulties of a campaign having Mexico City as its objective.

Letters written in February, 1847, describe the embarkation of troops at Brazos for Vera Cruz, and General Worth complains about the ingratitude of the government:

What a beautiful state of things exists at home. All parties by the ears and the high interest of the country being jeopardized to defend some artificial character or build up one of less importance, while my gallant and devoted officers who have served so nobly are called to another and yet more desperate service, without one word even of kindness and much less reward having been uttered or bestowed. For myself, so help me heaven, I am entirely indifferent.

General Worth was present at the siege of Vera Cruz. His first letter describing the beginnings of Scott's campaign to reach Mexico City was addressed to Mrs. Sprague:

Castle of Perote, Mexico, April 30, 1847

MY DEAR CHILD: General Scott remains at Jalapa, thirty miles in my rear, and prohibits my moving until he comes up. The way is open to the capital, which our force enables us to reach, but not, I fear, to hold without large reinforcements. There is no probability of another grand combat. The small portions of the Mexican army that escaped us at Cerro Gordo has totally dispersed, and they have not the means, torn as they are by factions and exhausted of resources, of assembling another.

Besides we have captured almost all their cannon—in all some 800—but they will now do as they ought to have done at first, commence the guerilla system, which, in other words, is a system of murder and plunder, by striking with small parties at our line of communications, and woe be to any stragglers.

General Worth's prophesy regarding the enemy's power of resistance was wrong, as the following shows:

Puebla, June 29, 1847

MY DEAR SPRAGUE: You will be, as usual surprised as myself at the place and date of this. I entered it on the 15th of May at the head of about 4000 good troops with all the flush and glow of victory in their hearts, and at the heels of a victory in their hearts, and at the heels of a beaten and disorganized enemy. In five days thereafter we could have been in the capital with but slight resistance, and it is my firm belief peace would have immediately resulted.

Three months have now passed since the rout of Cerro Gordo—the enemy has had time to recuperate in spirits, in men, and material. For instance they are assembled over 25,000 strong, have cast and mounted over sixty pieces of ordnance, have enveloped the city with a triple line of defense, enveloped the whole with water, presenting first a great impediment to our close approach: next, masking the secondary defenses, as ditches, troups de loups, etc.

Well, we did not advance! Why? Of that hereafter. Now it is understood we wait the coming of General Pierce, with some 2,000 or 3,000 men. He is understood to have been on route from Vera Cruz since the 2nd instant, and to this moment we have no reliable knowledge of his whereabouts. So our movement is entirely indefinite.

Here is the General's opinion about the proper method of ending the war and pacifying Mexico. Similar opinions have been expressed in the last five years:

> At or near the capital we shall undoubtedly have a very severe contest—probably the severest yet. That we shall triumph is not to be doubted, but at what cost? *Nous verrons.* At least, some will see, and where are we then? About the beginning of the war, which is not to be closed without one or two alternatives, to wit: Throw in 50,000 men, occupy many points, crush the enemy's miserable army at once, establish a base, and sustain and uphold it until its power is firmly established and the country tranquilized, or fix upon the boundary we devise, fall back upon and occupy it, from that point never to recede. As it is we control neither morally or physically a mile beyond the ground we stand upon, our line of communications cut, and infested throughout by guerillas, we gain victories and halt until all the moral advantages are lost. When we move, the enemy, with happy levity of character, will have forgotten the last defeat and again swell himself into a victorious mood.

This and other letters give hints of friction in the high command; apparently envy, jealousy and politics were conspicuous features of the campaign and influenced to a large degree the reports of battles written by certain officers. After the battles of Contreras and Churubusco, General Worth wrote as follows:

> I am satisfied and have no desire to be present at another battlefield, and such a field: More than thirty years of experience has filled my heart with satiety, if not with disgust, and I am quite content to leave other and younger aspirants the future fields. Three long hours of dreadful carnage, rivulets running blood, and fields where God's gifts and blessings were growing literally sowed with fragments of human flesh and bones. Four or five thousand maimed and crushed and wounded men within limited space is a fearful sight, and then the odor of human blood and festering wounds; even long use has not reconciled me to it.

My noble division has covered itself with honor. From circumstances to be explained hereafter I have no hope justice will be done it in the official report, but the whole army is its witness and will testify. My relations in a certain quarter are strange, but all susceptible of explanation. Alas, poor human nature! When I reach my country all things shall be put right.

My division holds Tacubaya, by the hill of Chapultepec, two miles from the city (City of Mexico).

The next letter to his daughter Maria was written after the battle of Molino del Rey and dated Mexico, September 23, 1847. In it General Worth tells how he battled on the causeways and "over the surface, now firm land, where Cortez contended for empire and struggled for victory." Stern measures were involved by Worth when his men entered the city:

The day we entered they commenced a fire upon us from the housetops, and cut down several of my officers and men. My friend Garland, who was at my side, caught a shell aimed at me. I caused the heavy guns to be turned against every house, whether palace, church, or convent, and after a few hours of such appliance, not regarding where or who it hit, quelled the dastardly villains, but it cost me some fifty brave fellows. If the general-in-chief will only hold every street responsible, and hang ten for every murder, we shall have order and safety; if not, not.

The remains of Santa Anna's army have gone towards the Pacific, and he toward the Gulf to embark. From present appearances our heavy fighting is over, but we shall have plenty of petite guerre, fine chances for the youngsters.

Time and again Worth wrote to his family that he longed for the day when he might join them, but he was generally pessimistic regarding the possibility of concluding peace. One of him most interesting letters was addressed to Secretary Marcy on this subject, and contained the prediction that Americans were destined eventually not only to overrun Mexico but the whole continent. The letter follows in part:

City of Mexico, October 30, 1847
To the Honorable W. L. Marcy, Secretary of War:

MY DEAR SIR: It is now, I think, some two years since I have written to you upon other than official subjects, and for reasons which I doubt not you have fully comprehended and appreciated. The official reports have advised you of the brilliant exploits of this army, but what is to be done next? . . .

Shall we retrograde and occupy the line we have proposed, or shall we overrun and hold the whole country? By adopting the first we shall in a measure abandon the war and bring ourselves into more or less contempt with the nations of Europe. I say abandon the war, because it is well known that the object in crossing the Rio Grande, and especially of the campaign from Vera Cruz to this capital, the geographical center and heart of the republic, was to compel, or, in the cant phrase of the day, to "conquer a peace." This peace will not be attained by withdrawing to a line, however generously that line may be arranged, and consequently the object for which the war was undertaken will have failed.

But it does not become a great nation like ours to fail in aught it undertakes, and hence I regard our honor as implicated in the prosecution of the war until either the object of it is obtained or the whole country subdued. Considerations of policy and of interest greatly strengthen these views.

That our race is finally destined to overrun this whole continent is too obvious to need proof. Like an axiom in mathematics, it is only necessary to state the proposition to ensure belief; and we may state it thus: put two distinct races in juxtaposition, one more powerful and superior in civilization, and it will absorb the inferior. The most that can be said in opposition to this is that we are somewhat premature, perhaps half a century. But what is half a century to the affairs of a nation like ours, thoroughly imbued with the progressive spirit? A mere point, which, like a point in mathematics should not enter into the solution of the great problem.

It being then a part of our destiny to overrun the country, a destiny which we can no more avoid, despite all the struggles of short-sighted politicians, than we can change the order of nature, the question is whether we shall complete the work we have already so nearly accomplished, or leave it to be undertaken de novo by our children? Having spent most of the blood and treasure which the conquest requires, shall we relinquish it and thus impose the same sacrifice upon another generation? But it is contended by a large and respectable party at home that further extension endangers the stability of our confederation, to which it may be answered that this doctrine has been the favorite theme since the adoption of the constitution.

The latter part of the war was marked by grave dissensions among the military officers. There were charges and counter-charges between General Scott on one side, and General Worth and Pillow and Colonel Duncan on the other. These differences led Scott to order the arrest of his three subordinates. Some of Worth's letters to members of his family contain references to the scandalous treatment he had received. In one he says, "Unless I mistake my countrymen, they will not quietly see one who has served with fidelity and some distinction trodden down in mere wantonness by a jealous and vindictive superior. His report on Cerro Gordo was a lie from beginning to end."

Again Worth remarks that he had received many letters from all quarters of the United States, which showed that he was the subject of all kinds of assaults from the partisan papers of Scott and Taylor. Finally the government in Washington was impelled to send a court of inquiry to Mexico to look into the quarrels of the generals, and on March 14, 1848 Worth wrote to Captain Sprague:

The court is endeavoring to quash the investigations, and will probably succeed. If the charges against Duncan and Pillow are withdrawn I have agreed for the good of the service and its harmony to abandon mine against Scott. My triumph has been complete, and I can afford to be magnanimous.

Chapter 21

Mr. Truman At Chapultepec

President Truman decided to pay a visit to Mexico in 1947 to cement the friendship between these two nations. It would be the first time a president visited that country. A more cautious man than Harry Truman might have hesitated to tread such doubtful ground. Mr. Truman didn't, and found himself acclaimed overnight as a hero in Mexico. The crowds in Mexico City were such as Truman had ever witnessed. Thousands of people poured into the streets to see and cheer an American president for the first time. Truly the trip was Truman's "Good Neighbor Policy."

While in Mexico City Truman announced that he would make an unscheduled stop at the cities historic Chapultepec Castle, where he would do more to improve the Mexican-American relations than had any president in a century. The next day the long line of automobiles pulled into the shade of an ancient grove of trees at Chapultepec. Mr. Truman stepped out of the lead car and walked over to a stone monument bearing the names of the Los Niños Heroes, six teenage cadets who had died in the Mexican-American war in 1847, when American troops stormed the castle. According to legend, five of the cadets had stabbed themselves to death, and a sixth jumped to his death from a parapet, rather than surrender.

The six cadets are honored by an imposing monument made of Carrara marble by architect Enrique Aragón and sculptor Ernesto Tamarez at the entrance to Chapultepec park. As President Truman approached, a unit of blue-uniformed Mexican cadets stood at attention. As the president placed a wreath at the foot of the monument, several of the cadets wept silently.

A current Mexican campaign to enlarge the monument was silenced during Mr. Truman's visit in 1947 for fear that it might revive the bitter memories of an old war. Presumably someone in the President's party suggested decorating the shrine, something which no previous American official had ever ventured to do. A colder, more cautious man than Harry Truman might have hesitated to tread such doubtful ground. Mr. Truman didn't—and found himself acclaimed overnight as a hero in Mexico. One healing touch of sentiment had opened more hearts than any round of banquets or set speeches could ever have done. Asked by American reporters why he had gone to the monument Truman replied, "Brave men don't belong to any one country. I respect bravery wherever I see it!"

Chronology

1836

March 06	Assault on the Alamo
March 26	Prisoners at Goliad executed.
April 21	Battle of San Jacinto.
July 04	United States recognizes the Republic of Texas.

1844

November 02	James K. Polk elected president of the United States.
December 06	Santa Anna deposed as president of Mexico.

1845

March 01	Annexation of Texas proclaimed by the United States.
March 04	James K. Polk inaugurated as president of the United States.
March 31	Mexico severs diplomatic relations with the United States.
June 03	Santa Anna goes into exile at Havana, Cuba.
June 15	General Zachary Taylor ordered to move his army into Texas.

July 04	Texas accepts annexation to the United States.
July 25	General Zachary Taylor arrives at St. Joseph's Island near Corpus Christi.
September 14	Jose Joaquin de Herrera elected president of Mexico.
September 16	John Slidell appointed as the new Minister to Mexico.
December 29	Texas admitted as the 28th state of the United States.
December 31	Herrera deposed as president of Mexico.

1846

January 04	Mariano Paredes y Arrillaga becomes president of Mexico.
January 13	Taylor's army ordered to the Rio Grande.
March 08	Taylor's army leaves Corpus Christi, Texas.
March 28	Taylor's army arrives at the Rio Grande opposite Matamoros.
April 25	Captain Seth Thornton's patrol ambushed and captured at the Carricitos Ranch in Texas.
May 08	Battle of Palo Alto.
May 09	Battle of Resaca de la Palma.
May 13	The United States declares war on Mexico.
May 14	Blockade proclaimed against Mexican ports.
May 17	General Mariano Arista evacuates Matamoros.
July 01	Mexico declares war on the United States.
July 14	General Zachary Taylor occupies Camargo.
August 16	Santa Anna arrives at Vera Cruz under order of safe passage from the U.S.
September 20	Battle of Monterey
November 14	Commodore Conner occupies Tampico with a 300 man landing party.
November 16	General Zachary Taylor occupies Saltillo.
November 18	General Winfield Scott appointed to command an expedition to Vera Cruz.
November 23	General Scott leaves Washington for Mexico.
December 06	Santa Anna elected president of Mexico.
December 27	General Scott reaches Brazos Santiago.

1847

January 03	General Scott arrives at Camargo.
January 14	General Scott departs for Tampico, and requisitions many of General Zachary Taylor's troops to go with him.
January 23	U.S. troops arrive at Tampico.
January 28	Santa Anna leaves San Luis Potosi and heads north to attack General Zachary Taylor.
February 22	Two day battle of Buena Vista begins.
April 02	General Scott's army begins their inland march to the City of Mexico.
April 18	General Scott defeats Santa Anna at the battle of Cerro Gordo.
April 19	American army occupies Jalapa.
April 22	General Worth occupies Perote.
May 04	Volunteers returned to Vera Cruz by General Scott for shipment home.
May 15	General Worth's army occupies Puebla.
August 07	Scott's army advances from Puebla to the City of Mexico.
August 19	Battle of Contreras.
August 20	Battle of Churubusco.
August 24	Santa Anna and General Scott agree to a truce at Tacubaya.
September 06	Tacubaya truce ends.
September 08	Battle of Molino del Rey.
September 13	Battle of Chapultepec.
September 14	U.S. Army occupies the City of Mexico.
September 16	Santa Anna resigns as president of Mexico.
September 26	Peña y Peña becomes acting president of Mexico.
October 07	Santa Anna relieved of his command of the army by the Mexican government.
November 25	General Zachary Taylor relieved of his command and returns to the U.S. to campaign for the presidency.

1848

January 08	Peña y Peña becomes acting president of Mexico.
January 1	General Scott relieved of his command in Mexico.
February 02	Treaty of Guadalupe-Hidalgo signed.
March 10	Treaty ratified by the United States.
April 05	Santa Anna goes into exile at Havana, Cuba.
May 30	Treaty of Guadalupe Hidalgo ratified by Mexican Congress. Jose Joaquin de Herrera again becomes the president of Mexico.
June 12	United States troops evacuate the City of Mexico.
July 15	General Worth departs Vera

References

The War in Mexico.
by Anton Adams
The Emperor's Press
Chicago, 1998

Jefferson Davis's Mexican War Regiment
by Joseph E. Chance
University Press of Mississippi
Jackson, 1991

Jefferson Davis
by Clement Eaton
The Free Press
New York, 1997

So Far From God—The U. S. War with Mexico 1846-1848.
by John S. D. Eisenhower
Random House
New York, 1989

Agent of Destiny—The Life and Times of General Winfield Scott.
by John S. D. Eisenhower
The Free Press
New York, 1997

Personal Memoirs of U. S. Grant. (2 volumes)
by Ulysses S. Grant
Charles Webster and Company
New York 1885

General Taylor and His Staff
by Grigg and Elliot
Grigg, Elliot and Company
Philadepphia, 1848

To the Halls of the Montezumas.
by Robert W. Johannsen
Oxford University Press
New York, 1985

Santa Anna
by Oakah L. Jones, Jr.
Twayne Publishers
New York, 1968

Antonio Lopez de Santa Anna
by Steven O'Brien
Chelsea House Publishers
New York, 1992

Origins of the War With Mexico—The Polk-Stockton Intrigue.
by Glenn W. Price
University of Texas Press
Austin, 1967

The Life and Military Service of General William Selby Harney.
by Logan Uriah Reavis
Bryan Brand and Company
St. Louis, 1878

The Scouting Expeditions of McCulloch's Texas Rangers.
by Samuel C. Reid, Jr.
G. B. Zieber and Company
Philadelphia, 1848

The United States and Mexico, 1821-1848 (2 volumes)
by George Lockhart Rives
Charles Scribner's Sons
New York, 1913

The New York *Times*.
The Internet

The Memoirs of Lieutenant-General Winfield Scott LLD (2 volumes)
By Winfield Scott
Sheldon and Company
New York 1864

The Rogue's March—John Riley and the St. Patrick's Battalion
by Peter F. Stevens
Brassey's Inc.
Washington, 1999

Lew Wallace, An Autobiography. (2 volumes)
By Lew Wallace
Harper and Brothers, Publishers
New York, 1906